Blue Falcon: a military phrase for someone who pretends to be your ally but ends up stabbing you in the back.

BLUE FALCON, a novel by Frank A. Ruffolo
www.frankaruffolo.com

First Edition, March 2019

ISBN: 978-0-9836803-6-9 (printed version only)

Printed in the United States of America

Frank A. Ruffolo

BLUE FALCON

A Jack Stenhouse Mystery

CHAPTER ONE

Wild migratory birds scatter and alligators dip under the murky water of the Everglades as the blades of the Broward County Sheriff Office's chopper thump through the thick and humid air. Jack Stenhouse and his new bride, Didi, (the perfect nickname for a gal with attributes to match), are in a futile battle with pesky no-see-ums and mosquitos while they watch for the chopper's arrival. Lost in thought, Jack stares at the 25-foot python that he has just shot in the head, and then shifts his gaze to the two human feet sticking out of its mouth.

"Well, Hon, this is a hell of a way to spend the last part of our honeymoon."

Smacking her thigh to kill a mosquito, Didi is not happy. "Shit follows you around like a shadow, Jack." Swatting at a bug on her arm, she adds, "Damn! When the hell are we going to get out of here? I'm becoming the main course!"

When the chopper arrives, it hovers overhead, looking for a dry spot to land in this river of grass. In doing so, it blows away most of the flying insects, inadvertently providing welcome relief to the honeymooners.

As they wait for the chopper to land, the couple notices sprays of water in the distance from several airboats that are also on their way to their location. One of the approaching airboats holds members of BSO, the

Broward Sheriff's Office, while the other airboats hold representatives of the city of Sunrise. The city is sending their own deputies to this crime scene because it is located close to the site of a hotel and casino complex that city legislators are hoping will be built nearby.

BSO Sergeant Walsh waits patiently while his airboat pulls slowly up to the shore, then he jumps out onto the bank before the engines are shut down. Looking around at his surroundings, his eyes widen in amusement when he recognizes Jack.

"Well, well, well, it really is the famous Jack Stenhouse! We heard you went up to New York. What are you doing way out here in the Everglades? Couldn't stay away from sunny Florida, eh?"

Jack flashes him half a peace sign in reply.

The sergeant smiles and then turns his gaze toward the large and very dead snake.

"Holy shit! I knew we had some pretty large snakes out here, but I've never seen one kill a human before! How'd you come across this thing?"

Before Jack can reply, two loud Sunrise police airboats also stop alongside the bank. All conversation ceases while the men wait for the City of Sunrise police officers to climb out of their flat-bottomed boats.

After approaching the group around the snake, one of the officers addresses the BSO officer.

"Hello there, Sergeant. We'd like to thank BSO for pointing out the location of this crime scene, but we'll take it over from here. This area is not under your jurisdiction."

Bristling at the smirking Sunrise officer, Sergeant Walsh barely masks his irritation. "Hold on, Slick. This is unincorporated Broward County, so it falls under the authority of the Broward County Sheriff's Department."

The officer from Sunrise smugly points his finger out over the water. "Sergeant, see that blue canal marker about twenty feet west? Well, that sign marks the boundary of the City of Sunrise. This area we're in was annexed by Sunrise last month in preparation for the building of a hotel and casino. So we thank you for your assistance, but *we'll* take charge of this crime scene now." He flashes the sergeant a short, humorless smile, and then turns to Stenhouse.

"Welcome home, Jack. What did you get yourself into now?"

Realizing that the Sunrise police officer is correct, the BSO sergeant informs his fellow officers that they will be leaving, and then he flashes the Sunrise cops the Florida state bird. The Broward group piles into their airboat and speeds off, with their helicopter following above them.

After the noise of the departing officers dies down, City of Sunrise Sergeant Jorge Octavio makes two phone calls: one to the city's forensics department, and the other to the medical examiner. Then he turns his attention toward Jack and Didi.

"As I was saying, what's the story here?"

With disgust for the Florida heat churning in his stomach, Jack wipes sweat from his brow with the back of his hand. Pointing to his wife, he says, "Didi and I are on a short layover in Fort Lauderdale before we head home. We just got off a cruise for our honeymoon and decided to take a guided tour of the Everglades before we leave for New York in the morning. Didi spotted the snake, and here we are."

"Honeymoon, eh? Congrats to you both. Finally made it legal?"

Didi smiles, but Jack offers no comment.

"Well," continues Octavio, "we'll take over now, thank you. NYPD has no jurisdiction here, either."

Jack was a homicide detective in Fort Lauderdale for many years before joining the New York City Police Department. He made a lot of friends in Florida, but also a lot of enemies. Sometimes he found it hard to tell his friends apart from his enemies, and sometimes he liked his enemies better than his friends.

"Thank *God* you'll be taking over," snaps Jack. "I really don't want to get involved in this crap. Look, I'm more than happy to let *you* stay here and feed the mosquitos. Here's my card; give me a call when you ID this guy."

Jack grabs Didi's arm and points her toward their tour ride airboat as hordes of buzzing, flying, and biting insects fill the hot, humid air around them.

As the guide pilots the boat back to its dock, Jack shouts to Didi above the engine noise, "This is the reason I wanted to leave Florida! It's too fucking hot here!"

Sergeant Octavio and his fellow officer remain on the bank in the sweltering heat, waiting for their CSI team to arrive. The crime scene techs will sweep the area and then transport the snake and its victim to the coroner. Octavio will wait while the M.E. releases the entombed body from the snake and performs an autopsy. Then he will accompany the body to the morgue.

Happy to be out of the Everglades and heading back toward "civilization," Jack and Didi are uncharacteristically quiet on the drive to their hotel near Fort

Lauderdale-Hollywood International Airport. Their flight to New York is scheduled for the next morning, which is none too soon for Jack; he is anxious to get back to work.

But Didi reminds him that they are still on their honeymoon, and there is still tonight.

In a quiet hallway in the West Wing of the White House, a cell phone buzzes.

"Yes?"

"Sir, the issue that needed to be resolved has been taken care of."

"Good. But I have more issues that need attention. You will soon be a very busy woman."

Jack is staring at his watch and pacing around the hotel room while he waits for Didi to finish primping for this last night of their honeymoon. They are planning to start the evening with dinner at a local restaurant, and then end with drinks and a show at a popular Fort Lauderdale night spot.

Both Jack and Didi grew up in South Florida, but strangely enough, neither of them had ever been to the Polynesian restaurant on Federal Highway. The tiki-themed restaurant, a must-see for tourists, is famous for its great Polynesian dinner show and exotic rum drinks that will knock you on your ass.

Jack is a good-looking man in his mid-thirties. Tall and with the chiseled body of a strong, muscular man, he has steel-gray eyes that can peer into your soul. A lifelong player, Jack has been in the company of many beautiful women over his lifetime and has even been married several times. His penchant for strippers is the reason that none of those previous marriages worked out, but he hopes that marriage to Didi, who happens to be an ex-stripper, is the one that will last.

Didi's first name is Deidre, but everyone calls her Didi—especially Jack. He loves how her nickname matches the size of her most notable features. Didi is in her early thirties, but she still looks like a teen-ager—a well-developed teenager. She's a real beauty, with brains to match, but her forty-fours overshadow her long auburn hair, narrow waist, and toned abs.

To pay her way through college, Didi worked as a pole dancer in an infamous gentlemen's club in Fort Lauderdale. She never intended to remain in that job for long—her dream was to own her own business—but life intervened, and the money was good. However, when she met Jack, she knew she had found the love of her life, and when he asked her to marry him and move to New York City, she agreed wholeheartedly. Then, after settling into Manhattan, she used the money she had saved while working as a stripper and opened a boutique selling sexy lingerie.

Finally finished dressing, Didi opens the bath-room door and steps out. When Jack looks up, he sees her double D's exiting the doorway long before she does. With wide eyes he takes in his bride—she is wearing a red vinyl cocktail dress that stops nine inches above her knees, and bright red, six-inch heels. Her ample breasts, straining at the thin straps that are holding everything up, look like they are ready to ex-plode into freedom. Jack stares at his wife in evident approval.

"Good God almighty, woman! I should stand up for you, but I really can't right now. Damn! You sure you want to go out now? We have room service, ya know."

Didi smiles and slowly saunters over to the couch. Bending over—a very risky move—she takes Jack by the hand.

"Come on, Babe," she says with a wink. "I want to see the show. We'll be alone together later."

Jack rises slowly and puts his arm around Didi so he can grab her ass. "Dee, nobody gonna' be lookin' at the show."

Shaking his head, Jack pockets his room key and starts to lead the way to the hotel room's door—until the sound of a ringing cell phone stops him. Sighing, he retrieves the offending object from his slacks.

"This is Jack," he answers.

"It's Sergeant Octavio. That guy inside the snake is, or was, Deputy Secretary of State Joe Cunningham! He was supposed to testify before Congress tomorrow at the impeachment proceedings against President Burris. Funny thing, though. The feds just barged in here and took control of the corpse. Hey, I gotta go now. I'll call you again later when it's more convenient."

CHAPTER TWO

Jack shaves slowly while staring through blood-shot eyes at his grizzled face. In the other room, Didi has already finished packing and is waiting for her husband to finish dressing.

When Jack creeps out of the bathroom, Didi exclaims, "Yikes! You look horrible, Jack! Your eyes are as red as my dress!"

Putting a finger to his mouth, Jack whispers pitifully, "Shhh... I need coffee and a morphine drip."

"Oh, right. Sorry, Hon. We'll get some coffee downstairs before we return the rental car. We have three hours until our flight."

Jack packs his shaving gear and cell phone charger and zips his luggage shut. Then he grabs his bag and slowly follows Didi out the door.

While they wait for the elevator, Jack's cell phone rings loudly, the sound exploding in his head. Fumbling to answer it as quickly as possible just to shut off the noise, he mumbles to himself, "Got to remember to put this thing on vibrate." And then he barks into the phone, "This better be good!"

"Jack, this is Sergeant Octavio," says the voice on the phone. "I had to cut our conversation short yesterday, so I'm calling back now. Our M.E. was only able to make a quick visual inspection of Joe Cunningham's body before a couple of federal black suits came in and took it away. All the M.E. could tell me is that there was blunt force trauma to the back of his head and that he must have been dumped in the Glades. Last night I tried to get into a condo he owns across from our hockey arena, but the FBI was guarding it. My police chief made some calls this morning, and I'm going to be let into his apartment today. Jack, this is the third witness scheduled to appear before Congress who died unexpectedly, and it looks like this one was murdered. They say that one of the others died of a heart attack, and that the other was in a vehicular accident."

"Yeah," responds Jack. "The one who died in a traffic accident was John Hastings from the State Department. He died on the Cross-Bronx Expressway last month. He was at our embassy in Sudan and was sent home after the recent attack there. Sue Wilkens also worked at the State Department, and she's the one who had a heart attack."

"Look, Jack, all of this smells. See if you can get more info on Hastings, and I'll get back to you on Cunningham after I take a look around his apartment. I'm also going to contact the D.C. police about the supposed heart attack of Sue Wilkens. Take care, Jack. Watch your back."

When Jack signs off, the elevator door finally opens.

"What's going on?" asks Didi.

"Before I answer," says Jack with a grimace, "do you have any Ibuprofen? My head is about to explode."

Jack manages to pop 600 mg just before the elevator reaches the main lobby. Then, on the way to the hotel restaurant for breakfast, he whispers to Didi, "The call was about our snake man from the Everglades. He was Deputy Secretary of State Joe Cunningham, and he was murdered before the snake got him. That snake must have been hungry, because they usually eat live prey." His eyes narrow. "The shit is about to get real."

But Jack hasn't told Didi the whole story. Not yet, anyway.

It's a beautiful day in D.C. Tourists are strolling around the National Mall, exploring the nation's monuments, memorials, and museums, and admiring the cherry blossoms that are in full bloom around the Tidal Basin. In the White House, President Howard Burris is working at his desk in the Oval Office while impeachment proceedings continue in full swing on the Hill.

In a rare moment of quiet contemplation, President Burris turns to stare out the window at the sunny D.C. morning, but his thoughts are quickly interrupted by Press Secretary Joe Conway, who hurries into the room and hands Burris an envelope.

"Good morning, Joe. What is this?"

"Good morning, Mr. President. This is my letter of resignation, effective immediately. I have been subpoenaed to testify before Congress, so I cannot in good conscience perform my duties as your spokesperson. It was a good ride while it lasted, sir. I will miss the West Wing."

President Burris stands, walks around the desk, and puts his arm around Joe's shoulders. "Could I try to change your mind?"

"No, sir. I have already boxed up my things. I wish you the best, sir."

Joe shakes the President's hand, and then leaves the Oval Office. When the President is alone again, he takes his cell phone out of the inner pocket of his suit jacket.

"Joe Conway just resigned. He was subpoenaed to testify before Congress."

Burris ends the call, sits back down at his desk, and buzzes for his secretary. "Get me Kevin Randel and Sherry Lawson."

CIA operative Frank Sansone has also received a subpoena to testify before Congress. The legislators want to know more about his involvement in the Sudanese embassy debacle. Frank suspects that he will be given a leave of absence from work while he testifies. He also suspects that he will now be followed wherever he goes. He isn't about to take any chances, especially after hearing about the death of Deputy Secretary of State Joe Cunningham on the news. Even though the official statement from the State Department did not mention foul play, Frank knows better.

Before he heads off to work, he plucks a small leaf from the basil plant that's growing in a pot on his balcony. Then, he carefully places the leaf in the apartment's door jamb, just above the deadbolt. If the leaf is still there when he gets home that evening, he'll know that no one has been in his apartment.

Frank also decides to vary his morning routine. Instead of taking his car to work at the old CIA campus, he walks to the nearby Metro station.

As he hurries toward the subway entrance, he notices a black Suburban SUV parked at the corner. After he walks down the steps to the train station, two black suits exit the vehicle.

After a short flight, the Stenhouse honeymooners finally arrive back home at their loft on the Lower East Side of Manhattan. Soon after dropping off their bags, Jack gives Didi a kiss and heads down to the First Precinct to see if he can get any information on John Hastings, the State Department employee who died recently on the Cross-Bronx Expressway.

While Jack is heading out of the Manhattan parking garage in his '68 Road Runner, the presidential impeachment hearings are just about to begin again in Washington, D.C.

IRS official Laura Leonard is as prepared as she will ever be to give her testimony to Congress. She will be questioned about her involvement in the IRS scandal involving the targeting of special-interest groups that just happened to hold viewpoints that are politically opposite from those of President Burris. The investigation's focus is on the Manhattan office of the IRS.

This latest scandal is having a negative impact on the Burris Administration. Amid scandal after scandal, and now the impeachment proceedings against him, President Burris's popularity rating has recently dropped into the single digits. However, none of that seems to worry him. Enveloped in arrogance, he continues to believe all is well.

Unconcerned, the President is waiting to begin a meeting in his office. Chief of Staff Kevin Randel has already joined him, but Assistant Press Secretary Sherry Lawson is running late. When she finally arrives and begins to apologize, Burris cuts her off from across his desk.

"Apologizing is for losers. Sit down. We have work to do," he barks.

Troubled by the knowledge that he is no longer employed at the White House, Joe Conway glumly picks up his box of belongings from the back of his Prius and heads toward his townhouse in Chevy Chase. As he walks up the sidewalk to his row house, a man approaches him from behind.

"Mr. Conway?"

At the sound of his name, Joe turns around. "Yes? Who are you?"

Showing a badge and ID card, the tall stranger continues. "I am U.S. Marshal John Powell. Because you are scheduled to testify later this week, Prosecutor Gutierrez and members of Congress are concerned about your safety. They have instructed me to place you in protective custody at a safe house until the hearing. There have been too many witnesses who have become 'unavailable' recently. Come with me, please."

"Well, I don't have any clothes or personal supplies..."

Taking Joe firmly by the arm, Powell leads him to his car.

"Not to worry, sir. We have already retrieved some of your belongings, and you can give one of the marshals a list of any other items you may need."

As the men enter a black sedan, a red-haired woman in a black SUV down the street takes multiple photos of them with an SLR camera. When the car drives off, the woman smiles and places a quick call to the West Wing.

CHAPTER THREE

When Jack enters his workplace at the First Precinct, the other officers and detectives turn and laugh.

"Hey, it's Robinson Crusoe back from Fiji! Did you need grass clippers to trim your skirt?"

Jack glares at his coworkers while rubbing his middle finger on the side of his nose, and he is puzzled at their reaction.

"What?" he retorts.

Detective Allison Giancarlo walks over, and with a huge grin, hands him her cell phone.

"Didi posted this video for everyone. Great moves, Jack!"

Jack frowns as he watches himself performing a drunken hula with three exotic beauties at the Polynesian restaurant in Fort Lauderdale. The performers had dressed him in a grass skirt with a coconut-shell bra over his Hawaiian shirt.

"Oh, fuck," he says with a groan. "I guess I had too many drinks. I don't remember this at all."

"Yeah, well, the whole world knows about it now, Jack. It's on the 'Net."

Shrugging his shoulders, Jack looks up as his office mates erupt in applause. With a sheepish grin, Jack acknowledges his fans and then tries to get down to business.

"Allison, is Rawlings in? I need to speak with him."

"Yeah, he's in his office. But why are you even here today? You aren't due back until Monday."

Speaking quietly enough so that no one else can hear, Jack replies, "Yeah, well, you heard about Cunningham, right?"

"Yeah, the Deputy Secretary of State. He was found dead in the Everglades, but we haven't heard anything else about it."

Pulling Giancarlo off to the side, Jack continues, "Didi and I were the ones who found him while we were on a tour of the Glades."

At this revelation, Giancarlo's eyes widen in surprise.

"Didi spotted him from our airboat on a bank off one of the main canals. Before the local police could do much of anything, the feds came in and booted the local guys off the case. But the Sunrise M.E. had enough time to determine that Cunningham was murdered. When we found him, he was sticking out of the mouth of a large python. But the M.E. found blunt force trauma to the back of his head."

Giancarlo is taken aback by Jack's news. "In the belly of a snake? Damn! It's no wonder you moved away from Florida."

"Yeah. You know he was slated to testify before Congress, right? His death makes one more witness who's been eliminated before the impeachment trial."

"Wow, I didn't think of that. So why do you need to see Rawlings?"

"I have a feeling that his murder is linked to a case up here. There's something odd going on. Remember that guy Hastings, the one they found on the Cross-Bronx? Well, he was subpoenaed, too. One of the sergeants in Sunrise—a Sergeant Octavio—is going to check out Cunningham's condo down there, and I want to take a look at our files on Hastings' death. That's why I need to see Rawlings."

As Jack starts walking toward Inspector Rawlings' office, he gets another ovation from the crew. Turning toward the group, he grins, and with a flourish of his arm, takes a bow.

Another meeting of the Presidential impeachment committee is about to begin before a joint session of Congress. After being sworn in, IRS official Laura Leonard takes a seat alongside her lawyer, while Special Prosecutor Juan Gutierrez prepares to begin the questioning.

"Good afternoon, Ms. Leonard. You have been subpoenaed to testify before us today to shed some light on the participation of your department of the IRS in targeting special-interest groups that seem to be in direct opposition to the goals of the current Administration. Can you tell us if you observed any irregularities in the processing of the department's workload? And if you did see anything irregular, do you know if your superiors were involved with it?"

Leaning over, Laura whispers to her attorney, and then leans forward toward the microphone.

"Mr. Gutierrez, under the guidance of my legal representative, I decline to answer that question on the grounds that it may incriminate me."

"Ms. Leonard, this is not a joke," responds Gutierrez with annoyance. "You were subpoenaed to testify before Congress and this special investigatory committee about the role you and your office had in certain transactions conducted by the IRS. Have you or have any of your staff postponed or denied any group's request for tax exemption due to their political agendas or beliefs?"

Again, Laura leans over to whisper to her lawyer and then addresses the microphone.

"Under the advisement of my attorney, I regret to inform you that I cannot answer that question on the grounds that it may incriminate me."

The reporters in the room click their cameras in unison as Special Prosecutor Gutierrez's face turns beet-red in anger.

"Before I hold you in contempt of these proceedings—in contempt of Congress—I will once again ask you to respond to these questions."

When Laura begins to lean toward her attorney yet again, Gutierrez blurts out in disgust, "Ms. Leonard, stop the theatrics and answer the question!"

Once again, Laura says, "On the advisement of my counsel, I refuse to answer your question on the grounds..."

Her response is cut short by Gutierrez as he slams the gavel down so hard that the handle breaks, and the gavel's head flies into the press box.

"That is enough!" he bellows. "You are now held in contempt of Congress. Sergeant-at-Arms, please escort Ms. Leonard out of these proceedings. There will be a thirty-minute recess."

Gutierrez stands up and stalks out after Laura, her counsel, and the sergeant-at-arms.

Jack knocks on Deputy Inspector Rawlings' door, then waits to be invited in.

"Stenhouse? You're back early." He motions for Jack to take a seat, and then adds with a smile, "Hey, congratulations on your 'performance'. You put on quite a show at that restaurant. Too bad we couldn't see it in person."

Shaking his head, Jack replies, "Thanks, Inspector."

His face grows serious. "I have a request, and I need the help of your office to get it done."

"What is it, Jack?"

"Remember that guy Hastings from the State Department, who died on the Cross-Bronx Expressway about a month ago, just before he was supposed to testify before Congress? Well, I was the one who found Joe Cunningham's body in the Everglades."

Groaning, Rawlings retorts, "That figures."

Ignoring his boss' comment, Jack continues. "Cunningham was also expected to testify before Congress."

At that statement, Rawlings' interest is piqued.

Jack fills Rawlings in on the rest of the story. "That must be why the feds came in and took over the investigation before the local Florida P.D. could get started on it. One of my contacts at the Sunrise Police Department was there when the feds arrived. He told me that the M.E. had been able to do a preliminary examination of the body, and he found that Cunningham was murdered—shot in the back of the head. If you're counting, this is the third subpoenaed witness that has ended up dead before they could testify. The other two deaths were...well, I consider them to be 'suspicious,' to say the least. My contact at Sunrise and I think all these deaths are related, and I want to review the file on Hastings to see what I can find."

Rawlings' interest, as well as his concern, has now intensified.

"Look, Jack, this is serious. If the feds are involved, the stakes have just risen sky high. And you think they're covering things up?" He shakes his head. "Go on and make your request through Lieutenant Conrad. I'll give Conrad a heads-up when he gets back in on Sunday, and I'll also call Inspector Hamilton at the 43rd Precinct. Now, go home and finish your vacation. When you come in on Monday, everything should be set up."

Then Rawlings lowers his voice as if someone might be eavesdropping. "Keep a low profile on this one, Jack. If the government is hiding something, you and your friend in Sunrise will be in deep shit."

Frank Sansone was greeted by his superior as soon as he entered the old CIA headquarters building in D.C.

"Come into my office, Frank. We need to talk."

Following his boss into a small, private room, the older man says, "Shut the door, please," and then takes a seat on the opposite side of a large oak-and-mahogany desk.

"Frank, I know you were subpoenaed to testify about the Sudanese incident. We sent redacted correspondence to Congress and to the special prosecutor, but under the Freedom of Information Act, we had to supply the full transcripts. I have to put you on a temporary leave of absence while you testify before the committee."

Frank begins to speak, but his boss holds up his hand. "To give you fair warning, three people who were scheduled to testify in the congressional committee investigation have ended up dead. Joe Cunningham's death is the most recent. He was murdered, but that information has not been provided to the public. The Secret Service and the FBI are now investigating all of the deaths. Remain vigilant, Frank. We've been watching various Administration officials, and we believe they're already starting to track you. Things may happen quickly."

Jumping out of his chair, Frank stands defiantly in front of his boss. "Look, if I think I've been compromised, I'm going to disappear. I'm not going to wait around to be number four. That's not a warning, it's a fact!"

Frank stomps out of the office while his boss calls out after him, "Don't do anything stupid, Frank!"

Frank Sansone is angry as he walks back to the Metro line for his fifteen-minute ride home.

Those fifteen minutes are the last normal ones he has before his life changes forever.

Joining the President at an emergency meeting in the Oval Office are his chief of staff, his press secretary, and several others of his closest staff members.

"Mister President, we need to devise a strategy that will offset all of this negative news. Another witness is dead, and your poll numbers are in the toilet.

You need to make a statement to the American people to calm things down."

Burris slaps a hand on his desk and jumps up from his chair. With veins popping out on his forehead and his face red with anger, he rebukes his staff.

"Fuck the people!" he yells. "The polls don't mean shit, Kevin! I received almost 60% of the vote, remember? I won a mandate from the people when they elected me, so in their eyes, I can do no wrong!"

From behind the Kennedy desk, Burris walks over to a window and stares outside in silence for several minutes. Then, suddenly and shockingly, his attitude and demeanor change drastically. Calmly, he turns around to face his new press secretary.

"Sherry, make an announcement and get me coverage on primetime TV. I'll give a statement tomorrow night from the Oval Office. I'll schmooze the public, the press, and Congress." Gazing out over the rest of the assembled staff, he issues further orders. "All of you need to get out there and get things started with our friends in the media. Thanks."

After everyone leaves, Burris sits back down at his large desk, once again alone in the Oval Office. When his private cell phone rings, he swivels his chair around toward the window to answer it.

"Yes?" he says. He listens for a moment, then says, "Okay, get it done."

CHAPTER FOUR

When Frank arrives at his Metro stop, he exits the train and walks up the steps to street level, three blocks from his row house. As he walks, he looks around carefully to make sure he is not being followed.

When he reaches his home, he stops first at his car, parked across the street from his house. Putting down the box containing personal items from his desk, he gets down on his knees to look underneath the vehicle. His car is a Japanese SUV that sits a little higher off the ground than a standard sedan, so inspecting the undercarriage is easy.

Immediately noticing a wet stain on the street, he touches his finger to the liquid and mumbles, "Brake fluid."

Grabbing his box of belongings, he crosses the street and climbs the front steps to his house, fumbling for his key while trying to hold onto the box. When he opens the door, he notes that there is no basil leaf in the door jamb. He looks intently around the small foyer, then enters the house cautiously, stepping around the mail that is lying on the floor. He walks slowly up the short flight of steps and places the box on a small table next to the hall closet. Then, he carefully inspects each room before he walks back down the steps, shuts the door, and retrieves the mail.

Mixed among several circulars is a manila envelope with no return address.

Frank walks back up the steps and heads to his bedroom on the second floor. Sitting on the bed, he turns the manila envelope over in his hands before slowly opening it.

Then, he begins to read about how his life is going to change.

The letter is from Joe Cunningham, the late Deputy Secretary of State.

"Ms. Leonard you are now in contempt of Congress and are facing jail time," states Juan Gutierrez, as he glares at Laura Leonard and her attorney in a small room in the United States Capitol Building. "I'm going to give you one last chance to testify, and I'm willing to issue you immunity from further prosecution. But only if you answer all our questions."

Laura leans over and whispers with her attorney. Then, she turns to the prosecutor.

"Mr. Gutierrez, how will you protect me from any...how shall I say this? Any possible retaliations for testifying? Three people have died over the last few weeks. All of their deaths seem to have been explained, but still... "

Gutierrez takes a deep breath before replying. "I will place you under house arrest and have federal marshals guard you. You will testify this Monday."

Laura looks at her attorney for approval. "Okay, let's do this," she says.

It's a typically hot South Florida morning. Offshore thunderstorms are spawning waterspouts over the ocean, within sight of Fort Lauderdale Beach.

About ten miles inland, City of Sunrise Sergeant Jorge Octavio, accompanied by an FBI agent, enters Joe Cunningham's apartment on the eighth floor of a high-rise condominium building. The agent remains near the door while Jorge inspects the apartment.

Walking through the living area and the bedroom, Jorge notes that there are no visible signs of anything unusual. He peers into drawers, closets, and cabinets, and finds—nothing. The only object that catches his eye as he snoops around the apartment is an oil painting on a wall near the living room.

The painting is an ocean scene and is set in an elaborate gold-leaf frame. Attached to the top of the frame is a small light fixture that is positioned to shine onto the canvas. The painting and its frame are not at all in keeping with the rest of the very modern Swedish décor.

"You guys scrubbed this place clean, right?" Jorge asks the FBI agent. "And you didn't find anything unusual?"

There is no response from the FBI agent.

"Hmm, I guess you're not going to share anything with me. Okay, look. I'm not going to go away, so if I should come across anything in my investigation—and I mean anything—I'll be sure to return the favor and not let you guys know about it, either. Just sayin'." Jorge scowls at the agent.

Continuing to walk around the apartment, he inspects the bathrooms and kitchen. Then he announces, "Okay, I'm done here. Don't let the door hit you in the ass on the way out."

With that, Octavio leaves the apartment, but the

FBI agent remains behind.

After reading the letter from Joe Cunningham, Frank Sansone realizes that he needs to go underground to protect himself from the corrupt Administration that is currently in power in Washington. It is crucial for him to immediately change his appearance and go off the grid as soon as possible.

Moving into survival mode, he packs a small backpack with minimal essentials—a change of clothes, a couple of pairs of underwear, some toiletries, and Joe's letter. Out of his armoire, he grabs a 9mm Glock, the $2,000 in cash that he has saved for a time like this, and a small metal box.

Next, Frank enters the master bath and pulls out a single-edge razor blade, a pair of tweezers, and a bottle of rubbing alcohol from the medicine cabinet. After pouring the alcohol over the razor and the tweezers, he lays them both on a tissue on the counter. Then, on his left hand, in the fleshy area between his thumb and index finger, he makes a small incision, about ¼ of an inch long.

Grimacing in pain, he dangles his hand in the sink, allowing his blood to flow down the drain in a constant stream. Grabbing the tweezers, he inserts the tip into the incision and fights against the pain to probe the area until he locates his target. What he removes from his hand is a small RF device the size of a grain of rice that all CIA agents are implanted with so their movements can be monitored.

After placing the RF device on the edge of the sink, he carefully washes the wound and applies pressure to stop the bleeding. Then he takes out a bottle of iodine and a jar of petroleum jelly from the medicine cabinet. Snatching a cotton swab from a small box on the counter, he swabs the wound with the iodine and frowns as the pain intensifies. Then, popping open the jar of petroleum jelly, he swipes out a wad with another swab and smears it over the wound. The jelly quickly clogs up the incision to impede the flow of blood.

After his hand is securely bandaged, he places the RF device into another tissue that he folds up and places into his pocket.

Now that the RF device is removed, Frank turns his attention to the metal box. He opens it and removes a bottle of spirit gum, a well-made prosthesis, and a fake mustache.

As skillfully as a makeup artist to the stars, he applies the spirit gum to the prosthesis and affixes it to his nose to alter its shape. Using theatrical makeup, he carefully blends the prosthesis into the skin tone around his eyes and cheeks, making it virtually impossible to detect. Then he attaches the fake mustache to his upper lip.

The next thing that he needs to change is his hair. Frank usually wears his hair in a short flat-top, but if he's going to become "invisible", that hair style has to go. Taking out a new razor, he shaves his head until he is completely bald.

With his transformation now complete, he cleans up the bathroom and walks back into the bedroom, where he packs the metal box into his backpack. After taking one last look around the room, he picks up his gun, grabs the backpack, and exits his row house.

Not looking back, Frank walks briskly toward

the nearby Metro station, but makes a quick detour when he comes upon an alley. Entering the narrow passageway, he approaches a dumpster, takes out his Android cell phone, and tosses the battery in. After he exits the alley, he takes the sim card out of the phone and throws the now-empty shell into a storm drain near the steps of the Metro station.

At the station, Frank buys his ticket and then stops at a kiosk selling "pay-as-you-go" cell phones. He buys a phone and has it activated on the spot.

Within minutes of his purchase, a train rumbles into the station and stops to unload its passengers. Just before entering the nearest train car, Frank furtively drops the sim card from his old phone onto the tracks between the car and the platform.

It is only a three-minute ride to the next stop on this line. Sitting by himself, Frank removes the RF device from the tissue that has been holding it. When the next station approaches, he rises from his seat and moves close to a woman who is near the door, waiting to exit. When she begins to leave the train, he drops the RF device into the woman's large purse, and smiles.

Now virtually untraceable, Frank exits the train and proceeds up to street level, where he hails a cab to the downtown bus terminal. There, he will take a Greyhound Bus to New York City. He knows that John Hastings was killed there and that Laura Leonard will probably be the Administration's next victim.

It is now Saturday evening, and Laura Leonard is scheduled to testify before Congress on Monday. FBI Agent Jim Medina is with Laura in her apartment near

New York's Battery Park, where she has been placed in protective custody until she testifies.

Laura and the agent have just finished a dinner of Chinese food that was delivered from a local restaurant, and she has turned on the TV to watch President Burris make his statement from the Oval Office. Neither of them is aware that a certain black sedan is parked down the street.

In D.C., Frank has just purchased a ticket for the next Greyhound bus to New York City, but it will not leave until 5:00 a.m. the next morning. He doesn't mind the wait, as it will give him time to review his plan.

Joe Cunningham's letter contains the home address of IRS official Laura Leonard, the next witness who has been subpoenaed to testify before Congress. Frank intends to go directly to Laura's apartment as soon as he arrives in New York City, to warn her about the danger of testifying against the Burris Administration.

As he sits on an uncomfortable bench in the lonely bus depot, Frank thinks about what he has to do and makes the best of his nine-hour wait. After a while, he closes his eyes and tries to get some sleep, but keeps one hand on his 9mm.

"My fellow Americans," begins President Burris, *"I am addressing you this evening to assure you that the charges leveled by conservative talk radio programs and cable news networks such as Fox News will be proven to be*

lies by my special prosecutor, Juan Gutierrez. Together with Juan, I will clear my name and my Administration of those false charges. My fellow Americans, I have done nothing wrong, and I will be vindicated in these matters. There is not even a smidgeon of corruption involving the IRS or the death of Ambassador Kingston, our late ambassador to the Republic of the Sudan. The so-called scandals are a partisan political ruse to taint my Administration and me personally.

"*This evening, I would also like to give you an update on the crisis in Iraq. I have assembled a coalition of allies to confront the radical faction that has taken over some of the country's northern territories. In addition, I have sent three hundred Special Forces advisors to Iraq to help protect our embassy in Bagdad. I will state again, as I have stated before, that there will be no boots on the ground in Iraq. I have a meeting later this evening with the Joint Chiefs of Staff to discuss further options that we may take, which would include manned and unmanned airstrikes.*

"*My fellow Americans, thank you for allowing me into your homes. God bless you all, and God bless the United States of America.*"

When the President finishes his speech, there is a knock at Laura Leonard's door in downtown Manhattan. Jim Medina un-holsters his weapon and turns toward the sound.

"Are you expecting anyone?" he asks.

"No, no one at all," Laura replies with eyebrows raised.

Approaching the door, Jim looks through the peephole and stares at a Secret Service identification badge.

"I know that you're looking at me through the

door," states a voice in the hallway. "I've been sent by the President to assist with Laura's protection. Code word, Lazy Eye."

Recognizing the password, Jim re-holsters his weapon and opens the door.

As the door swings open, a tall woman in the hallway Tasers Jim in the neck and watches as he falls helplessly to the floor, unconscious.

Shocked, Laura jumps up from the sofa and cries, "Who are you? What are you doing here?"

Without a word, the tall woman advances toward Laura, but Laura turns and runs into the bedroom, where she locks the door. Shaking, she tries to call 911 on her cell phone, but she is not quick enough. The tall woman kicks open the door and grabs her before she can make another move. She places Laura into a sleeper submission hold and forces a rag soaked in chloroform over her face until she is unconscious.

The tall woman drags her unconscious victim into the living room, where she drops her unceremoniously to the floor. Then, she walks over to the also unconscious Jim Medina. Removing a hypodermic needle from her pocket, she carefully unsheathes the thin metal needle and injects Joe with sodium pentothal to disable him for twelve to fourteen hours.

Redirecting her attention toward her target, she stows away the hypodermic needle and drags Laura into the bathroom. The mystery woman strips off Laura's clothing and scatters the pieces across the bathroom floor. Then she places Laura in the bathtub, closes off the drain, and turns on the faucet.

As the water begins to fill the tub, the mysterious woman takes the hypodermic needle, which is now empty, and injects an air bubble into the lingual artery at the base of Laura's tongue.

When the water reaches Laura's face, the female ninja forces her head underwater, causing water to fill her lungs and placing her into the throes of imminent death. When a coronary thrombosis attacks Laura's heart, she twitches and convulses, but the spasms subside as quickly as they began. The last indignity she is subjected to before her soul leaves her body is when her bowels and bladder evacuate involuntarily.

Calm and cool as she watches Laura die, the business-suited assassin smiles, reaches down, and gives Laura's right breast a gentle caress before she turns off the water.

Satisfied that her job is done, she stands and unrolls some bathroom tissue from its holder. Using the wad of tissue as a cloth, she carefully wipes down the room and anything in it that she may have touched. Then, using her elbow, she flushes the paper in the toilet and leaves the death chamber.

Intent on exiting the apartment, the woman heads for the living room, where she steps around Jim Medina, who is still lying on the floor. But when a thought occurs to her, she stops before reaching the door. Smiling deviously, she kneels down and kisses Jim, leaving a clear set of red lip prints on his cheek. Then, laughing aloud, she slinks out of the apartment.

CHAPTER FIVE

"That new problem we talked about has been re-solved," says the voice-mail message. After listening to this message, a cell phone in the West Wing goes silent.

Frank stares out of the window as his bus crosses over the Verrazano Bridge. The view of Lower Manhattan is clear, except for a slight haze over Lady Liberty, who, he is happy to see, is still standing guard in the harbor. It is about 8:00 a.m. Sunday morning and Frank should be at Penn Station within 30 minutes. From there, he will hail a cab and go to 71 Broadway.

This same morning, Jack is being awakened out of a dead sleep by the noise of a ringing telephone. Naked as a jaybird, he jumps out of bed and tries to answer the call quickly so he can shut off the annoying sound.

"Yeah? This is Jack. What's up? Okay... let me do my three S's, and then I'll be right there." Jack hangs up the phone and stares at a naked Didi trying to rub the sleep out of her eyes. Admiring his wife, all he can think of is the front bumper of a '58 Caddy.

"Gotta go, Babe. Looks like somebody killed someone."

"Thought you weren't going back to work until

tomorrow."

"Yeah, well, tell that to the murderer."

Jack exits the bathroom no more than twenty minutes later. When Didi squeezes past him to make her way in, he turns to stare at her ass and mumbles, "I am a *very* lucky man."

Grabbing his badge and his Glock, he walks back to the bathroom and pokes his head into the doorway. "See ya later, Babe," he says.

Within minutes, he is driving his Hemi Road Runner out of the parking garage, giving two quick beeps of the horn, and heading toward 71 Broadway.

Frank's cab stops about one hundred feet away from his destination because it can't go any further. There are blue and red lights flashing up ahead, with uniformed officers blocking all vehicles from entering the perimeter they have set up around a crime scene.

As Frank exits the cab, he notices a '68 Road Runner enter the perimeter with blue lights on the dash. His first thought is, "Who is this cowboy?"

Frank makes his way through the small crowd that always seems to gather around misery, and stops at a line of police tape. Calling out to one of the officers, he remarks, "So, Road Runners are now special issue to you guys?"

"Huh? No, that's Detective Stenhouse. He's with Homicide."

Playing the part of a curious onlooker, Frank asks, "What's going on, Officer?"

"Don't know. Guess someone died."

"Yeah, by the looks of things, it must have been a

VIP."

Frank has a pretty good idea who must have died, and he is very troubled that he couldn't have gotten there sooner. Saddened by his inability to prevent the tragedy, he watches glumly as reporters spill out of news vans and satellite towers fly up to the sky like weeds. One of the local female journalists gets set to begin her broadcast ten feet from where he is standing.

"This is Judy Fine with WPIX TV. I am standing in front of 71 Broadway, where another witness who was set to testify before Congress has died. IRS official Laura Leonard was found this morning by U.S. Marshal Jim Medina. No details have been released, so we don't know if Ms. Leonard's death can be attributed to natural causes or to something much worse. I have asked local officials for more information, but they have had no comment."

The reporter stops and looks over her shoulder at something off screen. "Hold on. It appears that the FBI has arrived. Let me see if I can get a statement from them."

Judy runs over to the group of persons exiting a black sedan, followed closely by her cameraman. Each of the new arrivals is wearing a windbreaker with the letters "FBI" stenciled on the back, even though only one of them is from the FBI. Two of them are actually from the CIA, and the other is a U.S. Marshal.

"Excuse me," she says, holding out her microphone, "I'm with WPIX TV. Can you tell our viewers how Laura Leonard died? Was she murdered?"

As the group walks past Judy, a female FBI agent responds to her without breaking stride.

"We have no comment at this time," she says, as

the officers continue toward the building's entrance, leaving the reporter in the lurch.

Not surprised by their unresponsive attitude, Judy once again faces the camera. "Well, it appears that the FBI is keeping a tight lid on this situation, which leads me to believe that there may be more to this story than what we have been told. This is Judy Fine for WPIX-TV, at a murder scene at 71 Broadway."

When the reporter returns to her news van, Frank walks away from the scene. His new destination is an hourly hotel a few blocks away that he knows is frequented by local "working girls." He has taken a room there several times before while doing his thing for the Company, so he knows that it's the perfect place for people who want to drop off the grid. He plans to stay there until he can contact Detective Stenhouse, the Homicide Detective with the '68 Road Runner.

On the way to the hotel, he stops at a small cell phone shop where he purchases another pay-as-you-go phone and has it activated. After leaving the store, he covertly strips down his current phone and throws individual pieces of it down several of the storm drains he passes on his way to the Midnight Hotel.

Laura's residence is filled with police and FBI agents combing over every nook and cranny. When Jack arrives at the door, he stops to place protective coverings over his shoes before he enters the apartment. Jack's partner, Allison Giancarlo, is already there.

"Allison, what's the skinny?" asks Jack as he looks over at the EMTs attending to Jim Medina.

"We got another government witness dead," replies Allison. "It's Laura Leonard." Nodding to the FBI agent lying on the floor, she adds, "He was supposed to be guarding her. I haven't taken his statement yet. He was the one who contacted 911."

Allison motions for Jack to follow her into the bathroom. "It appears that she drowned in the tub, but the CSI guys haven't arrived yet. We don't know what happened with Medina, either."

"Well, let's go find out," says Jack.

When the partners reenter the hallway, Jack sees a familiar face among the assembled officers.

"Maria?" he inquires.

At the sound of her name, FBI Agent Maria Assante turns around.

"Jack! How the hell are you?" she asks enthusiastically when she recognizes the face behind the voice.

Jack gives his friend a handshake that changes into a quick hug.

"I thought you were transferred to D.C.," he states. "What are you doing back in New York?"

"I'm on point with a special team to investigate the deaths of government witnesses. We were sent here to investigate the Hastings case." She looks around. "And now, this one."

"Wait. The feds who took control of the Hastings and Cunningham cases—that wasn't the Bureau?"

"No, it wasn't us. So far, the only presence we've had are some guards that I placed at Cunningham's Florida condo. Everything is classified; that's why this special team is here. I suspect that my next trip is going to be South Florida."

Over their shoulders, they notice that Jim Medina is trying to stand but is still a bit unsteady. Jack reaches down and grabs his arm, helping him to his feet. Medina thanks Jack, and then looks back and forth between Jack and Maria, who are looking at him quizzically.

"Hey!" he states emphatically. "I was overcome by a guy claiming to be a Secret Service Agent! Laura and I had just finished dinner when there was a knock at the door. I went to investigate, and when I peered through the door's peephole, I saw his ID. He spoke to me through the door, and said the President sent him to assist with Laura's safety, and he gave me the code word. But when I opened the door, I guess he had a stun gun. That's the last thing I remember."

The assembled officers who were listening to Jim's explanation stare at each other uncertainly. Then Jack addresses one of the EMT officers. "You got a mirror?"

Fumbling through his gear, the EMT pulls out a small mirror and hands it to Jack.

"Jim, you say the guy at the door was some guy from the Secret Service?"

"Yeah, I saw the name on his ID badge. Allen Vanierri. Why?"

Jack hands Jim the mirror, and after taking one look at his face, he is aghast. "What the fuck?" he asks with disbelief.

"You and Laura were only eating dinner?" Jack asks.

Befuddled, Jim continues to stare into the mirror. "Yeah. No... Yeah," he finally replies. Swiping at the lipstick on his cheek, he continues, "That guy kissed me?"

"You're saying that this 'guy'—the Secret Service

agent—was wearing lipstick?"

"Well...I never saw his face directly. I heard his voice through the door and saw his photo through the peephole. The name on the ID was Allen Vanierri."

Maria takes Jim's arm. "Can you walk? We need to get you to our sketch artist so we can get a good look at this so-called 'Allen.'"

At that, Jack blurts out, "Hey, this is our case!"

"Jack," replies Maria. "Ms. Leonard was under the protection of the federal government. We're taking control of this case now."

"Oh, no," Jack insists, "we're doing this together. I'm comin' with ya. I was the one who found Cunningham in the swamp, so I got skin in this game. Allison," he addresses his partner, "can you accompany the M.E. with the body and observe the autopsy? I'm going down to the Bureau with Assante. Call me later, okay?"

Upset, Maria grabs Jack firmly by the arm. "Look," she declares with a scowl. "I'm going to let you in on this, but only because we're friends. You need to remember that it's our lead, though. Got it?"

Taken aback by Maria's tone, Jack, responds, "Hey, calm down, Wonder Woman. I'm only doing my job."

Just then, the CSI team walks in, accompanied by the medical examiner.

CIA operative Frank Sansone is nearing the Midnight Hotel at the same time as Jack is leaving Laura Leonard's apartment with Jim Medina and the FBI. Frank is scheduled to appear before Congress on Monday, but he know that when he does not show up, a search for him will be triggered. He intends to hide until he can speak with Detective Stenhouse, and until he feels it is safe for him to come back out.

Meanwhile, former Presidential Press Secretary Joe Conway is entering JBAB—Joint Base Anacostia-Bolling—in Southeast Washington D.C., accompanied by two U.S. Marshals. He is being taken to a secure area at this combined Naval support facility and Air Force base, and will be guarded there 24/7 until he appears before the special prosecutor on Wednesday. The U.S. Marshals Service has been instructed to spare nothing to ensure that Joe appears at the hearing as scheduled.

That is everyone's expectation, anyway.

CHAPTER SIX

As he ducks into a dark alley, Frank observes the blue and red lights of speeding police vehicles without being seen.

He waits until the commotion on the street dies down, and then leaves the alley to continue walking to the no-tell motel. But after a few minutes, a distinctive '68 Road Runner also passes by. Muttering at Stenhouse's retreating vehicle, Frank vows, "We'll be talking soon, Detective."

When he finally reaches the Midnight Hotel, Frank reaches for the door handle to enter the building, but he quickly steps aside when two disheveled persons exit in a hurry.

There is no cheerfully decorative front desk area in the lobby of Frank's chosen hideout. Instead, the dimly-lit room showcases yellowing and peeling wallpaper and a cast-iron grate that is crudely bolted across a cutout in one of the walls. The unpleasant odor of bleach, pine, and urine permeates the room.

When Frank approaches the grating, a fat, tattooed man peers at him through the opening and belches.

"Rooms are paid in advance," he intones. "Cash only, fifty bucks a night. You get clean sheets once. If you stay more than a day, you can clean them yourself. There's a washer in the basement."

Without a word, Frank passes three hundred dollars cash through the gate and watches as the man's eyes light up. He knows that it's probably not very often that he sees that much money at one time. The man greedily grabs up all the cash and then passes a ledger under the grate. "Sign the last line, and then print your name."

When Frank returns the ledger, the fat man takes a key off the rack and says, "Okay, Mr. Ben-Hur, you're in Room 305. Right up those stairs—the elevator's broken."

Frank takes the key and heads up the stairs, where he is immediately joined by a 'working girl' who is just coming home for the day.

"Want to have some fun this morning, Stud?" she asks.

Turning his head toward the well-endowed, mini-skirted woman trying to look twenty years younger than she is, he states, "You can't afford me," and continues on his way.

When he reaches his room on the third floor, he looks around before inserting the key into the door and sees the mistress of the night, whose room is also on this floor, flashing him half a peace sign.

The room Frank will be holed up in is stark and bare. Its furnishings consist of a bed, a chair, and a small table with a tiny TV. The dreary cell is illuminated by a bare light bulb hanging from the ceiling, and one dirty window that provides a view of a brick wall.

Nevertheless, Frank is satisfied, and sits down on the bed. He wants to be off the grid, and this place meets all of his expectations.

"This is the composite drawing of Allen Vanierri from Medina's description of the ID photo he saw," explains Maria as she hands Jack an artist's sketch of the suspect.

"Typical jar-head," he comments.

Just then, another agent walks into the room and hands Assante a file. She reviews it quickly and blows out a frustrated sigh. "Well, it looks like Allen Vanierri is a ghost."

"A what?" asks Stenhouse.

"This guy was a Secret Service agent for President Burris, but he died in a helicopter crash in Sweden. His last known address is a townhouse in Columbia, Maryland."

"He died in Sweden? Why was this 'ghost' in Sweden?"

"It says here that he resigned from the Secret Service about three years ago and was on vacation there. Apparently, he was taking a helicopter tour of a glacier when the chopper went down."

Jack stares at Maria. "Yeah, you know that's bullshit, and I don't believe in ghosts. Maria, the Bureau can get access to info that I can't. Can you check with the Secret Service and find out why he resigned? Also, check travel records out of Sweden for this guy, or girl, or whatever."

"We're already on it, Jack."

Jack ignores her. "New York has cameras all over the place, but interestingly, there are no security cameras at 71 Broadway. There have to be cameras along the street, though. Let's see if we can pick up an image.

Medina said they'd just finished watching the President's statement on TV when the guy knocked on the door, so we have a timeline."

Sighing, Maria says, "Jack, I'll get with Interpol on the travel thing, but we're already checking the cameras. I'll call the Secret Service myself to find out why he resigned."

When Jack's cell phone rings, he glances at the screen before answering.

"Allison? What's the skinny?"

"Hi, Jack. Preliminary results from the M.E. say Leonard drowned and also had a heart attack. He's not sure yet which one occurred first, but there was water in her lungs. Oh, and your federal friends came in and took the body."

Jack immediately ends the call and grabs Assante by the arm. "What's this shit about? Allison told me you guys just took Leonard's body."

Maria yanks her arm out of Jack's grip. "Hold on, macho man. We didn't take anybody." Maria places her face close to Jack's and stares into his eyes. "Jack, you grab me again like that, and I'll break your arm. CAPEESH?"

"Hey! Back off, Wonder Woman. I'm just tired of the federal government coming in and shutting down my investigations. First it's Hastings and Cunningham, and now, it's Leonard. And who knows what happened with this Vanierri Secret Service guy, or girl? This whole thing stinks. We got a congressional committee investigation going on about possibly impeaching President Burris, and people are dying all over the place. So, excuse me if I don't trust you guys as far as I can throw ya. But I promise I won't do that again—unless you start covering shit up."

"Sorry, Jack. I've been chosen to lead a team involving the U.S. Marshal's office, the FBI, and the CIA. We also believe that something stinks at 1600 Pennsylvania Avenue, and we think the Secret Service is involved in whatever's going on. I bet they're the ones who took Laura Leonard."

"And probably Joe Cunningham, too," adds Jack.

"Go home, Jack. I'll contact you as soon as I get any new information. I'm not going to cover anything up, but you should be very vigilant. If the witnesses connected to the Burris probe are being targeted, we may be next on the list."

Jack sighs but leaves the office, freeing Maria to continue to review Allen Vanierri's file in relative silence. At an adjacent desk, her CIA partner sends out requests for CCTV footage from the neighborhood cameras that might give insight into the mystery Secret Service agent.

Across the room, George Ipsocky, a U.S. Marshal, ends a call with the Secret Service, and calls out to Maria. "Hey, I got some info on this Vanierri guy. My contact with the Service told me that there were rumors that Allen Vanierri had a, well, how shall I say this...an 'inappropriate' sexual relationship with President Burris, and he was forced to resign because of it. My guy said Vanierri was a cross-dresser."

"Wow, I always suspected Burris was a switch-hitter," says Maria. "That may explain the lipstick on Medina's face. Look—place a call to Interpol to see if they can get anything about Vanierri's death out of the authorities in Sweden. If they don't cooperate, I'll have two of the CIA team—probably Ralph and

Joan—contact their CIA sources in Stockholm." Suddenly, a thought occurs to her, and she waves her hand dismissively. "Hold on... never mind about that. We'll just go through the Company for that info."

Back in D.C., a secret cell phone conversation begins.

"Yes?"

"Conway is in lockdown. I'm not going to be able to take care of that issue at this time."

"He won't say anything, so I'm not concerned. Concentrate on Sansone."

"Well, that's another problem. Sansone is missing."

"What? He's CIA. He was there—he knows. Look, the CIA will find Sansone. All of those agents have implanted tracking devices."

"That doesn't matter. He won't be found if he doesn't want to be found."

Shutting down the call, the red-haired assassin stares at her Android screen. *Mr. Joe Conway, Press Secretary, is the one who may spill the beans. But not if I can help it.*

Laughing, the assassin heads to Sansone's house to see if she can find any clues as to where may be hiding.

CHAPTER SEVEN

Jack is deep in thought. With a cup of coffee up to his lips, he's studying a whiteboard detailing the information they have so far about the Leonard case: a mystery Secret Service agent, a timeline based on the President's speech, and lip imprints on Jim Medina's face.

When Detective Giancarlo returns to the precinct from the autopsy, she stops at her desk, and then joins Jack at the whiteboard.

"So far," she informs him, "we got a lot of nothing. The FBI sent a consultant to help with the investigation. They're still examining the body, but it looks like Leonard suffered a heart attack, which probably caused her to slip under the water and drown."

"That's 'probably' a lot of bullshit," snaps Jack. "Do we know why our 'kissing agent' was at the apartment?"

"Maybe he was there to kill Leonard, but she was already dead?"

"No, Allison, that dog won't hunt. We're missing something."

"Hey, Jack!" calls a fellow officer. "You got a call on line three."

Jack walks over to his desk and picks up the phone. "Stenhouse here."

"Detective, Laura Leonard was taken out and so were John Hastings and Sue Wilkens. I'm next. Remember Cronos? Meet me at that abandoned warehouse at

5:00 tomorrow morning."

"Wait! Who are...?"

The line goes dead.

"DAMN IT!" shouts Jack.

"What the hell was that all about?" asks Allison.

"Some guy said Hastings, Wilkens, and Leonard were murdered, and that he was next. He wants me to meet him at the Remus warehouse at 5:00 tomorrow morning."

"What does he mean, he's 'next'?"

"Maybe he's another witness who's been subpoenaed. Tomorrow's Monday. I'll find out what this guy wants before I come into work. Then, when I get here, maybe Conrad will have the Hastings file ready for me."

Special Prosecutor Juan Gutierrez is at home with his family when he gets a frantic call from an associate working on the Burris investigation. "Mr. Gutierrez, we have a problem. Frank Sansone is missing."

Gutierrez is shocked but doesn't let on to his family. "Hold on, let me go into my office." Once he is alone, Gutierrez questions the caller. "Okay, what do you mean, he's 'missing'?"

"We tried calling him, but there was no answer. We also sent marshals to his house, but he's not there."

"I'll contact his boss at the CIA," declares Gutierrez. "They can track him through his chip."

Juan ends the call and then quickly contacts Sydney Bishop, Frank Sansone's CIA superior. Sydney is also enjoying his Sunday off, so when his phone rings, he is surprised to see Juan Gutierrez's ID information pop up on the screen.

"Juan? To what do I owe this call on a Sunday?"

"Frank Sansone is missing, and he must have deactivated his phone. We can't get a GPS signal on it—nothing. We need you to activate his tracker."

"That's not good; I hope he hasn't gone silent. I'll contact our boys at Langley to get a trace started."

Sydney ends the call and immediately places a request with his office for surveillance of an agent.

In a dark sub-basement of an undisclosed location, a CIA operator triggers Frank's chip and tracks the blip that appears on the screen to the National Zoo. He quickly places a call back to Sydney Bishop.

"Sir, we got a hit at the National Zoo. I guess he likes animals."

"Keep tracking him. I'll call Gutierrez so he can send in the cavalry. When he gives me his marshal's cell number, I'll contact you, and you can patch the tracer onto his marshal's phone."

Jack is staring at the whiteboard and shaking his head. "Allison, we're going to need help with this one."

Allison's reply is lost when they are interrupted.

"Jack, I got something for you," says a voice.

Turning toward the sound, Jack smiles at his boss. "Lieutenant Conrad! I didn't expect to see you until tomorrow."

"Yeah, well, my contact gave me a call and, well... here." He drops the Hastings file on Jack's desk and fixes an intent gaze on his detective. "Now, go home, Jack. Spend time with your new bride. I have a feeling you won't be seeing much of her in the next few weeks. Allison, that goes for you too. Go home."

Jack looks at the file, and then at Conrad and his partner. "Lieutenant, I think this investigation is going to lead to influential people in our government."

"Take it where it leads, Jack, but be very careful. We're now knee-deep in this shit, but it seems that someone doesn't want to be found."

Jack thanks the Lieutenant and picks up the file. He gives a high-five to Detective Giancarlo and then heads out the door for home.

A team of U.S. Marshals is causing a stir as they walk determinedly through the National Zoo on a chilly Sunday afternoon. Thousands of people have flocked to the zoo to see the various animal exhibits, and when the team of black-suited agents passes by, they leave a trail of startled gasps in their wake.

Clint Jessup, the deputy U.S. Marshal in charge of this team, receives a link on his phone from the sub-basement at Langley as the group heads down Olm-stead Walk, the park's central pathway. After he clicks on the link, a blip appears over a map of the zoo. As he watches the image, the blip turns onto the Elephant Trail and enters a restroom.

At the direction of Jessup, the marshals sprint toward the zoo's elephant area. On the way, Clint mo-tions for two of them to accompany him down the pathway near the small animal exhibit, while he sends the others to the far end of the trail, near the lemur exhibit. All of them are being stared at by the visiting families and tourists, their black suits standing out like a sore thumb.

When Clint and his companions arrive at the restroom building, Agent Sansone's target blip is still inside.

Cautiously, Clint and one of the agents enter the men's room while a third stands guard at the entrance and prohibits anyone else from entering. There is soon a crowd at the scene, as the elephant area is one of the zoo's major attractions.

Inside the restroom, the urinals are empty, but one of the stall doors is closed. After a flushing sound, the door opens to reveal an older man who walks over to the sink and washes his hands. It is not Sansone. Puzzled, Clint checks his cell phone and sees that the blip is still in the restroom building.

Addressing the other agent, he says, "This guy is in the ladies' room." They hurriedly exit the men's room and then wait impatiently for the target to appear outside of the ladies' entrance.

A man, who is standing nearby with his son, is also waiting outside of the ladies' room.

When a woman and a young girl leave the restroom and walk past Clint, his phone reacts instantly and beeps loudly. At the sound, the three marshals approach the woman, along with the remaining agents who have just arrived from the far end of the path.

Clint stops the woman and displays his badge.

"Excuse me, ma'am. I'm U.S. Marshal Clint Jessup, and I need to speak with you."

The woman's husband approaches with their son, but he is stopped by the other marshals. "Why are you stopping my wife?" he demands from a distance.

The husband watches incredulously as one of the marshals passes a wand around his astonished wife's body. The marshal stops the wand when the chirping alert becomes a steady tone. Turning to Clint, he says, "It's in the purse."

"Ma'am, I need to see your purse," demands the lead officer.

The woman reluctantly hands it over while her husband begins to spout their constitutional rights.

Clint quickly searches through the deep, dark chambers of the leather cavern, pushing aside pieces of candy, various beauty items, lint, and gum wrappers. Finally, he removes what looks like a grain of rice, and hands the purse back to the woman.

"Where did you get this?" he asks.

The woman peers at the tiny object. "I have no idea what that is," she says.

Another marshal shows her a photograph of Frank Sansone. "Do you know who this man is? Have you ever met him?"

The woman looks at the picture and says, "I have no idea who he is, and I've never met him. What's going on?" she demands.

At this point, her children are crying, and her husband is livid. Clint tells one of the agents to take the children and their father off to the side while he continues to talk with the now worried and frightened woman.

"Ma'am, I need to speak with you in private. Would you like some water or soda?" Clint takes her by the arm and guides her to a nearby vending machine.

"Yes, water would be good," she answers shakily.

Clint makes the purchase, and hands a bottle of cold water to the woman while leading her to a round table with a large metal umbrella. After they are seated, he waits for her to take a drink and then continues his line of questioning.

"Okay, ma'am, what is your name?"

"Mrs. Silvia St. James."

"Mrs. St. James—Silvia. Can you tell me what your routine has been in the last twenty-four hours? You say you don't know this man, yet you have his tracking device in your purse."

Still a little shaky, Silvia takes another sip of water. "Well, I'm a legal secretary for the law firm of Gutierrez and Phillips here in Washington. I was called in to work yesterday to help with a deposition. I took the Metro around 5:00 in the afternoon, and returned home around nine that night."

Clint's interest is piqued. "Gutierrez and Phillips? Is that Special Prosecutor Juan Gutierrez?"

"Yes, but I'm not working on that case, thank God."

"Did anyone approach you, or talk to you, or bump into you on the train?"

Silvia chuckles sarcastically. "Come on now, it's a train. People bump into you all the time. But I don't remember seeing that man."

"What line did you take on the Metro?"

"The Green Line. I took the Green Line."

Satisfied that Mrs. St. James is not a threat, Clint ends the conversation. "Thank you, Silvia. I'm sorry for any inconvenience to you and your family."

Clint also apologizes to Mr. St. James, and then motions to the rest of the marshals. As the team leaves the zoo, Clint places a call to his office.

"We have a problem," he begins. "Sansone removed his tracker; he went dark. All we did here was scare a lady and her kids and piss off her husband. Sansone must have dropped the RF device into her purse. She took the Metro Green Line on Saturday, and since Sansone lives near Branch Ave, he probably took the Metro that day as well and passed the tracker off to her. Get Metro Police involved, and circulate his photo at the airports, bus, and train stations. Also send it to the car rental companies. Sansone is on the run."

Didi expects Jack to be home from work any minute. She is preparing his favorite dinner, meatloaf and mashed potatoes, in her very special way—wearing fishnet stockings and six-inch heels under a black leather apron that strategically ends twelve inches above her knees and has two thin straps that are struggling to encase her assets.

When Jack opens the door and takes one look at his wife, all of his previous plans for the evening are pushed to the back of his mind. Jack may want to review the Hastings file, but that is going to have to wait until after dinner and dessert—if he still has the strength.

Later that evening, after watching an uninteresting program on the small television set in his room, Frank finally decides to remove his disguise and prepare for bed. Staring into the cracked bathroom mirror, he begins by pulling off the fake nose. "Well, Frank," he sighs, "tomorrow should be an interesting day."

As he walks out of the bathroom, the wails of police sirens waft up from the street below, and the sounds of moaning and gasping seep through the thin wall of the adjoining room.

CHAPTER EIGHT

It's five a.m. on Monday morning, and the Big Apple is slowly waking. Jack is exhausted as he drives to the old Remus meat-packing warehouse near FDR Drive. It is way too early for him to be up. He got very little sleep, but smiles at the memory of last night...oh, that tiny black apron...

The sight of the warehouse brings him back to reality. The last time he was here was months ago, but with remnants of crime scene tape still dangling and swaying in the morning breeze, the place hints at death even now.

At the front entrance, he briefly inspects the door, which seems to have been forced open, and then cautiously makes his way inside with his gun and flashlight pointing the way. It is pitch dark in the main warehouse, so Jack swivels his flashlight from side to side to look around.

Suddenly, a voice booms down from an upper floor at the far end of the building.

"Shut off the light, Jack, so that we can proceed with our meeting. And put your fucking gun away. If I wanted to kill you, you would have been dead already."

Jack holsters his weapon and turns off the flashlight. "Okay, who are you, and what do you want from me?"

"Who I am will be known to you real soon. For now, you can call me 'Ben-Hur.' Watch the news. I came to New York to warn Laura Leonard, but I was too late. The body you found in the Glades—Cunningham—I reported to him in Sudan. I was at the Sudanese Embassy, and I know what happened there. So did he. He sent me a package that included a letter from him that said he was probably going to be killed. The letter details stuff that will rock this country, and he left proof of it all, a lot of proof, but I don't have any of it. Witnesses are being killed, and it's all coming from 1600 Pennsylvania Ave."

"That's a hell of a story. What evidence do you have that the President is involved in murder?" asks Jack.

"I don't know have any evidence, but I know it exists; Cunningham gave me a clue. His letter says, 'Things are hidden from plain sight. Look where it cannot be seen.'"

"What the hell does that mean?" growls Jack.

"I don't know yet, but I do know that we can't meet like this again. If they find out that you're on their trail, you'll be followed, your phone will be tapped, and you may be the next one to be hit. Get a pre-paid cell phone so we can keep in touch. A dumb phone, not an Android phone. We'll use it as a burner; I don't want our calls traced. I'll send a courier to your office this afternoon. Give him the cell phone's number. I'll contact you again soon."

"Oh," the voice continues, "two more things. First, the media is going to report that Joe Cunningham had a gambling debt, and that's why he was killed. But that's bullshit—there was no debt. Someone is being set up to take the fall. Have your sergeant friend in Florida check out the casino down there and get him to check Joe's place. The second thing has to do with Hastings. The M.E.'s report will say that he went into diabetic shock, and that's what caused his deadly crash. But Hastings wasn't diabetic. Have your M.E. check Leonard's body carefully. She was killed, and so was Sue Wilkens. Now, go to the back of the building and stare at the river for five minutes."

Jack tries to stall the mystery man. "Hold on a second. You just made a lot of accusations. What am I supposed to do with this information? And when will you call? I have a lot of questions."

"No questions," replies 'Ben-Hur' firmly. "Just go out back. *Now*."

Fumbling his way in the dark, Jack reaches the back receiving door, and exits the warehouse. Then he walks over to the sea wall and waits. As he watches a tugboat chug down the East River, he hears the front door of the warehouse open and then slam shut. No longer waiting the prescribed five minutes, he runs around the building to see if he can spot the mystery man, but all he encounters is a quiet parking lot and the slowly-awakening FDR Drive.

Disappointed, he climbs into the only car in the lot, his beloved '68 Road Runner. Starting up the beast, he gives two quick beeps of the horn and heads to work.

On the way to the First Precinct, he thinks about what the mystery man said and decides to stop at a small phone and media store near the office later that morning.

On the commuter train from New York to D.C., the red-haired assassin sits quietly and concentrates on her next target. Even though she was told that he would not be a problem, she is taking no chances. She will do this one as a favor. Joe Conway is a dead man.

"This is Sam Larson, CBS News Washington. As you have probably heard by now, IRS official Laura Leonard has died of a heart attack. Another mysterious tragedy among the group of witnesses that was scheduled to testify before Congress. And my sources have told me that another witness who was supposed to testify today, CIA Operative Frank Sansone, is now missing. There have been no comments on either of these mysterious circumstances from Special Prosecutor Juan Gutierrez or the White House. However, Mr. Gutierrez is holding a press conference at 11:00 a.m. today. Perhaps he will provide some insight as to why all of his witnesses are ending up dead or missing. This is Sam Larson in Washington."

At 5:45 in the morning, the First Precinct's Homicide Division is a lonely place. Clutching the Hastings file, Jack walks over to his desk, and begins to read it over a cup of steaming coffee. He never got the chance to look it over last night—Didi had other ideas.

After a while, he puts the file down and dials Sergeant Octavio in Florida.

"Jorge, its Jack."

Awakened way too early, the sergeant displays his annoyance. "Jack, its fucking 6:00 in the morning! What the hell do you want at this hour?"

"Look, I got an informant on the murders of those witnesses."

"Murders, plural? There's been another one?"

"Yeah, it looks like there are four now—John Hastings, Joe Cunningham, Sue Wilkens, and Laura Leonard."

"Oh, yeah. I heard about Leonard on the news yesterday. But what about that informant?"

"I think the guy is CIA, and he knew Cunningham. He says a report is going to come out that Cunningham had a gambling debt, and that he was hit because of it. The thing is, though, according to this guy Cunningham had no gambling debts. He also says that you need to go back to Cunningham's apartment. He says Cunningham left a clue there about the killings. Take this down, these are the words to the clue."

"Yeah, okay, let me get a piece of paper. It's fucking 6:00 in the morning, you know that?"

Jack ignores Octavio's complaint. "Here's the clue: 'Things are hidden from plain sight. Look where it can't be seen.'"

"What kind of clue is that?" Octavio grunts.

"Check out the condo and let me know what you find there. And get someone to visit the casino he frequented. Call me at my office number at the First, not on my cell. And Jorge, be careful. You'll probably be followed."

Jack ends the call and walks over to the whiteboard, where he adds Hastings and Wilkens to the growing list.

Allison Giancarlo finally makes her way into the office at 8:00. By now, Jack is on his third cup of coffee and needs to see a man about a horse. Waving at Allison, he scurries to the men's room down the hall.

Allison drops her things at her desk and looks at the updated whiteboard. Then, she thumbs through the large file on Jack's desk.

"Find anything interesting?" asks a voice. Turning, Allison sees FBI Agent Maria Assante approaching.

"Hi, Maria. The Bureau is up early today."

Looking puzzled, Maria asks, "Where's Jack?"

"Right here," says Jack as he walks back to his desk with another cup of coffee. "Any news yet?"

"Yeah, replies Maria. "Allen Vanierri was on President Burris's Secret Service detail three years ago. We have an agent in Stockholm looking for documents related to his visit to Sweden, and the Swedish Police Service is checking records at the Karolinska University Hospital. He was taken there after the crash."

"Great," Jack says with a nod. "Well, I got some news as well. It seems that I have a 'Deep Throat.' A guy contacted me yesterday; he's probably with the CIA. He says the information that will be released about the deaths of John Hastings and Sue Wilkens won't be true. He says they're going to say that Hastings was diabetic, but he wasn't. According to this guy, he was murdered, and so was Wilkens. He also says they're going to say that Cunningham was hit because of a gambling debt, but according to my contact, Joe didn't have any gambling debts. I'm having that story checked out in Florida as we speak. Oh, and he also says that Leonard didn't have a heart attack, that she was murdered, and that her killing is related to the others."

"Do you have any idea who this guy is?" asks Allison.

"No, but he must have a wicked sense of humor.

He wants me to call him 'Ben-Hur.' "

After the snickers die down, Jack continues. "And as if all that wasn't enough, he laid out a real bombshell before he left. He said all this shit is coming from the White House."

"The White House?" Maria exclaims. "He said Burris is involved?"

Instead of answering, the always quick-witted Jack replies, "You know what you get when you cross an elephant and a rhino?"

Maria closes her eyes and shakes her head. "Okay, so don't answer me," she says with a smile at the corners of her lips. Then, she gets serious. "I think I know who 'Ben-Hur' is, Jack. Frank Sansone was due to testify today, but he's missing. Play along with him and keep his cover. If it's Frank, he's CIA, and if he gets any indication that we're looking for him, he'll disappear into thin air."

"He got a letter from Cunningham. Joe knew he was being targeted, and the letter says he left a clue in his apartment."

Maria snorts, "Our guys went through that apartment thoroughly, and they found nothing."

"Yeah, I know. I also sent my contact at the Sunrise Police Department there, and he didn't find anything, either. But I told him to go back."

"Jack, I need you on my team," decides Maria. "I'm going to talk to Deputy Inspector Rawlings."

Jack has mixed feelings about that. He wants the action, but he suspects that this case is going to be big, and he doesn't want to leave his new wife for too long. "You know, if Rawlings approves putting me on your team, Didi is not going to be happy."

Maria knows this but dismisses his comment with a shrug of her shoulders.

"This guy 'Ben-Hur'," says Jack, "wants me to buy a pre-paid phone to get off the grid. He's sending a courier down here to get the phone number, so I'm going over to that Slam Mobile outlet down the street."

Maria nods in agreement. "Okay. When you get back, call your contact in Sunrise. I want to go down to Florida myself, and I want you to come with me. Someone is working very hard at covering things up. We'll check out the apartment and the casino together."

She looks at the whiteboard again. "I'll make arrangements to leave tonight. That will give you time to get your new cell phone number to 'Ben-Hur.' I'm going to have the Secret Service look into the Hastings and Wilkens cases, and we'll do another autopsy on Leonard. If they find anything new, we should know about it by the time we get back."

While he's anxious to work with his old friend Maria, Jack remembers that he already has a partner at the First.

"Allison, stay close to the Bureau on the Leonard case. I'll pick up a new phone for you as well. We can call each other off the grid if we need to."

Allison is uncomfortable with this arrangement but agrees to do her part for the team. "Okay, Jack, what if the President's involved? How the hell are we going to get into that circle?"

Jack smiles. "ELAPHINO!" he shouts.

Maria groans and rolls her eyes. "You just had to say it, didn't you?"

"What the heck does that mean?" asks Allison.

"It's one of Jack's 'cute' sayings," she says with air

quotes. "It means, 'Hell if I know.' "

Now, Allison rolls her eyes.

Smiling, Jack turns to leave for the cell phone store while Maria goes off in search of D.I. Rawlings to request Stenhouse's help on the case.

Remaining behind, Allison reflects on the interaction she just witnessed between Jack and Maria. *They must be really good friends,* she muses. *They're acting like an old married couple!*

"Doctor, I'm Agent Sam Cummings with the United States Federal Bureau of Investigation, and this is Inspector Christian Malmstrom."

"Yes, Doctor," interjects Malmstrom, "I'm with the National Police Department, but I'm also working with Interpol and our American friends. We are here to talk with you about a former patient of yours, one Allen Vanierri."

At the Karolinska Hospital in Stockholm, Dr. Johan Borgstrom gestures to a couple of chairs across from his desk. "Please sit, gentlemen. How can I be of assistance?"

"Doctor," begins Inspector Malmstrom, "Agent Cummings is investigating a murder in the United States that may be linked to Mr. Vanierri's death at this hospital."

"Oh?"

"Yes. We have information that Mr. Vanierri was injured in a helicopter crash about three years ago and was transported to this hospital, where he died from his injuries."

Doctor Borgstrom is stunned. "No...no, that is

not exactly accurate."

With his interest piqued, Cummings inquires, "How so, Doctor? Isn't it true that Allen Vanierri's life ended here?"

"Well, Agent," smirks Doctor Borgstrom, "I would have to answer yes and no to that question. There was no accident. When Inspector Malmstrom called me to schedule this meeting, I looked up the records of Mister Vanierri."

He opens a file on his desk and presents a photograph of Allen Vanierri to Sam Cummings. "This is the man in question, is it not?"

Cummings nods in agreement.

Borgstrom sits back and smiles. "Allen Vanierri came here three years ago for gender reassignment surgery. He began hormone therapy before his arrival here, and we continued that therapy for three months before his surgery. Mr. Vanierri also had his Adam's apple reduced and had breast and facial enhancements. He was hospitalized here for one week and then went through physical and psychological post-surgery sessions for about three more weeks. So, yes. Allen Vanierri's life ended here. He became Ellen."

Inspector Malmstrom looks at Agent Cummings, and then at Doctor Borgstrom. "So, there was no helicopter crash or declaration of death?"

"No, nothing like that at all." Thumbing through the file, the doctor produces another photograph.

"Gentlemen, meet Ellen."

Slack-jawed, Cummings and Malmstrom gape at the photo of a red-haired woman, and then look back at each other.

"Doctor, may I have that photograph?" asks

Agent Cummings.

"Yes, of course." Borgstrom hands the photo over. "Is there anything else I can do for you? If not, I have surgery in twenty minutes."

Inspector Malmstrom stands and says, "No, thank you, Doctor. You have been very helpful."

After shaking the doctor's hand, the two men leave his office and walk down the hospital hallway in silence. However, after only a few steps, Inspector Malmstrom comments, "The U.S. must be a very progressive country to allow this type of person to be one of your President's personal bodyguards."

"Ha! You don't know the half of it," retorts Sam. Handing the photo of Ellen Vanierri to Christian, he asks, "Hold this up, please. I need to take a photo of it to send to a fellow agent in New York."

Using his Android phone, Cummings captures the image and forwards it to Agent Assante. After the image is sent, he gives Maria a call.

"This is Assante."

"Hi, it's Sam Cummings in Stockholm. I just sent you a picture of Allen Vanierri, or should I say, Ellen Vanierri. Allen's life did end here, in a way. He's now known as Ellen."

Sam hears a gasp on the other end of the line but continues. "I'm going to check into airline departure records here, and I'll also go to our embassy to see if they have any information on this 'new person,' Ellen Vanierri. I'll call you if I find out anything."

"Okay," says Maria. "Let me open the file you sent." After a short pause, she exclaims, "Holy shit! Wait until I show this to Jack!"

CHAPTER NINE

"Another key witness in the impeachment proceedings of President Burris is now missing. CIA Agent Frank Sansone was subpoenaed by Special Prosecutor Gutierrez to testify before Congress this morning, but according to the U.S. Marshal's Service and his superiors at the CIA, Mr. Sansone is nowhere to be found. So far, one witness in this investigation has been murdered, and three other witnesses have died suddenly. However, there have been no comments from either the White House or Mr. Gutierrez about these bizarre developments. One must wonder if anyone else will willingly testify against the President. This is Gloria Patrone, CNN Washington."

It is now late morning, and Ellen Vanierri has made her way back to her townhouse in Annapolis. After checking her mail, she walks into her bathroom and begins to transform her appearance for her next job.

While she gathers her makeup and other paraphernalia, the nagging headache she has had all day increases. Opening a bottle of Ibuprofen, she takes three pills this time, because two do not work anymore. Then she closes her eyes for a few moments and rubs the back of her neck.

This self-pampering only lasts a minute, however. Shaking off the pain, she continues with her preparations.

Ellen works carefully and precisely. She applies several types of prosthetics to change the appearance of her face, adds brown-tinted contacts to mask her beautiful blue eyes, and slips on a long, gray wig over her red hair. All of these measures add at least fifty years to her appearance. Then, to complete the transformation, she pulls out a walking cane from the umbrella stand near the front door and leaves the house.

Ellen will take a cab to D.C. and exit the vehicle near the National Mall. She will then 'hobble' over to the Metro entrance and take the Green Line to Branch Avenue. There, she will attempt to get into Sansone's house. She had thought her next target would be Conway, but if it turns out that Sansone suits her fancy, he'll be next.

The Big Apple is wide awake now. People are flowing through her crowded streets like life blood flowing through her veins.

Jack is back at the First with his new dumb phone. He writes a quick note to the desk sergeant with instructions for him to give the phone number to the courier who should arrive later that day. Then he goes up to his office, where Maria and Allison are reviewing the video tapes they requested, which are from an ATM across the street from Laura Leonard's apartment.

"Huh. I leave for a few minutes, and when I come back, you guys are watching Netflix!"

"Ha, ha..." deadpans Allison, not taking her eyes off the screen.

Maria hands Ellen's photo to Jack. Puzzled, he

looks at it, flips it over to check out the reverse side, and then flips it to the front again. "Who the hell is this?" he asks.

Placing a steadying hand on Jack's shoulder, Maria answers, "That's Allen Vanierri, now known as Ellen Vanierri."

"Ha! Really? He had a little nip and tuck done in Sweden? Well, I guess that explains the lipstick, then."

"Yeah," Giancarlo chimes in, "and that rumored 'affair' with Burris just became more…involved."

Suddenly, Allison sits up straight in her chair. "Hold on, I think I got something." She stops the tape, rewinds it, and then hits Play. "Look at the timeline. There's a tall redhead in an overcoat entering the building just before the end of the President's speech."

"Good job, partner!" says Jack with a slap on Allison's back. Turning to Maria, he asks, "Can you get your guys to enhance that image so we can get a better view of it? This redhead could be our killer. And then we need to get the enhanced photo circulated to the troops."

"Will do, Jack," agrees Maria. "And our guy in Sweden is trying to establish a paper trail on Ellen Vanierri from when she left his country." With a big grin, she adds, "And by the way, I got reservations for us to leave for Fort Lauderdale this afternoon at 2 p.m. You're officially on my team."

Jack grins in reply, but then says, "Shit! That means you're my boss! Oh, well." He looks at his watch and continues, "I need to get home to pack, and I need to tell Didi what's going on. I'll meet you at the terminal at one o'clock."

"Oh, one more thing, Jack," says Maria. "We

towed Sansone's, or 'Ben-Hur's', SUV into the garage. Its brake lines were cut."

Jack gives a low whistle. "Well, then, I'd go dark, too."

Before leaving for home, Jack hands a piece of paper to his partner. "Allison, this is my new cell number. Don't forget to get yourself a burner, too. And please make sure that courier gets my new number."

Jack needs to talk to Didi before he catches his flight. He climbs into his beast, which he left double-parked in front of the First, to head to her boutique on the Lower East Side. If he can flow through the city's veins freely and not get stuck in a traffic embolism, he should get there in about twenty minutes. That will still be cutting it short, though. He only has about an hour and a half to get to the airport.

On his way to enter the crowded byways, he places a call to Sergeant Octavio in Florida through the Roadrunner's onboard phone system.

"Hey, this is Stenhouse. I'm coming down there today with an FBI agent from Washington. Both of us are assigned to the case. I'll call you in the morning, and we can all go down to Cunningham's place together."

Enthused, Octavio responds, "Good, because I was told to back off by my boss. New phone?"

"Yeah, it's a prepaid, so it can't be traced easily. I'll use it for a couple of days and then switch to another one. See you tomorrow."

In the lobby of the Midnight Hotel, Frank Sansone picks up the receiver of one of the last pay phones in Manhattan and wipes it down thoroughly before placing a call to Xtreme Couriers. The delivery service employs maniacs on bicycles to scream through the streets of New York on a mission to transport urgent packages. Frank is very familiar with this service because they are very discreet.

"Hi. Yeah, I need one of your guys to go to the First Police Precinct and pick up a letter from a Detective Jack Stenhouse. I'll pay cash when the letter's delivered to me at the Midnight Hotel, Room 305. My name is Ben-Hur."

An old, gray-haired lady is slowly making her way down Branch Avenue. When she sees a man sitting in a car parked outside of Frank Sansone's house, she walks near enough to get a quick look inside and immediately notices the coiled wires of a communications device trailing from the back of his ear down into his shirt.

Smiling, the old woman taps the driver's side window with her cane and waits for the man to lower the window. Then she asks haltingly, "Excuse me, young man, I'm a little lost. Can you tell me where the Metro station is? I'm trying to visit my great-grandchildren, but I think I took a wrong turn."

"Sure, ma'am. It's back in the other direction, about two blocks down. Are you sure you can make it there?"

Sighing, the old lady wobbles a little on her cane. "Well, I am a bit tired. Oh, do you think you can take me there?"

The man thinks about it for a minute and then agrees. "Sure. Okay, let me help you into the back."

The man gets out of the car and circles around to help the old lady into the back seat. When he leans in to help her with the seat belt, she grabs his collar and yanks him in with her. Quickly, the woman Tasers the U.S. Marshal and he falls limply to the floor of the car. She then injects him with a sedative and exits the car.

As the "old lady" makes her way across the street, she mumbles, "What a jerk."

At 26 Federal Plaza, the New York field office of the FBI, Agent Loretta Fusco is cleaning up the surveillance video obtained from a camera across the street from Laura Leonard's apartment building. She has been trying to enhance the image of the tall redhead, but when she notices that the woman's reflection appears in the glass door of the building, she uses that to capture her face. When she's satisfied with her work, she digitally removes the enhanced image from the video, and clicks Print.

Photo in hand, she immediately places a call to Agent Assante. "Hey, Maria," she says into the phone. "This is Fusco from Forensics. We got her."

Jack surprises Didi while she is cashing out a customer at her boutique.

"Jack, what are you doing here?" she asks. "Is anything wrong?"

Smiling, Jack walks behind the counter while Didi is still bagging the customer's lingerie and gives her a kiss as he squeezes her ass.

He waits until the customer leaves, then asks, "Remember the guy we found inside the snake in Florida?"

"How can I forget that, Jack? It was horrible!"

"Well, that guy was one of the people who has died or gone missing after being subpoenaed to testify before Congress in the President's impeachment trial. Maria's back in town on assignment, and she asked me to join the special task force that's trying to find out who's killing those witnesses. I'm going down to Florida with her later today, and we're going to search the 'snake man's' apartment. I've also been contacted by someone who I think was scheduled to testify today, before he placed himself among the missing."

Wide-eyed, Didi remembers watching news coverage of the missing witness. "Oh, I saw that on TV this morning! It's a CIA guy named Frank Sansone, right? He's the one who disappeared. You think he's your informant?"

"Yeah. Remember that warehouse the serial killer used a few months ago? I met him there, and he told me to use a pay-as-you-go phone to get off the grid. But Babe, I have to go now. I have to go home and pack, and then I have to get to the airport. I'm going to leave my baby parked outside. Here's her keys. Use her while I'm away, but be gentle with her. I'll take a cab home from here."

Jack gives Didi a hug and an extra-long kiss, and then leaves the boutique. On the sidewalk outside the store, he hails a cab and waves at Didi, who is watching him through the boutique window.

Frowning with worry, Didi remains at the window until the taxi cab drives off. She knows that this assignment must be dangerous, because Jack never lets her drive his baby.

Still searching through Frank's row house, Ellen has not yet found anything that has piqued her interest. Knowing that every CIA operative worth his or her pay makes plans to go underground if necessary, she starts looking for evidence of Frank's special stash for emergency situations. When she doesn't find anything like that in the house, she knows for sure that Frank Sansone has gone rogue and that he is now 'invisible.'

When she is ready to leave, she cautiously checks up and down the street to see if she is being watched, and then walks stiffly down the steps. With an old lady's shuffle, she slowly makes her way down the street to the nearest Metro station. On the way, she decides to put Frank's whereabouts on the back burner for now and instead turns her attention to Joe Conway, the former press secretary.

While Jack Stenhouse and Maria Assante are making their ways to Kennedy Airport, a courier is entering the First Precinct building. Bicycle in tow, he approaches the sergeant on desk duty.

"Hey, how are ya? I'm supposed to pick up a letter from Detective Jack Stenhouse."

The desk sergeant was waiting for him, but he no longer has Jack's note. Allison Giancarlo took possession of it a little while earlier and instructed him to call her when the courier arrived.

"Yeah, okay, hold on," says the sergeant. "I'll get it down here." Picking up the phone, he calls Allison.

"Detective Giancarlo, the courier is here for that letter."

"Okay, I'll be right down." Allison searches for the note in the accumulating pile of work on her desk and then takes the elevator down to the front entrance.

When the doors open, she is confronted by the sight of a tall and taut twenty-year-old ready to take on the Tour de France. Although Allison is happily married, window-shopping is not illegal. She approaches the young man slowly so she can get a better look at him, and directs her attention to his tight ass.

"Here ya go," she says as she hands him the letter. "Sooo, tell me. Where are you taking this letter?"

"I can't say, ma'am. But you can try to follow me...if you can." He says this last remark with a sarcastic smirk, knowing that Allison would never be able to keep up with him while he darts in and out of traffic on his bike. He also knows that she has been staring at his ass.

"Well then, who sent you here?" asks Allison.

Holding the precinct door open with one hand and guiding his bike through with the other, he turns and winks at Allison. "Ben-Hur."

Clear of the door, the courier hops on his bike and heads down Varrick Street toward Broadway. Bobbing and weaving through cars, trucks, and taxis, he is like a Heisman running-back on a bicycle.

When he arrives at the Midnight Hotel, he and his bicycle enter the lobby.

The dimly-lit room still reeks of bleach, urine, and pine, but a new aroma is now wafting through the background—semen. Keeping the bike close, he carries it up the stairs to the third floor as fast as he can, since the odor is overpowering. When he reaches the third floor, he passes a man who is having his pipes cleaned by a woman old enough to be his mother. He tries not to notice and searches instead for room 305. When he finds it, he knocks and announces, "Xtreme Courier for Ben-Hur!"

A loud voice from inside the room asks, "Is it a package or an envelope?"

Staring at the door, the courier speaks back at the voice. "An envelope."

"Slide it under the door," says the voice.

Bending down to push the envelope through, the courier looks over to the mini-skirted woman down the hall, who is motioning for him to be next. Realizing that he may not get a tip, the young man says, "You know, I need to get paid for this delivery. I rushed here as fast as I could, and I almost got hit by a bus."

Waiting for a response, he is soon rewarded by an envelope that is slid back out toward him.

"Your payment is enclosed, and a tip is included. Now leave quickly, before my neighbor has her way with you. And if you want to see your next birthday, you won't tell anyone that you were here."

Nervously, the courier picks up the envelope and dashes down the steps. In addition to what the voice said, he's determined to leave the building as quickly as possible because the awful smells would gag a maggot, and because he wants nothing to do with that woman who is smiling at him with missing teeth.

After the bicycle courier left the First Precinct, Allison Giancarlo contacted Xtreme Couriers to see if she could find out who sent them to pick up Jack's letter. But the only information they would give her without a search warrant was the name of the bicycle courier who made the pickup. On the off chance that the guy had a record, she plugged his name into the police database and was rewarded with a hit.

Now, address in hand, Giancarlo has arrived at a studio apartment on Grove Street in Greenwich Village. She's going to stake out a position in front of the young stud's building to wait for him to arrive home.

Within the hour the young man returns, bicycle and all. When he ascends the steps to his front door, Detective Giancarlo bounds out of her car and approaches him.

"Kyle Branks?" she says. "I need to speak with you."

Surprised, Kyle looks down at her from the top step. "How the hell did you find me?"

With a smirk, Allison replies, "A police badge opens up a lot of doors. Where did you drop off the envelope?"

Street-wary Branks replies, "Look, I can't tell you anything. He warned me to keep my mouth shut. Arrest me if you want, but I'm not telling you squat."

Undeterred, Allison presses on. "Mr. Branks, you need to know that you're impeding a police investigation by..."

"Like I said, Detective," interrupts Branks, "I'm not telling you anything. Get a warrant and arrest my ass. I'll get a lawyer, and we'll dance around for a while."

The two of them stare each other down until Kyle remembers that Allison was staring at his ass back at the police station. Turning around to show her his good points, he smiles and gives her a wink before he grabs his bike and heads inside the apartment house.

Staring after him, Allison can't help thinking, *I wouldn't mind dancing with* that *for a while!* Then she sighs and jumps back in her car, not noticing that two black "suits" are exiting a sedan parked up the street.

After Allison leaves the area, they head up the stairs to Branks's apartment.

CHAPTER TEN

On the two-hour flight to Florida, Jack uses the downtime to catch up on a little sleep, while Maria reads a book in the seat beside him. When they arrive at Fort Lauderdale International Airport, they are approached by an FBI agent who was waiting for them in the luggage pick-up area.

"Hi, I'm Agent Tim Coffers. Welcome to Florida."

"You mean, welcome back to this hell-hole," quips Jack. The blast of hot air he felt as he stepped out of the plane and into the bridgeway reminded him of why he left the state.

"Well, at least it doesn't snow here," Coffers replies with a smile. "I reserved two rooms for you at the Holiday Inn in Sunrise. You'll be meeting with Sergeant Octavio at 8:00 a.m. tomorrow."

With a smirk, Jack gazes at Maria. "Oh, damn. You mean we won't be sharing a room?"

"In your dreams, Jack, in your dreams," says Maria with a shake of her head.

When the trio leaves the comfort of the air-conditioned terminal, they are immediately struck by the thick humidity of South Florida. Jack sighs with discomfort but thankfully makes no comment this time.

Following Tim, the group snakes their way through the parking garage to his black SUV. Maria updates Agent Coffers on the drive out of the airport.

"We now have a photo of our mystery woman,

Ellen Vanierri. Agent Fusco in Forensics lifted it out of a CCTV camera. And we had an incident the other day in D.C. The agent who was in an unmarked car on surveillance detail outside of Frank Sansone's place was taken out by a 'little old lady.' "

"And I've been contacted by an informant," adds Jack. "He won't give me his name, but we're pretty sure it's Sansone. He's using a pay-as-you-go phone to contact me and told me to get one as well. He's the one who gave me the lead on Cunningham."

Maria provides Coffers with more details. "Sansone is CIA, and he was knee-deep in shit in Sudan. He, Cunningham, Wilkens, and Hastings knew what was really going on there. And now that Cunningham, Hastings, and Wilkens are dead, it's no wonder that he went dark."

"You're right, Maria," says Tim. "Remember those rumors that went around the Bureau about that operation in Sudan? If they're true, they put the POTUS in a rather compromising position." Tim glances at Jack in the rearview mirror but doesn't provide any further details.

Frustrated, Jack blurts out, "Guys, what the fuck aren't you telling me?"

Maria looks at her old friend. "We can't say anything else right now, Jack. Not until we get more evidence."

Placing his arm around Maria, Jack lowers his voice suggestively, "Well, if we were sharing a room, we could get into some pillow talk, you know."

Removing Jack's arm, Maria shakes her head again. "Jack, you're a married man now! And that would never, ever happen, even if you weren't married. Besides, Didi is my best friend, and I don't think you want me to tell her what you just said, do you?"

"Shit, she already told me that if she ever decided to switch teams, you would be the first."

Surprised at the turn the conversation in the back seat has taken, Coffers breaks in. "Shit is right! What the hell is going on between you two?"

"We're just old friends, Tim," laughs Jack. "There's no problem, just some insolence between best buds."

Maria chuckles. "Yeah, Jack is a dog, but his bark is worse than his bite."

Realizing that what she has just said might lead to more 'suggestions,' Maria puts a hand over Jack's mouth. "Don't say a word, Jack!" she admonishes.

Jack just laughs as the SUV travels down University Drive.

Sansone is sitting on his bed eating Chinese take-out. After a few bites, he picks up his phone and places a call to Jack at his new cell phone number.

"Good evening, Jack," he states when Jack answers the call. "Having fun?"

"As a matter of fact, I am. I'm at an Irish Pub with an old FBI friend enjoying a Guinness, Frank."

Annoyed that Jack has guessed his identity, 'Ben-Hur' exclaims, "To you, my name is Ben-Hur! Got it?"

"Yeah, whatever...'Ben.'"

"Fuck you. Call me when you get to Cunningham's."

"Hey, quick question," says Jack before Frank ends the call. "What the hell went on in Sudan?"

Now even more annoyed, 'Ben' retorts, "Listen, Slick, I don't answer questions. You got that? Call me from Cunningham's, or not. I don't give a flying fuck if you do, or if you don't."

The line goes dead.

On the other side of the table, Maria was listening to Jack's side of the conversation while eating her fish and chips. "Was that your mystery man?" she asks.

"Yeah, 'Ben-Hur.' He wants me to call him when we get to Cunningham's."

"What did he say when you called him 'Frank' and asked about Sudan?"

Jack removes the bottle of Guinness from his lips and smiles. "As they would say across the Pond, he told me to 'piss off.' "

Juan Gutierrez is in his office, making a list of new witnesses to subpoena. When he's done, he hands a piece of paper with four names written on it to the U.S. Marshal who is standing in front of him. "Get subpoenas issued for each of these people and place all of them, save one, in protective custody."

Reading over the list, the marshal raises her eyebrows in shock. "You're going to subpoena the President?"

Juan replies, his voice dripping with sarcasm, "Yeah, I'm pretty damn sure *he* won't end up dead or missing."

Ellen is busily working on her computer, using Secret Service access to get information on the Anacostia-Bolling joint Navy and Air Force base's maps and personnel files. She is pleased that her access has not been blocked. But as the old saying goes, "It's not who you know, but who you blow." Within minutes, she finds exactly what she needs, and laughs out loud.

"This is going to be fun!"

Early the next morning, Jack makes his way down to the hotel's complimentary breakfast area to wait for Maria Assante to join him. When she still hasn't appeared by 7:42, he begins to get a little antsy, since Tim Coffers is scheduled to meet with them at eight.

Just before he's about to storm up to Maria's room, she finally walks in and picks up a blueberry muffin. After pouring herself a cup of coffee, she sits down nonchalantly at Jack's table.

Annoyed by her tardiness, Jack breaks her chops. "Fashionably late this morning, aren't we? Sleep well?" he snaps.

Maria rubs her middle finger against the side of her nose before replying. "We still got fifteen minutes, Jack, and our ride isn't even here yet."

"Yes, I am," says Coffers as he takes an empty seat at their table. "You two ready?"

"According to Maria, we got fifteen minutes," says Jack gruffly. "Grab a cup of coffee and chill."

"Nah, I already had my coffee," states Tim.

"Okay, then. I gotta see a man about a horse. Is your car out front?" asks Jack.

"Sure is."

"Well, then, I'll see you in a couple."

Maria takes several gulps of coffee and then,

muffin in hand, follows Agent Coffers out to his car. Within minutes, Jack walks out and jumps in the car with them, ready to go.

While Tim guides the car toward the Sunrise Police Department's headquarters on Oakland Park Boulevard, Jack calls ahead to ask Sergeant Octavio to meet them in front of the building.

After picking up Octavio, the group continues west to Joe Cunningham's apartment.

When they arrive at Joe's unit, yellow crime scene tape is still attached to the front door. The building's custodian unlocks the door with a master key, and then leaves them to conduct their business in private.

Pushing the yellow tape aside, the group enters the unit and shuts the door behind them. Then they split up, each one searching a room, looking at, in, and behind everything. In the kitchen, they even lift the tiles of the drop ceiling, but the only thing they find is a couple of dead spiders.

After a thorough search of the apartment, Sergeant Octavio comments, "There doesn't seem to be anything here. But you know what? That painting in the hall looks out of place to me. Its frame is old-style, but the rest of the decor is Scandinavian-modern."

Walking out into the hallway, the crew takes another look at the painting. Maria moves it aside to make sure there's nothing behind it, and then, just as she is about to take it down from the wall, Stenhouse comments, "Hey! The bulb in that fixture attached to the frame is a black light. Has anyone turned it on?"

"No," they all answer, so when Jack flips on the switch, everyone gapes in surprise.

Appearing in a blue glow across the front of the

painting are ten numbers: 8640961989.

"That must be what 'Ben-Hur' meant by, 'Things are hidden from plain sight. Look where it can't be seen.'" mutters Jack.

"Yeah, but what the hell do these numbers mean?" queries Maria.

Jack shakes his head. "Hell if I know."

Grabbing a notepad, Maria writes the numbers down. "It could be a phone number," she suggests.

Octavio looks thoughtfully at the blue numbers, and then turns to Jack and Maria.

"Look, before we leave here," he says, "I need to ask you guys a question. The feds booted me off this case pretty quickly, but now you're here again, and you're asking for my help. What's up with that?"

"Sergeant, it wasn't us who took you off the case," responds Maria. "That's why we're here now."

After looking around the apartment one more time, the group locks the door from within and shuts the door.

On the elevator ride to the lobby, Maria tests her theory that the numbers are a phone number by punching them into her cell phone. When the call connects, she listens to a recording with widening eyes, then abruptly disconnects it.

"Well, that's not it," she says. "I just dialed a phone sex operation. 'Pay as you go to increase your flow,' they say. Right down your alley, Jack."

Jack scratches his forehead with his middle finger while Maria laughs.

"I'll give the numbers to the guys in Forensics," she says. "Maybe it's a code or a serial number or even a safe deposit account." Jack, Tim, and Octavio simply grunt in response.

On the way to the parking lot, Maria adds, "On another subject, we need to stop at that Indian casino in Hollywood to see what they can tell us about Cunningham's gambling habits. The County picked up a local loan shark, and they're charging him with Cunningham's murder. But if what your informant said is true, Jack, then the charges against that guy are just a red herring. He'll have to be released, and we'll be back at square one, trying to find Cunningham's murderer."

"Maybe the guy was forced to confess," suggests Octavio.

As the group is climbing back into Tim Coffer's SUV, Jack taps him on the shoulder with some directions. "Let's get Octavio back to work. After that, we'll stop at the casino, and then visit the loan shark."

On the way to Sunrise police headquarters, Maria places a call to her office in Washington and gives them the sequence of numbers from the painting. Then she writes them down on a piece of paper that she hands to Octavio so he can run them against local sources.

"Guys," comments Jack, "I still have some contacts at the Fort Lauderdale PD. If they're the ones who arrested the loan shark, you two can visit the suspect, and I'll talk to my pals in Homicide. After we leave the casino, drop me off downtown."

CHAPTER ELEVEN

The Seminole Indian casino in Hollywood is a sprawling, two-hotel complex with a vast gaming area and a large theater for concerts.

Tim is permitted to leave his black SUV parked out front, after each member of their group shows their credentials to the tribal police officer on duty. The trio was careful to check in with the tribal officer before entering the complex, because technically they are no longer in the United States. Once they entered the casino's property, they passed into tribal territory, and they must now abide by Seminole laws, not U.S. laws.

The officer hands them off to a second Seminole police officer who escorts them to the office of the casino manager, announces their presence, and then leaves.

The manager is standing at a two-way observation mirror that overlooks the casino floor. He doesn't acknowledge their presence or give any indication that he cares a damn about who they are.

Minutes tick by as the three of them wait to be recognized. Finally, Jack speaks up, rather loudly.

"Excuse me!" he barks.

But there is no response from the manager. Jack looks at Maria and Tim and then says again, even more loudly, "Hey, Slick! We don't have all day, and I'm sure we could shut this place down if we wanted to. I know you got hookers parading around downstairs."

At that comment, Jason Stork slowly turns around and eyes the three 'intruders' in his office.

"Hookers here, this early in the morning?" he says with a laugh. Then, narrowing his eyes, he adds, "You know you have no jurisdiction here, right?"

Walking up to Jason, Maria stands nose to nose with him. "I'm FBI, and I have jurisdiction everywhere, got it? Now sit down at your desk, or we'll drag your lazy ass out of here to get our questions answered properly."

Surprised that he has been confronted, Jason complies and takes a seat at his ornate desk. "What can I do for you?" he asks.

Looking around, the trio spots a few chairs. They pull them up to the desk and, after they are all seated, Maria begins the questioning.

"Did you know a customer by the name of Joe Cunningham? Was he a regular here?"

"You mean the Deputy Secretary of State? Yes, we've met."

"Was he a heavy gambler?"

"He liked blackjack, and he was here the night before he was found dead. I read about it in the newspaper. The article said he had a substantial gambling debt, but we never had a money problem with him."

"Was he a frequent gambler, Mr. Stork?"

"A few thousand here and there. He was very good. Mostly won, I think."

"Was he alone the night before he died?" asks Jack.

"I remember seeing him walk in that night, but let me get the pit boss for the blackjack tables. He would know better."

Picking up the phone, Stork barks out an order, and within minutes, there is a knock at the door.

"Come on in, Vince," calls Jason.

A stocky but well-built man, looking more like a wrestler than a pit boss, walks into the office.

"You need me, Mr. Stork?"

"Yes, Vince. These people would like to ask you a few questions about Mr. Cunningham."

"Oh, you mean the guy that was found in the swamp?"

"That 'guy,'" snaps Maria, "was the Deputy Secretary of State. Was he alone the last time you saw him?"

"No, he was with a tall redhead. She looked like a pro."

Jack glares at Stork. "No hookers here, eh Jason?"

Maria pulls out her photo of Ellen Vanierri and shows it to Vince. "Is this the woman?"

"Yeah. They sat at the table for a while, and then both of them left about 10:00."

Maria gives a sideways glance at Jack and then turns to the pit boss. "Did Joe Cunningham have a gambling problem, Vince?"

Abruptly, the casino manager stands and walks over to the window overlooking the casino floor. Watching his boss, Vince replies haltingly, "Cunningham didn't have a problem—we did. The guy never lost."

Maria, Jack, and Tim look at each other and then, in silent agreement, they all stand in unison.

With a nod to the pit boss, Maria addresses the manager. "We want to thank you for your cooperation, Mr. Stork, but we may need to ask you some further questions. Here is my card. If you think of anything else that we should know, please call me at my cell number, or leave a message for me at the Bureau."

Before the group leaves Stork's office, Maria also gives her business card to the pit manager.

On the elevator ride down to the casino floor, Jack is the first to speak.

"Shit!" he exclaims. "That loan shark isn't involved at all. Sansone was right; there was no gambling debt, so the charge that he murdered Cunningham for money owed doesn't hold up. This looks like a cover-up. Didn't anyone down here investigate the casino? What the hell is going on, and who the hell is behind this? Drop me off at the Fort Lauderdale PD. I'm going to talk to the guys there, and one of you needs to talk to that loan shark to see what he knows."

Earlier that day, Ellen prepared herself for her next job. She altered her appearance once again on the assumption that her identity has been compromised. Green-tinted contacts now hide the blue of her eyes, and a blonde wig masks her short-cropped hair.

Now that she looks different, she needs to get a new set of passport photos taken so she can produce updated ID documents if she needs them.

Before leaving the townhouse for the nearest passport photo store, she pops several Ibuprofen to quell her near-constant headache.

On the way to the car, she briefly ponders whether she should slow down, wondering whether the fast pace is what's causing her headaches. She quickly shrugs that notion off and drives away, determined to continue with her plan.

Conway is on lockdown, but she will get in. Tonight she will retrieve her key.

After dropping Jack off at the Fort Lauderdale police station, Tim and Maria have continued on their way to the Broward County Jail. The team is splitting up for the next few hours so they can cover more ground in a short amount of time.

On the way into his old haunt, Jack is surprised by the touch of a hand on his shoulder.

"Want your old job back?" a familiar voice asks.

Spinning around, Jack grins broadly. He is happy to see someone he knows, but he is twice as happy that he no longer has to see this person on a regular basis.

"Captain Jeffers! How the hell are ya?" he asks his old boss.

"Getting old, Jack. What brings you back down here?"

"I'm on a task force with Maria Assante and her FBI team to investigate Joe Cunningham's death. I stopped here today because I need to speak to the guys who interrogated Tommy Giordano."

"You mean the punk who confessed to killing Cunningham?"

"Yeah, but we don't think he did it."

"Well, you're a little late. The feds just came in and took that case away from us."

"Oh, crap! Not again!"

"What do you mean, 'not again'? What's going on, Jack?"

"I don't know, but the guys who came here weren't from the Bureau. Someone wants to bury this case."

"Okay, come on up," says Jeffers. "The detectives who were involved are here today. I'll bring them into my office, and we can all sit down and have a chat."

Jack follows his old boss into the Homicide Division, where they weave their way through the desks toward Jeffers' office. On the way, Jack stops to greet several officers, so Jeffers leaves him behind and walks off to collect Detectives Joe Arnold and Centrale Davis, the two officers involved in the Giordano arrest.

Centrale is a rookie, but Joe has been with the department for ten years, so he knows Stenhouse. When he catches sight of Jack entering Captain Jeffers' office, he laughs heartily.

"Stenhouse? What the hell are you doing here? I thought you never wanted to come back!"

"Yeah, Joe, shit happens," deadpans Jack.

"It sure does," he agrees. Then, gesturing to the man sitting beside him, he adds, "This is Centrale Davis, my partner."

Centrale reaches a hand out to Jack. "Your reputation precedes you, man. Just call me 'Trale."

"Good to meet ya," says Jack, seating himself near the two detectives. "But let's make this meeting short and sweet. I'm here to talk to you guys about Tommy Giordano. I was told that he turned himself in and then confessed to the murder of Joe Cunningham. Did you guys check his story out?"

"No, there was no need to," replies Joe. "Giordano said that Cunningham owed him money, but wouldn't pay up. He said Joe thought no one would go after him because he was from the State Department."

'Trale adds, "Yeah, the guys from Washington

said the murder weapon belonged to Tommy, and that his fingerprints were on it. They also said his DNA was present at the scene."

"Are you sure about that? Who came here from Washington?" challenges Jack, frustrated at the disinterest of the Fort Lauderdale detectives in confirming evidence. "Where were those guys from? FBI? CIA? NSA?"

Listening to this exchange, Captain Jeffers speaks up to defend his team. "Hey, hey, Jack! Who's on trial here? They had government IDs from Homeland Security and clearance from the State Department!"

Remembering how much he hates his old boss, Jack retorts, "Yeah, well, only the FBI and the Justice Department are the ones with the authority to investigate the Cunningham case, along with the special prosecutor and Congress! It seems that evidence is being snatched up by people who are claiming to be from the government, but they're not one of us!"

"So, if your group is the one investigating the case, what have you found out?" asks Jeffers with a sneer.

Gritting his teeth, Jack works hard to keep his cool. "Based on what we know so far, we don't think the loan shark murdered Cunningham. My team and I went to the Seminole casino today to check out the debt story, and we found out that Cunningham didn't have a gambling problem. In fact, they said he won most of the time. We may have a suspect, though; a woman was seen with Cunningham at the casino the night he was killed."

When his phone rings, Jack looks at the caller ID.

"It's Assante," he announces. "Let me take this

call."

Rising from his seat, he walks over to the other side of the room, where he can speak with a little privacy. "Yeah?" he says into the phone. "What's up?"

Jack is quiet for a few minutes while he listens to Maria, and then he shouts, "Are you fucking kidding me? What the hell! Who found him? Okay, okay! We gotta get back to New York. Yeah, I know... See ya later."

Jack ends the call, but not in the way he'd prefer. Cell phones don't lend themselves to the dramatic actions of desk phones. What he really wanted to do was to slam the phone down in disgust, but instead, he clicks a button and looks around the room, scowling at Fort Lauderdale's finest.

"Tony Giordano hung himself in his cell! How did that happen, huh? Wasn't anyone watching him? Everyone who's tied up in this shit is ending up dead or missing! Captain, Maria Assante is on her way here to pick me up. We're going to fly back north later today. Guys," he says, looking around at the assembled officers, "you need to watch your backs."

Sergeant Octavio is hovering over the forensics team while they attempt to decipher the 8640961989 day-glow message.

"So far, we got nothin', Sergeant. It's not a bank account number or a legitimate phone number; it just goes to that sex line. And it's not a GPS coordinate."

"Did you try splitting the number up?"

"Yeah, still nothing."

"Well, shit. It has to mean something. Keep looking."

CHAPTER TWELVE

When Tim and Maria were at the Broward County Jail, they were shocked to find out that the loan shark they were supposed to interview had committed suicide. Tim waited while Maria phoned Jack with the news, and then he drove her back to the Fort Lauderdale Police Department to pick up Jack. Now, he's bringing them both to Fort Lauderdale International Airport so they can catch their flight back to New York.

After dropping them off at the departure area, Tim drives out of the airport and immediately comes upon a detour created by the airport's expansion project. The detour forces him onto Federal Highway/US-1, a road he has traveled often without incident. Today, however, a black Humvee suddenly pulls alongside his SUV and forces it down an embankment, into four feet of standing water.

Stunned by the sudden impact, Tim works frantically to unlock his seatbelt and doesn't notice the four men who are approaching his vehicle from behind. When they reach the car, two of the men yank open the driver's side door and pull the bewildered agent from his vehicle. At gunpoint, they carry him to their Humvee and then speed away.

At the airport, Maria and Jack brandish their badges at the security line, which allows them to breeze through the checkpoint. Walking determinedly through the terminal, they head directly to their gate for the short wait for their flight. Three and a half hours later, they arrive at New York's La Guardia Airport.

Neither one of them had checked a bag, so as soon as they leave the plane, they exit the terminal and make their way to the taxi stand, which they are dismayed to see is surrounded by a lengthy line of fellow travelers.

Never a patient man, Jack is soon frustrated by the probability of a long wait.

"You know, Maria, it looks like getting separate cabs from here is going to take an act of Congress, so why don't we share a ride? You can have dinner at our place, and then I'll drop you off at your hotel."

"Okay, that works for me, Jack. Oh, wait! It looks like we got a quick ride after all."

While Jack was talking, he was also flashing his NYPD badge in the direction of traffic, and a yellow shuttle van has just stopped at the curb in front of them, ignoring the rest of the people in line.

Grateful for another one of the perks of the badge, Jack and Maria climb into the back of the van. But before they can buckle up, the driver speeds off, and the passenger doors lock shut. Searching the interior, the officers notice that there are no door handles. In a panic, they flash their badges at the glass partition and shout, "Hey! Stop this vehicle! We're law enforcement officers!"

But there is no response from the driver. Then, while they are trying to decide what to do next, a milky gas suddenly seeps into the back of the van. Immediately going into emergency mode, the duo unholsters their weapons and continues to scrutinize the van's interior.

"Jack, this area looks like it's bullet-proof!" shouts Maria.

With the unknown gas continuing to fill the vehicle's sealed-off area, the partners quickly become light-headed, and then eventually pass out. The mystery driver watches them in his rearview mirror and then speaks into his wrist.

"Targets acquired. Will rendezvous in twenty minutes."

Alone and handcuffed to a chair in a dark room, Tim Coffers has been calling out for over an hour but has received no response.

Just as he resigns himself to having to spend a lot of time in that black room, a disembodied voice that sounds like a cross between Darth Vader and Godzilla penetrates the darkness.

"Agent Coffers, listen, and listen well. You are delving into areas that do not concern you. Soon enough, you will learn who we are and what we are capable of. Now, please tell us what you have learned about Joe Cunningham."

"FUCK YOU!" yells Tim into the darkness, letting the voice know how he feels about their question and their treatment of him. "*You* are the one who's delving into something you don't want to become involved with, and you will learn soon enough what *we* are capable of. I'm not telling you shit!"

Out of the dark, an air-powered hypodermic needle is suddenly placed on Tim's neck, and he is injected and drugged.

Jack Stenhouse and Maria Assante are unconscious and unaware of their whereabouts. After being
exposed to a mystery gas in what they thought would
be an uneventful airport taxi ride, they were taken to
a sub-basement in the heart of New York City's Wall
Street district where they were propped up on metal
chairs, and canvas bags were placed over their heads.

Watched by several men dressed in black, the
two prisoners are slowly returning to consciousness.
As they awaken, the only effects of their exposure to
the mystery gas are splitting headaches.

Disoriented by the darkness of their head coverings, each of them immediately attempts to remove
the canvas bags from their heads, only to discover that
their hands are tied behind their backs. This lack of
sight increases their other senses, so when they hear a
rustling sound behind them, they come to attention.

"You two will have a slight headache for about
two hours," says a voice, before its owner removes the
bags.

Now free to look around, Jack and Maria see several men standing around the room, and they promptly
protest their situation.

"Who the fuck are you?" spits out Jack in
anger. "NSA, CIA, or some covert government bullshit
agency?"

"Well, hello to you, too, Jack," responds the man
who removed their head coverings. "To answer your
question, we are a special operations detail attached to
a—now, how shall I phrase this?—a 'concerned govern-

ment agency.' "

Chiming in through the pain in her head, Maria shouts, "Are you the feds who took over our case?"

"Well, we haven't actually taken it over," responds the man calmly. "Let's just say that we're actively supervising its progress."

As only he can, Jack adds his two cents' to the discussion. "Bullshit!" he yells. "You're holding a federal agent and a New York City police officer against their will, and if I..."

"Now, hold on a minute, Jack. We're not 'holding' anyone, and if we were, there would be nothing you could do about it. In fact, we could make you two disappear rather easily. As they say in this town... *capeesh*?"

Sensing that this person is the leader of the group in this sub-basement room, the two partners are unnerved to note that he is rather cheerfully ignoring everything they have to say.

"You're here because we need something from you," the man continues. "As you are quickly discovering, some of our own are involved in this... ahem...'problem' in our government. We are a tight-knit group, and we are determined to get this situation resolved."

"What 'situation' are we talking about?" asks Maria.

"We believe that the witness' murders are either the result of a personal vendetta involving someone high up in the government, or a coordinated effort directed by some entity at the White House. We cannot be tied directly to your investigation, but we will help you as much as we can. We want the two of you to be the point persons on our team. Maria, we already contacted your fellow agent, Tim Coffers, and asked him to back off, but that did not go well. Therefore, we want you to call him and tell him to leave this thing alone. If your investigation leads you closer to the White House, we will help you behind the scenes, but before we do, you'll have to provide us with definitive proof that the White House is involved."

Jack and Maria are stunned. Several times they attempt to get the leader to reveal the name of the group he's associated with, but he won't budge on that issue. Nevertheless, they agree to work with him. They are as determined as he is to discover the truth about the alarming events surrounding the President's impeachment hearings.

After discussing the details of their working agreement, the leader says, "Okay, now we're going to take you out of here. But before we do, we need to place the bags back over your heads so we can preserve the anonymity of this place." Smiling, he adds, "It doesn't exist, you know. We'll call you soon. Oh, and your headaches shouldn't last much longer."

The duo allows the men in black to cover their heads once again, and then passively follow directions as they are led out of the building. Within a short time, they are dropped off in front of Jack's apartment, and their weapons are returned to them.

Once the yellow van is out of sight, Jack places a call with his dumb phone.

" 'Ben,' he says firmly, "don't ask any questions, just do as I say. Get a new phone right now. Then call me at the First in the morning."

Tim Coffers is slowly coming back to reality after his own ordeal with the mystery group. When his cell phone rings, he opens his eyes to search for it and quickly identifies his current situation.

"Oh, shit!" he groans loudly. He is back in his SUV off the side of the road, in four feet of water.

Annoyed as hell, he hits the answer button hard.

"Yeah? What the fuck is going on?" he barks.

"Tim? It's Maria. You probably have the same headache I do. Now take a deep breath and pay attention to what I'm about to say."

The sleepy city of Cumberland, Maryland is located south of Wills Mountain State Park in the northwestern part of the state. Once central to the western migration across the Appalachian Mountains, Cumberland is now largely forgotten and is one of the poorest cities in the nation.

In the rural lands surrounding the city, a skilled gunsmith is working his craft on a project for Ellen Vanierri. The gunsmith has been hard at work in his barn for a while now, and is ready to advance to the next step. He takes a paintball sniper rifle, opens up the regulator ports, and switches out the .68 caliber barrel with a .270 from an old Remington. Then he carefully adjusts the flow of compressed nitrogen on the extra tank that he had previously fastened to the gun's barrel.

With the now-decreased size of the barrel's bore and the increased nitrogen flow from two tanks instead of one, the muzzle's velocity has risen to 739 feet per second, instead of its previous 335.

In a standard paintball gun, projectiles are gravity-fed from a large container. However, this newly-crafted weapon requires its projectiles to be loaded one at a time, using compressed gas and the bolt action of a Remington rifle.

After some test fires, the machinist makes an adjustment. He removes the gun's barrel and shortens its length to make the weapon more portable and easier to break down for transportation.

Within a few more hours, he has reached his objective. The silent killing system he has created is not heavy, and it can easily fit into an oversized attaché case. The sniper rifle itself weighs four pounds, and even with the addition of two nitrogen tanks, the entire package works out to a relatively light ten pounds.

Pleased with his work, the man inserts his prized creation into a custom-fitted aluminum case and places a call to his customer.

"This is Trent. Your order is ready for pickup."

Ellen Vanierri disconnects the call and grins with delight. Grabbing her keys, she immediately heads out the door for the drive to Cumberland. On the way to claim her prize, she will stop at a distributor of scientific equipment to purchase a cylinder of liquid nitrogen and a small cryogenic chamber with an internal holding rack.

Her trip to Cumberland and back will take about five hours.

Five hours until my next project is begun, Joe Conway.

After their calls to "Ben-Hur" and Tim Coffers, Jack and Maria walk up to Jack's apartment.

Jack didn't have time to let Didi know that he was back in town from his trip to Florida, so she is surprised when he opens their door and enters with Maria. She is happy to see them both, though, and doesn't mind having an extra guest for dinner.

Postponing the inevitable as long as possible, Jack waits until their meal is finished to let Didi know that he has to go back to work. He finds it painful to explain that, even though he's back home, he's still on duty and is not free to be with her right now. Understanding the demands of Jack's job, Didi smiles and shoos her husband and his partner out the door.

With a kiss goodbye, Jack promises to call Didi as soon as he can. Then, he and Maria head down to the building's garage where Jack fires up his beast for the drive to Maria's office at 26 Federal Plaza.

Heeding Jack's advice, Frank Sansone has just purchased a new cell phone at a nearby media store, after dismantling and discarding the old one. On the way back to the hotel, he stops at a Chinese restaurant and orders takeout for two, then continues on to his hole-in-the-wall hideout.

When he enters the hotel's lobby, his nose is once again assaulted by the familiar aroma of urine, semen, and bleach, and doesn't notice the two black suits who are driving by in a black sedan.

Quickly climbing the steps up to the third floor,

he places a box of sweet-and-sour pork on the floor outside of his neighbor's door and knocks lightly.

When the veteran hooker opens her door, she stares at the box at her feet and then looks down the hall at Frank, who is slipping his key into the lock of his room. He gives her a slight nod, and she smiles.

The hooker has been trying to recruit Frank as a new client and hopes that his offering will be the ice-breaker. "If you want a freebie," she calls out, "just whistle. You know how to whistle, don't ya?"

Ignoring the comment, Frank shuts the door behind him and grins. "Yeah," he mutters. "Just pucker up and blow."

Night has fallen over D.C., and Ellen is recreating her image once again. She studies several photographs of Captain Jane Tingsdale, an IT officer at the Anacostia-Bolling Air Force Base in southeastern D.C., a woman who can easily pass as Ellen's sister.

After changing her hair color and skillfully applying theatrical makeup, she is satisfied that she can "become" Tingsdale, a critical part of her plan.

Jane Tingsdale has chosen to live off-base because of the active social life she maintains when she's not on duty. The Purple Peacock, an LGBT bar near her townhouse, is her favorite hangout.

Still wearing the captain's "look," Ellen is clicking through the many photos Jane has posted of herself and her friends on social media websites when an idea for her next step begins to germinate.

One of her clicks has sent her to a page announcing a birthday bash at the bar the following evening.

When a comment from Tingsdale indicates that she will be there, Ellen decides to attend as well, for she knows that she will have no problem fitting in with Jane's crowd.

Satisfied that she has a plan, she shuts down her laptop and heads to the freezer, where she removes several ice molds of .270 projectiles. Taking the frozen bullets out of the molds, she opens the door of the cryogenic chamber she purchased on the way to Cumberland and places them on a rack above a layer of liquid nitrogen. Then she closes the door and carries the unit to her fenced-in backyard, along with the aluminum case that contains her newly-created sniper rifle.

Ellen's townhouse is in a secluded area of the city, and her backyard is not visible to any of her neighbors. At the far end of the yard, she has set up a watermelon and a block of gel to mimic the consistency of the human body.

Removing the rifle from its carrying case, she assembles it quickly and pulls on a pair of protective gloves. Then she opens the nitrogen-cooled cryogenic chamber, takes out a frozen bullet, and chambers it into the rifle.

Quickly, she aims and fires. A muffled "fump" sends the ice bullet into the watermelon, but it shatters when it hits the hard rind. Taking out another projectile, she repeats the sequence on the gel target and receives the same result. The ice bullet is not dense enough to inflict a kill shot.

Disgusted, she removes the gloves, packs up the rifle, and slams the cover of the miniature freezer shut, but catches the tip of her pinkie finger in the process.

"Shit! Damn it!" she growls. With blood trickling

down her finger and onto the ground, she stares at her hand and scowls. Then, suddenly, she begins to laugh.

Trailed by Jack, Maria walks into her office, where she is met by her boss and two men dressed in black.

"Sir, we were detained by…" she begins to explain until she is interrupted by her boss.

"Yes, I know," he says. "These men filled me in on what happened. I spoke to Tim Coffers in Florida, and also to his boss. He has been dismissed from the case. I also contacted Sergeant Octavio at the Sunrise PD, and told him to back off."

"Okay," acknowledges Maria. "Have we been able to decipher that hidden message yet? You know, those numbers we found?"

"No, we're still working on it."

Shifting his attention to Stenhouse, the special agent-in-charge declares, "Jack, we need you to contact your informant."

"You mean Sansone?"

In reply, one of the men in black speaks up. "Yes, Sansone was knee-deep in this mess. We're going to need him to come in at some point. Someone high up in the White House is leading this operation, and we fear that the President may be the one who is championing it. Obviously, we're going to need convincing proof of our suspicions, but for now, the only thing we can do is work behind the scenes to help you get it. We can't be involved in the investigation until you get us a direct link to the players; that is, until you get undeniable proof of their involvement. Then we'll go into action."

Maria looks at the two black suits. "And who are you?"

"Who we are is of no concern to you. Let's just say that we're on special assignment with Homeland Security, which allows us to open doors that you can't. Jack, we need you to 'encourage' Sansone to cooperate with us, and to assure him that we'll keep him safe."

"Oh, yeah? How do we know that you're not part of the problem, or that you'll just kill him off if I get him to come in? How do we know that you're not keeping me on the case just to get to Sansone? I won't give him up, not yet; I don't trust any of you. Too many people have ended up dead, and I'm not sure your hands are clean, either, especially after what some of your 'friends' put us through when they picked us up at the airport. I'm beginning to have second thoughts about all of this."

Looking apologetically at his partner and friend, Jack states, "Maria, I'm with you, but not with these two. If you still want me on your team, meet me at the First tomorrow. As for now, I'm outta' here."

Turning his back on the group, he exits Maria's office.

After the door slams shut, Maria looks at the men in black but directs her comments to her boss. "Sir, I'll continue with the investigation, but I need Jack's help. I'm in for now, but I'm not sure that I believe you guys, either. I need all the info you have on the other deaths, and I also need whatever info you have on the President and his staff."

Suddenly realizing that one of the black suits is the one who held her captive, she turns to the man and kicks him in the balls. "Now, do you CAPEESH?"

Jack is back home after leaving Maria's office in a huff. When he enters his loft apartment, he finds that all the lights are out and that several candles are lighting the way into the bedroom. Wondering what's going on, he calls out, "Didi?"

In response, Didi peeks her nose out of the doorway to their bedroom, but that is not the first thing Jack sees. His wife is wearing a black lace teddy that accentuates her womanhood.

"I thought you'd like to ease your mind after a hard day," she says with a wink.

Mouth agape, Jack stares at his woman. He is normally not at a loss for words, and one would think he would be used to this type of thing by now, but Didi has a way of bringing out the beast in him.

"Well, don't just stand there, Jack."

Moving quickly, Jack approaches his wife, lifts her up, and swoops into the bedroom.

CHAPTER THIRTEEN

Jack walks into the First with a cup of coffee and a can of Coke. He is not hung over this morning but is trying to wake up after less than one hour's sleep. Maria is waiting at his desk, along with his partner, Giancarlo.

"Too much Single Barrel last night?" winks Maria.

"No, too much Didi," he mumbles. "But it was worth it."

Seizing the chance to rib her partner, Allison teases, "You know, Jack, Red Bull works better. Get into the 21st century, will ya?"

"Hey, I'm old school," he smirks. "Would Sam Spade drink Bed Bull? Fuck no!"

After their laughter dies down, Maria brings the crew back to business. "Okay, guys, we got new info on the autopsies."

While the team in New York is busy working on the case amid bustling office activity and ringing telephones, it is relatively quiet in western Maryland. The country air is crisp and clean, and the only sound is the crunching of gravel and the scurrying of squirrels as Ellen walks up to a small building in Cumberland. Although the structure resembles a barn, it is actually a machine shop, with work benches, lathes, and drill presses in place of hay and barnyard animals.

The shop's machinist, who has just started his work for the day, looks up in surprise. "Ms. Vanierri? Back so soon?"

Ellen nods. "Trent, you did an excellent job, but I need some changes, and I need them quickly." She places an aluminum case on a work table and continues.

"This works great as is, but I need it to be more portable, and I need to be able to conceal it better. It should be more like a handgun than a rifle. I also need to be able to load more than one round at a time. The rounds will be frozen, so the chamber must be cold enough so they won't melt."

Trent reaches under his work table and pulls out two canisters. "Look at these nitrogen chambers. Is this what you're looking for?" When Ellen nods, he continues. "Okay, then two of them would be needed to produce the muzzle velocity you want." He picks up the rifle and examines it. "I can shorten the length of the barrel, but I'll need to cool down the bolt assembly and munitions chamber to accommodate your request. And both of them will have to be polished and coated to prevent jams at the temperature you're talking about."

Turning the rifle around in his hands, he considers his options.

"What I could do is put a cylinder into the stock to hold the liquid nitrogen, and then port it to the chamber and bolt assembly. The only problem would be the compressed gas tanks. I can run them parallel to the barrel, but the bolt assembly needs to be accessible. I could run one under the barrel and one to the left, but it's going to be clumsy."

Ellen has some ideas of her own. "Can you create one large cylinder instead of two, and run that alongside the barrel, like a sawed-off double-barreled shotgun? And can you give me a pistol grip like the ones they use on the tactical shotguns designed for law enforcement and military?"

Trent is silent for a few minutes while he thinks things through.

"Well," he finally responds, "the grip would have to be large enough to hold your coolant. I could put a thumb hole through it and then create a hip holster like the one that old TV Western character with the sawed-off Winchester had. But you would need to wear gloves to protect your hands from the cold. The wooden stock I'd use would give you some insulation, though."

After making some quick calculations he adds, "Wow, this is going to be expensive. It'll cost you three thousand dollars, and it'll take me at least a week to get it all done."

"Come on," declares Ellen, "that's double my original cost! I'll give you two thousand, and I need results in twenty-four hours."

Throwing the gun on the table, Trent insists, "Can't be done! The polishing and coating will have to be done outside, and then there's the testing. I can have it for you in three days."

Ellen is fuming; she does not like to be challenged. But before she can respond, she suddenly closes her eyes and takes a deep breath, as another massive headache makes her skull feel as if it's being squeezed in a vise.

Then, just as suddenly, she opens her eyes and stares daggers at Trent.

"Not good," she snarls. "Too fucking long! How about using aerospace lubricants to withstand the cold temperatures?" she proposes through clenched teeth.

Trent is firm in his resolve; he knows he's right. "No, no, no, that will change the chemical composition of the frozen projectiles. Look, Ellen, even if you gave me five thousand, the best I could do is three days. Take it or leave it. Or you can take it to someone else."

Trent knows there is no one else, and so does Ellen, but she joins the dance anyway. "Today is Tuesday. Three days from now will make it Thursday. I need it by Thursday morning, or sooner."

"Okay, I'll tell you what. Let's split the difference," says Trent, handing her some concessions. "Twenty-five hundred, and you'll have it Thursday morning. But that means no sleep for me, so I need payment up front. Money talks and bullshit walks."

Ellen agrees and whips out ten one-hundred dollar bills. With a smirk, she counts them out on the table between them. "You get the other fifteen hundred on Thursday morning—early Thursday morning, before dawn—and don't fuck it up. Now, get me a glass of water. This discussion gave me a headache."

"Let's go over what we know so far."

"Okay," begins Maria, "there's John Hastings. He went into diabetic shock; low blood sugar. A large concentration of Glucotrol showed up in his blood work, but Sansone told Jack that he wasn't diabetic. So why was a drug that lowers blood-glucose levels in Hastings' system?"

Jack's curiosity is piqued. "Do we know if he

was taking any medications on a routine basis? Was he under a physician's care?"

"Don't know, Jack. I got a search warrant for his house in Massapequa. We'll go out to Long Island later. Now, as for Laura Leonard and Sue Wilkens, both of their autopsies revealed puncture wounds under the base of their tongues. We believe air bubbles were injected into their lingual arteries. So, we got three witnesses who were murdered and one who's on the run—Frank Sansone. And there's also Tony Giordano, a loan shark who confessed to a murder and then just happened to commit suicide. We also got the Secret Service, the black suits from who knows where—maybe Homeland Security, or even the Secret Service itself—and an arrow pointing to the White House. The common denominator in all of this is the Presidential impeachment investigation."

Jack stares at Maria for a moment and then walks over to the whiteboard. "Looks like we're in deep kimchee on this one."

"Yeah, Jack, and the assassin may be a crossdresser whose whereabouts are currently unknown. We were able to track her from Sweden to Montreal, but then she disappears."

"That's because we don't track people who enter the U.S. through the Canadian border. We're screwed in that area."

"Yeah, she seems to have gone off the grid. Unless we get lucky or she screws up, she's going to be hard to find."

"Don't worry, they always screw up," states Jack. "Let's take a drive out to Massapequa. We need to… "

Before he can complete his thought, he is interrupted by his ringing desk phone.

"Stenhouse."

"What's the skinny?" asks a familiar voice.

Holding his hand over the receiver, Jack mouths, "Its 'Ben-Hur.' " Then into the phone, he says, " 'Ben,' we got detained by some men in black. They're looking for you, and they're watching us. They want you to come in. It's for your protection, or so they say. I have a new phone, so contact me like you did before, and we'll talk privately."

Jack ends the call without waiting for Frank to reply, but Frank got the message. He'll send another messenger to the police station to pick up Jack's new phone number and to convey his. But this time, he won't use a bicycle courier service. He'll just send Jack a pepperoni pizza.

On the way out of the station, Jack gives the desk sergeant an envelope for the next messenger that Frank sends, and asks him to hold the response from Frank that he is expecting to receive in return.

Ellen's upcoming rendezvous at The Purple Peacock requires the perfect outfit, so she is out shopping. She needs to be sure that she will catch the attention of her next target.

In rural Maryland, Trent has disassembled the rifle and is now machining the new configuration. When that's done, he'll polish the bolt assembly. After that, he'll drive down to Baltimore where his plater will Teflon-coat the modified assembly and the munitions chamber he created to hold Ellen's frozen projectiles.

Trent is planning to wait at the plater's until the process is completed.

When the gun is ready, he'll trek back to his barn in Cumberland to create a new stock, and a new coolant chamber and tank for the compressed gas.

Trent knows that if he wants to complete this job on time, he's going to need a lot of coffee and super-energy drinks to help him stay awake during the next forty-eight hours.

Forty minutes after leaving Manhattan, Jack, Allison Giancarlo, and Maria Assante arrive in the town of Massapequa.

With the aid of a GPS navigation system, they successfully negotiate the winding streets and eventually arrive at their destination, a Cape Cod home on New Hampshire Avenue, with yellow siding and a brick facade that help it blend into the tree-lined landscape.

Taking the lead, Maria directs Jack to park in front of the house and then guides the trio down a short path that meanders under an oak tree well over seventy-five feet high. At the front door, she addresses the two Homeland Security officers who are pulling guard duty.

"Hello, gentlemen. I'm FBI Agent Maria Assante, and these are NYPD Detectives Jack Stenhouse and Allison Giancarlo. We have a search warrant to enter this house."

Placing the document into the sentinel's outstretched hand, Maria and the rest of her group wait patiently while the sentinel reviews it carefully. When he's satisfied that it's in order, he nods to his partner, who hands each of them a set of nitrile gloves and paper shoe wraps. When they have donned their protective gear, the sentry turns and unlocks the door to the home of the late John Hastings.

The first room the group passes through is a great room that connects to the kitchen. To the left of the kitchen is a hallway that leads to a bathroom and two bedrooms.

Leaving the women to search the great room and kitchen areas, Jack walks down the hallway to the rest of the house. When he reaches the bathroom, he enters and opens the door of the medicine cabinet. Noticing a bottle of Jalyn, he shouts, "Hastings must have had prostate problems. We need to test these pills to see if they've been tampered with."

After dropping the prescription bottle into an evidence bag, he enters the room across the hall, which looks like it was used as a den. On one wall of the room is an old black light poster of a peace sign, but the special light fixture needed to view it properly is not nearby. After a few minutes of searching the room alone, he is joined by Allison.

"Why would someone hang a black light poster without a black light?" she asks.

Jack has been mulling over the same question. "Well, they wouldn't," he answers. "There's a floor lamp over there, but it has one of those new fluorescent bulbs in it. There must be a place in the house where he stored extra bulbs and stuff. I'll take a look around."

Jack leaves the den and starts searching through closets, finally making his way to the kitchen pantry.

On an upper shelf, he locates a paper bag containing new light bulbs, and finds an ultraviolet one.

"Got it!" he shouts. Returning to the den, he switches out the fluorescent bulb in the floor lamp and turns on the light. Immediately, the colors in the peace poster pop, but the colors are not what Jack and Allison are staring at.

Splashed across the multicolored peace sign is a familiar number: 8640961989.

CHAPTER FOURTEEN

After completing their search of John Hastings' home on Long Island, Maria and Jack drop Detective Giancarlo off at the First Precinct and then continue on to the FBI forensic lab at 26 Federal Plaza. They want to get the Jaylin medicine bottle dusted for fingerprints and the drug capsules tested for contamination.

While they're at the lab, they also check with one of the code specialists on their progress in deciphering the meaning of the 10-digit number they originally found at the Cunningham condo. They are disappointed when he tells them that they still haven't learned anything meaningful about the mysterious numbers.

Frustrated by the slow pace of the investigation, they sit down grudgingly in the lab area to wait for the Jaylin results. Soon, Jack's cell phone buzzes.

"Stenhouse. Yeah? Pizza, huh? Okay, give it to me. Yeah, I got it. Thanks."

He ends the call and says, "That was Allison. Sansone sent me a pizza. He wrote his new cell number inside the cover with a message saying he'll call me later."

"Agent Assante, we got something!" calls out one of the forensic scientists.

Jumping up from their seats, they rush over to see what they found. "What is it?" they ask expectantly.

"We found fingerprints on the bottle that belong

to Hastings, but we also got a partial print off one of the capsules, and it's not his."

The forensic expert sends the partial print to a separate terminal where a technician runs it through the FBI database. Within seconds, he gets a hit.

"Allen Vanierri!" they exclaim when the name and photo of the partial print's owner pop up on the screen.

"Well, I guess he didn't change everything," notes Maria with a mischievous grin.

"Yeah, and that's great for us," replies Jack.

Maria requests several printouts of the fingerprint and the FBI's information on its owner, and then thanks all the technicians in the lab for their quick work.

"Maria," says Jack, "I'm going back to the First to wait for Sansone's call. I'll ask him about Vanierri and that weird number. He may know something about at least one of them. And can you ask the black suits about Vanierri? We need all the help we can get before someone else winds up dead."

"Okay, Jack. I have a few things to catch up on here, so call me after you talk to Sansone."

With a wave of his hand he turns to leave, but then remembers something and stops short. Looking back at Maria, he says, "You know, we never did have that dinner, did we? If I remember correctly, some goons very rudely interrupted our plans. Do you want to come over tonight? I'll let Didi know you'll be there so she can get some takeout."

"Okay, that sounds good!" replies Maria with a smile. Very quickly, however, her mood changes. "Hey, Jack, things around here are getting pretty complicated. If the evidence leads us to the White House, we'll be in D.C. again soon, and who knows what may happen there."

"Yeah, and if it gets that far up the food chain, we may even make it onto the evening news!"

Back at his workshop, Trent is concentrating on welding the new nitrogen tanks together. When that's complete, he will manufacture a wooden stock and a new barrel. After that, he will modify a standard hip holster to hold his new creation.

There will be no sleep in Trent's immediate future.

Sitting at his desk at the First, Jack picks up the phone to call his colleague, Sergeant Jorge Octavio, in Florida.

"Hey," he says when Octavio answers, "this is your old pal, Jack Stenhouse. Have you had any luck with those numbers?"

"No, nothin', and we were told to let it go. We had black suits all over our building. I tried getting back to Cunningham's, but that place has more guards around it than Fort Knox. Any news on your side?"

"Not really, except that we found that same string of numbers up here, at Hastings' place. Keep vigilant, Jorge, and if you find out anything at all, let me know immediately."

As soon as he hangs up with Jorge, his throwaway cell phone rings, causing him to let out a frustrated sigh. *No rest for the weary*, he thinks as he hits the answer button.

"What do you want, Jack?" a familiar voice demands even before Jack can get out a hello.

Jack wonders how Sansone knew that he intended to call him.

" 'Ben!' " he responds, "How the hell did you...? Oh, never mind," he says instead of continuing. No time for such questions. "Look, the feds, I don't know who they are—the NSA, the Secret Service, MIB, the X-Files—whoever they are I don't trust them, but they want you to come in. Okay, I told them I would relay that message, and I did. Now, I have a couple of questions for you."

"I don't answer questions, remember?"

"Well, you better start answering them, because things are heating up. Listen, we found the same series of numbers at Hastings' place that we found at Cunningham's. Do you know what the hell they mean?"

A few moments of silence ensue while "Ben" decides whether to answer or not.

"Okay," he finally says, "all I know is that Cunningham and Hastings had certain information that doesn't show the President in a very positive light. I was told that those numbers are clues to where the information is hidden."

"Hmm... Okay, question number two. What's the deal with Allen Vanierri?"

First, Jack hears a deep sigh on the line, and then " 'Ben' " says, "Vanierri was in the Secret Service, on President Burris's personal protection detail. It was rumored that he had a sexual liaison with the President and that he was forced to retire because of it. The official word was that he died in a helicopter accident, but Cunningham had conflicting information that said there was no accident. What you need to do is find Cunningham's hiding place. That's all I have to say for now. Ciao."

"No, wait...! Damn!" Jack tries calling " 'Ben's' " number back, but there is no answer.

Realizing that there is nothing else he can do now, he uses the Android phone to call Didi at the boutique. "Hey, Babe, I'm done for the day and Maria is coming over for dinner tonight. I'll pick you up in a few minutes so we can get some Chinese."

Ellen is primped and plumped, ready for her rendezvous at The Purple Peacock. Tonight, she is wearing a long, dark-haired wig, a short black cocktail dress, and carrying Rohypnol, a powerful depressant that affects the central nervous system.

Satisfied with her looks, she leaves her house to move one step closer to former presidential press secretary, Joe Conway. Captain Tingsdale is her key to entering the Anacostia-Bolling Base, where Joe is being held in protective custody before his appearance at the Presidential impeachment hearing.

Didi is preparing the dinner table while Jack is in the kitchen partitioning out the egg rolls, egg drop soup, rice, sweet-and-sour chicken, and of course, the fortune cookies. When the doorbell rings, Didi smiles and runs to the door.

"Maria!" she squeals. "It's so great to see you again!" Hugs and kisses follow while Jack turns and gazes at the two women.

"Hold that pose," he leers. "I need to get a camera, and then join in on the fun!"

Maria flashes half a peace sign at her crime-fighting comrade and gives him a disapproving scowl. "In your dreams, Jack."

"Hell! How did you know?" he retorts slyly.

Maria is not wearing her customary FBI-type clothing tonight. Instead, she is wearing a short black skirt with a white pullover sweater. Jack doesn't know who to look at first—Maria, or his wife.

Didi notices Jack's interest and frowns at her husband. "Our eyes are up here, you know."

"You have eyes?" he asks with feigned innocence.

When Didi answers him with "the look," he just winks at her. "Come on and sit down before the food gets cold."

Maria laughs. "You're the one who needs to cool off, Jack."

"Not a chance of that happening while you two are sitting in front of me!"

After they seat themselves at the table, all conversation stops while they help themselves to the food. When their plates are full, Jack turns to Maria.

"Any results from the tests on the Jalyn pills?"

Bristling at hearing a "work" question, Didi breaks in before Maria can answer.

"Jack! You said there wouldn't be any shop talk tonight! Now, open the wine and be a good host."

"Just this one thing, Didi, and then we'll turn off the 'office'."

Maria glances at Didi, who nods her head slightly. With the "okay" from her friend, she responds to Jack's question.

"The Jaylin capsules were actually filled with Glucotrol. That's how it got into his system. So after ingesting the pills, Hastings must have gone into shock from a low level of blood sugar. He was on his way home from a morning breakfast appointment in Manhattan when it happened, so he must have taken the pill after he ate. You know, Jack, this Ellen chick is a piece of work, but Didi's right. That's enough company talk for now. Pour me some wine, would you?"

Jack pours for the ladies and asks, "Listen, gals, how about we play some strip poker after dinner?"

Nearly choking on her wine, Maria retorts, "Jack! You're a married man now, but you haven't changed a bit! And there's not a snowball's chance in hell that *that* would happen anyway!"

"No, no, no, I don't want to play," he says with mock seriousness. "I thought you and Didi could play, and then I could just watch. Hehehehe!"

Maria shakes her head while Didi reaches under the table and grabs Jack's manhood, which isn't too hard to find at this point. Then, Didi leans close to him and whispers, "Later, Jack. After Maria leaves." Then Didi gives Maria a wink.

"You know, Jack," says Maria after acknowledging Didi's wink, "your behavior reminds me of a joke I heard a long time ago."

"Oh, yeah? Which one?"

Smiling, Maria responds, "I'm glad you asked. An old man is walking down the street. At the corner, he sees a young man approaching women, whispering in their ears, and getting slapped. As he moves closer, the routine continues, slap after slap. When he finally reaches the young man, he asks, 'Hey, bud, what are you saying to those women?' With a look of concern on his reddening face, the young man replies, 'I'm just asking them if they want to get laid.' The older man laughs and says, 'Shit, man! You keep asking them *that*, and you're gonna get slapped *a lot!*' "

"But I bet he gets laid a lot, too!" says Jack, ending the joke in his own inimitable way.

The burst of laughter that follows encourages more laughter and good conversation among the three good friends, as they enjoy each other's company for the rest of the evening.

Meanwhile, at the barn in Maryland, Trent hasn't had time to stop for a dinner break. He is still hard at work, determined to finish Ellen's job before her deadline.

He has already shortened the barrel of the gun and is now shaping the oak stock to accept the tubing and small cryogenic tank he created to keep the weapon's assembly cold. After that, he needs to manufacture a cartridge for the frozen nitrogen, and then connect all the components together so he can alter a hip holster to fit it.

When he takes a minute to glance at the clock above his work bench, he notes that he is ahead of schedule. Maybe he can get a couple of hours of sleep in after all.

The Purple Peacock is jam-packed tonight with lots of overly-aroused females, so when Ellen struts in, all heads turn to gaze at the new arrival. Playing it cool, Ellen deliberately ignores the many faces that are ogling her. With poise and self-assurance, she pushes through the crowd searching for her target, and eventually spots Jane Tingsdale standing at the bar.

Sauntering over, she intentionally positions herself where Tingsdale won't notice her. Then she orders a drink and watches her target carefully. At just the right moment, she moves closer and "accidentally" bumps into Jane, causing the woman to spill her Appletini cocktail drink.

"Oh, I'm so sorry!" exclaims Ellen. "Let me buy you another one—or maybe two or three..." she adds suggestively.

Jane looks at Ellen and her now-empty glass, and then places a hand on Ellen's arm. "That would be wonderful," she purrs.

"The pleasure is all mine," responds Ellen coyly. "My name is Ellen, by the way." Leaning closer, she adds, "And I hope I'll have the pleasure of pleasuring *you* sometime *very* soon."

CHAPTER FIFTEEN

The alarm sounds like a siren. Jack grabs the little monster in an attempt to silence the morning's intrusion, but when Didi catches sight of him cocking his arm to throw the sleep terrorist against the wall, it's her cue to spring into action.

In an instant, she grabs his wrist and pulls it toward her. "Not again, Jack! I am not buying another alarm clock!" she insists.

Jack rolls over onto his wife. "Well, then, you can wake me up instead!" he says sleepily.

Didi pushes him away and gets out of bed. "You need to get to work, Jack, and so do I. But why don't we shower together to save some time?"

Before Didi can take another breath, Jack is already in the bathroom, turning on the water. "Come on in, Babe, and don't forget to drop the soap!"

There was no need for an alarm clock at the Tingsdale home this morning, as Jane was awakened early by noises from her kitchen. When she emerges from her bedroom, she finds Ellen busily making coffee.

"What the hell happened last night?" she asks groggily.

"Well, you drank too much, and I had to help you home. You were barely able to guide me here, though. Too many Appletinis, I guess." Ellen stops what she's doing and looks over at Jane.

"I know you need to get ready for work, and I haven't showered yet. Want to join me?"

With a smile, Ellen takes Jane's hand, and the two women walk together into the bathroom, their morning coffee forgotten.

Ellen's plan has just passed Phase One—she has succeeded in gaining the confidence of her new friend. Phase Two will be to get access into the base where Jane works.

After working most of the night, Trent is taking a well-deserved nap. The rifle's conversion is almost complete. The only thing he still needs to do is to assemble all of the components together and then modify a holster.

When the gun is ready for testing, he will procure some liquid nitrogen from a store in town. He has already frozen water into the shape of the bullets he will use during the test, but he is wondering what Ellen intends to use as her live ammo, since water is not dense enough to penetrate flesh. Even if the water is frozen, it will not pierce soft tissue; it will just shatter on impact.

Because of their morning tryst, Jack's and Didi's morning routine was disrupted. They both scrambled to get dressed and out the door and then hopped into Jack's Road Runner for the ride to Didi's boutique. After dropping Didi off, Jack drove directly to the First and parked in the first available space. Just as he's about to exit the vehicle, his "special" phone rings.

"Yeah?" he answers, still a little distracted from his quick drive to work.

"Don't talk, just listen," says "Ben" on the other end of the line. "We need to meet this morning. Be at the Statue of Liberty in one hour. I'll contact you again once you're there." The call ends as abruptly as it began.

Jack runs up into the office to tell Giancarlo where he's going and then heads back down to his car for a trip to the Liberty Island ferry. As he drives out of the police station, he doesn't notice the black Ford sedan that is following several cars behind him.

The morning traffic in Manhattan is brutal, and the ten-minute drive to the ferry dock at Battery Park takes almost forty minutes. There is no place to park nearby, so he pulls up onto the central square, drawing the attention of a Homeland Security officer who is standing near the ticket booth.

"Hey! You can't park there!" the officer yells as he rushes over to Jack's vehicle.

Quickly flashing his NYPD ID, Jack declares, "I'm on official business, bud. Keep an eye on her, will ya?"

"And who the hell are you?"

Not in a good mood after all his rushing around this morning, Jack lowers his head and takes a deep breath to calm himself before responding to the security officer's challenge.

"My name is Detective Jack Stenhouse and I'm following a lead, officer. Here's my ID. I need to get onto the next ferry to Liberty Island."

The Homeland Security officer takes a good look at Jack's ID, then returns it and motions him toward the ferry that is preparing to leave the dock.

Boarding just in time, Jack manages to find a place among the tourists crowding around the railing, where he can watch the boat pull away from shore. As the ferry chugs out into the open water of New York Harbor, he notices that back on land, two black suits have exited a black Ford sedan and are walking toward the water's edge. When one of them lifts up his hand and talks into his cuff, Jack realizes that he's being followed.

When the boat is far enough away from shore, he strolls around the deck and periodically looks back at the New York skyline, watching it become smaller and smaller as it recedes into the distance. When a mist forms and a slight drizzle begins to fall, the tourists head inside the cabin to stay dry, but Jack remains outside, wanting to be alone with his thoughts.

His solitude is short-lived, however. Almost immediately, a voice penetrates the mist and the silence—a voice that he recognizes.

"Don't turn around, just stand there and listen," the voice commands. "I wanted to tell you this in person, in case our phones are being tapped. I believe that one of the Secret Service agents who sympathizes with the President will use you to get to me. I think I've already been compromised, so I'll have to disappear for a while. But I'll contact you again. Be wary. I'm being targeted, and so are you."

"I know. I was followed here today." When there is no response to that comment, Jack speaks again. "Did you hear me? Are you still there?"

When there is still no answer, Jack turns around to find himself alone on deck.

Fortunately for the many tourists, the weather

has cleared up by the time the ferry pulls into the dock at Liberty Island.

As soon as the gangway is lowered, the sight-seers stream toward Lady Liberty, while Jack searches through the crowd and wonders, *which one of you is Frank Sansone?*

Since it is still early in the day, no tourists have re-boarded the ferry for its next stop at Ellis Island. Consequently, Jack is the only rider on this leg of the sightseeing cruise. As the ship passes the Lady of the Harbor, he gazes fondly at the iconic statue.

At Ellis Island, Jack remains on board. He doesn't disembark until the ship returns to its dock at Battery Park.

On the way back to his car, he is approached by the Homeland Security officer, who has been waiting for him.

"That was a quick trip," the officer comments.

"Yeah, the lead ran dry. Hey, can you tell me where the two suits with the black sedan went after I boarded the ferry?"

"Those guys left as quickly as they arrived. They sped outta here before I could get near them. I guess they were with one of the other federal agencies. They with you or after you?"

Gazing at nothing in particular, Jack is quiet as he mulls things over. Before long, he breaks away from his thoughts, pulls out his mirrored sunglasses, and puts them on.

"I don't know who they are," he says, by way of answering the officer's question. "Thanks for watching my ride."

Heading toward his car, he stops a few steps away

when he remembers something.

"Oh," he says, as he fishes in his pocket for a photo of Frank Sansone. "Did you see this guy this morning?"

The officer studies the photo carefully before he replies. "No, I can't say that I did."

Shrugging his shoulders, Jack thanks the officer again and walks over to his baby. After climbing in, he fires it up and gives two quick beeps of the horn before pointing it toward the First.

This time, he is very careful to be aware of everyone who is driving behind him.

Sansone is now on the move. In a New York State of mind, he heads to the bus terminal at Penn Station to purchase a Greyhound bus ticket to the city of Plattsburgh.

His destination is his family's old cabin on the shore of Lake George in upstate New York. It's the perfect place to hide out, and he intends to make the cabin his new home. Since it has no TV or Wi-Fi, he will be completely off the grid.

To test his suspicion that he's being followed, Jack changes direction. Instead of driving to the First Precinct, he heads toward the FBI's New York field office at 26 Federal Plaza. And just as he suspected, a black sedan trails behind him at every turn.

After turning right on Worth Street, he stops at a red light at Broadway and puts the car into neutral. With the car running, he grabs a spring-loaded punch out of his glove box and exits the vehicle. Walking back three cars to the black sedan, he draws his gun and places the punch on the driver's side window. He presses it into the glass, then waits until the spring-loaded point jerks forward and blows out the window.

He points his Glock at the startled black-suited driver and his similarly-clad passenger and announces, "Hi, guys! I'm Detective Stenhouse. In case you lose me, I want you to know that I'm heading over to 26 Federal Plaza. See ya later!" Then Jack back-steps to his ride at the head of the line of cars that is still waiting for the light to change.

Once he's back in his car, he places a blue police emergency light on the dashboard and takes off through the red light.

When he arrives at the FBI building, he parks and walks up to the door, all the while looking over his shoulder for his shadows. But the now-windowless sedan and its occupants are nowhere to be found. Sighing with relief, he heads inside the building.

But when he arrives at Maria's office door, he is stopped short by the sight of two more black suits who are talking with her.

"Who the hell are these goons?" he asks with extreme annoyance.

Looking up at the muscular bodies standing in her doorway, Maria responds, "These are Agents James Smithfield and Corrie Johnson, Jack. They're with the Secret Service, and they have joined our little task force."

Visibly upset, Jack lets the suits know exactly how he feels about them. " 'Joined' the team, my ass! You mean, they *infiltrated* the team." He points toward the street below. "I just outed two of you who were following me. And by the way, I'm not paying for the window."

With a puzzled expression, Agent Smithfield turns toward Agent Johnson and then looks back at Jack. "We have no one following you, Detective."

"BULLSHIT!" Jack yells furiously. "Two of your guys followed me to the Statue of Liberty, and then to Worth and Broadway, where I formally 'introduced' myself."

"It wasn't us, Jack," assures Corrie, "but that's why we're here. An agent in the Secret Service is conspiring with the President. It's a current agent, not Vanierri. We don't know if he's working with Vanierri, or if he's just running interference for the President, but we need to reach your contact, Frank Sansone, before he or Ellen does. We need to take Sansone into protective custody before he's silenced like the others."

Jack is not convinced, but decides to play the game.

"Oh, yeah?" he growls. "Well, that's why I'm here. I went to the Statue of Liberty this morning to meet with Sansone. Frank must have seen them follow me there because he bolted before he said very much. I don't know where he is now. He said he would contact me again, but he didn't say when. He also told me that Cunningham and Hastings hid the information they dug up on your rogue agent. And without any help from the Secret Service, we already found a clue that may tell us where it is. We're still working on cracking that code."

"Jack, these guys are here to help us," says Maria

calmly, trying to reassure Jack. "You need to trust them."

Squinting at Maria, Jack stares at her like a sniper zoning in on his prey.

"I don't fucking trust them as far as I can throw them," he sneers. "But I guess I'll keep my friends close, and my enemies closer."

Shifting his glare to the suits, he spits out, "The 'Secret' Service just wants to cover this thing up, right, guys? What about the trumped-up confession by the loan shark down in Florida, who was then conveniently found dead in his jail cell?" Pointing at the two agents, he declares, "You guys are behind all of this bullshit!"

Recalling the case of the Florida loan shark, Maria challenges the suits. "Explain that one away," she demands.

"Look," says Agent Smithfield, "we know that there's an ex-agent who is going around killing people, and a current agent who is somehow involved with him, or her. By the way, that loan shark is not dead. He's alive and well, and in the witness relocation program. Apparently, he was working with Ellen Vanierri. That's why we went down there, and that's why we're here now. Sixteen Hundred Pennsylvania Avenue is waist-deep in blood, but we need a direct link to the White House before we can take them down."

With a frustrated glare at Jack, Agent James Smithfield continues. "Once we get that link, you're going to need our help to get in there. So, whether you like us or not, we *are* going to work together, got it?"

In a more conciliatory tone, the agent adds, "Look, there's nothing more in New York that ties into this case. Special Prosecutor Gutierrez is choosing more witnesses, and we know for a fact that he may subpoena the President. Agent Assante, we suggest that you move yourselves down to Washington. We believe that Vanierri lives in the area, and all the other players are there as well. Jack, those numbers you found are also being worked on by our guys. But again, we all need to get down to D.C."

As the Greyhound bus passes through the city of Newburgh, Frank stares mindlessly out of the window. He plans to disembark at the Lake George stop and then walk five miles around the lake to the old cabin where he remembers spending summers as a child.

Jack needs to let Didi know that he will be going out of town again, so he drives over to her boutique. When he enters the store, he catches her by surprise.

"What's wrong, Hon? Why are you here at this time of day?" Didi is concerned, because it's not like Jack to visit her at work unless something is going on.

"Dee, Maria and I have to go to back to D.C. as soon as possible. The case is heading toward the White House, and we have to follow where it leads. I don't know how long I'll be gone."

Didi is not happy. It seems that ever since they got married, Jack has been away from home more than not. She gives him a hug and tries to hold back her tears while they hold each other tightly, the two of them becoming one, neither one wanting to let the other go.

After a moment, Didi whispers into Jack's ear so that the customers don't hear.

"Why don't we go into my office for a goodbye quickie? A little something to remind you of what you'll be missing."

"That's my girl," Jack says with a smile, "knowing what I want before I even ask."

CHAPTER SIXTEEN

Jane has been in a state of excitement the entire way home from work. All day long, her thoughts had turned to Ellen, to fantasizing about having a wild interlude with her before dinner. Before she left for the office that morning, the new lovers had agreed that Ellen would remain at her house that day so they could continue to get to know each other when Jane returned from work.

As Jane enters the kitchen from the door to the garage, her only thought is to find Ellen and to get things started quickly. So when Ellen springs at her from behind the open door, she is shocked and doesn't react fast enough to fend off the attack.

Ellen uses the few seconds of inactivity to hit Jane across the temple with a bronze statuette that she had taken from the living room. When Jane crumples to the floor, Ellen quickly binds her hands and legs with duct tape and places a wide strip of the tape across her mouth. Then, she inserts two straws into her nostrils and applies a quick-hardening gel over Jane's nose. Her intent is to make a prosthesis that will complete her transformation into Captain Tingsdale.

Fifteen minutes later, she removes the mold from Jane's face and drags her nearly-dead body into the garage.

Returning to the kitchen, Ellen opens Jane's purse to retrieve her car keys and then unlocks the car's trunk. Effortlessly lifting Jane's body, she drops it unceremoniously into the temporary sarcophagus of the trunk, as if it were a bag of manure.

Early the next morning, Ellen will drive Jane to Cumberland, but she will return to D.C. alone.

Phase Two is now on its way to completion.

Once again, Jack leaves the keys to his baby with Didi and takes a cab home. After packing his gear, he calls Assante and asks her to pick him up on her way to LaGuardia Airport. Next stop, BWI—Baltimore-Washington International Airport.

Jack does not like having to leave his new bride again, but he is nonetheless determined to do whatever it takes to catch the evildoers.

This evening, there is a significant amount of secretive action going on in a dimly-lit barn in western Maryland. Trent has successfully inserted the liquid nitrogen tank into the gun's stock, and he is now ready to test-fire the newly-created silent weapon.

After placing the firearm into the holster on his hip, Trent walks over to a small freezer in a corner of the barn. With gloved hands, he removes the mold containing four of the frozen projectiles he had prepared earlier. Concentrating, he carefully opens the breach and places each of the projectiles into the cooled chamber. When the gun is locked and loaded, he turns toward a set of honeydew melons that he placed on a large pedestal opposite the barn door.

Trent eyes the melons and takes a stance like a

gunfighter about to enter a duel. Then, imagining himself as a gunslinger going for his weapon, he reaches into the hip holster, removes the gun, and fires. With a muffled thump, the frozen water projectile splatters onto the target but doesn't penetrate it. He repeats the action three more times until he is satisfied that his creation is working perfectly, even though the frozen bullets aren't quite right.

With a laugh, he says to no one but himself, "Well, the gun works, but it seems that frozen water won't kill a person because it's not dense enough." Shaking his head, he adds, "I have no idea what she has in mind."

Before calling it a night, he opens the gun and checks the chamber to see if there is any residue of melted water. Finding none, he re-holsters the weapon, removes the belt from his hip, and heads to bed for a couple of hours of sleep before the morning delivery deadline.

Jack settles into his room at the Grand Hyatt Hotel, four blocks from FBI headquarters at 935 Pennsylvania Avenue. He accepts the special pampering of a good hotel, even though he knows that his expenses are being paid by the taxpayers of the United States, through the FBI.

He hopes that the pleasant surroundings will enable him to get a good night's sleep, since he doesn't know how much rest he'll be getting as the case goes on.

With the evidence appearing to be focusing on Ellen Vanierri and her trail of death, he expects that he'll be very busy, very soon.

Ellen is back at her own home now, but Jane's Camry, with Jane in the trunk, is sitting at the curb in front of her house. Ellen is in the bathroom, carefully and methodically applying makeup and highlights to disguise the new prosthesis covering her face. When she places contacts in her eyes to change their color and covers her hair with a wig that mimics the now-dead Jane, she transforms herself into the spitting image of Captain Tingsdale.

The only difference between her and Jane is that Ellen's legs are longer, and this difference is enough to effectively convert the skirt of the captain's conservative Army uniform into a mini-skirt. Ellen smirks as she regards herself in the mirror. *Almost looks like the stage gear of a naughty stripper-soldier—not the usual garb of a typical base captain.*

Fortunately for Ellen, though, the weather has turned cool, and she can now cover the too-short uniform with a long overcoat. The addition of the coat will do two things—it will hide both the skirt and the new weapon she has commissioned.

Ellen looks at her watch; it is now 2:00 a.m. She pops some Ibuprofen, grabs Jane's purse and her military base ID, and then begins the drive to Cumberland in Jane's Camry.

CHAPTER SEVENTEEN

After three hours of driving, sunrise is still almost two hours away but Ellen's trip to Cumberland is almost over. Taking advantage of the darkness to cover her sins, she stops at a desolate bridge overlooking Wills Creek and pushes Jane's body over the railing into the cold water.

A short while later, she makes another stop for a quick phone call.

"Trent, I'll be there in less than thirty minutes," she says curtly, ending the call without waiting for a response.

Twenty minutes later, the Camry pulls up in front of Trent's barn on a secluded back road. Even though it's early—a little after 5:00 a.m.—Trent is alert and waiting inside the barn. When the crunching of gravel announces Ellen's arrival, he opens the barn door to greet her. Ellen pushes past him without acknowledging his presence.

Trent is surprised but chooses to dismiss her boldness. Instead, he inquires, "Got a new car?"

"Borrowed it from a friend," Ellen announces dispassionately. "Am I going to be pleased?"

Trent stares quizzically at Ellen through the barn's dim morning light, sensing that something is different. "Got the cash?" he asks.

"You'll get it after I see it in action," she says.

Trent continues to stare at Ellen. Something about her looks different, but he can't put his finger on what it is. Deciding that it'll have to wait until later, he turns and heads to his workbench while Ellen follows anxiously behind.

At the table, Trent hands out the holster and modified hip rifle. Immediately, Ellen puts down a small box she has brought in with her and reaches greedily for her prize. Trent notes that the box contains a small cooling chamber but makes no comment. However, when Ellen opens up her long overcoat to put the holster on, he notices the uniform.

"Joined the Army?" he asks.

Ellen's only response is a smirk while she straps the holster on, pulls on insulated gloves, and adjusts the weapon on her right hip.

"This baby ready to fire?"

"Yeah, I already filled the liquid nitrogen chamber in the stock. There's a port on the butt of the stock that can be unscrewed," he explains. "You pour the nitrogen in there, but be careful not to spill any. Pull the bolt back, and then you can load four projectiles. You'll have to re-chamber it after every shot, though."

He watches as Ellen removes the gun from the holster. "I thought the nitrogen would only last about thirty minutes," he adds, "but I found that the gun will operate up to one hour before it needs to be charged with more coolant. You can test it with some of the frozen projectiles I made earlier."

"No need," interrupts Ellen, as she opens the cooling chamber containing her ammo stash. "I brought my own," she says, loading two of her projectiles into the rifle.

"Well, I set up a watermelon for you," says Trent helpfully.

"No need," she repeats.

Turning quickly, Ellen fires and puts a round directly into Trent's chest. The machinist stands there in shock for a couple of seconds, and then, wide-eyed, looks down at his chest and then up at Ellen, who is chambering another round. He is barely able to squeeze out a "fuck you" before he collapses to the floor, face first.

Calmly, Ellen walks over to Trent's limp body, which is quickly bleeding out on the cold barn floor, and puts another round into Trent's back. Laughing with delight, she shouts at the now-dead machinist, "Looks like I saved some money here, Trent! Besides, don't they say dead men tell no tales?"

Still laughing, she re-holsters the rifle, retrieves her cold-ammo box, and heads toward the barn door. But before turning the knob, she looks back at Trent and calls out, "It works great Trent! It really, really works great! Hehehehehe!"

Back at the Camry, she decides to leave the gun and holster on to see if she can wear the weapon while driving, but she can't make it fit beneath the steering wheel. Dissatisfied but not discouraged, she removes the gun from the holster and places it on the floor. Then she drives toward the highway for the trip back to her place.

When she arrives home, she will pick up more ammo, recharge the weapon with more liquid nitrogen, and head to her next target—Joe Conway.

Sitting alone in the hotel's restaurant, Jack peers solemnly at his breakfast of grits and eggs-over-easy while he contemplates what he and Assante may be doing in D.C. over the next few days. Deep in thought, he picks up his cup and sips his coffee silently, until a jingling sound from his phone announces an incoming text message.

Clicking on the messaging icon, he gazes goggle-eyed at a photo of a naked Didi lying in their bed. His first thought is to wonder, *Why am I here, and not there?* But his second thought is not as pleasant. *How the hell did she take this picture?*

Still admiring his bride, he doesn't notice that Maria Assante has walked up to his table.

"Nice picture, Jack," she comments dryly as she takes a seat across from him.

Quickly turning over his phone, he looks up sheepishly. "Hey, warn a guy, will ya?" he says a little too harshly, and then turns away so that Maria can't see he's embarrassed.

"Want some coffee?" he asks, to try to change the subject.

Jack is surprised by his reaction to Maria catching him that way. He has mellowed a bit since his marriage, and being embarrassed is a new feeling for him.

"No, thanks, I already ate," responds Maria. "You ready to go?"

"Yeah, but not to where *you* want to go."

"Jack, I mean, go to *work*," says Maria with a roll of her eyes.

"Give me a minute to eat something," he answers

gruffly.

Maria watches as Jack gobbles down some of his breakfast, signs his room number on the receipt, and takes a long gulp of coffee. Finished with his meal, he announces, "Let me hit the head, and then I'll meet you in the lobby."

When they leave the table, Jack glances at his watch. It is 9:00 a.m.

Across town, Ellen has displayed her forged Jane Tingsdale ID and has easily entered the Anacostia-Bolling base.

Blissfully unaware of the danger he is in, Joe Conway is getting ready to take his morning shower in a guarded private room on the fourth floor of the base hospital.

Ellen is smugly confident that her mission will be successful. During their one night of passion, Jane was very forthcoming about several things, one of which was bragging to Ellen that she knew where Conway was being kept at the base.

Ellen drives around to the back of the hospital but doesn't park right away. Instead, she cruises up and down the parking lot, checking the building's façade for security cameras. When she's convinced that there are none in this area, she parks the Camry and unlocks the trunk. Then she opens the passenger side door and picks up the gun from its resting place on the floor.

But caution being her forte, she stops to check her surroundings once more. Swiveling her head around for the umpteenth time, she makes sure she is not being watched before she slides the weapon beneath her overcoat and into the holster that is still on her hip. After pulling the coat closed, she moves to the trunk to retrieve the rest of the materials she needs.

Working within the trunk, she pulls on her gloves and carefully removes four frozen projectiles from their deep freeze. Then she loads them into the weapon and locks the car.

Walking with firm intent, she heads directly for one of the hospital's back entrances, where she unlocks the security door with Jane's ID badge.

Without difficulty, she navigates uncontested through corridor after corridor, finally entering the stairwell that leads to her destination.

When she arrives at the fourth floor, she opens the door a crack and peeks down the hallway, not surprised to see a U.S. Marshal standing in front of Conway's room. Without hesitation, she unholsters her weapon and approaches the officer, with the gun still hidden under her coat.

At the sound of the stairwell door opening, the marshal turns his head toward the approaching woman, but before he can confront her, she raises her rifle and fires. A muffled thump sends a deadly projectile between the joints of his vest, deep into his chest and lungs. He gasps, and then slumps to the floor.

Rushing over to the dying marshal, Ellen quickly searches through his pockets for the electronic key to Conrad's room. Finding it, she immediately unlocks the door and enters the room, but Conrad is nowhere in sight.

"Hey, Sam, is that you?" Joe calls out when he hears a noise outside the partially-open bathroom door. Ellen surmises that Sam must be the now-dead marshal.

She chambers another round, walks toward the bathroom door, and waits. When Conway exits, she hits him in the chest with another frozen messenger of death, and watches dispassionately as he falls backward and smashes his head on the tile floor.

Never leaving anything to chance, she re-chambers and fires one more round. Then, she exits the hospital while Joe Conway bleeds out on the floor.

On her way out of the base, Ellen hears the sirens of military police vehicles wailing over the street noise of Washington, D.C. Smiling at herself in the rearview mirror, she announces, "Now that that's done, I'm pretty hungry. I think I'll get some pancakes."

When Jack and Maria arrive back at the FBI building, they find that their Secret Service partners haven't made it in yet, so they settle themselves in Maria's office to wait.

During a lull in their conversation, Maria's boss suddenly bursts into the room and orders, "Head over to Anacostia-Bolling—now! Conway's dead!"

Shocked, the colleagues bolt out of their chairs.

"What the hell happened, sir?" asks Maria, her voice rising in dread.

"I don't have all the details yet. All I know is that Conway and the U.S. Marshal guarding him were killed a short time ago. Military police are checking the hospital's video cameras for a glimpse of the shooter, but I want your asses down there as well. The Secret Service guys will meet you there."

With knowing looks, the partners shout, "It's got

to be Ellen!"

After leaving Cumberland, Ellen drove the Camry back to D.C. When she arrived at Jane's house, she parked the car in the street instead of the garage, and transferred her killing paraphernalia from the Camry to her SUV. Then she left the keys in the car's ignition and the doors unlocked, and drove home. She's hoping that the car will get stolen, and in this neighborhood, there's a good chance that it will.

The crime scene at the Anacostia-Bolling base hospital is buzzing with activity. When Jack and Maria arrive at the scene, they find Secret Service Agents James Smithfield and Corrie Johnson waiting for them in the lobby. Together, they all head up to the fourth floor.

Before entering the hallway outside of Joe Conway's room, they stop to put on gloves and booties to prevent contamination of evidence. The "shoe condom" booties produce a noticeable squishing sound as they hurry toward the room.

The first victim they encounter is the dead marshal. After asking a few questions of the crime scene techs, Agent Smithfield elects to remain with the team in the hall while Maria, Jack, and Corrie proceed into Joe's room.

They introduce themselves to the FBI forensic and CSI techs in the room, and then crouch down beside the M.E., who is examining Joe's body.

"What's the skinny?" asks Jack.

The medical examiner looks at Jack with a puzzled expression and says, "Well, we got some entry wounds, but we're not sure of the caliber. One of them is in his chest, and the other one is right here, in his back."

"What do you mean, you're not sure of the caliber?" asks Maria. "Where are the rounds?"

"Well, there aren't any," the M.E. responds.

"What do you mean?" asks Jack. "Aren't there any exit wounds? Spent cartridges?"

"No, Detective. There aren't any exit wounds, just the two entry wounds. And there are no shells, bullets, or spent cartridges."

Narrowing his eyes, Jack looks intently at Conway's body. "Can you take a guess at the size?"

"Well, my best guess is that it was between a .222 and a .38."

"Hmm. No exit wounds and no spent cartridges. Do you think the shooter used some of those fabled 'ice bullets'?"

"No, that couldn't have happened," chimes in Maria. "Ice won't work, because water isn't dense enough to enter flesh. The ice would shatter from the force of the impact. Did anyone on this floor hear gunshots?" she asks the M.E. "Could these be wounds from arrows that were subsequently removed from the body?"

"No shots were heard, Agent Assante, but these wounds couldn't be from arrows. The entry point on the back indicates that whatever the type of projectile it was that hit this guy, it was deflected when it bounced off a rib. An arrow would have made it straight in. Besides, there is no indication of anything being withdrawn from the body."

"Agent Assante!" shouts a member of the CSI team from across the room. "We found an electronic key card on the floor. That's how the shooter gained entry to the room. He must have taken it from the marshal."

Having completed his review of the crime scene out in the hallway, Agent Smithfield has moved inside the room. Joining his colleagues around Joe's body, he declares, "They found no bullets in or around the marshal, and there are just entry wounds, no exit wounds. Same here?"

"Yeah," says Jack. "We need to take a look at the hospital's videos to see if we can determine what type of weapon was used, and who the perpetrator is. Or rather, we need to confirm that Ellen Vanierri is the one who did this."

"Maria," continues Jack, "why don't you stay up here with Smithfield. Corrie can accompany me to the security office to check the video tapes. We'll also take a look at the entry logs into the building. If the perp came in through the lobby, there should be a notation in the logs. But, if he, or she, came in through a different door, he would have needed an electronic key card or an ID badge to gain access to the building."

While Johnson and Stenhouse head to the security office, Maria waits with Agent Smithfield and the forensic and CSI teams for the bodies to be transferred to the morgue.

Ellen has changed her clothes and her appearance again, this time to revert to her lovely self. She is relaxing on the couch with the TV on, but is not paying much attention to what's on the screen, until there is a news flash.

The talking head informs the audience that Special Prosecutor Juan Gutierrez has announced that he will subpoena President Burris to testify by deposition in the impeachment proceedings.

Surprised by the news, Ellen mumbles, "Well, I guess he's my next target."

Then she turns off the TV and lies down to take a nap.

CHAPTER EIGHTEEN

Jack and Secret Service Agent Corrie Johnson are staring at footage from the hospital's security cameras. They are in the building's security office with Police Corporal Denali.

"We were told earlier this morning," offers the corporal, "that Captain Jane Tingsdale's badge was used to access a side entrance. If you take a look at monitor three, I'm re-running a video from that hallway."

The group sees nothing unusual in the corridor until Denali points at the screen. "There! I believe that is Captain Tingsdale." He pauses the video to allow Jack and James to study the grainy image, while on a nearby computer terminal he pulls up a photo of Jane Tingsdale. "Here, guys, take a look. This is Captain Tingsdale's ID photo."

Staring intently at both images, Jack says, "The video is not as detailed as I would like it to be, but damn, it sure looks like her."

"Jack," interjects Corrie, "this is a video of the hall outside of Conway's room. Corporal, replay this one, would ya?"

With a quick flick of a button, the second video plays, showing Jane Tingsdale exiting the stairwell and approaching the U.S. Marshal. As they watch, Agent Corrie declares, "There it is! She's pulling out what appears to be either a shotgun or a sawed-off rifle. The marshal stands up and then... Well, she obviously pointed it at him, but I didn't see any flash or smoke, did either of you? The marshal jerked to one side and then fell, so it's obvious that he was hit by something."

As the recording continues to play, Jack points out, "Look, Corrie, she's taking the marshal's electronic key, and now she's going into the room. But you know what? Something's not adding up. What reason would Tingsdale have for killing Conway? What's the connection? And what the hell did she kill him with? Something doesn't smell right. I still think Ellen Vanierri's involved, but how do we prove that?"

Corrie thinks for a moment and then says, "You know, there's a gunsmith nearby that the Secret Service uses for special projects that involve some of our more unique applications. The man is a genius. His name is Trent Daniels, and he lives on a small farm in Cumberland, Maryland. As a former member of the Secret Service, Allen, or Ellen, would probably know about this guy. It looks like we need to take a road trip."

"Good idea. And we also need to do more research into Vanierri's past. Ellen may be living in the D.C. metropolitan area. I'll call Maria and ask her to get Ellen's address, and I'll also let her know that we're going to go visit Daniels."

While they wait, Corporal Denali makes copies of the recordings. The men thank him for his help, and then pass the tapes on to the FBI team that is still working at the hospital.

Three hours later, they are well into their trip to Cumberland.

Ellen is also on the move. She is trailing the Special Prosecutor, hoping to find a spot to ambush and neutralize her new target.

Jack is in one of his favorite places -- behind the wheel of the Road Runner. With Agent Johnson riding shotgun and feeding him turn-by-turn directions, they have been making good progress toward Trent's farm.

So when they come upon a sea of blue lights that blocks their path onto a small wooden bridge, they are curious. Jack maneuvers the beast close to the various local and State of Maryland police cruisers, and parks. Since it looks like they won't be able to travel on this road for a while, they exit the vehicle and approach an officer at the scene.

Displaying their IDs, Jack asks, "What's going on here, officer?"

"A local found the body of a woman in the creek. They're just pulling her up now."

"We're following a lead on a homicide," interjects Corrie. "Can we see the body?"

"Sure."

The officer leads them through the assembled crowd toward the rescue team that is in the process of lifting the body over the railing and placing it on the ground. When Jack and Corrie are close enough to take a good look at it, they are shocked that they recognize it.

In unison, they shout, "That's Tingsdale!"

Pulling out his cell phone, Jack places a call to Maria while Corrie addresses the lead officer. "We need to drive through here STAT! Clear the way for us!"

Racing back to the beast, they barely get the doors closed before Jack drives forward in a hurry, causing the assembled police vehicles to part like the Red Sea. As they speed away from the bridge, they wonder whether Trent will be able to shed some light on what happened at the bridge.

Agent Smithfield is watching an FBI medical examiner conduct Joe Conway's autopsy. Maria joins him after she ends her phone call from Jack. At the next table, the same medical procedure is being performed on the U.S. Marshal.

The M.E. takes tissue samples from the wounds in Conway's chest and swabs them onto a small glass strip. Then she places the glass under a microscope for closer analysis.

"I can see no foreign matter here. There are no fragments of any kind," she announces after scrutinizing the image.

Puzzled, Maria questions the doctor. "What could have caused the wound?" she asks.

"I have a theory about this, but let me analyze it further. I need to take more samples of the internal wound, and then place them in the spectrum analyzer. We should have more information in about thirty minutes."

While Maria waits patiently for the M.E. to continue her work, James Smithfield excuses himself to make a phone call.

Meanwhile, Jack and Corrie have arrived at Trent's cabin. They exit their vehicle and walk up the porch steps, where they knock several times on the front door. When there is no answer from within, they step off the wooden deck that encircles the house and walk around the structure, peering into each of the windows. As far as they can tell, there is no one inside.

They huddle near the car and discuss their options while looking around at their surroundings. When Corrie notices a light under the nearby barn door, he points at it and declares, "Trent must be working."

Immediately, the men turn and walk up the gravel drive. At the door to the outbuilding, they knock again, but when there is no response here either, they try the handle. Finding that it is unlocked, they slide open the door slowly and call out before entering Trent's machine shop.

After only a few paces inside, a stench that is all too familiar to a homicide detective assaults their noses. Immediately unholstering their weapons, they continue forward until they reach the large, wooden work table. Peering over the table, they discover the body of Trent Daniels lying in the middle of a pool of dried blood.

"Damn!" exclaims Corrie, while Jack covers his nose to mask the stench. "Ellen must have wrapped this one up as well!"

Looking around for a pencil, he bends down and uses it to probe a noticeable wound on Trent's back. After straightening up, he sighs in frustration. "No bullet, Jack."

"You probably won't find an exit wound, either."

Splitting up to search the shop, the pair soon locates various paintball and hunting rifle components scattered about the open room. As they examine each of the assorted objects, they eventually come upon a large cylinder resting on the floor in a corner.

"Isn't that a container for liquid nitrogen?" asks Jack.

"Yeah, and these are molds for .270 rounds," adds Corrie as he holds up the objects for Jack to see.

When Jack spots a small freezer at the side of the room, he walks over to it and opens the door. Finding another mold inside it, he puts on a pair of nitrile gloves that he sees nearby, and removes the mold. Then he unclips the restraints and cracks it open.

Staring wide-eyed at the contents, he turns to Johnson. "We got ice bullets here! .270 ice bullets!"

"Wow! Trent must have modified a paintball gun to shoot a .270 round!" cries Corrie. "That must be the weapon Ellen's using in the video!"

"Yeah, but we know that ice won't work," states Jack. "So what the hell did Ellen use?"

Jack places another call to Maria.

"Hey. We got another body up here in Cumberland. It looks like Ellen offed her gunsmith, and she's using a modified paintball gun for the murders. I'll send you the GPS coordinates; you need to send your M.E and CSI guys up here. We still don't know what she's using for bullets, though."

"We *do* know what she's using!" shouts Maria. "We just got the info! And get this... Ellen is using her own blood for the bullets! The M.E. found two different blood antigens in Conway's wounds, and they're the same ones in the wounds of Sam Collins, the marshal who was killed with him. We cross-referenced the blood type with the records on Allen Vanierri, and got a match."

"Wow! Good work, Assante!"

"Yeah, and that's not all. We also think we know

her next target. Gutierrez is subpoenaing the President!"

Jack agrees. "Yeah, Gutierrez is a prime target."

"Jack, I'm going to his office now. I've volunteered to be his personal bodyguard."

Concerned for his friend, Jack is silent while he thinks about this revelation. Then he states the obvious. "That will put you square in the crosshairs, Maria. Are you sure you want to do that? Don't do anything stupid. You can volunteer someone else."

"Look, Jack, I'm a big girl. Besides, who's better than me to catch this bitch? You and Smithfield will be my back-ups. Just stay close. Meanwhile, I'll send CSI up there, but you need to get your ass back here to protect mine. Johnson can catch a ride with the CSI crew."

Like a ninja assassin, Ellen silently stalks Special Prosecutor Gutierrez, quickly learning his daily routine. Every day during lunch, Gutierrez jogs from the Washington Memorial to the Lincoln Memorial, and then runs along the Potomac River to the Jefferson Memorial, eventually returning to Washington's giant obelisk.

Plan in place, she will do her thing tomorrow. But today, she will head to the spa.

Gotta keep up the beauty routine, she smirks.

CHAPTER NINETEEN

Local and national news teams go wild with their reports that another witness has been killed—and this one was in protective custody on a military base.

While Congress waits for a deposition from President Burris, the impeachment proceedings against him have been put on hold. He has forty-eight hours to comply with their request. However, that is not the reason for the hold. The real reason is that no one else wants to testify before Congress. Witnesses who had previously pledged their cooperation have now backed away from their commitment.

Ellen has done good work.

At the law offices of Gutierrez and Phillips, Juan Gutierrez is in his office, going over a new list of potential witnesses to contact, while down in the lobby, Maria Assante has entered the building and asks to meet with him. Within minutes, he walks out to the reception area.

Offering his hand, he says, "Agent Assante? I'm Juan Gutierrez. How may I help you?"

Maria shakes his hand, and then gives him the news. "Mr. Gutierrez, it is my belief, and the belief of the FBI, that because of the recent assassination of Joe Conway, we need to place you under our protection. Effective immediately, I have been assigned as your personal bodyguard. From now on, I will be at your side at all times. It is most unfortunate that we cannot take you into protective custody, but due to the duties you need to perform, that it is not an option. A team has been created to act as my backup, but the members of that team will remain anonymous at this time."

Although the prosecutor has heard what Maria has said, and understands the seriousness of the situation, he dismisses her nonetheless. "I appreciate your concern, Agent, but I have my own bodyguards. I don't need the help of the FBI."

Still grasping the prosecutor's hand, Maria squeezes it tightly. The strength of her grip stuns the prosecutor, who is becoming increasingly uncomfortable as he unsuccessfully tries to make her let go of his hand.

"Sir," states Maria firmly, "this is not a request, but a statement of what is going to happen. I will remain with you in this office, and I will accompany you to your home. I will be with you 24/7. I have a protective vest for you to wear while you are in public, and I will be your shadow until we can remove the threat against you."

Trying not to show that he is in pain, Gutierrez answers, "Very well. Yes. Okay, I agree. I think we can stop shaking hands now."

Maria smiles as she unscrews the vise. Rubbing his hand, Gutierrez asks, "Does the FBI have any idea about who may be killing all of these people?"

"I can only give you the standard response, sir: The situation is under investigation, and we cannot comment at this time."

"However," she adds, "I can tell you that the trail of blood is linked to a person or persons who have been or are still involved with the White House. That is all I can say at this time, and that is why we feel your life is in extreme jeopardy."

"Agent, are you saying that Burris is involved in all of this?"

"Sir, I am not saying anything. We are following leads, and right now, the leads are pointing to 1600 Pennsylvania Avenue. Mr. Gutierrez, we feel that you are being watched, so I recommend that you change your daily routine. If I may, I suggest that you leave the office early today. Perhaps you could continue your work at home."

Surprised and annoyed at the same time, Gutierrez' expression changes from wide-eyed astonishment to distrust. "Well! This is a lot to take in." He looks around, not quite knowing what to do. Finally he looks at Assante and huffs, "Okay, we'll move things to my house. I'll be right with you."

While Gutierrez talks to his colleagues about his new setup, Maria leaves a message on Jack's phone.

"Jack, I'm about to accompany Gutierrez to his house, and I'll stay there overnight. I'll send you the GPS coordinates. Meet me there when you get back into town."

Finished with her spa treatment and back at home, Ellen has returned to business. She is now in her bedroom, pulling down a heavy case from her closet. The case contains a KBP VKS sniper rifle with a Leupold Mark 4LR/T 30mm scope and a suppressor.

She pulls out the rifle and checks the chamber, then loads ten rounds into the magazine. Satisfied with the weapon's readiness, she places it back into its foam-lined case, latches the case closed, and carries it to the front door, where she stuffs it into a duffel bag filled with fishing gear.

Her next task is to make a phone call.

She dials the Crimson Boat House. "Hello? I need to rent a 16-foot boat for a day of fishing. I'll pick it up around 10:00 a.m. tomorrow."

To reserve the boat, she uses a prepaid, reloadable debit card that cannot be traced. When she arrives at the marina, she will pay the balance in cash.

Standing in the hallway, she goes over her plan one more time and is pleased to realize that everything is now set into motion. With nothing further to take care of tonight, she decides to go out for dinner. But first, she makes another phone call.

"Don't worry," she says into the phone. "Your latest problem will soon be resolved."

Detective Stenhouse and Agent Smithfield have arrived at Special Prosecutor Juan Gutierrez' house. Maria has been waiting for them, so when she sees their car, she walks outside.

"Guys," she says, "tonight I need you to be vigilant, and tomorrow morning, I need you to follow me. I'm going to stick to Gutierrez like glue. I have a bad feeling that Ellen Vanierri is going to try something real soon. A team at the Bureau is combing through records at the property appraiser's offices for the D.C., Maryland, and Virginia areas, trying to find out where she lives. We don't know if she's listed under her name, a relative's surname, or another family member's name."

Jack is still concerned and expresses his feelings.

"Maria, this is a very dangerous bitch. You'll be in harm's way at all times. Please re-think this."

"Vanierri is ex-Secret Service," interrupts Smithfield, "and 'she' has access to weapons that will make a protective vest useless. I suggest that you quarantine the prosecutor instead of letting him leave the house."

"Yeah, well, how did that work out for Conway?" Maria snaps. "Look, I'll be fine. Just cover my ass." Giving Jack a sidelong glance, she adds, "Be nice, Jack."

Although he is still worried, Jack hides his feelings for now.

"Okay, then," he says. "Smithfield will stay here tonight because we can't both be here at the same time. One of us has to get some sleep. Get me a ride back to the hotel, and I'll take over in the morning. Jim can sleep during the day."

Looking closely at Maria, Jack slips once again into worry-mode.

"Maria, you know this whole scenario is fucking stupid, don't you? Vanierri could off both you and Gutierrez at the same time!"

Placing her hand on Jack's shoulder, Maria tries to soothe her friend.

"I'll be fine, Detective. Juan has a private bodyguard, and with you as my guardian angel, I know I'll be okay. I'll see you tomorrow, Jack."

Maria walks back into the house and closes the door. Then she places a call to arrange for Jack's ride back to his hotel.

Jack stares at the closed door and turns to Smithfield. "I got a baaaad feeling about this," he says with a frown.

Smithfield nods, then turns away to hide a smile.

After enjoying an excellent meal at her favorite restaurant, Ellen has returned home. Because she needs to get a good night's sleep, she skips TV viewing for the evening, and instead turns off all the lights and heads off to bed. Tomorrow, she will be up early for her "fishing" trip on the Potomac.

Across town, Jack ends a call to Didi and also heads off to bed. He wants to be sharp tomorrow, for he fears the worst.

CHAPTER TWENTY

Juan Gutierrez' house is one of the nicer ones on the block. His 3,000-square-foot brick-faced Tudor is located near Glover-Archbold Park in Northwest Washington, D.C.

Jack parks the "piece of shit" vehicle the FBI issued to him in front of the house, behind the P.O.S. sedan where Agent Smithfield spent the night on guard duty.

He exits the car and walks up the steep front steps, ready to knock at the front door. But before he can raise his hand, the door is opened by Maria, who steps aside to allow Agent Smithfield to exit around them. Nodding hello to Jack, Smithfield continues on his way out the door. He seems to be intent on getting to his car quickly so he can drive home to get some sleep. Later that day, he is scheduled to meet them at the Lincoln Memorial.

After Jack steps into the house, Maria closes the door and starts to lead Jack inside, but Jack places a hand on her arm and stops her. With a frown, he quizzes her. "Smithfield spent the night inside?"

"No, Jack," she responds with a sigh. "He came in for breakfast."

Relieved, he says, "Okay. What's the plan for today?"

"Well, we stop at Starbucks around 9:30 for a quick breakfast, and then we head to Gutierrez' office.

You will hang out in the lobby until 11:30, which is when Gutierrez takes his late-morning jog around the D.C. Mall. He usually starts at the Washington Monument, heads down to the Lincoln, runs along the river to the Jefferson, and ends back at the Washington Monument. But today, he will stop at the Jefferson. We have a car ready to pick him up there."

Jack is shocked. "A fucking jog? Are you fucking kidding me?"

Disgusted, Maria shakes her head. "Yeah, can you believe it? He won't back off, no matter how much I protest. He wants to jog! The area is relatively open, but we must be extra vigilant."

Raising his eyebrows, Jack asks, "You up to the jog?"

"I hope so. It has been awhile."

Their conversation continues as they walk further into the house. "I'll lag a few car lengths behind by car," decides Jack. "Then I'll monitor you after you pass the Lincoln Memorial. I don't think anything will happen in front of the monument on the central Mall. Too many people there."

"Jack, do you think Ellen will try something in broad daylight, with all the tourists and other people around?"

"That bitch will do anything, and I think this whole bodyguard thing is a bad idea anyway. This jog—it's fucking crazy!"

Maria shrugs as they wait for Gutierrez.

When the special prosecutor is ready to leave for work, he is followed out of the house by Maria, his new "shadow," his personal bodyguard, and Jack. The two bodyguards ride with Gutierrez in his Jaguar while Jack trails behind them in his black P.O.S. sedan.

A few minutes after 10:00 a.m., Ellen boards the boat she rented for the day. The dockhand who helps her into the vessel comments, "That's a large bag for a day of fishing, ma'am! What do you have in there?"

"Oh, it's my fishing gear. It's easier to carry this way."

After listening to the dockhand give her a brief tutorial on water safety, Ellen starts the engine and drives the boat to her "fishing" spot, twenty minutes away.

To keep himself alert while he waits for the special prosecutor to leave the office for his daily jog, Jack studies all the people who are walking in and out of the building's lobby.

At exactly 11:30, Maria, Juan Gutierrez, and the bodyguard exit the elevator in jogging shorts and various styles of running gear.

When Maria is close to him, he pulls her aside and states, "You know, you two are going to be very uncomfortable with those Kevlar vests on."

"I know, but I'm thankful that the weather is turning cooler. Besides, we'll burn up more calories this way. Just be glad that you're not jogging heavy along with us," she says with a smile.

Still not able to shake the uneasy feeling that he's had since yesterday, Jack's reply is a frown of consternation.

The special prosecutor and his escorts are on their way to the Washington Memorial to begin the day's jog. Jack will wait for them in the unmarked FBI sedan at Ohio Dr. SW, just south of the Lincoln Memorial. Unbeknownst to any of them, Ellen is 150 feet offshore on the Potomac River, about fifteen yards south of Jack's position.

Jack is restless as he sits alone in the sedan. After a while, he finally sees Gutierrez, Maria, and the bodyguard to come into view. As he watches them, he also glances periodically into his rear and side view mirrors to make note of the passing automotive and boat traffic.

Having just passed the Lincoln Memorial, the group is now on the path that runs along Ohio Dr. SW, on their way to the Jefferson Memorial. When they are abreast of Jack, he pulls into traffic and follows behind them slowly in the right-hand lane.

Jack is grateful that the area is relatively free of people this morning. It is a beautiful day, but there are only a few tourists and joggers on the walkway. Off to the side, there are also several couples sitting on blankets near the water, enjoying picnics in the pleasant D.C. weather.

With blue skies above and laughter and Frisbees floating through the air below, all is serene for the moment in our nation's capital. Although Ellen is ready to put her latest plan into action, no gunshots will be heard, so the devastation she is about to unleash will not excessively disrupt the perfect Currier and Ives setting.

Maria and Juan's bodyguard are keeping the special prosecutor between them as they jog. The bodyguard is on the river side while Maria is running close to the street.

Earlier this morning, when Ellen arrived at her chosen site on the Potomac River, she anchored the fishing boat and placed an empty hook attached to a weighted line over the side. At the appointed time, she plans to hunker down beneath the gunwale and use the side of the boat as her shooting platform.

For most of the jog, Gutierrez had been content to remain in the middle of his "pack," but without warning, he suddenly puts on a burst of speed and surges a few paces ahead of the others.

That surge of speed is the last mistake Gutierrez ever makes.

Jack wasn't the only one who was watching the group as they jogged past. Ellen has also been watching them.

As soon as she sees her prey move away from the security of his bodyguards, she seizes the opportunity and releases two quick shots. The 12.7 x 55mm projectiles streak noiselessly toward their target.

Certain of her aim, she is disappointed as the first shot whizzes by the prosecutor's head and hits a woman on a blanket twenty feet away. But the second shot rewards her with the sound of exploding bone and the sight of a spray of blood that covers Maria with pieces of the prosecutor's head.

Two more rounds aimed at the bodyguards track down-range from the prosecutor as he is dropping to the ground. One of them hits the bodyguard in the thigh and breaks his leg, and the other hits the trunk of a nearby tree.

At the sound of the whizzing bullets, Maria immediately draws her weapon and raises it up to her line of sight, sweeping the gun along the river as she searches for the shooter.

Shouts and screams from joggers and picnickers break the silence of the day and echo across the Potomac, but Maria doesn't hear any of it. Neither does Jack, who pulls the sedan over to the side of the road and jumps out.

Ellen's next shot hits a jogger in the leg and sends him sprawling to the ground, and her last bullet hits the barrel of Maria's Glock. The force of that bullet flings Maria's weapon into her forehead, knocking her to the ground.

Disgusted with herself for leaving the two bodyguards alive, Ellen throws the rifle onto the deck of the boat and begins to weigh anchor. As she does, an amphibious D.C. duck tour boat full of tourists passes between Ellen and the shoreline, blocking her from the view of the frantic passersby on shore.

When Jack saw the prosecutor and the bodyguard being hit, he knew the prosecutor was dead and the bodyguard was alive because of where they were shot. However, he didn't see Maria get hit, so when she fell, he ran over to see what happened.

Relieved to see that she is just knocked out, he leaves her on the ground and runs back to his car to grab the radio and call for EMTs and police backup.

Reassured that with the emergency call placed, help will be on its way, he runs down to the river's edge to scan the area for the shooter. But all he sees is the typical boat traffic navigating north and south, none of them aware of the recent carnage on land. He can't see the craft that Ellen is piloting, as she is using the large duck boat as cover. And by the time the sound of multiple sirens blasts through the D.C. area, Ellen is well on the way toward making her escape.

When he doesn't find anything incriminating on the river, Jack runs over to the bodyguard, who is bleeding profusely. Removing his belt, he wraps it around the guard's leg and pulls it tight to stop the bleeding. Then he walks over to Gutierrez, although he knows he can't do anything for him.

The EMTs arrive quickly. Fanning out, they tend to the wounded bystanders first and then check on Maria, who is slowly coming around. She waves them away, but the large knot in the middle of her forehead is concerning. Jack helps her on her feet as more EMTs arrive along with D.C. police, FBI, and Secret Service. Within minutes, a swarm of officers has descended over the area and cordoned it off from curious bystanders.

Twenty minutes later, Ellen is back at the marina. The dockhand who helps her tie off asks, "Catch anything today?"

Ellen chuckles. "Got three good ones, but I let them go. It was a good sporting morning."

She tips the dockhand, pays her boat rental bill in cash, and heads home.

Holding a cold compress against her forehead,

Maria sits quietly on the rear step of an emergency vehicle. Concerned for her, Jack puts his hand on Maria's shoulder and says, "You need to get checked out by the EMTs. You were out for a while. You may have a concussion."

Maria stares at the ground, dejected. "I'm fine Jack, but I failed. I didn't stop the attack. I should have been more vigilant and directed my attention toward the river. How's the bodyguard?"

"He'll be okay. He has a shattered femur, but he's young and will heal fast. The EMTs found a round in his leg and another in a tree. They look foreign. I'm guessing they're 12 to 13mm. I gave one of them to the CSI crew. We didn't hear any shots, so the shooter must have been using a suppressed weapon. You're lucky you drew your gun when you did, otherwise your head would be like the prosecutor's."

Gritting her teeth, Maria feels the bump on her head. "We have to get this bitch, Jack!"

At that moment, James Smithfield approaches through the milling officers. "Hey! I just heard this on the news! I was sleeping late this morning. How did it all go down?"

"I saw the whole thing, Jim," answers Jack. "I think it was Vanierri, but she must have been on a boat in the river. It looks like she used a Russian semi-auto suppressed, took six quick shots, and now we have another dead body and a bunch of injured bystanders. Check the boat rental places and get in touch with HQ. Hopefully, they found where the bitch lives. Oh, and let's get in touch with that duck tour boat ride company. One of their boats was passing by when the shots were fired. We need to talk to everyone on that ride.

Maybe one of them saw something."

Maria interjects, "Look, I gotta go home and change. Then we need to get to the Bureau to de-brief. James, can you stay here until they're done with the crime scene? You can check in with us later."

Frank Sansone is walking down Lake Shore Drive, carrying the food and supplies he bought in town. Before he left D.C., he called the local utility company and had the electricity turned on at the cabin, and then, when he arrived in town, he stopped at the utility company and paid cash for a few months in advance.

He passes motel after motel and then turns down a dirt road, where towering maple and oak trees line the way and songbirds keep him company. All is quiet and peaceful in this area of the country, and the contrast with D.C. makes it seem as if he's left the real world behind.

Feeling secure, he stops for a minute to admire the sunlight filtering through the leaves, and then continues his trek back to the cabin. Unfortunately, he doesn't know that a black vehicle has pulled onto the road at the turnoff from Lake Shore Drive.

Entering his family's log cabin, he busies himself by unpacking his food and supplies and wiping down the kitchen that hasn't been used in a few years. Just as he is finishing up, the sound of breaking twigs and footsteps on the gravel at the front of the cabin grabs his attention.

Peering cautiously out of the window in the living room, he sees two black suits slowly making their way up the driveway, with suppressed weapons drawn and aimed at the cabin.

When one of them splits off to go around back, Frank grabs his Ruger P95DC, screws on a suppressor, and quickly dispatches the intruder at the front of the house with a 9mm to the head. When he turns his attention to the back of the cabin, he is just in time to see the second attacker enter the house through the back door.

Firing three more shots, he quickly ends his brief interaction with the two uninvited visitors.

Wasting no time, Frank searches through the pockets of the dead men and is not surprised to discover that they were with the Secret Service. He confiscates their IDs, weapons, and car keys, and within minutes, has stuffed their belongings and all of his gear into the trunk of their car. Firing up the engine, he heads south on State Route 9N.

Near I-87, he stops at a Walmart and buys another pre-paid phone to replace the one he threw into Lake George before arriving at the cabin. In the parking lot, his first call is to Jack.

"Stenhouse, watch your ass. I just eliminated two Secret Service dicks. Don't trust anyone! I'll call you when I get back to D.C."

When the brief call ends, Jack stares at his phone. Steam seems to escape from his ears as he puts the phone back into his pocket.

"What the hell was that about?" asks a surprised Assante. "I've never seen you look so angry!"

"That was Sansone! The fucking Secret Service found him, and he just took two of them out! He warned me that the Secret Service was involved and that they would come after us, too. Fucking Smithfield! I never trusted him, or Johnson. We need to break the code on that mystery number, and we need to get to Vanierri!"

In response, Maria shakes her head. "Jack, we're stuck with the Secret Service on this one. We're going to need their cooperation if this ends up at the White House."

Fuming, Jack growls, "Then give Smithfield some busywork to keep him occupied. Make him feel needed, but keep him uninformed. There's a mole somewhere, and I think it's him. And where's Johnson?"

"He's with the M.E. They're reviewing the autopsies of Trent and Tingsdale. Listen, Johnson gave you the lead to Trent, so I don't think he's involved. He wasn't part of the Presidential detail, but Smithfield was."

Jack glares at his friend. "Keep your friends close, and your enemies closer. Right now, I don't trust anyone but you."

CHAPTER TWENTYONE

President Burris is in the Oval Office with his closest advisers.

"Within two days of each other, Gutierrez and Conway are dead, and I still have a deposition to give. How do we spin this in my favor?"

Public Relations Director Conner Shinley suggests, "Mr. President, it may be too late to spin this. All the current polls show your approval rating in the single digits, and party leaders are calling for you to resign. I suggest that you give a primetime statement to the American people assuring them of your complete support of the congressional proceedings, and offering any resources you can to finding the person or persons responsible for the killings. But I'm afraid, Mr. President, that even if you do all of this, including humbling yourself before the people of this nation, you may still not survive this term. You may either be impeached, or as I said before, be forced to resign."

With a hand on President Burris's shoulder, Chief of Staff Kevin Randel presents alternative suggestions.

"Mr. President, you need to appoint another special prosecutor. I suggest Gutierrez's partner, Joy Phillips. You must reassure the public that you have nothing to hide and that you have done nothing wrong. Show your disdain for these killings and vow to assist in exposing the killer and anyone else who is behind this mess. Mr. President, it's going to be tough to climb out of this. But if we're able to resolve this issue and nothing else happens, you may survive. However, you must be prepared not to."

Burris rises from his chair, stares at the floor, and then looks at Randel.

"Set up a time with the media for this evening, and get Phillips on the phone. And get my speech writers in here, now! I gotta wow the dumb public tonight, and dazzle them with my bullshit!"

After his advisors have left the Oval Office, he waits a few minutes, and then pokes his head out of the door toward a Secret Service agent who is standing in the hallway. "Jason, come in here, will ya?" he asks.

Jason Goodie enters the Oval Office and waits for directions from his boss.

"Jason, let's take a walk outside in the garden. I have something to discuss with you, and I want complete privacy."

Just before they walk out of the door toward the Rose Garden, Burris's speech writers are ushered into the office by his secretary. Annoyed that they arrived so quickly, Burris bellows, "Hang tight for a few! I'll be right back!"

When the men are alone in the Rose Garden, Burris leans toward his bodyguard and whispers, "Jason, I'm currently getting hammered by events involved with my impeachment proceedings, so I need a diversion, something that will redirect the attention of the news media, especially Fox News. I need you to put into effect that plan we discussed."

"You mean Operation Blue Falcon?" asks Jason.

"Yes. You, Smithfield, and the others have been very close friends. More than friends. I need this done soon so we can get those media bastards talking about something else. I'm going to give a primetime statement tonight about the death of that fucking prosecutor, Gutierrez. Get the operation done today. In fact, have it done before 9:00 tonight."

Ellen is soaping up in the shower when she hears her cell phone ring. Cursing, she turns off the water and reaches over to the sink to get the phone. When she bends her head to look at the screen, she feels lightheaded, but recovers after a few seconds. She blinks her eyes and clicks the answer button.

"Ellen, you need to back off for a while. Blue Falcon has been launched. Lay low. I'll get back to you soon."

Ellen is not pleased. She returns the phone to the counter and turns the water of the shower back on.

"So, it's Blue Falcon," she fumes as she washes her hair. "Well, it's about time! Okay, I'll lay low, but only until it's over. Fuck him, and the horse he rode in on!"

As the hot water cascades down her neck, she laughs with the knowledge of what is about to be unleashed.

The team of several officers is standing before a whiteboard containing a timeline of recent events. Maria has received reports from FBI field agents, but before she discusses them with the others, she must first get Smithfield out of the way.

"James, I need you to check out Galaxy Scientific in Bethesda. That must be where the liquid nitrogen was purchased. Drive down there with photos of Vanierri and Trent."

"Okay, I'll leave right after this meeting." He is not pleased that he was asked to leave.

Maria realizes that he's trying to stall, and wants no part of it. "No, there's really nothing new that we're going to discuss today. Get down there now. We'll bring you up to speed if anything comes in while you're gone."

"Look," James persists, "I should be here in case there are any updates."

Staring him down, Maria adopts a more commanding tone. "Jim, I need you at the distributor. It's a link that we need to have confirmed. I'll fill you in later."

Reluctantly, Smithfield leaves the room.

Maria waits until he is gone before continuing to speak.

"Well, that was awkward," she says. Then she gets down to business.

"Actually, we do have new info. The owner of the Crimson Boat House confirmed that Ellen rented a fishing boat from them this morning. We sent a CSI team over there, but the dockhand had already started to clean it so they could rent it out again. We impounded the boat, but we don't expect to find anything in it. Johnson is at the boatyard, interviewing all the workers."

"Okay, sounds good," says Jack.

"We also have reports from that tour boat. Some of the passengers saw a woman in a small boat throw a fishing pole into the water before she raced away from the area. And we have a lead on where Ellen may be staying. Margaret St. Rocquefort is Ellen's late mother's sister. She owns a townhouse in Annapolis but is currently living in Paris. We requested a search warrant for the townhouse, but the judge said we need to provide more evidence that Ellen is linked to the case before he'll grant the warrant. The Bureau contacted Interpol and asked them to question the aunt. Due to the time difference, we won't hear anything from them until tomorrow at the earliest. Meanwhile, we dispatched a surveillance team to Annapolis to watch the townhouse. If Ellen shows up there, we'll get her."

"Wow, looks like we're finally making some progress," says Jack with a smile to the rest of the team.

Then he turns to Maria. "But what's up with that judge? He needs *more* info? We got her blood type in the wounds of dead people! What the hell?"

Drawing a breath, Maria tries to calm herself before replying to Jack's angry comments.

"You're right, Jack. We already went back to that liberal judge with the blood evidence, and now we need to wait for his reply. So, that's it for now. Let's go over what we have so far."

Maria adds the new information to the whiteboard, which is already filled with a long timeline of events and photos of the suspects and their victims.

"First of all, we have Allen Vanierri as the suspected killer. He's an ex-Secret Service agent who is now known as Ellen after a sex-change operation. We have Frank Sansone, a CIA agent who went underground and can't be found, and John Hastings, a State Department employee who was poisoned. The list of people who were murdered is a long one: Deputy Secretary of State Joe Cunningham, ex-Press Secretary Joe Conway, State Department employee Sue Wilkens, Captain Jane Tingsdale, and the U.S. Marshal who was guarding Conway. Special Prosecutor Juan Gutierrez was assassinated, and there is also a dead gunsmith and some wounded tourists. With the evidence increasingly pointing to someone at the White House, the Secret Service is making their presence known by mucking up the works. And then, among all that bullshit, the CIA has credible information about a terrorist threat to blow up the Lincoln Memorial, but they're not letting the public in on it. And if that's not enough, the country is in the middle of a congressional investigation of an incumbent President." Maria shakes her head in disgust. "But there is one silver lining."

"Oh, yeah? What's that?" asks Jack.

"That lead on where Ellen may be living."

"Oh, right. But what's that about a terrorist threat? I guess we don't have to worry if the CIA is on it," says Jack sarcastically.

Turning to the whiteboard, Jack studies it for a moment and then states, "Hey, you know what? You forgot the numerical message that no one can decipher—86401961989. We really need to get a break on that fucking number."

At that moment, Corrie Johnson walks into the room with an agent from the forensics team and hands Assante a note containing more information. She looks it over quickly and then shares it with the group.

"Well, it looks like Trent bought a paintball rifle and a .270 Winchester hunting rifle. There were components of each at his place. We also found a plater who did some work for Trent."

Placing the note on a desk, she looks around the

room at the members of her team.

"We know that there were traces of Teflon in Joe Conway's wounds and that Trent purchased liquid nitrogen and the tanks to hold it. We also know that Ellen put her own blood into bullet molds and froze the molds in the nitrogen. That's the link the judge needs to issue a warrant to search her house. Now that he has that info, I promise that I'll get a warrant from him, if I have to sit in his office and wait for it myself. Then maybe we can finally get this bitch. Corrie, you need to visit the plater to wrap this all together. See if there's a link to the Teflon and what they plated for Trent, and find out when they did the work for him."

Corrie nods his approval and exits the meeting, prompting Jack to make a note of his reaction.

Walking up to Maria, he remarks quietly, "You know, Smithfield balks every time we ask him to do anything, but Johnson does what he's told, with no complaints. You may be right, Maria. Johnson may not be the one involved in this shit after all."

Secret Service Agent James Smithfield is at Galaxy Scientific reviewing sales records. When he receives a phone call, he steps out into the hallway to answer it.

"Hello?"

"Hey, Jim. They got a warrant for Vanierri's place. They're on the way there now."

Smithfield ends the call and places one of his own.

"Look out for FBI and SWAT. Stay vigilant. Love you."

As he leaves the plater, his cell phone buzzes with a text message. The message is brief and contains only two words: Blue Falcon.

The following morning proves to be a fruitful one. Interpol's interview with Ellen's aunt provides valuable information for the investigators. Apparently, Ellen is living at her aunt's house in Annapolis so she can watch over it while her aunt is in Paris. When Maria adds this information to the evidence about Ellen's blood, she is finally able to secure the search warrant.

Now that they have permission from the judge, the team goes into high gear. In just a few hours a plan is devised to swarm the townhouse and search it thoroughly.

Later that morning, a quiet street in Annapolis is suddenly filled with FBI agents and SWAT teams. Jack and Maria are there, protected by bulletproof vests in the event that Ellen is at home. With the rest of the team, they spread out along the street and await the go signal.

But before anyone approaches the townhouse, a projectile hurled through a second story window explodes on the pavement below, stunning the agents who are gathered there. Automatic weapon fire then erupts from the house and causes the agents to duck and run for cover.

Looking down the street, Jack sees that several of the agents have been wounded and are lying on the ground in pools of blood. When he recognizes one of them, his eyes open wide in horror.

"Maria!" he shouts.

Without regard for his own safety, he runs to his friend's side, only to find that a .228 round has entered Maria's neck and destroyed her jugular vein.

As Maria bleeds out uncontrollably and drowns in her own blood, Jack tries vainly to compress the wound. He clutches her hand and shouts, "Stay with me, Maria! Don't you dare leave!"

Maria, sensing her fate, peers calmly into Jack's tear-filled eyes. Unable to make a sound, she mouths, "Goodbye, Jack."

Jack is helpless as his friend and colleague's once-tight grip goes limp and her beautiful, bright eyes dilate and go blank.

Unable to hold back his tears, he holds Maria's limp body and says his own goodbye. But when he looks up and becomes aware once more of the action still going on around him, rage and the need for revenge quickly take over.

His eyes become laser-focused on the scene before him. When he catches sight of a SWAT team member holding a battering ram to knock down the front door, Jack reacts. As bullets scream through the air, he rushes to the agent, snatches the ram from him, and runs toward the front door. When the SWAT leader realizes what he's doing, he barks out an order: "Tear-gas that bitch, and follow Stenhouse!"

Canisters full of the harsh chemical rain down inside the townhouse just as Jack and five of the SWAT team members reach the front door.

"Jack, wait!" one of them shouts. "You're not wearing a mask!"

With the determination of a raging bull, Jack stares down the masked SWAT warrior. *"Fuck it!"* he yells, and delivers a powerful swing with the ram that blasts the door open. Then, in one quick move, he drops the ram, pulls out his Glock, and enters the residence.

Once he has his bearings, Jack looks up the small flight of stairs in front of him—and sees Ellen staring back with a mask over her face. In an adrenalin-fueled rage, he flies up the stairs and tackles her before she can react. Tumbling to the floor, they land with Jack on top of the assassin.

Impervious to the toxic cloud around him, Jack rips off Ellen's mask and pistol-whips her. As Ellen's bones crack and blood gushes from her face, the SWAT leader bounds up the stairs and yells to his troops, "Get him off her!"

Two muscular agents jump into the fray, each of them struggling mightily to pull Jack off of his now semi-comatose victim. As Jack kicks, curses, and coughs, they forcibly pull him down the stairs and lead him out of the house.

Outside on the lawn, Jack coughs deeply and washes his eyes with a bottle of water. He tries to compose himself while he watches the EMTs scurry around him, attending to the many wounded agents. Moving to the curb, he sits down near the covered body of his good friend and tries to catch his breath.

Behind him, EMTs are bringing Ellen out of the house on a stretcher. Without delay, they load her into an ambulance and rush her off to the hospital. Two FBI agents follow behind the ambulance to guard her at the ER.

Also exiting the townhouse are FBI SWAT members carrying three weapons—a fully automatic AR-15, a suppressed 12.7 x55 KBP VKS, and a wild-looking nitrogen-powered rifle.

When the CSI team arrives, Agent Gomez, the SWAT team leader, sits down on the curb next to Jack.

"You messed her up pretty good," he says. "If I had gotten to her first, I'd have done the same thing." He puts a hand on Jack's shoulder. "Take a break now and go back to your hotel. There's nothing more for you to do here today."

Jack is still filled with rage and the need for re-venge as he watches the M.E. take Maria's body away. With red-rimmed eyes, he turns to Gomez. "Listen, you need to have Forensics check out the bitch's phone. Somebody tipped her off, and I think I know who."

He stands up and winces in pain as the adrenaline begins to wear off. "Now, if you will excuse me, I'm gonna go somewhere and get shit-faced. And I'm taking one of your cars."

Gomez stares at Jack's back as he leaves the crime scene. And predictably, just as Jack disappears from sight, Smithfield arrives.

On the way back to the hotel, Jack dreads the phone call that he will have to make to Didi, and regrets that he won't be there to console her.

Across town, in the private study of the West Wing, a phone rings. "Ellen has been arrested," the caller says.

The call ends with the phone being flung across the room.

Jack is sitting at the bar in his hotel downing

anything he can think of to try to drown out the pain of losing his friend. When coverage of the Annapolis crime scene fills the bar's wide-screen TV, he watches and listens dully as the reporter states the fate of a downed FBI agent. There is no mention of the agent's name because the family has not yet been notified.

In deep sadness, Jack raises his glass of bourbon, neat, in tribute to his fallen comrade.

The day's events have not yet ended.

A man wearing jeans and a hoody to cover his face slowly walks down the National Mall toward the Lincoln Memorial.

Forty minutes before this, Mohammed Qatari, also known as George Wilson, a recent college dropout and convert to Islam, had been playing video games in his rented apartment. When his phone rang, he answered it and heard, "Allah calls you to the Blue Falcon." Placed into a trance by the pre-programmed phrase, Mohammed walked to his closet and dutifully donned a deadly vest.

As usual, the Lincoln Memorial is full of tourists looking up adoringly at the great statue of our sixteenth President and taking selfies at his feet. Mohammed climbs the stairs to join them, but when he arrives at the top, instead of taking in the view, he yells "Allahu Akbar!" before detonating his vest of C4 explosives packed with BBs.

As a curtain of death extends outward and copper pellets splash across the reflecting pool, chaos, death, and destruction descend upon the nation's capital. Screams of terror follow the bomb's concussion wave all the way to the Oval Office, where President Burris is looking out of the window and smiling. When his aides barge into his inner sanctum, they tell him what he already knows.

Moments after the explosion is heard in the hotel bar, the TV cuts off the Annapolis feed and replaces it with reports of the terrible act of death and destruction that occurred at the Lincoln Memorial. When the lethal projectiles were ejected over the Mall, seventy-eight people were killed and over two hundred were injured, some of them critically. Lincoln's left foot was damaged, and the statue and the interior of the monument were splattered with parts of Mohammed Qatari and the blood of innocent tourists.

Because he is now "three sheets to the wind," Jack is probably the only one in the bar who is not paying much attention to the news. Shrugging his shoulders, he finishes another drink and mumbles, "Well that's one way to divert attention."

While Jack continues to drink away his sorrow, the bar's patrons gather close to the TV, hanging on every bit of information the talking heads can provide.

Inevitably, Jack's cell phone buzzes. He pulls it from his pocket, checks the screen, and does his level best to keep his eyeballs from dancing around in his head so he can read the incoming phone number. At the same time, he wonders whether he should bother answering the call at all. When he finally realizes the caller is Didi, he fumbles to answer it before it goes to voice mail.

"Dee... ah... Didi?" he slurs.

"Jack, are you all right...? Oh, no, you're drunk, aren't you?"

"Yeah, Babe, but not drink, uh, drunk enough."

"Jack, I was watching the news about the suspect you guys think was responsible for killing all the witnesses, and they mentioned that an FBI agent was killed. But then they flipped to the attack at the Lincoln Memorial. What the hell is going on over there?"

Trying hard to clear the cobwebs from his mind, Jack answers, "I'm at my hotel, drunk as a skunk. And I have some really bad news for you. The agent who was killed was Maria! That fucking bitch shot her!"

There is a sharp intake of breath on Didi's end, and then silence until Didi cries, "Oh, God, no, Jack! Oh, my God! I'm coming there to be with you!"

"Didi..."

"Oh, no—Maria! I'll take the shuttle train in the morning!"

"Didi, listen..."

"I love you, Jack!"

Didi ends the call and begins to weep bitterly. Little does she know that D.C. is now completely shut down, with no traffic coming in or going out.

When Jack puts his phone back in his pocket, the shifting scenes on the large TV screen catch his eye and shock him back into semi-normalcy. Instructing the bartender to charge his drinks to his room, he leaves a generous tip and heads for FBI headquarters.

CHAPTER TWENTYTWO

After the blast at the Lincoln Memorial, social media explodes when messages from Amman Kobouli, a general with the Syrian caliphate, takes credit for the attack and insinuates that the caliphate had help from Iran. When the Ayatollah of Iran hears about the general's claim, he immediately places a call to the Syrian caliphate's leader.

"What have you done?" he bellows. "Burris has done little to affect you, and now you have awakened the devil. They will annihilate you! They will annihilate us!"

"I have done nothing!" Mahmoud Kattani sputters. "And I do not know what this is about. I spoke with General Kobouli, and he swears upon Allah that he has done nothing wrong!"

The exchange between the Iranian Ayatollah and the Syrian caliphate leader continues with accusations on both sides, until a cruise missile hits General Kobouli's house in Syria, killing him and his family instantly.

The bar he is staying at is only a few blocks from FBI headquarters, so Jack decides to hoof it. The walk does him good, because he is almost sober by the time he walks into the building and makes it up to the floor where Maria's office was.

When he enters the open staging area, he spots Senior Special Agent David Percal carrying a box of Maria's personal effects. Impulsively, he blocks his way and reaches into the box to seize the picture that is lying on top. It is a photograph of Maria, Didi, and himself that was taken at a restaurant in Florida. The FBI agent tries to take the picture back, but Jack resists.

"Look, Slick! I'm taking this photo of my friend! You gotta problem with that?"

Jack stares defiantly at the agent until Maria's boss, the Special Agent-in-Charge, intercedes.

"It's okay, Dave," he says calmly. "Jack can have that photo."

When the other FBI agent is no longer within earshot, Dave turns to Stenhouse.

"Are you okay, Jack? If you want some time off or someone to talk to, I can arrange that for you."

Jack inhales and looks down at the photo. "I'll be okay. I'm a big boy."

"Alright. But if you change your mind, we can help. Oh, hey," he says, motioning to a man who is walking toward them, "there's an old friend of yours here to see you."

Looking inquisitively at the man walking toward them, Jack barks, "And who the hell are you?"

"Hello, Jack," says the stranger. "I'm 'Ben-Hur.'"

As soon as Didi got off the phone with Jack, she went online. For about thirty minutes, she has been logging into multiple websites to try to book a flight to D.C. for the next morning, but nothing is available. Finally, she manages to grab a late-night flight into BWI and gives Jack a call.

At the FBI office, Jack's phone rings while he's staring at Sansone.

"Yeah?" he answers without taking his eyes off Frank. "Hi, Babe. I can't talk right now. Tonight? Okay, see ya later."

With bloodshot eyes, Jack continues to gawk at his previously-unseen informant.

"Well, well, well," he begins, "so it's Frank Sansone. Glad to see that you're out and about, 'Ben.'"

"Yeah, good to see you, too. Look, the Secret Service has been trying to stop me from testifying for a while, and now they pulled off this false-flag operation at the Lincoln Memorial to deflect attention away from the hearing itself. They're the ones behind the bombing at the Mall. Hastings and Cunningham found out all about their plan, and when I got tipped off about it, they tried to shut me up as well. I'm sure they're going to charge me with killing two of their men, even though that's exactly what I did. I killed them before they killed me. And that's why I'm here now."

"Let's take this somewhere more private," suggests David. They nod their agreement, and the discussion stops while they follow the senior agent to his office.

When they enter the office, Dave shuts the office door, and then motions to Frank to continue.

"The key to what's going on are the numeric messages you got from Cunningham and Hastings. Solve them, and you solve the whole thing. By the way, I think the two agents who followed you in Manhattan, Jack, are the ones I just terminated. We can't trust anyone from the Secret Service. If rumors are correct, there's a scandal brewing in that agency that you won't believe."

"What rumors? What kind of shit is going on at the White House?" asks Jack.

"There's talk that the President is bisexual," says Frank matter-of-factly. "And that Allen Vanierri left the Service because he was having an affair with Burris. That much is well-known—in certain circles. The real skinny is that there are a lot more people involved in that circle—other agents and personnel on Burris's staff. When Allen became Ellen, Burris kept in 'touch,' with her, so to speak."

Wide-eyed, Jack probes for more information. "What the hell are you sayin', Frank? That President Burris is directly involved in all of this shit?"

"Hey, follow the trail, will you? Joe Conway, the ex-press secretary, was homosexual. Ellen is really a man, and key people are now dead. And just before he was killed, Cunningham told me that he found out about something big and that he was going to spill it before Congress. He said there was a covert plan, a false-flag diversion labeled 'Blue Falcon,' that could be trotted out whenever it was needed. He hid all the info about it somewhere, and the numeric message you found is a clue to where it is. Figure that out, and solve the killings." Turning his head toward Percal, he adds, "Follow the trail, and look into the Praetorium. It's a bathhouse in Alexandria, Virginia, and Burris is a member there. Conway was a member and so is Vanierri, and I'm sure you'll find other names on their member list that you're familiar with."

With a glance at Jack, Dave notes that he seems about ready to blow his top. "Jack, I'll get on this," he hastens to assure the detective. "Now, listen, we contacted Maria's parents, and they're flying into BWI late tonight. The Bureau is setting up a memorial service for Maria. It's scheduled to take place at the Basilica of the National Shrine of the Immaculate Conception in forty-eight hours. We're contacting Fort Lauderdale P.D. and NYPD, and so far, they're both promising to have a significant representation of their forces at the service. Maria's brothers in the military are also petitioning for leave time to be there."

"Sounds great, Dave. I'll be at BWI later tonight to pick up my wife, so I could pick up Maria's parents at the same time. But I thought her brothers were cops?"

"They were cops, but they enlisted. Jack, we booked them into a room at your hotel, so this will work out well. Now, take some time off, Jack."

Turning to Frank, he declares, "We're going to put you into a safe house. We contacted the CIA, and they're in full agreement with our plan."

Sansone barks a short, humorless laugh. "No offense, but I'll go with the Company plan on this one. They're in a better position to provide for my safety. Your past efforts have been—how shall I say this?—subpar, to say the least, don't you think?"

Percal concedes the point by nodding his head. "Okay, Frank. Burris is scheduled to make a statement tonight at 9:00, but he may do it sooner. It's now almost six. The whole city is in lock-down, so traveling around D.C. tonight is going to be a nightmare. Burris has local and state police, and the National Guard and Homeland Security controlling the streets, so Jack, your NYPD badge isn't going to get you anywhere. I'll have one of my agents drive you back to your hotel now, and later, he'll take you to the airport."

Not yet one-hundred-percent sober, Jack replies, "Thanks, but I'll walk back to the hotel so I can clear my head. Have your guy come and get me. My wife's flight gets in at 9:00."

"Will do. The Assantes should arrive at about 10:00, so you won't have to wait long."

President Burris has indeed pushed up his scheduled speech. At 6:15 p.m., the networks cut over to the White House for a special announcement from the President.

"My fellow Americans. I speak before you this night with a heavy heart. Today, a lone terrorist in our nation's capital has killed and injured many innocent people. This heinous act against our homeland will not go unanswered. The caliphate in Syria has taken responsibility for this cowardly act at the Lincoln Memorial, and we have proof that the terrorist received logistical and financial support from the government of Iran. Again and again, I have promised that there would be no direct involvement of our military in a ground war in the Middle East but now, because of this act, we are fully involved.

"After this speech, I will consult with the Joint Chiefs of Staff and will then announce troop deployment to the Middle East within twenty-four hours. This atrocity against the lives of innocent people must be responded to without prejudice.

"Congress is currently locked up in a frivolous attempt to smear my Administration, but our country has been drawn into a war. Therefore, I will go before Congress tomorrow to ask for approval of my actions. During this

time of tribulation, I suggest that Congress postpone their investigation and stand behind their Commander-in-Chief. I ask your help in contacting your elected representatives to tell them to stand behind me as President of the United States. Together, we will prevail against the evildoers and send them down to the gates of hell. We will follow them and destroy them no matter where they are, be it in Syria, Iraq, or Iran. The full power of the United States military will be unleashed against them, along with the force of our NATO allies. I have already received commitments from them to join us in this fight. We will prevail, and we will not falter.

"God bless all of you, and God bless the United States of America."

After the TV cameras are turned off, President Burris walks back to the Oval Office with his chief of staff. On the way, he leans over to his aide, and with a cynical smirk on his face, whispers, "Now, *that* is *sure* to tie the shorts of those assholes in Congress up in a knot!"

CHAPTER TWENTYTHREE

"In a joint statement issued today, the Speaker of the House and the Senate Majority Leader have announced the postponement of the impeachment proceedings on President Burris due to the terrorist attack at the Lincoln Memorial. They want to present a united Congress to the American people, to bring the country together in support of our wartime President.

"This is Sam Dubarry, Fox News Washington."

Back at his hotel room, Jack is in the shower. When his cell phone rings, he bolts out of the bathroom to try to answer it, but the call has already gone to voicemail.

"Jack, it's Percal," the voice says. "You need to get your ass back here, pronto. I'm sending a driver to your hotel now; he'll be there in a few minutes. We found some information in Ellen's townhouse and on her phone, and we have someone here that you may want to talk to."

Within twenty minutes Jack is back at the FBI building, wet hair and all. When Percal spots him, he motions him over to a small room located next to the interrogation room.

"What's up?" asks Jack.

"We found some bullets made from frozen blood in Ellen's freezer, and there were wigs, face prosthetics, and theatrical makeup all over the place. When we checked her phone, we found that she received a call from Smithfield just before the raid at her place and that she also made calls to an encrypted phone in the D.C. area. We contacted NSA to have them look more closely at her phone records. Smithfield is obviously the mole! We got him!"

Through a two-way mirror, Jack stares hard at James Smithfield, who is sitting quietly in the interrogation room. As anger and rage boil up from his gut and finally reach his face, he asks in a low, barely-controlled voice, "What did that shithead have to say?"

"Nothing. He just sits there and smiles down at the table."

"Oh, yeah? Just give me five minutes, with no interference from anyone. Get me an old phone book, and I'll take care of the rest."

Reaching into his pocket, Jack pulls out a small leather sap, a mini billy club, and gives Percal a wink. He replaces the club in his pocket when another agent offers him a large phone book.

"Come in with me," he tells the agent. "I'll need your assistance."

Smithfield is startled when Jack slams the phone book down on the table in front of him.

"Hello, James," he says with contempt. "You just killed a friend of mine, so let's talk, shall we?"

"I'm not telling you two *anything*," sneers Smithfield. "Where's my lawyer?"

Focused on his mission, Jack ignores Smithfield's question and proceeds with his plan.

"Now, now, James. You know I'm going to get the information I want out of you one way or another. Your lawyer will be here in five minutes, but first you need to talk to *me*."

"Okay, Jack, here goes: *fuck you*."

Unruffled, Jack grabs the chair in front of him and moves it underneath the surveillance camera that is bolted high up on the wall. Standing on the seat of the chair, he reaches up and unplugs the camera, then climbs back down.

Watching Jack warily, Smithfield is now clearly nervous. He knows that Jack has just prevented the recording of anything that is about to transpire in that room and he is anxious about what is to come next.

In the next moment, he finds out.

In one quick move, Jack pushes the table up against the suspected mole and pins him to the wall.

"Now, you should *really* start talkin', James. Who's behind all this shit? You? Ellen? Burris? Who?"

Straining to speak against the pain of the table compressing his ribs, James grunts, "That's for me to know, and for you to find out."

Jack pulls the sap from his jacket pocket and slams it on the table, causing Smithfield to stare at it in shock.

"You can't hit me with that!" he protests. "It'll leave a mark, and I'll sue your ass!"

Jack simply laughs and turns to the other agent. "Hold him down by his head."

When the agent complies, Jack leans against the table and places the phone book against the side of

Smithfield's head. Smithfield struggles and calls for help, but Jack ignores him. Instead, he slams the sap against the book hard enough to jolt him, but not hard enough to knock him out.

"There ya go, James. No marks."

Bending down, he peers into Smithfield's eyes. "How's your head, buddy? What do you want to tell me now?"

There is no reaction from Smithfield until Jack raises the sap again. Then, in an attempt to prevent another blow, James blurts out, "Jack, you don't understand!"

In response, Stenhouse smacks the book again, which causes James to howl in pain.

"Okay!" he groans. "It's the West Wing! And there's more!" But just as he is about to speak again, the door to the interrogation room opens.

Furtively, Jack places the sap back in his pocket and turns in time to see Dave Percal entering the room with Smithfield's lawyer.

"He needs some aspirin," Jack advises Percal. "I think he has a migraine."

Taking in the scene, James' attorney glares at Jack and the assisting agent. He repeatedly threatens a lawsuit against them while he helps his client shuffle out of the room.

After they're gone, Dave states the obvious.

"It doesn't look like your interrogation procedure worked, did it? We still need to get concrete information that directly links the murders to someone at the White House. Right now, all we have are the phone records. We'll have to jump on any leads the NSA can get from Ellen's phone."

Jack nods, and then stands on a chair to plug the security camera back in. Looking down at Percal, he says, "Dave, the FBI knows that Burris is behind all this shit, and they also know that members of the Secret Service are protecting his ass. Sansone says that those numbers we found are a coded message and that it's the key to unlocking all of the secrets. Any luck figuring out what the hell they mean?"

Jack climbs down from the chair, and then he and Dave move the table back into its customary place in the room.

"No," Dave replies, "we don't know anything about the numbers yet. So far, they don't make any sense at all."

"How about Ellen? What's going on with her?"

"She just came out of surgery and is still unconscious. They had some reconstruction work to do. You messed her face up pretty good, Jack. But the doctors think she'll be able to talk within twenty-four hours. Well, not talk, exactly. Her jaw is wired shut. You know, you almost killed that bitch."

" 'Almost' only counts in horseshoes and hand grenades," sneers Jack. "Hey, can you get me that ride to the airport now? I gotta pick up my wife and the Assantes."

Immobilized in her bed, Ellen tries to open her eyes, but the morphine coursing through her veins is making her too drowsy. With a cloud of confusion filling her mind, the last thing she can remember is Jack Stenhouse's face.

After a fitful sleep, she tries to open her eyes

again and is startled to realize that her left eye is swollen shut. Then, when she tries to call out, she finds that she can't open her mouth. Panicking, she moves her arms and quickly realizes that her right arm is stuck with IV tubes, and her left arm is handcuffed to the bed. With her right eye opened as wide as possible, she turns her head until she sees the shadowy outline of a figure standing near the door. While she can't focus on the figure clearly enough to know who it is, she nevertheless raises her left hand, chuckles drowsily, and gives the image half a peace sign.

After being released into his attorney's custody, Secret Service Agent James Smithfield is on his way out of the police station. His lawyer arranged for bail and agreed that James would wear an ankle monitor and reside at his home. He also agreed that James would be under 24-hour surveillance until his trial.

Thus far, Smithfield has been charged with interfering with an investigation. However, the federal prosecutor is also trying to get him charged with the murder of Maria Assante. Because James knows that more shit is about to hit the fan, he told his lawyer that he wants a plea deal.

As the world awaits the outcome of the vote of the United States Congress to support or reject President Burris's declaration of war, it is holding its collective breath over the likelihood of a devastating response from Iran in the event of an affirmative vote.

Jack has just been dropped off at BWI airport, where he will wait for Didi to arrive and then pick up the Assantes. The FBI driver will wait for him in front of the terminal—his FBI credentials provide special parking privileges.

Inside the airport, Jack's NYPD ID has also provided him with special privileges. Even though he is not a passenger, he was allowed through the TSA checkpoint and is now at the gate, waiting for Didi's plane.

CHAPTER TWENTYFOUR

When the passengers from Didi's flight first begin to appear at the jetway entrance, Jack moves over to a spot that will allow him to see her as soon as she walks into the terminal.

In the midst of the passengers flowing around him towing their carry-on luggage, he focuses on the jetway and watches anxiously for a glimpse of his wife.

When he finally catches sight of her walking in his direction, he breaks into a large grin, and when Didi spots her husband, she runs into his arms and hugs him with tears in her eyes. The couple embraces, seemingly in an alternate universe, as people throng past them oblivious to their tender moment. Didi cries tears of sadness over losing her friend, and tears of joy at not losing her soul mate. With two hearts beating together as one, Jack kisses away Didi's tears and comforts his wife.

"Dee, everything is okay. Maria gave herself valiantly to the job she loved. She died doing exactly what she wanted to do."

Didi sniffles and grabs a tissue from her purse, trying in vain to wipe away the makeup that is streaming down her cheeks. "Damn it, Jack, I must look like a clown."

"You look beautiful, Babe. You just need to freshen up a bit."

Jack picks up Didi's carry-on, puts an arm around his wife, and guides her toward the restroom.

While he waits for Didi, he checks his watch and calculates that the Assantes will arrive in thirty minutes.

Jack had wanted to meet Maria's parents, but not under these circumstances.

Back at the FBI office, Senior Special Agent David Percal is pulling an all-nighter, reviewing information the team recovered from Vanierri's residence and Smithfield's and Vanierri's phones. He posts the latest information on a whiteboard with a timeline of events in the case and looks everything over again and again. When he finally connects the dots, his eyes widen in surprise, and he immediately places a call to the federal prosecutor for the District of Columbia.

"Evening, Carl. It's Dave Percal. Sorry to bother you so late. Have you heard anything from the FISA judge about Burris's phone?"

Under the Foreign Intelligence Surveillance Act, the United States Foreign Intelligence Surveillance Court can be contacted around the clock for warrants against Americans and foreign nationals, if there is credible evidence that they are involved with terrorists, spies, or other "foreign powers."

"No, he needs more evidence linking him to your case before he'll ask the NSA to get the records released. But if he does that, it will surely open up a can of worms."

"I know, but I have what he needs."

"Oh, yeah? Well, it better be good; we were lucky with Smithfield's phone. They were able to get confirmation that he warned Vanierri about the raid on her place. That's how we were able to rescind his bail and get him re-arrested. I'll bring that info to you in the morning."

At the airport, Didi emerges from the restroom refreshed and in a better state of mind. Jack smiles as she approaches him in her tan trench coat and high heels. Placing his arm around her, he whispers, "Got anything on under that coat?"

"Jack! Seriously?" she says, giving his shoulder a shove.

"Hey, I'm only human, you know."

"Yeah, I know," she replies with a roll of her eyes.

As they walk to the gate to pick up the Assantes, Didi inquires, "How will you know who they are, and how will they know who you are?"

"I have a little sign with their name on it."

"Ha! Like a chauffeur?"

"Yeah, I guess so."

The Assantes' flight from Orlando arrives at the gate five minutes early. While the passengers file through the gate area, Jack notices a woman who looks just like Maria. Motioning toward her, he whispers to Didi, "That has to be Maria's mom. They look like twins!"

At that moment, Tony Assante, Maria's father, notices the sign Jack is holding. Before boarding their flight, he received a text message from the FBI letting him know that Stenhouse would be meeting them at the airport. Holding his wife's hand, he approaches Jack.

"You must be Jack. Maria has spoken of you many times." Tony shakes Jack's hand and gives him a hug, stunning Jack with his strength. It reminds Jack of how strong Maria was.

Jack offers condolences to the couple, and then introduces his wife. After everyone exchanges greetings, he announces, "A driver from the FBI is waiting for us outside. It's almost impossible to travel through D.C. right now because of that asshole terrorist, but the FBI can get through. They reserved a room for you at the hotel we're staying at, so as soon as we get your luggage, we'll get you settled."

Tony stops Jack from saying anything further by grabbing his arm with an iron grip. Fighting back tears, he asks, "Where is my daughter? Where is Maria?"

Taken aback by the question, Jack looks uneasily at Mrs. Assante before he replies.

"Mr. Assante, Maria was taken to the funeral home the FBI uses. She will remain there until the memorial service, which will take place two days from now. A viewing has been arranged for tomorrow, so we'll take you both there in the morning."

Mr. Assante insists on seeing his daughter. "Jack, I want...we want...to see our daughter now, please."

"Um, sir, it's late, and D.C. is rather unsettled. I believe there may be a return to normalcy by tomorrow morning."

With a tear in his eye, Tony Assante stares at Jack and states firmly, "Jack, I absolutely insist. We want to see our Maria now."

Jack takes a deep breath and sighs. "Mr. Assante, I'll do my best. First, let's get your luggage. Then when we're outside the terminal, I can get a better signal on my phone, and I'll make some calls. I can't promise anything, but let's see what happens."

Listening to the conversation, Maria's mother walks up to Jack and places her hand on the side of his face. Speaking softly, she murmurs, "Thank you, Jack. Thank you."

Late that night, a radiologist who is hard at work at the hospital has just begun to study the results from Ellen Vanierri's MRI. Staring at the images, he notices a dark mass near the brain stem. He picks up the phone and calls a colleague to consult with him about what he is seeing, and then places a call to Ellen's doctor.

Ellen is having trouble sleeping, so she tries to sit up even though she is handcuffed to the bed. The movement causes her to feel dizzy, so she lies back down and presses the call button for a nurse. Her legs feel numb, and she feels throbbing pain at the back of her head and all over her face.

While she waits for the nurse, she tries to block out the pain by closing her eyes, but as soon as she does, the room begins to spin around, and she becomes nauseous. She panics at the thought of having to vomit, because with her mouth wired shut and only a small opening between her upper and lower jaws, she could very well choke to death. But she can't hold it back.

When the nurse enters the room, Ellen's head is hanging over the bed rail, and unidentified stomach contents are spraying all over the floor.

The ride from the airport is long and quiet with

the knowledge of what is to come. They are being driven directly to Stanton's Funeral Home, located near the Basilica of the National Shrine of the Immaculate Conception.

Even though it's late, the FBI was able to get an attendant to open the facility so the Assantes could have some private time with their daughter. The public viewing will be tomorrow from 11:00 a.m. to 7:00 p.m. and a memorial service will be held at the Basilica at 10:00 a.m. the following day. After the service, Maria's parents will accompany her body back to Florida for burial.

When the car pulls up to the funeral home, Jack glances at his watch and notes that it is almost midnight. Considering the death and chaos of the afternoon, the D.C. streets are relatively quiet this evening. But the National Guard troops that are stationed at each intersection may be a contributing factor.

A lone funeral home attendant motions the car around to the back, where several hearses are parked in a row. The couples exit the vehicle in silence and wait for the attendant to open the back door.

Maria is lying in a simple wooden coffin that has been brought into one of the viewing rooms. Jack and Didi remain respectfully behind while the proud but heartbroken parents approach their daughter.

At the sight of their daughter lying in a casket, Mrs. Assante sobs uncontrollably, causing Didi's tears flow to like a river.

As he holds his wife close, Jack's sorrow is overcome by a rising rage, which allows him to remain stoic, like a marble statue devoid of emotion.

While the Assantes pay homage to the daughter

they love, the minutes tick away like hours. Finally, the couple leaves their daughter's side and sits down wearily in the first row of chairs.

Seizing the chance to pay their own respects, Didi grasps Jack's hand and pulls him toward the coffin. Jack is hesitant as he walks forward with her. He fears that his composure may crumble as soon as he catches the first glimpse of his friend and colleague.

However, when they finally arrive at the coffin, he is surprised and relieved to see that Maria looks as beautiful as ever. Dressed in a black suit, she looks as if she will be waking up soon to report to the Bureau for duty. Her FBI badge has been placed just below her hands, and a silk scarf hides her fatal wound. The one thing that gives it all away is a set of rosary beads that her mother lovingly draped around her fingers.

When Jack reaches out to touch his friend's hand one last time, a solitary tear trickles slowly down the side of his face. But beside him, Didi is a wreck.

CHAPTER TWENTYFIVE

The majority of D.C. is finally back to normal, except for the areas around the Lincoln Memorial and the nearby reflecting pool. Those places are still cordoned off with crime scene tape, but workers have been allowed in to clean and repair the statue of President Lincoln.

The mood of the nation in the wake of the terrorist attack at one of our most cherished monuments has essentially guaranteed that Congress will vote to authorize military action against Iran and the Middle Eastern caliphate, but Jack couldn't care less.

While he and Didi wait for their breakfast in the hotel restaurant, Jack checks his watch for the umpteenth time. It is now almost 8:00, and he is anxious to get to work. The FBI has assigned a driver to the Assantes while they are in town, but Jack is content to walk the few blocks to his temporary position at the Bureau.

Noticing that her hubby seems preoccupied this morning, Didi reaches under the table and rubs his thigh.

"You were your old self last night," she coos.

Jack smiles. "Keep rubbing my leg, and I won't be able to stand up, let alone go to work today."

Dave Percal joins them just as the waiter arrives

with their orders. He slips into an empty chair at their table with some very interesting news for Jack.

After he greets Didi, he asks her, "How did it go last night with Mr. and Mrs. Assante?"

"Oh, it was very sad. Maria's parents are taking this pretty hard, but it was good that they had time to see her."

"Yes, I'm glad we were able to arrange that for them. I can't imagine how they are feeling. It must be awful to lose a child," he says.

When he turns his attention to Jack, he is all business. "I have some news for you, Jack. They discovered a tumor near Ellen Vanierri's brain stem last night, and it's inoperable. She has brain cancer, and may only have a couple of months left, at most."

At that news, the hand that Jack is using to hold his coffee cup stops in midair. "Are you serious?" he asks.

"Yes, it's true. And based on the phone records we got from the NSA, Smithfield is no longer on house arrest. He has been re-arrested and taken back into custody. As soon as you're done here, we need to get to the hospital to speak with Vanierri. I don't think she'll say anything to us, but who knows? The key seems to be that damn numeric message that Cunningham left."

"Gotta go, Babe," says Jack to Didi. He finishes his coffee and scarfs down some eggs. "Can you pay the check? I'll see you later, at the wake."

"Okay, Jack. I'll be with the Assantes today. Love you."

After giving Didi a quick kiss, Jack and David leave the restaurant.

While Percal drives them to the FBI, he fills Jack

in on the Assantes' other children.

"Maria's two brothers are in the military. One of them is on his way back from Germany and should be arriving this morning. He wants to surprise his parents, so they don't know he's coming. The other son has just left Afghanistan on a flight to Kuwait, and must wait there for the next flight out. He won't make it to D.C. in time for the wake or the memorial, so he's going to fly directly to Florida for the burial."

"Okay, thanks for letting me know. What's the plan for the memorial service?" asks Jack.

"We're expecting representatives from the Fort Lauderdale Police Department and the NYPD at the church, and of course, there will be a sizeable contingent of federal agents from D.C. and New York."

Jack has heard Dave's update, but he is also thinking about the case. Slipping into detective mode, he puts everything else at the back of his mind and gets down to business.

"Any news from the bathhouse?" he asks.

Percal also turns to the problem at hand, understanding that Jack is on a mission to resolve the situation in honor of his fallen comrade.

"Yeah, the membership roster reads like a list of 'Who's Who' in Washington. Names on that list belong to White House staff, the House of Representatives, and the Senate."

"How about the Secret Service?"

"Yeah, that too, and some of the agents are still on the President's detail."

"Fuck it! Burris is looking more and more like a Roman Emperor! First we need to break Ellen, and then we need to find a way to turn Smithfield."

"Yeah, but if neither of them talks, we're back to square one."

In a private room at the police station, James Smithfield is waiting for his lawyer. His shackled ankles are making it difficult for him to walk, but nervous energy is forcing him to shuffle back and forth around the room. Beads of sweat are glistening on his brow, and his hands are repeatedly moving over his hair and face.

Finally, a distinguished-looking man in a gray business suit walks casually into the room.

"It's about time you got here!" seethes James.

"Relax, Jim. Traffic is a little messy in D.C. these days. Sit down—we need to talk."

Smithfield seats himself at the metal table and stares into his lawyer's eyes. "Okay, what's up?"

"Well, I've been told that Ellen Vanierri has terminal brain cancer. The feds are on their way to interrogate her this morning."

James is surprised by the news but dismisses it quickly. "Look," he says, "if she says anything to them, I'm toast!"

His attorney responds sternly. "No, *you* look. You *are* toast. They got your conversation with Ellen from your phone—remember when you warned her about the NSA? Your best course of action right now is to spill everything. I contacted the prosecutor and the FBI as you asked me to, and requested a plea deal from them for immunity."

"Okay, but shit, if I talk, I'll be killed. I want relocation and a new identity, or the FBI gets nothing."

Dave Percal and Jack Stenhouse have stepped into the hospital elevator on the way to Ellen's floor. When the doors close on them, Jack takes advantage of the privacy to speak candidly.

"Dave, you're going to have to take the lead with Ellen. I'll stand nearby and listen to everything. I'm afraid that I'll lose it if I'm too close to her when she starts giving us shit."

"Maybe you shouldn't be there at all then."

"No, I want to see that bitch. Besides, maybe my presence will 'influence' her to talk. *Capeesh?*"

After exiting the elevator on Ellen's floor, they begin to walk toward her room but are stopped in the hallway by her attending physician.

"This is a private floor. What business do you have here?"

After examining their IDs, the doctor issues a stern command. "Gentlemen, Ellen's health is deteriorating rapidly. She has a very aggressive type of cancer and is now severely impaired from the waist down. Her speech is also compromised far beyond the fact that her jaw is wired shut, no thanks to you."

Beginning to simmer, Jack gives the doctor a piercing gaze, and then announces icily, "Doc, if it were up to me, that bitch wouldn't be here at all. Personally, I don't care what condition she's in. So lead, follow, or just get the fuck out of the way. We're going into her room, *now.*"

He pushes his way past the doctor, and Dave follows silently as Jack walks toward the guards who are stationed in the corridor outside of Ellen's room. The guards know Dave, so there is no need to flash their IDs again.

Inside the room it is quiet, and it looks as if Ellen is sleeping. The only sound is the steady beeping of the cardiac monitor that is keeping track of Ellen's heartbeat.

Realizing that they will need to wait until Ellen is alert, they lean against the wall and watch for signs of movement. After a short while, Ellen opens her eyes. When she does, the first thing she focuses on is Jack, which results in intensified beeping of the cardiac monitor. Jack just stares at her and grins.

Calm and professional as always, Agent Percal begins the interrogation.

"Ms. Vanierri, I am Senior FBI Special Agent David Percal, and I need to ask you a few questions." He picks up an Android tablet from the bedside table and hands it to Vanierri. "You can answer me with this. We know about your condition, so I hope you will answer my questions truthfully."

Dave waits for a response, but when it's obvious that there won't be one, he continues.

"First, let me first tell you what we know. You're an ex-Secret Service agent, and you're sexually involved with President Burris. You have been charged with four murders and are linked to a fifth. We believe that you have been acting under the direction of the White House, so we need to know who your contact is in the West Wing."

Percal waits while Ellen taps out her response on the tablet. When she flips the screen toward him, he reads the message while Jack looks on.

I will not admit to an alliance. I acted alone.

Percal takes a deep breath, while behind him, Jack increases his sniper-like stare.

"Ms. Vanierri, we currently have a colleague of yours in custody—James Smithfield. His attorney has informed us that he wants to make a plea deal for immunity from prosecution."

Immediately, the beeping of the monitor increases, and Ellen's heart rate goes sky-high. This alarms a nurse at the nursing station, who enters the room within seconds of the monitor's change in status. "Gentlemen, you are endangering my patient's fragile condition, and I must ask you to leave," she declares firmly.

Taking hold of the nurse's arm, Jack deftly guides her out of the room. "We understand your concern, ma'am, but we need to get some answers from her. So, back off. *Please.*"

Visibly upset, the nurse walks off in a huff to get the attending physician.

When Jack re-enters the room, Percal is reading Ellen's tablet. Turning it toward Stenhouse, he displays her latest response. The two-word message is a combination of a verb and a pronoun.

Jack pushes Percal aside and walks up to Vanierri's bedside. Leaning over, he whispers in her ear so quietly that Dave can't hear him.

"You know that soon you're going to be a dead woman, or man—whatever. As far as I'm concerned, I should have ended your existence when we tussled back at your house. But actually, I'm glad that you're already suffering in this life because you're surely going to suffer in the next. You know, we're going to get Burris one way or another, so I can safely say, *fuck you, bitch!*"

At that, Ellen's heart rate begins to go through the roof again, so before they are chastised by hospital staff for the second time, they decide to leave the room. As they nonchalantly saunter down the hallway, they are passed by a scurrying physician and head nurse.

As the elevator door opens, Percal looks over at Jack.

"Burris is obviously the key here, but we still have no clear connection between him, Ellen, and the murders. And what the hell did you say to set her off like that?"

Jack just smiles. "Let me at Smithfield again, or did he really want to cop a deal?"

Before Percal can reply, a text message arrives on his phone and he reads it as they enter the hospital lobby.

"I need to call the office about Smithfield."

After Jack left for work, Didi took a seat in the hotel lobby to wait for the Assantes. At 10:30 a.m., she is absently watching the hands of the clock on the wall opposite her when the Assantes enter the lobby and motion for her to join them.

"Deidre, would you like to join us for breakfast?" asks Mr. Assante.

"Thank you, but I already ate breakfast with Jack. I can have another cup of coffee, though."

Mrs. Assante touches Didi's arm to get her attention.

"Didi, we know that you and Maria were good friends. Maria spoke very highly of you and Jack, and we feel as if we already know you both."

Didi smiles at Maria's mother and gives her a hug. Then the three of them enter the hotel's restaurant.

After the waiter takes their order, a tall, well-built Marine in Dress Blues walks into the restaurant. Thinking that he looks like a younger version of Mr. Assante, Didi taps Mrs. Assante's shoulder and nods toward the young man. At the sight of the uniformed officer, Maria's mother gasps and grabs her husband's arm with one hand while she covers her mouth with the other. With tears in her eyes, she exclaims, "Oh, my God! It's Jacob!"

James Smithfield has been moved to an isolation cell at Maryland's Joint Base Andrews Naval Air Facility, with a rotating group of Marine guards stationed outside of his door to ensure his safety.

At the present moment, Jack Stenhouse, David Percal, and Smithfield's attorney are sitting together in a small room, waiting to talk to him.

After a brief delay, the shackled prisoner is escorted into the room by a guard, who guides him over to a table, unlocks his ankle shackles, and loops them through the retaining ring on the floor.

Smithfield's lawyer waits for the guard to leave before he addresses Jack and Dave.

"I have consulted with my client, and we concur. James will cooperate with your investigation in exchange for immunity and entrance into the witness protection program."

Percal glances at Stenhouse and Smithfield, and then looks back at the attorney.

"What makes you think that we want, or need, his cooperation, or that any information he has is valuable to us?"

"We contacted the Attorney General's office and the federal prosecutor assigned to this case, and they both seemed eager to gain Mr. Smithfield's cooperation."

Percal is intrigued by the prospect of gaining critical information. He leans toward Stenhouse and whispers, "Keep them occupied; I'll be back in a minute."

Rising from his seat, Percal announces, "I need to make a phone call. Jack will entertain you while I'm gone."

Dave's absence creates a void that is filled by unspoken tension, and Jack's cold, sniper-like stares at the Secret Service agent increase the level of stress in the room.

"So here we sit again, James. You wouldn't happen to have a phone book handy, would ya, Jimbo?"

The taunt causes beads of sweat to form on Smithfield's forehead, so Stenhouse leans forward and presses on.

"Because of you, I lost a very close friend the other day. The murder of a federal agent brings the death penalty, so I hope they tell you to pound sand before they give you a deal. You know that we're eventually going to link this whole mess together and end this shit with or without your help. So as far as I'm concerned, you are nothing but a dead man walking."

When Percal returns, he sits down and says,

"Okay, tell me what information you have, and I'll let you know if we accept your proposal."

Agitated by the terms, Smithfield's attorney responds quickly. "No way! You accept our proposal now, or there will be no sharing of information."

Percal studies the lawyer and then addresses his client.

"Maria Assante—remember that name? She's dead because of you, you piece of dirt. Immunity is not going to happen, but we will take the death penalty off the table and go for a lesser charge. But everything depends on the type of information you have for us. Take the deal, or take death by injection. It's your call. If you don't agree, we're through here."

Smithfield and his lawyer confer in whispers. Then, the attorney asks Percal, "What are the lesser charges?"

"That will depend on the level of your client's cooperation, and the value of the information we receive. So the ball is in your court."

Smithfield considers his options while he stares at Percal, and then at his lawyer. With a sigh, he says, "Okay, I'll tell you what I know."

CHAPTER TWENTYSIX

Sergeant Jacob Assante has taken a seat at the table with his parents and Mrs. Stenhouse. Even though he hasn't slept in almost thirty hours, he shows no ill effects. Didi stares at the young man as he eats a breakfast of grits and eggs.

"How long have you been in the military?" she asks.

"Five years, ma'am. I've been deployed in Germany for three."

Didi is taken aback by his response, but not because of his years in the military. This is the first time she has been called 'ma'am'.

"You must be very proud of your sons," she comments to Mr. and Mrs. Assante.

Mr. Assante puts his arm around Jacob's shoulder. "Jacob, Vincent, and Maria are our pride and joy. We have been blessed with wonderful children."

Jacob hugs his dad and then turns to Didi with a serious expression. "Who did this? Who killed my sister?"

Didi doesn't know how to answer the question, and she's not sure if she should even attempt it.

"Jacob, I'm not sure if I can answer that, but my husband, Jack, is working on the case. He'll be with us later, so you can ask him."

Mrs. Assante leans over and rests her head on her son's shoulder.

"Maria was doing what she wanted to do," she tells her son, "just like you and Vincent. Vince is on his way home, too, but he won't make it in time for the memorial service. He'll meet us at the funeral in Florida." With a dab at her eyes, she gives her son a shaky smile. "Now, let's all have a nice breakfast together. We're going to be at the funeral home for most of the day."

Jack stares at Smithfield. "So, you're ready to spill it now? This better be good, Slick."

Before speaking, James takes a deep breath and slowly exhales. "When Ellen Vanierri was still Allen, he was a Secret Service agent on President Burris's detail and was having an affair with the President. He was one of at least six other agents assigned to the White House who were involved in a special clique around Burris. All of them knew what was going on."

"Did they all belong to the Praetorium?" asks Stenhouse.

"Yes," Smithfield replies, not surprised that Jack knows the name of their hangout. "Although I wasn't part of the inner circle, I did attend various gatherings at the bathhouse, and at 'special' parties held at the White House. The agents on the Presidential detail had a unique codename for Burris that was different than the official one we used while we were working. Whenever we communicated privately with each other about the President, we called him 'Caligula.' "

He smiles weakly. "The name kind of fit him, you know? Ellen, or shall I say, Allen, was selected to be the scapegoat for what was going on at the bathhouse. She was supposed to take attention away from there because many influential people frequented the place. Many times when we were there, we would see someone we knew or had heard of—from White House staffers to members of Congress—both men and women.

"When Allen left the States and then returned as Ellen, Burris resumed their relationship. Nothing had changed between them, although Allen had changed dramatically. When the impeachment proceedings began, a group of us got together at the White House and pledged our allegiance to the President. The two agents Sansone eliminated were part of the group that..."

"Who else belongs to that 'group,' " interrupts Jack tensely.

"Me, Allen—or Ellen—and three more who are still working at the White House: Jason Goodie, Sharon O'Neil, and Leon Travis."

"Who are...?"

David Percal holds up a hand to prevent Jack from asking another question and directs his attention to Smithfield.

"Do you know anything about Blue Falcon?"

Smithfield's eyes widen, but he leans back in his chair and stares at the floor. "I've heard the name," he murmurs, "but that's all I know about it. I'm not part of the elite four—that would be Ellen, Jason, Sharon, and Leon. Blue Falcon was rumored to be something that Burris was planning. That's all I know."

Fuming, Stenhouse bursts in. "That's bullshit! You know more than you're saying! What the hell is Blue Falcon?"

"Careful, Detective," warns Smithfield's lawyer.

Still staring at the floor, Smithfield shakes his head. "I got nothing more. Nothing."

Rising from his seat, Stenhouse presses both of his hands onto the table and stares at James. "Did Ellen work alone, or was she directed to kill?" he snarls.

Shaken by the question, Smithfield looks up at Stenhouse. "I don't know. She may have been directed by someone from the beginning and was just carrying out orders, or she may have acted on her own and 'encouraged' to continue."

Dave Percal asks, "What was your role in all of this?"

"I was her mole," James responds with a sigh. "Ellen asked me to give her information from time to time, and that's what I did. You guys need to concentrate on the members of the Praetorium bathhouse and the people in the inner circle, especially the three agents who are still working close to Burris."

Neither Jack nor Dave believe that Smithfield is telling the truth about his lack of inside knowledge.

"As far as I'm concerned," says Dave, "all you have given us is crumbs. I think you know a hell of a lot more than what you've told us. We'll be sure to investigate that 'inner circle,' but what you've said is basically worthless. I'll talk to the prosecutor, but I haven't heard anything that leads back to anyone of importance, just to other Secret Service agents. It's your word against theirs, and your word ain't worth shit."

Dave stands and gestures to Stenhouse. "We're done here unless you have more to say, and you'd better make up your mind real quick about that, or this deal is off the table."

Jack and Dave walk out the door, leaving Smithfield with his attorney.

After they exit, a guard enters and unshackles James from the restraining ring. As the prisoner shuffles down the corridor, Dave and Jack, who have been standing in the hallway, shake their heads at him in disgust.

"That guy knows more than what he's saying," states Jack. "Burris is the one who's orchestrating everything; I just know it. We need to examine the President's phone records."

"The FISA judge needs a more definite link to the President before we can even think of doing that, Jack."

"What's FISA?"

"It's short for the Foreign Intelligence Surveillance Act, and it's used to decide whether to grant government requests for wiretapping, data analysis, and other types of monitoring within the United States. Let's begin by interviewing some of the names on the Praetorium list. I'll get my guys to start with the White House staff." He looks at his watch. "It's time to get to the wake, so I'll have someone drive you over there. I'll be there later."

"What about Leon, Sharon, and Jason?"

"We can't do anything that will tip them off, but we'll keep them under surveillance. Our next step would normally be to contact Homeland Security Secretary Olsen, but he's a member of the Praetorium. Since we don't know if he's involved, I'll have to ask the federal prosecutor to contact the FISA judge. We need the NSA to give us the phone records of those Secret Service guys."

"Corrie Johnson is a Secret Service agent. He and Smithfield are the ones they sent over to help us."

"Yeah, Corrie may be a good lead in the Secret

Service. His name is not on the Praetorium list, and he was never on the President's detail."

Jack shakes his head. "This Administration sounds like it would fit in really well in ancient Rome."

CHAPTER TWENTYSEVEN

The viewing room at Stanton's Funeral home is filling up fast. Mr. and Mrs. Assante are sitting in the first row of seats on the right with their son, Jacob, who is in full military dress. Behind them are Jack and Didi.

It seems as if every agent from the D.C. office of the FBI is coming to the wake to pay their respects. Maria's casket is surrounded by flowers, and to the left of the casket, a small table is filling up with Mass cards. Representatives from law enforcement in New York and Fort Lauderdale are also trickling in, albeit slowly, because travel into the D.C. area is still limited after the attack at the Lincoln Memorial.

When Detective Allison Giancarlo from New York's First Precinct arrives, she sits down in an empty chair next to Jack.

"Hey, how you doin'?" she asks with concern.

Jack is surprised to see her, but he's happy that someone from the First Precinct has shown up. Placing his arm around his partner, he gives her a hug. "Hey you. How are the guys back home?"

"SSDD Jack. Same shit, different day." She gazes at the casket. "This is so awful. Maria was one of the good guys."

"Tell me about it," says Jack. "I miss her already." A thoughtful pause ensues, and then he suggests, "Let's change the subject, okay? How'd you get to D.C.? Fly, drive?"

"I drove in. The First will be sending more guys to the service tomorrow. How the hell did this happen, Jack?"

"The shooter was tipped off. When we got there, she started firing at us, and Maria got hit. She was gone within minutes."

Jack sighs. "Let me introduce you to her parents."

As Jack stands up, Didi leans over his chair to give Allison's hand a squeeze. Then Jack guides his partner over to Maria's family. Hugs and handshakes bring tears and warm memories of Maria, while behind them, David Percal waits patiently for his turn to pay respects to the family.

Moments later, Allison leaves the group and turns toward the casket. Kneeling in front of Maria, she prays silently for her fallen colleague.

After David expresses his condolences to Maria's family, he walks over to greet Jack, who is once again seated next to Didi.

"Let me introduce you to my wife," says Jack proudly.

"Mrs. Stenhouse, it's a pleasure to meet you."

Jack tells Didi, "Dave is the lead FBI agent on the case, and he was Maria's boss."

After some small talk, David motions to Jack. "Let's step outside. I have some news for you."

"Be right back, Babe," says Jack.

Didi gives Jack's thigh a squeeze and watches as he follows Percal out of the room.

In the lobby, David asks a representative of the funeral home for a private area where they can talk, and they are guided to an empty viewing room at the end of a hall. When they are alone, David starts talking.

"Jack, our forensic lab and CSI team were able to piece together a wallet they found at the bombing. The terrorist who blew himself up was George Wilson, also known as Mohammed Qatari."

Wide-eyed, Jack asks, "Who is he? Any links to the Secret Service or the Administration?"

Percal shakes his head. "The thing is, Jack, this guy is a 'ghost.' He doesn't exist. The ID we were able to piece together from the wallet was a driver's license, but the number on it is not listed anywhere. It was a fake, and a good one. His name doesn't appear anywhere else, either—no Social Security number, no address, no telephone—nothing. Like I said, he was a 'ghost.' "

"So, it was planned."

"Yeah, Sansone was right. It was a red herring, a false-flag diversion for something else, and we're at another dead end."

Uneasy, Jack stares quizzically at Percal. "What the fuck? The President is killing off witnesses and blowing up the Lincoln Memorial? Even if we can prove it, how the hell are we going to arrest the President? What prosecutor is going to request *that* warrant? Certainly not the Attorney General, who's so far up Burris's ass, every time Burris smiles, you see his face."

"Yeah, and our Attorney General is also being investigated. He's accused of sending guns into Mexico without being able to trace them, and then trying to cover up that whole mess."

"What the hell do we do now, Dave? Where do we go? How the hell do we get to the President, if everyone around him is connected to each other?"

Jack slams his hand on the back of a chair in frustration, and Dave sighs and runs his fingers through his hair.

"There are two people we can trust," says Dave. "Corrie Johnson and Frank Sansone. I have a meeting tomorrow with FBI Director William Decker. He's ex-military and not exactly a Burris supporter. Ellen's cell phone was one of those prepaid phones, and the call records show that she dialed the President's private phone number. But that's all we have right now. We have the phone numbers, but no recordings of their conversations. However, even if we do get the goods on Burris, convicting him is going to be almost impossible. The repercussions of arresting a sitting President are, well..."

"Yeah, we are fucking screwed, blued, and tattooed."

Sunrise, Florida Police Sergeant Jorge Octavio is in the kitchen preparing an early dinner while his wife watches TV in the family room.

"Hey, Hon, come here," she calls. "There was a freak accident on I-595."

Jorge walks in from the kitchen in time to hear the report.

"This is Joe Storm on the scene at the New River Canal near I-595 and Flamingo Road. As you can see behind me, there is a covered body lying on the roadway. About thirty minutes ago, a motorcycle driver was forced off I-595. He flew over the overpass and crashed onto Flamingo Road. His name is being withheld until his family is notified."

As the camera pans back, Jorge rushes closer to

the screen to get a better look at the view behind the reporter.

"Holy crap! That's it!" Jorge gives his wife a kiss and immediately places a call to Jack Stenhouse.

Jack's phone rings while he and David are walking back into the room where the wake for Maria Assante is being held. Glancing at the screen, he comments, "It's Sergeant Octavio from Florida. I'll take it outside."

As he walks back into the lobby, he swipes to answer the call. "Octavio! What's goin on, man?"

"Jack, I got it! Those numbers—8640961989! I got it!"

"Hey, hey, hey, slow down! What have you got?"

After taking a deep breath, Octavio speaks more calmly. "Jack, those numbers are on a bridge over the canal on Flamingo Road: 864096. I just saw them on a news report about an accident there."

Excited by this information, Jack responds, "And 1989 must be the year the bridge was opened! Get ahold of Tim Coffers at the FBI office down there, and get a team to search under that bridge. I'll catch the earliest flight I can."

Rushing back into the wake, Jack locates Percal and gives him a big smile. "We got it, Dave! We got the link! I'm going down to Florida in the morning!"

CHAPTER TWENTYEIGHT

Styrofoam cup of coffee in hand, Jack stands in front of the Holiday Inn in Sunrise, waiting for his ride. When a black P.O.S. sedan pulls up Jack just stares at it, until the passenger side window opens.

"Hey, I'm not your personal chauffeur," calls Tim Coffers. "Get in, will ya?"

Jack rubs the side of his nose with the middle finger of his left hand, and then he pulls the latch on the door and climbs in, careful not to spill his breakfast. To Tim, he smirks, "This is how you treat your guests in beautiful, sunny, Florida?"

"Yeah, whatever. Mornin', Jack," responds Coffers. "Octavio and a dive team from BSO—you remember the Broward Sheriff's Office, right?—are en route to the bridge, along with our CSI guys."

With blue lights flashing on the dash and grill, the black sedan pulls out onto University Drive heading south, then west. Within a few minutes, it joins a sea of blue lights lining the bank of the New River Canal north of Interstate 595.

Tim and Jack exit the sedan and join Sergeant Octavio, who had arrived a few minutes before.

"Hey," greets Jorge as he shakes hands with Jack and Tim. Pointing at the bridge, he says, "The date the bridge was opened is stenciled onto the concrete barrier wall on the east side of Flamingo Road."

"Okay, we'll take a look later. What's going on

now?" asks Tim.

"The divers are in the canal under the bridge. We already searched the banks on both sides of the canal but found no indication of disturbed areas. The divers are trying to see if anything is underwater, but it's very murky down there, and visibility is low."

The men walk along the canal toward the bridge and stop when they see CO_2 bubbles rising from under the surface.

The three police divers who are scouring the murky bottom have retrieved something of interest. The first diver who surfaces gives a thumbs-up while the other two rise with a large aluminum box that they swim over to a nearby flat-bottomed boat.

In that area of the canal, the bank is too steep for the divers to climb out, so the dive team attaches one end of a rope to a handle on the side of the box, and then tosses the rope's other end to the trio on shore. Sergeant Octavio catches the line and attempts to pull the box up the bank, but it's heavier than he thought. Seeing him struggle, Jack joins in, and with the two of them grunting loudly, they finally manage to pull the locked case up onto the shore.

When it's free of the water, Tim Coffers moves down the bank to study it more closely.

"Let's get this back to our lab in Miami," he declares. "Our team can open it up there. It appears to be waterproof, and it's still fairly clean. It doesn't look like it's been in the water very long."

Jack is eager to see what's in it, and doesn't want to wait for the trip down to Miami, and the subsequent red tape that will ensue before the case can be opened.

"Look, all we need are some bolt cutters to open

this padlock," he counters as he peers out at all of the police and FBI personnel around them. "Any of you guys got a bolt cutter?" he yells.

From one of the flat boats in the canal, a BSO diver calls out, "Hey, Coffers! You guys need this?"

In a flash, a large bolt cutter is swung onto the shore by one of the divers in the boat, and it lands precisely at Jack's feet. As excited as a kid opening gifts on Christmas morning, Jack grabs the cutter and clamps it onto the lock, snapping it in two.

Within seconds, the team is staring at the contents of the opened chest. On the top of a pile of official-looking documents from the State Department are three DVDs. Jack hauls them out and reads the titles on each label. "This one is named 'Cunningham,'" he states, "and this one is called 'Skyhook, Vaya con Diablo, and Blue Falcon'. The last one says 'Praetorium.'"

Suddenly wide-eyed, Jack flips back to the DVD labeled 'Blue Falcon.' "You know, Sansone said there was an operation called Blue Falcon that involved the President. This must be the shit Cunningham was killed for! Octavio, you got a forensic team at police headquarters in Sunrise, don't ya?"

"Yeah. They're not as advanced as the FBI in Miami, but we got one."

"Well, that settles it. Sunrise is closer than Miami. We gotta go there to take a look at these DVDs. Maybe we can solve all of this bullshit sooner than we think."

"Hey, sorry to put the kibosh on your thunder here," interrupts a sergeant with the Broward's Sheriff's Office. "That box was retrieved from the New River Canal, which is under the jurisdiction of Broward

County. If that box goes anywhere, it goes to the Sheriff's office on Broward Boulevard."

Furious at the sergeant's posturing, Jack jumps down his throat, bellowing, "Bullshit! That's one of the very reasons I left this fucking town!" He snarls and continues, "This is a *federal* investigation, so that trumps your sorry ass! And as a member of this *federal* task force, I'll take this evidence wherever I damn well please."

Alarmed by Jack's reaction, Coffers holds him back by his shoulders.

"Look," he says calmly to the sergeant, "we'll take this back to our FBI lab in Miami, and that will settle everything. Sergeant, I suggest that you leave now, because I'm about to let Stenhouse here past me, and then I'll join in on the fun. Got it?"

The Broward County sergeant backs off, realizing that he has now become a pariah to the entire assembled group of law enforcement personnel from Sunrise and the FBI. After he leaves the scene, Tim Coffers peers at Jack.

"Man, the veins on your forehead were about to burst! We're going to take this over to Sunrise forensics to view the recordings. Miami's too far. I just told him that so he'd leave. After we take a look at everything, we'll take it all back to Washington with us."

Jack looks like he wants to spit. "You think it's bad in Washington? It's all bullshit politics down here in Florida." He shakes his head in disgust. "But let's get going. We got a President to fry."

After a quick trip north on Flamingo Road, they arrive at the headquarters of the Sunrise Police Department, where Octavio leads them to a room containing a large-screen TV that is connected to a DVD player.

Placing the lock box on a table, Stenhouse opens it and pulls out the DVD marked "Cunningham." He inserts the disk into the DVD player, and hits "play."

At first, static and "snow" fill the screen, disappointing the trio and causing them to wonder whether the disk is damaged or blank. But just as Tim is about to hit "eject," an image suddenly appears on the screen. At first, the only thing visible is an empty desk, but in the next moment, Joe Cunningham walks onscreen and sits behind the desk.

"Hello, my name is Joe Cunningham, Deputy Secretary of State. I am recording this in the event that I am killed because of the evidence I have gathered against the present Administration. With the help of CIA employees John Hastings, Frank Sansone, and several of my State Department subordinates, I have accumulated evidence of the illicit activities of President Howard Burris. The evidence I will present also implicates Secretary of State Hilda Canton, who at the time of this recording is in a coma as a result of a brain hemorrhage. What you may not know is that Ms. Canton's injury was caused by a fall against a granite coffee table while she was in a drunken stupor.

"The information you are about to see will implicate Hilda Canton, Attorney General Ellis Handelman, Vice President Jeff Borden, and President Howard Burris, as well as a group of Secret Service agents that President Burris describes as his "Posse."

"Please review each DVD without prejudice, so that all facts are treated objectively. God bless you all, and God bless the United States of America."

When Joe's image is replaced by more "snow," the men stare at the screen in silence, with mouths agape.

The stillness in the room is so loud that it is overpowering.

After a couple of minutes, Jack turns to his compadres and murmurs, "Holy shit on a shingle!" Then Coffers mutters, "We are about to blow a hole through this entire Administration! What the hell have we gotten ourselves into?"

Jack reaches out and inserts the DVD marked "The Praetorium," and within minutes, they are watching what appears to be a scene from ancient Rome. Men and women, men and men, and women and women, are comingling in organized chaos, like an image from a Jackson Pollack mural. The scenes of decadence include images of President Burris with Allen Vanierri and White House staff members, as well as prominent members of the D.C. establishment.

With a grunt of disgust, Coffers reaches out and ejects the DVD with a quick jab of his finger. "I don't think we need to see any more of this. Those images are now burned into my retinas for life. I'm sure the written report that Cunningham left will suffice."

Tim inserts the last DVD into the player. With increasing unease about what may be on this last recording, the officers wait anxiously until Cunningham's image once again appears on screen.

"I am Joe Cunningham, Deputy Secretary of State. If you are viewing this, I have been killed because of the information I have gathered, which I will now disclose to you.

"I will begin with Operation Skyhook. This covert mission is one of the reasons that President Howard Burris may be impeached, because it involves illegal activities in support of the government of Iran.

"The person in charge of spearheading Operation

Skyhook was Vice President Jeffrey Borden. He directed the mission under the pretense of negotiating a treaty with Iran, and he was aided by Secretary of State Hilda Canton. Ms. Canton directed State Department employees and members of the CIA stationed at the U.S. embassy annex in Sudan to transfer jet fighter replacement parts to the Iranian government so they could sustain their aging fleet of attack aircraft. Under the current sanctions against Iran, those parts should have been unavailable to them, but President Burris had no qualms about violating the terms of the sanctions. He believed that if we supplied the replacement parts to Iran's military services, the leadership of the country would then cooperate with the West and dismantle their nuclear weapons program.

"Of course, Burris's plan did not work at all. Iran went along with the farce and played us for the fool. And when spies in Tehran notified the Saudi government about Burris's scheme, the Saudis informed the Kuwaitis, and then both countries jointly reported everything to Al-Qaida in Sudan. Although Al-Qaida is an enemy of the Saudi and Kuwaiti governments, they are all enemies of Iran, and politics makes strange bedfellows.

"Al-Qaida subsequently attacked the U.S. embassy compound to stop the parts from being smuggled to Iran, and in that attack, we regrettably lost our ambassador and five other good men. Although she was warned beforehand, Secretary of State Canton did not permit the consulate's security to be increased, because she did not want to draw attention to Operation Skyhook. And contrary to what has been reported in the media, an order not to interfere in the rescue of our men at the annex came directly from the White House. My written report outlines the details and timelines of those events.

"Now, I will discuss Operation Vaya con Diablo. This mission was directed by Attorney General Ellis Handelman, with the approval of President Burris. Under Handelman's instructions, the Department of Justice approved the purchase of assault weapons from various dealers in Texas and Arizona, and sent them into Mexico so they could find out who was using them against us along our southern border. Apart from this being a bad idea, the guns were shipped into Mexico in such a haphazard fashion that the DOJ soon lost track of hundreds of the rifles and handguns. And in order to disguise this ineptitude, Department of Justice officials blamed local DOJ officers for the missing guns. But that is not all. Handelman was paid off by the drug cartels in Mexico to keep the guns flowing across the border, so that's why, even though we couldn't keep track of what was going on, the mission was never aborted. You'll find timelines of the events in my written report, along with evidence of the direct involvement of the White House, and the names of the Mexican officials and criminals who were complicit in the scheme.

"Finally, I will discuss the last and most vile plot—Operation Blue Falcon. With the mood of the country turning increasingly against him, President Burris was forced to confront the fact that his house of cards would eventually crumble. So, to get the country to rally behind him while he was still in office, he devised a distraction that would cause the impeachment proceedings to move off the public's radar. But to make the diversion work, he needed to implicate Iran, one of the country's major enemies. He knew that if any information was leaked about the truth of Operation Skyhook, he was toast.

"The diversion Burris devised was the bombing at the Lincoln Memorial. It was put in place with the help of

his 'posse' of Secret Service agents, which everyone knew about. Without his knowledge, the bomber was indoctrinated as a sleeper agent, to be activated upon command. He was placed in the D.C. area and told to go about his business. Just before his activation, his life history was removed from the 'grid,' and he was turned into a virtual 'ghost'—a person who doesn't exist. My written report contains further details about Operation Blue Falcon.

"As I continued to gather information about all of these schemes, I began to fear for my life. I heard rumors that Allen Vanierri, now Ellen, was acting as Burris's vigilante to silence me and anyone else who got in the way of the President's legacy. As you know by now, John Hastings, who worked under me at the State Department, is dead. He knew about the President's schemes, and so does CIA Agent Frank Sansone, who helped me compile all of this information. I hope that Sansone is still alive.

"Be assured that everything I have discussed in this recording will eventually be corroborated. Be vigilant, for this information will take down the current Administration.

"If you decide to pursue criminal charges, you have a daunting task ahead of you—you must confront and charge a sitting United States President with crimes against the homeland and crimes against humanity."

When the image on the TV screen fades back to "snow," Sergeant Octavio reaches up and turns off the DVD player.

In the ensuing quiet of the room, the three officers reflect on everything they have just heard. But after a while, their musings are interrupted by Octavio, who comments sullenly, "We are in deep shit! Our lives won't be worth a damn! What the fuck are we going to do? How the hell can we arrest the President?"

Coffers rises from his seat and sighs. Looking at Octavio, he says, "First, we gotta get all this stuff up to Percal in D.C. No, wait. Before we do that, we need to make copies of everything before we let it out of our hands. One copy should stay here in Florida, and there should be a copy for me and one for Jack, so that if any of us turns up dead or the originals disappear, the evidence will still be around. Jack, you'll need to get back to D.C. with one of the copies. I'll send an electronic version to the FBI in New York. Octavio, don't say a word about this to anyone. Once we get this stuff to the FISA judge, all hell will break loose."

Draping his arm around Coffers' shoulder, Jack declares, "Mark my words, Tim, this is going to leak out somehow, and then we'll see how the roaches run for cover. We should talk to Smithfield and Vanierri again soon, and also to Sansone. And we need to find someone in the Secret Service who's clean—someone who's not involved in all this bullshit."

"Yeah, you're right."

"You know what?" adds Jack. "I need to get back to D.C. Get the copies made and then give me the originals. I'm going to take them with me. Can you book a flight today?"

"I'll do better than that; you can use one of our private jets. We'll get you there within four hours."

Listening to the conversation, Octavio stares gravely at Stenhouse and Coffers. "Vaya con Dios, guys," he advises.

On the way back to Washington, Jack stares out

of a small window at thirty thousand feet while his mind drifts back to the first time he saw Maria Assante. She was turning heads at Fort Lauderdale Police headquarters, as she always did wherever she went. Glancing at the aluminum case at his feet, he sighs and then closes his eyes, only to have his thoughts turn toward the funeral he is missing at the Basilica of the National Shrine of the Immaculate Conception in Washington.

Scores of blue-uniformed police officers from New York and Fort Lauderdale are sitting in the pews at the Basilica next to their FBI comrades from D.C. and the Big Apple. At the front of the church are Maria's parents and her brother, Jacob, in his Marine dress uniform. Immediately behind the Assantes are Deidre Lee Stenhouse, Senior FBI Special Agent David Percal, and Police Detective Allison Giancarlo, with her husband, Mario.

The Assante family is trying desperately to hold back their tears as the pastor wraps up his eulogy, but when the basilica's bells begin to toll the nation's respect toward its fallen heroine, their tears are impossible to stop.

The first chime rings out over Washington, D.C., while the FISA judge signs an order for the NSA to release President Burris's cell phone conversations.

The second chime reaches Ellen Vanierri in her hospital room and triggers shudders of her weakened body. When her heart monitor begins to produce a constant, high-pitched tone, the nurses and doctors on her floor rush to her aid.

The third toll is heard while a private telephone call is being answered by Attorney General Ellis Handelman.

And the fourth peal is heard while Vice President

Jeffrey Borden is talking on his cell phone.

Standing alone in the Rose Garden, President Burris feels a cold wave of fear pass over him while he listens to the tolling of the bells in the distance. The sound incites in him a feeling of isolation and vulnerability, so he is startled when Agent Jason Goodie suddenly appears at his side.

"Excuse me, Mr. President," says Jason. The agent leans close and whispers confidentially that Ellen Vanierri has died.

Knowing that a response is required from him at the death of a trusted member of his security detail, President Burris murmurs standard words of shock and sorrow but does not say anything further. The trusted agent waits for instructions, but seeing that nothing will be forthcoming, moves quietly back into the White House.

When the President is sure that he is alone again, he turns away from the iconic building and chuckles, grinning broadly.

CHAPTER TWENTYNINE

As soon as Jack's flight lands at the D.C. airport, he makes a beeline for FBI headquarters. But since so many of the agents are attending Maria's memorial service, the building is almost empty. While he waits for their return, he makes use of the relative quiet to place a call to his wife at their hotel knowing she is there by now. He wants to let her know that he's back in the nation's capital after his short trip to Florida.

When the agents finally begin to trickle in, he watches eagerly for David Percal, and as soon as he sees him, he hands over the aluminum case.

"Dave, this is the evidence that Cunningham collected. We made copies of everything, but these are the originals. Guard them well."

"Great work, Jack! I have good news for you, too. The FISA judge has authorized the NSA to release Burris's phone records. We'll proceed with our investigation as soon as the records are decrypted."

"Wow, it looks like we're finally getting the ball rolling," replies Jack.

"Yeah, and I have one other piece of news for you," adds Dave. "Ellen Vanierri died."

"What?" cries Jack.

"Apparently, she had a massive brain hemorrhage, and didn't make it."

"Fuck! We needed to interrogate that bitch again! What about Smithfield? Any updates on that jerk?"

"Yeah, we contacted his lawyer and told him about the new evidence you found, and now he agrees to spill his guts."

"Funny how that works, isn't it? But do we need his testimony now? Don't we have enough damaging information without it?"

"We do have a lot, but we're going up against a sitting President, so we need all the evidence we can get. I'm going to get the stuff you found over to our team so they can check it out. We need to make sure it's legit before we use it. My contact at the NSA says they should have the President's phone records for us within forty-eight hours, so there's not much more we can do today. I'm going to have Smithfield brought here in the morning, and I've asked Frank Sansone to come in as well."

Percal smiles sadly. "You missed a good service this morning, Jack. The Assantes are leaving tomorrow with Maria's body. I overheard Deidre say that she and Detective Giancarlo are having dinner with them tonight at the hotel. Go and say your goodbyes. I'll see you tomorrow."

Jack looks at the aluminum case, and then back at Percal. "What the hell are we going to do, Dave? How do we go about arresting the President of the United States?"

Percal shakes his head. "I haven't the slightest idea."

It is now late in the day, and there is a sudden flurry of activity at the White House as Attorney General Handelman and Vice President Borden meet with the President and his chief-of-staff in the Oval Office.

"Gentlemen, we need to keep calm," begins Burris.

Visibly shaken, Vice President Borden sputters, "Mr. President, my source told me that the information Cunningham left behind will fry us all! My name is stamped on the Skyhook mission, so I can't remain here to add fuel to a burning Administration." Reaching into his suit jacket pocket, he pulls out an envelope and hands it to President Burris. "Mr. President, I'm handing in my resignation. I will announce my decision to resign at a press conference tonight. As you know, I recently had a brief stay in the hospital for some tests, so I'm going to use my health as an excuse to leave office. This whole thing is falling down around us!" Turning to the chief of staff, he declares, "Kevin, I'm out."

With that, the Vice President rises from his seat and shakes President Burris's hand. Then, with head bowed, he leaves the room. The remaining men stare at the retreating Vice President in a state of shock.

A moment of awkward silence ensues, after which Chief of Staff Kevin Randel advises, "Sir, you will need to make an announcement about his resignation."

But before Burris can respond, the Attorney General adds, "Mr. President, you're going to need to make two announcements. I'm also resigning, and I will state family issues as the reason. I will make my announcement in the morning. Shit is about to hit the fan, sir, and I suggest that you take a good, hard look at what has been going on here. Your presidency is definitely at risk."

Handelman hands a resignation letter to Burris and leaves without a goodbye or a handshake. He just walks out of the room.

Burris is livid. "What the fuck? Are you also a quitter, Kevin? Are you going to leave me, too? Well, I won't give you the fucking satisfaction! Get the fuck out of my office! Get the fuck out of the White House!"

"Calm down, Mr. President! I'm not going anywhere."

"Calm down?" Burris laughs hysterically. "You're fired! Get out of here before I have the Secret Service throw you out!"

Slamming his tablet computer on the floor in anger, Randel leaves the office in a huff. Immediately, Burris picks up his desk phone and calls his secretary.

"Get Johnson and Lawson in here right now," he orders.

Within minutes, Sherry Lawson, assistant press secretary, and Victoria Johnson, Burris's personal advisor, step into the Oval Office.

"Sit down and listen," commands Burris. "We have work to do." He addresses his assistant press secretary first.

"Sherry, Borden and Handelman just resigned, and I fired Kevin. You need to figure out how to spin that. And get the speech writers in here. They need to draft a statement that I can make in the morning. Now, go out and get started."

Taken aback by the President's abrupt attitude, Ms. Lawson quickly exits the Oval Office. After she's gone, Burris turns toward Victoria.

"It's about to hit the fan, Vickie," he says worriedly. "What do we do now? What do I do?"

Victoria takes Burris's hand and states soothingly, "I know exactly what you need, Mr. President. Come on, let's go upstairs."

Entwining her fingers with the President's, Victoria begins to lead him out of the Oval Office. But just outside the door, she stops to whisper to the Secret Service agent on duty.

"Call the posse together and join us in the President's bedroom. We're going to have a party."

While the President and his personal advisor walk off hand-in-hand, the agent speaks softly into his lapel mic. "Caligula wants his posse upstairs."

Jack, Didi, Detective Giancarlo, and Giancarlo's husband are sitting at the bar in the hotel lobby while they wait for the Assantes to join them for dinner. They are chatting amiably until their attention is diverted by a news flash that interrupts the program on the TV above the bar.

"We interrupt this broadcast for an address to the nation by Vice President Borden. We will return to the Nationals game as soon as possible."

The picture on the screen switches to the Vice President, who is standing behind a podium with his wife and family by his side.

"My fellow Americans, I come before you tonight with a sense of disappointment and regret.

"As you may have heard, I was hospitalized briefly last week for some tests that were considered to be routine. However, the tests revealed a condition that neither I nor my physicians knew that I had. I have been informed that I am suffering from sick sinus syndrome, a condition that causes my heart to beat too slowly, and my doctors have recommended that I have a pacemaker installed immediately.

"After deep reflection, I have concluded that my

health and my family are my first priorities; therefore, with the approval of President Burris, I have resigned from my position as Vice President, effective immediately.

"Until my replacement is named, I will remain as a consultant to our President, and I will assist him in choosing my replacement. I am sorry that I am not able to complete the job you elected me to do, and I thank you for your support. God bless you, and God bless America."

Vice President Borden walks off-screen, accompanied by his family. Then the station reporter breaks in.

"Vice President Borden has resigned from office, stating medical reasons for his departure. However, one must wonder if the events surrounding this Administration have prompted his abrupt resignation. We have contacted the White House for comment and have been informed that a statement will be issued in the morning.

"Our sources in the Administration have told us that Borden's resignation may not be the only one. We have learned that there was an emergency meeting at the White House earlier today, attended by both Vice President Borden and Attorney General Handelman. That meeting may be related to the press conference that Attorney General Ellis Handelman is scheduled to conduct tomorrow morning at 8:00. This is Bill Jenkins, NBC News. Now, back to the game."

Allison Giancarlo turns to Jack with a quizzical look, but he is quietly sipping his bourbon on the rocks.

"You have info on this, don't ya?" asks Allison.

"The only thing I can say right now is that all hell is about to break loose."

At that moment, Mr. and Mrs. Assante enter the bar area accompanied by their son, Jacob.

"The lobby is all abuzz," states Mr. Assante. "The Vice President just resigned, and they're saying that the Attorney General will be next. Maria told us that she was working on something big, but she wouldn't say what it was. She did say that it would rock Washington, though."

Jack places his empty glass down on the bar. "Be prepared, everyone; more shit is coming down. Maria was partially right; there's more here than meets the eye. What's going on will rock Washington, but also the whole nation, and worse. History is repeating itself—Nero is fiddling while Rome burns. But look, tonight we're going to honor your daughter and my good friend, so let's concentrate on that."

CHAPTER THIRTY

The next morning, Jack files into FBI headquarters with a cup of black coffee in one hand and a cola in the other. Too much booze and too much Didi left him with only one hour's sleep.

Percal and Sansone stare at Jack, who looks downright morbid. With a smirk on his face, Frank Sansone announces, "Okaay! Dead man walking here!"

Jack removes his sunglasses, puts down his coffee and cola, and flashes half a peace sign to the now-laughing Sansone. Dave Percal watches but just shakes his head.

"Damn, Jack," continues Sansone, "close your eyes before you bleed to death. Getting pretty old for this shit, ain't ya?"

Jack sits down slowly and stares at his coffee. As blood pounds into his head like clapping thunder, he struggles to make a coherent sentence. "My tongue is asleep, my hair hurts, and my teeth itch. And I can't even make a fist..."

He makes a heroic effort at a grin. "But I did have fun last night. So, what's the skinny for today?"

"Well, in case you haven't heard," responds Dave, "Handelman resigned this morning, and Burris is going on TV soon to make a statement. Borden and Handelman must have gotten tipped off about what you found."

Jack takes a gulp of soda. "Yeah, they're like rats

leaving a sinking ship. What about Smithfield? Hey, Frank, did Dave fill you in about the stash we found?"

"Yeah, that's why I'm here. Smithfield is waiting down the hall with his lawyer. You up for this, Jack?"

"That's what Didi said last night," chuckles Jack.

While the others laugh, Jack glances at the door. "Let's get this shit over with," he says. "Didi goes back to New York later today, and I gotta take her to the airport...if I'm still alive by then."

The men walk toward the interrogation room, and then split up. Jack and Percal wait outside the door while Sansone enters the room next door to view the proceedings through a two-way mirror.

Still wearing his sunglasses and carrying another cup of coffee, Jack downs 600mg of ibuprofen and asks Percal to do the talking.

Agreeing to take the lead, Dave opens the door, and Jack follows him into the room. They seat themselves across the table from James Smithfield and his attorney, and then Percal begins the conversation, speaking as tersely as possible.

"Look," he states, "we have corroborating evidence from documents left by Cunningham that you and the President are guilty of crimes against the nation. Tie that up in a bow along with your damaging phone records, and it doesn't look like we need anything else before we charge you. So, what's it gonna be? You ready to talk now?"

Smithfield looks over at his lawyer, and when he is given a positive nod to proceed, he says, "Cunningham left his account of what happened, and that opened Pandora's Box. With that information you could impeach Burris for sure. I know that Cunningham links him to Blue Falcon, but what I have is the proof you need that will fry that murderous bastard. I got copies of letters, emails, and recordings of meetings with Burris. I was part of the in-crowd at the Praetorium, and I was close to Allen while he was still on duty at the White House, before he became Ellen. Burris's posse—his 'special' group of Secret Service agents—includes agents that are still at the White House. Before Allen left the Service, he pledged his loyalty to Burris, and he told me that Burris wanted to retain his expertise as a private enforcer 'for special assignments.' At one point, Burris ordered me to check out the groups that wanted to investigate him, and that's when two of the agents that were part of his posse were taken out by Sansone."

Jack interrupts as he stares at Smithfield through his shades. "Look, Slick. Ellen is dead, so what you're telling us now is only your version of the story. Where's all the information that links Burris to this shit?"

Leaning over to his lawyer, Smithfield confers with him in whispers. Then he reaches into his attaché case, retrieves a key, and places it on the table.

"This key will open the locked drawer of a desk in the captain's quarters of the U.S.S. *Torsk*, which is the World War II sub that's been turned into a floating museum in Baltimore's Inner Harbor. In that desk, you will find information that directly links President Burris to the bombing at the Lincoln Memorial. The information links Secretary of State Canton, Vice President Borden, and the late ambassador to Sudan to Operation Skyhook. Operation Blue Falcon was created to cover up Skyhook, and I was part of the team that indoctrinated George Wilson, the man who bombed the Memorial.

You will find all of the background info on these projects in that drawer, with electronic copies of all the other information I told you about. My attorney has the originals."

"Anything else?" asks Percal.

"Yeah. Burris wanted to cover his ass in case the Sudanese operation went south. When it all fell apart, he assumed the American people would ignore what happened in Sudan if he started a war with Iran. If war broke out, he didn't think the GOP would continue to pursue the scandals in his Administration, but after they gained control of the House and Senate, they moved to impeach.

"But even with all this evidence, I don't know how the hell you're going to get to President Burris. His 'special' Secret Service agents guard him 24/7, and all of them have pledged their undying loyalty to him, above and beyond the usual Secret Service pledge that we all take. There will be a bloodbath at the White House if you attempt to go after the President, so I give you this warning: all of you are being watched and followed. Burris has friends in the Bureau, in the U.S. Marshals Service, and in the DOJ. I suggest that you get the military involved, because they hate him."

Smithfield points at Jack and David. "You two guys, as well as you, Sansone," he adds as he peers into the two-way mirror, "are already marked and set to be erased. Trust no one. Maria was targeted first, and now they have their sights set on you and me. But I'm done talking. I want military protection that is way better than Conway's was."

Taking the key off the table, he holds it up. "Gentlemen, with this and Burris's phone records, you have all the information you need to arrest the President of the United States. God protect us all."

Percal grabs the key out of Smithfield's fingers and then goes out into the hallway to speak to the two agents who are waiting there.

"Take him to the Marine barracks on 8th and place him under Marine guard. I'll get Decker to make the formal request to hold him there."

Percal waits in the hallway while Smithfield and his lawyer are escorted out of the interrogation room, and then he walks back into the room to speak to Jack.

"Jack," he says, "I have to speak with the Director. We need to pay a visit to the U.S.S. *Torsk* in Baltimore."

"Okay. I gotta take my wife to the airport, so I'll do my husband thing first, and then I'll meet you there. I need a car, though."

Percal reaches into his pocket and throws a set of keys to Jack. "Take mine. I'll see you in Baltimore in a couple of hours. Tell Sansone to sit tight. I'm going to request a Marine Guard for him, too."

When Sansone hears Dave's comment through the two-way mirror, he runs next door and confronts Percal in the interrogation room. Nose to nose, he declares, "I am *not* going to be locked up with some damn Marines! The Company has a safe house they can sequester me in. I'll feel *much* safer with them." Shaking his finger, he says, "You two need to watch your combined asses! Some of those Secret Service guys are ex-black ops. If they want you dead, you're dead. Remain vigilant. If something looks out of place, it probably is."

Percal nods, and without saying another word, heads to the FBI director's office.

After four cups of coffee, Jack is feeling almost normal when he walks into the hotel to fetch Didi. She is in the lobby, waiting for him with her luggage.

"Ready, Babe?" he asks. "I borrowed a car. I'll drop you off at the terminal, and then I gotta get back to work."

To Didi, Jack seems a little distant, so she looks questioningly into his bloodshot eyes.

"You're not telling me something, Jack. What's wrong?"

Holding Didi close, he whispers into her ear. "We're going after the President, and some people aren't happy about it." He picks up Didi's luggage and walks her over to the car.

Didi is scared—she has never seen Jack this concerned. Not wanting to show her fear, she remains silent as they drive to BWI airport, but in her mind, she can't shake the feeling that something is about to happen.

Something bad.

CHAPTER THIRTYONE

Jack is late, and Dave Percal is annoyed. He's been waiting for thirty minutes next to the U.S.S. *Torsk* on the pier at Baltimore's Inner Harbor, and he can't wait much longer.

"Where the hell are ya?" he asks irritably when Jack answers his cell phone call.

"I'm stuck at a traffic light on East Pratt Street. Where's a good place to park in this town?"

"Think out of the box, okay?" responds Dave. "Turn toward the harbor at South Gay Street and continue driving onto the Harbor Walk to Pier Three. I'll let Harbor Security know that your vehicle will be on the promenade. I'm waiting near the sub."

When the light turns green, Jack finds the street where he needs to turn, and with blue lights flashing from the borrowed sedan's front grill, he drives down the walkway to the water's edge as tourists stare and scamper out of his way. When he spots Percal, he parks the car and jumps out.

"Nothing like making a memorable entrance!" he says with a grin.

Watching from a short distance away is the driver of a black SUV, who transmits Jack's and Percal's location through his shirt cuff, and then drives off.

It is a beautiful, sunny day in Baltimore. Crowds of tourists are milling about, enjoying the sights along the city's historic seaport while hordes of seagulls are squawking above and making their presence known.

To reach the *Torsk*, Jack and David have to cut through a crowd of people that is completely unaware that the pair of them is about to unseat their President.

Well, almost everyone.

A Baltimore law enforcement officer on duty at Pier 3 leans against a black sedan and speaks into the microphone attached to his uniform shirt.

"Targets are on the way to the *Torsk*. Will inform when they return."

When Jack and David reach the veteran submarine that is now part of the collection of historic ships on display in the harbor, they present their badges and IDs and request the services of a private guide to escort them into the bowels of the vessel.

When the guide arrives, they follow him down a narrow ladder that leads into the torpedo room. Then they make their way into the operation room, past the crew quarters and galley, and into the area that houses the officers' quarters.

When they arrive at the captain's quarters, they are confronted by a rope that is strung across the doorway to prevent tourists from entering the room. Peering into the tiny space, the men see the captain's bunk and a small desk attached to the wall. The desk consists of several drawers and a large compartment that appears to be locked.

"We need access to this room," declares Dave to the guide, who obediently removes the rope barrier.

Now free to enter the room, Dave walks directly over to the desk and inserts the key that Smithfield gave them. When the large compartment unlocks, he opens the door, reaches in, and removes the contents.

Then he re-locks the door and hands the key to the guide.

"Here," he says. "I believe this is yours."

A few minutes later, the men have climbed up the stairway and are back on land.

As they walk away from the sub, Jack asks, "What did you find down there?"

Without comment, Dave shows him a small flash drive.

"Holy shit! There must be some good stuff on that thing. But I'd go crazy under the water in that tin can! There's no room down there at all!"

With the flash drive tucked safely into David's pocket, the pair continues walking to the car Jack parked at the end of the pier.

When they reach the "cop" on duty, he gives them a nod, and once they are past him, he speaks surreptitiously into his uniform mic once again.

"Targets are back," he whispers.

At the same time as Jack and David are climbing into Dave's sedan, a large garbage truck is pulling off Pratt Street and heading down the Harbor walkway, taking the same route that Jack had taken earlier.

As Dave prepares to put his car into gear, the last thing he sees in the rear view mirror is the grill of the large truck as it smashes into the rear of the vehicle.

Conveniently, the garbage truck's driver has jumped to safety from the vehicle before impact. From a safe distance, he watches indifferently as the force of the collision catapults the sedan into the harbor.

Inside the car, Jack and Dave are dazed, but conscious. They struggle to exit the car while it still remains afloat, but the force of the water against the doors prevents them from being opened. As water fills the car's interior, David calls out, "We need to let the car fill with water, so the pressure equals out! Then, we can open the doors!"

"Bullshit!" responds Jack. "I'm not dying in Baltimore!"

With the water level now at his neck, Jack unholsters his Glock and shoots out the driver and passenger windows. Now completely exposed to the water, the car submerges quickly, but the large openings allow the pair to squirm out of the windows like NASCAR drivers exiting their vehicles. Swimming to the surface, they cough and sputter while their ears ring from the underwater gunshots. And as they look back at the pier, they realize how lucky they are. The garbage truck that hit them is hanging halfway off the dock. If it had followed them into the water, they might not have gotten out of the car alive.

Shaken by the crash, the men don't notice that a crowd of tourists is lining the pier and screaming in horror. The only thing they care about at the moment is the Baltimore Harbor Patrol go-fast boat that is pulling up alongside them.

When the harbor patrol officers drop them off at a landing area on Pier Two, they are met by a contingent of FBI agents who rushed over from their nearby office.

While all this was going on in Baltimore, Didi was in the air at 35,000 feet, on the way back to New York City. At the moment the car entered the water, she felt a cold shudder that shook her to her bones, and her thoughts went immediately to Jack.

"Oh, God!" she mouthed.

Wrapped in blankets, the pair of soaked officers sits in the back of an emergency vehicle. With bleary eyes, Jack glances over at David, who is not looking healthy at all. Suddenly squealing "BUICK!" David turns his head just before the foul harbor water that fills his stomach spews out, along with his undigested breakfast. He moans and spits, wiping his mouth with the end of the blanket.

"Gesundheit," Jack smirks.

"Shut up," Dave mutters. Wiping his mouth again, he says, "We gotta get the flash drive over to the lab before the salt water corrupts it."

Jack stares at the harbor through bloodshot and burning eyes. Then he mumbles, "Sansone was right. That had to be the work of the Secret Service."

He pulls out his drenched phone and looks at it ruefully. "I hope you guys have some rice back at the lab. We gotta dry out our phones. And we need to get into some dry clothes," he adds with a shiver.

Just then, a black stretch Cadillac drives onto the pier. FBI Director William Decker exits from the back of the vehicle and approaches the soaked FBI agent and NYPD task force member.

"You two okay?" he asks with concern. "As soon as I heard, I dropped everything to come down here personally. Did you find anything on the sub?"

Reaching into his pocket, Dave pulls out the flash drive and holds it up with a grin.

Decker smiles. "Good job! Now, come with me. I'll drive you both back to headquarters."

Hesitant, Percal says, "Sir, we're both dripping

wet with harbor water. We'll ruin your car."

The director shrugs it off. "Hey, so I'll have it cleaned. Let's go."

Jack and Dave follow Decker back to his Cadillac. Then they climb into the back of the vehicle and Decker's driver drives off the pier, back onto Pratt Street.

Nearing Camden Yards, the driver prepares to turn onto I-395 on the way to I-95 but quickly realizes that I-395 is backed up. Hoping to bypass the congestion, he continues on to Russell Street, which parallels 395. When he approaches the intersection of Russell and West Hamburg Street, a black SUV runs the red light and plows into the side of the car. The impact sends the vehicle fifteen feet sideways into a left-hand spin, and shakes the occupants like a martini.

With Decker's car stopped in the intersection, another black SUV enters the street and disgorges a group of men in black Kevlar masks who discharge a volley of automatic weapon fire at the crippled Cadillac.

Bullets zing past and hit the car, denting the outside of the vehicle, but Decker exclaims, "Hey, don't worry! This car was one of the President's armored vehicles!"

However, right after has he said that, his driver shouts, "They hit the front! We can't steer! We can't move!" and then he blurts out ominously, "Oh, shit!"

The Cadillac's occupants peek out of the car's front windshield, but all they can see is an armor-clad, ninja-style warrior destroying the side window of one of the black SUVs in the intersection with a shoulder-mounted rocket launcher.

As he prepares to fire again, he is joined by three black Humvees that converge on the scene and expel a group of black-ops soldiers, who engage the Cadillac's assailants in a rapid-fire weapon gun battle.

Realizing that they are now outnumbered, the attackers back off and scurry into their undamaged SUV. Tires squealing, they leave the area in a hurry.

With the attackers now gone, one of the masked avengers approaches Decker's vehicle to check on its occupants.

The car's driver has already exited the vehicle, but the passengers are still inside, trapped by doors that won't open. Working together, Jack pushes on his door from the inside while the Black Knight pulls on it from the outside until the door flies open, allowing Jack, Dave, and Director Decker to climb out safely.

As the men thank the masked avenger, he removes his Kevlar mask to reveal a familiar face.

"Sansone! How the hell? What the hell?" exclaim Jack and Dave in unison.

Frank cuts them off. "You're welcome," he smiles smugly. "We had a feeling that something was going to happen in Baltimore when we intercepted some radio chatter. So I decided that you might need backup, and took a ride over. Anyone need a lift?"

As soon as Didi's plane lands at Kennedy International Airport, she calls Jack's cell phone. However, the only thing she hears on the other end of the line is the standard recording that "your party is unavailable." Now she is more concerned than ever for her husband, so after leaving a message, she says a silent prayer for his safety.

Jack and Dave gratefully take Frank Sansone up on his offer for a lift back to FBI headquarters. In the quiet of the car ride down I-95, Jack's thoughts turn from trying to analyze the day's events, to thinking about his wife. Glancing at his watch, which is still functioning after its bath in the harbor, he realizes that Didi must have already landed in New York.

"Hey, Frank," he asks, "you got a phone I can use? Mine's kinda wet."

"Yeah, sure," says Frank, laughing as he hands Stenhouse his cell phone. "Try not to go swimming with this one, okay?"

Jack gives Frank the bird before he grabs the offered cell phone.

When Didi's phone rings, she is on the taxi line at the airport. When she doesn't recognize the number displayed on the screen, her first inclination is not to answer the call, but then she changes her mind.

"Hello?" she asks with uncertainty.

"Hey, Babe, how was your flight?"

"Oh, Jack," she says with relief, "I was so worried! I got such a bad feeling on the flight. Are you okay?"

"Fine as wine, Babe. Just calling to say I love you."

Jack flashes the bird again as his comrades in the car throw kisses his way.

"Why are you on this strange phone number?"

"Dee, I'm fine. My phone got a little wet, that's all. I dropped it in the Inner Harbor. But I gotta go now, so I'll call you later. Ciao!"

Didi breathes a sigh of relief as she ends the call.

"Shit follows that guy around like a shadow," she mumbles, as a cab pulls up to the curb.

That morning, President Burris lays out his plans in an address that is carried live on all the major networks.

"My fellow Americans, the American spirit that has kept this country at the forefront of world events for centuries will continue unwaveringly into the future. We are a resilient people, and we will bounce back stronger than ever in the wake of any and all setbacks.

"I am confident that I will continue on as your President after the investigations into my Administration are ultimately dismissed. Certain persons are attempting to term matters handled by me and my subordinates as scandals, but I have done nothing wrong, so their efforts are futile. Any such accusations will eventually be deemed to be untrue.

"The bombing at the Lincoln Memorial has dealt a severe blow to our country, but we will rebound from this crisis and our nation will survive. Our distinguished members of Congress are prepared to approve military action against the evildoers responsible for the bombing, and I ask all of you to stand beside our troops and your President as we prepare to exact swift judgment against our foes. I have contacted our close allies, and have received firm commitments of cooperation from Great Britain, France, Germany, Israel, and Australia. We have also received unprecedented support from China and Russia, as well as from Saudi Arabia and Kuwait, and many other nations around the world have pledged logistical and supply chain backup for this mission that we have codenamed Operation Swift Justice.

"*Now, I must discuss certain events that have occurred in the past twenty-four hours. It was with a heavy heart that I accepted the resignation of two Patriots, Vice President Jeffrey Borden, and Attorney General Ellis Handelman. Both of these men have served the nation above and beyond the call of duty, and they will leave a void in this Administration that will be hard to fill. Please keep Jeffrey Borden in your prayers for a swift return to good health, and please give your moral support to Ellis Handelman and his family as they try to work through some personal issues. While Vice President Borden won't be able to fulfill the demanding duties of the Vice Presidency, he has nevertheless volunteered to consult with a committee that I have established to recommend replacements for both open positions.*

"*As we enter this critical time for our country, I have also found it necessary to revise the structure of my White House staff. Victoria Johnson, my closest advisor, will become my Chief of Staff, effective immediately. She will replace Kevin Randel, who has been dismissed. This change will result in a more cohesive and efficient operation during this time of war.*

"*As Thomas Paine said in 1776, 'These are the times that try men's souls.' May God bless you all, and may God bless the United States of America.*"

CHAPTER THIRTYTWO

After being reunited with a shower and dry clothes, Jack and David are feeling refreshed and are ready to begin working again—but first, they need to take care of a few things.

All officers of the law know how critical it is to keep their firearms in tip-top shape, so at the moment they are sitting in the FBI's forensic lab, cleaning and oiling their weapons after their dunking in Baltimore Harbor.

When Dave is finished, he looks over at Jack, who is still working on his Glock. The untraceable pistol that Jack carries on his ankle is lying on the table, waiting to be reassembled.

"Hey, Jack, give me your phone," interrupts Dave.

"What for?" asks Jack. "You gonna rice it?"

"Yep. I'm going to have an agent rinse it in fresh water and then remove the battery and SIM card and dry them with a hair dryer. After that, he'll place all the pieces in a bag of rice. They already put mine in there. With luck, our phones should be good as new in twenty-four hours."

"Okay. It's in a duffle bag with my wet clothes. I was gonna ask about doing that. I hope the salt water hasn't already done its deed."

"Where's the duffel bag, big guy?"

"I left it in your office after we showered and changed. Hey, any luck with the flash drive?"

"Yeah, we should have something soon. When you're done here, go over to the situation room. I have some news that will knock your socks off."

Percal leaves the lab to get the duffel bag while Jack reassembles his weapons.

When the guns are back in working order; Jack heads downstairs to the situation room. Percal, sub-agents on the case, and representatives of the forensics team are already gathered there.

Taking the nearest seat, Jack watches Percal as he approaches a large whiteboard at the front of the room. On the board is a timeline of events, with photographs of Ellen Vanierri, James Smithfield, each of the murdered witnesses, and the assassinated Juan Gutierrez. Other photographs tacked onto the board include the murdered Secret Service agents, the Lincoln Memorial bomber, and Maria Assante, whose photo is recognizable by the black mourning sash placed across it. The photos are arranged in the form of a pyramid, with a photo of President Burris at the top.

Before speaking, Percal looks out over the room full of agents. When he spots Jack at the back, he motions for him to come up front.

With Jack beside him, he begins talking to the assembled group with inner power and stern conviction.

"Okay, people, we can now proceed with our plan. The two new pieces of the puzzle that we just received are reinforcing our belief that the evidence is taking us to the very top. The President's phone records and recordings directly implicate the President in the multiple murders carried out by Ellen Vanierri, and the flash drive from the U.S.S. *Torsk* contains conversation transcripts and copies of emails that directly link him to Operation Blue Falcon. They also confirm that Attorney General Handelman and Vice President Borden knew about that operation. We are very fortunate to have that flash drive, because the data it contains is confirmation of the information from Joe Cunningham, the testimony and files from Agent Smithfield, and statements by Frank Sansone.

"Regarding today's attacks in Baltimore—the garbage truck was reported stolen earlier in the day, and the SUVs that were used in the attack on Decker, Jack, and myself, were rented and prepaid in cash. We ran the name on the ID that was used to make the SUV reservations, but it belongs to another 'ghost;' that person does not exist. Our assumption is that the Secret Service was involved in both attacks.

"But now that we have all this information, we still have one glaring problem—who do we take it to? How do we arrest and indict a sitting President of the United States for domestic terrorism, conspiracy to commit murder, and treason?"

Not expecting an answer, he continues. "I have already submitted the evidence against Handelman and Borden to Joy Phillips, the new special prosecutor. She will continue Juan Gutierrez's investigations of the incident at our embassy in Sudan, and the DOJ's gunrunning operation. I have also scheduled a meeting with Director Decker to evaluate the best ways to pursue this to the White House.

"This case is very complex, and without each and every one of you, we would not be where we are today. I thank all of you for your diligence in investigating every lead."

Turning toward Stenhouse, he adds, "And I particularly want to thank NYPD Homicide Detective Jack Stenhouse for his invaluable assistance."

With a pat on Jack's back, he pauses to acknowledge a smattering of applause from the assembled agents.

"But now, Jack, your job is done, and you can take a break. I'll be sure to contact you again after we develop a definitive plan to go after Burris."

Turning back to his audience, his mood becomes somber.

"Now I need all of you to listen very carefully to my next order. You must tell *absolutely no one* about this case. If *any* of this gets out, I will blame all of you collectively, in one broad stroke. That's it for now."

Understanding that the meeting is over, the FBI agents rise from their seats and mill about in small groups.

While the agents are chatting, Jack takes Dave's elbow and pulls him over to a corner of the room. He has been stunned by Dave's pronouncement that his services are no longer needed, and is resolved to reverse that decision.

Glaring at his colleague, Jack states rather forcefully, "Dave, I need to be at the meeting when you discuss Burris's takedown. Actually, I *deserve* to be at that meeting!"

Percal places one hand on Jack's shoulder and looks into his eyes.

"Jack, there is no doubt that you were an important factor in this investigation. But now, we're facing a potential Constitutional crisis. We have a monster as President, and no Vice President to take his place. And standing in our way is a group of ultra-loyal Secret Service agents that will stop at nothing to protect him—you've seen that for yourself. This is a political firestorm in the making, and I don't think a solution will come about very quickly. The Bureau will have to handle this now."

Before Jack can protest further, he smiles at him reassuringly.

"But don't worry; you'll be back in D.C. as soon as it all gets ironed out. Go home to your wife now, and take a well-deserved break!"

With a pat on Jack's arm, Percal exits the room.

Jack is not happy at being dismissed. He stares at the whiteboard and studies the photos of President Burris and Maria Assante. Contemplating everything that has happened, he places a hand over Maria's photo and declares, "I promise you, Maria, I *will* get this fucker."

With renewed resolve, Jack leaves the now-empty room and heads back to his hotel. He will book a first-class flight back to New York and charge the fare to the Bureau.

FBI Director Decker is on the phone, so David Percal waits patiently outside of his office door until the director's secretary can announce his presence. When the secretary motions him over with a nod, Percal enters his boss's office.

Unaware of that meeting and its agenda, President Burris is enjoying his day. He has just started a round of golf at a beautiful golf course on the outskirts of the nation's capital.

CHAPTER THIRTYTHREE

"President Burris? Are you absolutely sure about this?"

Dave Percal stares at Director Decker and nods his head in reply to the Director's question.

Sighing, Decker rises from his seat and begins to pace about the room.

"My God," he says, "we have to arrest the President! There's a bunch of armed thugs protecting the bastard, and we have no Vice President. The Attorney General has resigned, and the bulk of the staff over at DOJ are Burris supporters. If we are actually able to find someone who's willing to take this case on, it will definitely leak out."

Throwing an alarmed look at Percal, he states rhetorically, "Do you know what will happen if the press gets wind of this? It will throw this country into complete shock! The stock market, which took a beating after the bombing, will go into freefall again, just like it did after 9/11!"

He continues to pace while thinking aloud. "But if we're successful, Clifton Bradley, Speaker of the House, will become our new leader." Decker sits down behind his desk, and both men stare at each other in deafening silence.

"Mr. Decker, wasn't Bradley the Chairman of the Joint Chiefs of Staff before he retired and ran for office?" asks Dave.

"Yes, but where are you going with that?"

"Look, he's ex-military," says Percal as he rises from his seat, "and he'll be the new president once we clear the crap away. So, we need to get him up to speed on the case and ask for his input on how to proceed. Joy Phillips, the new special prosecutor, can issue the indictment against Burris, but we're going to need an unbiased team to get to him. We need to create a plan that won't alarm his protectors."

Decker smiles broadly. "Another 'false flag!'... That's perfect!" Walking quickly out of the office, he barks an order to his secretary. "Get Speaker of the House Bradley on the line—NOW."

Jack has checked out of his hotel and is now sitting in an airport shuttle on his way to Reagan National Airport. He's feeling vulnerable since he no longer has the dumb phone that he was using to stay off the grid, and his water-logged cell phone is in his luggage, in a plastic bag full of rice.

As usual, the late-afternoon traffic in D.C. is dreadful, and with his nerves on edge, he is continually looking out of the windows for anything suspicious. The Secret Service tried to kill him twice today, and he is not a happy camper. Once he gets to the airport, he hopes to buy another go-phone so he can check in with Didi.

Halfway through the ride, a black SUV suddenly cuts off the shuttle. Jack automatically reaches for his weapon, but quickly realizes that it was nothing but a stupid driver. With a sigh of relief, he pats his firearm and silently urges the traffic to dissipate so the shuttle can get to the airport.

Speaker of the House Clifton Bradley is in the Longworth Cafeteria on Capitol Hill, enjoying a BLT with one of his aides. Bradley is a chiseled Marine veteran in his late fifties, who led several campaigns in Iraq and Afghanistan. His 6-foot 4-inch frame is still fit, trim, and toned, and with his square jaw and flat-top haircut, he could have been the model for that famous GI action figure of the 1970's.

Bradley and his aide are discussing current House activities involving approval of the war on Iran when another aide from his office rushes up to his table.

"Mr. Speaker, FBI Director Decker is sitting in your office. He says he needs to speak with you—he says it's urgent."

Ever stoic, Speaker Bradley replies to his aide's excitement with practiced indifference.

"I'm having a well-deserved lunch break, Stanley. Tell Decker to wait."

The aide responds meekly, "Sir, he said it concerns a Constitutional crisis that needs to be addressed immediately."

That comment piques the Speaker's interest, so he takes one last bite of his sandwich and puts a twenty-dollar bill on the table.

"Okay, let's go," he says.

Within minutes, Bradley and his aides are at the door of the Speaker's office, a stark, mahogany-lined room containing a large mahogany desk and a couple of chairs. The only decoration is a blue carpet, emblazoned with the Marine Corps emblem encircled by stars.

When Bradley enters his office, Director Decker rises to greet him. "Mr. Speaker," he begins, "I'm sorry to interrupt your lunch, but I have urgent business to discuss that will shake this nation to its core."

"You sound so serious, Bill," says Bradley as he towers over the Director and gives him a firm handshake. "Let's talk."

Closing the door to his office, he motions for Decker to sit, and then takes a seat behind his desk.

"Okay," he says, "what's this all about?"

Without wasting any time, Decker launches into a tale to end all tales.

"Mr. Speaker, I know that you have been occupied for a while by the impeachment proceedings against President Burris, and I know how important those proceedings are. But you and I know that it has been replaced in the media by the recent terror attack at the Lincoln Memorial. While we know that it was a serious event, there are things about it that you need to know—things that will influence public opinion about the current Administration."

"Hmm. Please go on."

"As you are aware, the Bureau has been investigating the murders of the witnesses who were scheduled to appear before Congress for the impeachment hearings. We now have evidence—actually, it is concrete evidence—that President Burris himself approved and directed each of those killings. We also have evidence that incriminates the President, Vice President Borden, and Secretary of State Canton in illegal activity in Sudan. In addition, we have conclusive evidence that the bombing at the Lincoln Memorial was a staged diversion concocted by Burris, Borden, and Ellis Handelman, and Victoria Johnson may have been involved as well."

"These are very serious charges, Decker."

"Yes, they are, Mr. Speaker. But we are preparing to arrest and indict the President of the United States, the ex-Vice President, and the former Attorney General. The Secretary of State is still in a coma, but if she ever returns to good health, we may indict her as well. However, we have a major problem, sir."

Speaker Bradley does not seem to be overly surprised by these revelations. "Beyond our country having a murderous President and an evil Administration? What other problem could trump those?"

"Burris has a contingent of ultra-loyal Secret Service agents who will protect him over and above the call of duty. They will fiercely prevent any actions from being taken against him, even if they are required by the Constitution. They already attacked one of my agents, and they even attacked my car in Baltimore earlier today. If it wasn't for the assistance of the CIA, I would not be talking with you now."

"What do you mean? I didn't hear about an attack against you today."

"No, we suppressed all information about the attacks, so the local media outlets won't be reporting anything about them. What you *will* hear later today is that an FBI training exercise was held in Baltimore to prepare for possible attacks against a Presidential motorcade. That is the story we're giving out."

"So what you're saying," interrupts Bradley, "is that if you get to Burris, I will become the next President, but getting to Burris could produce a bloodbath at the White House. 'Constitutional crisis' was an understatement, Bill."

"Mr. Speaker... Cliff... It is well known that the military is not a great fan of this President. We need to devise a plan to get to the President that will not alert his armed guards, and who better to pull this off than the military?"

"You're not suggesting a coup!" shouts Bradley as he jumps out of his chair.

"No, no, not at all! But how about a false-flag operation of our own—a diversion that will get the President away from his guards?"

Bradley ponders this thought as he walks over to a painting of Thomas Paine, one of the most influential propagandists of the American Revolution. "Have you presented this evidence to a federal prosecutor yet?"

"That's another problem. Handelman has staffed his department with hardline party supporters. I was hoping that we could pursue this through the special prosecutor who was appointed for the impeachment hearings."

Bradley sits back down in his chair. "That won't pass muster," he states, and then pauses to consider another thought. "I do know one prosecutor who works for Handelman that we can trust. She's ex-JAG. We can go through her, and we can also use Joy Phillips."

Pinching the bridge of his nose, he declares, "Bill, these are truly more of those times that will try men's souls. Let me wrap my head around all of this. I'll call a meeting this afternoon with a few of the people I trust at the Pentagon. The prosecutor you need to talk to is Anita Nicollazzi; she's in the D.C. office. I'll give her a heads-up about all of this shit, but you need to get her together with Phillips ASAP."

Bradley walks around his desk, and Decker stands to accept his outstretched hand. With a grip that almost crushes Decker's hand, Bradley asserts, "We'll get that bastard, Bill. I'll try to delay Congress' confirmation of military action, but the people want it. They don't know that the bombing was a setup. We'll have to act fast, because if we don't there's going to be war."

On the way to the airport, Jack had intended to purchase one of those outrageously expensive cell phones in an airport shop so he could call Didi, but he has another idea as he passes through security.

After clearing the checkpoint, he spots a TSA agent who is standing outside of the area and sweet-talks her into allowing him to borrow her phone.

"Hey, Babe!" he announces cheerfully. "There's been a break in the case. I'll be home in a couple of hours for a little tickle and grab."

"Well, I'll have to go out and get some whipped cream!" is what he hears on the other end of the line.

With Jack's mind now wandering to wonderful places, he stops on the way to the gate to buy a latte, but not because he's thirsty. He needs a break because at the moment, he's finding it very difficult to walk.

CHAPTER THIRTYFOUR

"Hello? This is Nicollazzi."

"Ms. Nicollazzi, this is William Decker. I have some information to share with you."

"Yes, Director Decker. I was expecting your call."

"Excellent. I need you to be at my office tonight at seven o'clock."

"Oh, but this is short notice," she replies haltingly. "I have plans to... "

"Cancel your plans. Be at my office at seven," replies Decker before he slams the desk phone's handset down roughly onto its cradle. "Can't get that effect on a cell phone," he says with a grin.

Scrolling through the list of contacts on his cell phone, he calls Joy Phillips next.

"Joy, it's Decker. I have some news that will knock your socks off. Shit, I have some news that will rock the Constitution! Be at my office at seven."

Moving the phone away from her ear, Joy stares at the screen for a second, not happy with what she has heard. Placing it back against her ear, she says, "Well, hello to you, too, Bill. I'm fine. How are you?"

"Yeah, yeah," says Decker.

Knowing that she won't get anything more out of Bill, Joy asks, "Okay, what's this shit about?"

"We got the goods that Gutierrez needed to get the case moving forward. See you later, and be prepared to be amazed."

Decker ends the call and takes a quick look at his Rolex. It is 5:45 p.m., enough time to grab a quick bite and be back in the office for one of the most important meetings he has ever held.

From opposite ends of Washington, D.C., two women are driving to the FBI building on Pennsylvania Avenue. Joy Phillips is anxious to hear what Decker has on Burris, and Anita Nicollazzi is pissed off about cancelling a hot date, and can't wait to let Decker know exactly how she feels.

At the same time, Speaker of the House General Clifton Bradley is sitting in a secure meeting room in the Pentagon, waiting for two of his fellow generals, and an admiral.

The wood-paneled room is sparsely furnished, with only an octagonal oak table and chairs for functionality, and an American flag in a bronze base for décor.

Bradley watches as his friends and colleagues enter the room and take their seats. When all the greetings are completed, he gives a silent order, and the room's door is locked. Turning to those assembled, he begins the meeting.

"I have brought you all here tonight to inform you about a matter that is exceedingly crucial to this country. It is my belief that it is the most important thing to occur since 1776."

Raised eyebrows and expressions of surprise erupt around the table as Bradley pauses for effect.

"Now, before you ask any questions, let me explain. As all of you know, President Burris is currently being investigated for possible impeachment, and several of the witnesses who were scheduled to testify before Congress in those proceedings have either been killed or have gone missing. Furthermore, our righteous legislators are about to allow our boy to throw us into another war.

"Now, what you do not know is that our President is the one who is directly responsible for all of the murders, as well as the attack at the Lincoln Memorial."

Amid audible gasps from everyone around the table, Admiral Reynolds speaks up.

"General, what you are saying is treasonous! What proof do you have that these accusations are true? I must warn you to think carefully about what you are about to say."

"Admiral Reynolds—George—those files in the center of the table contain all the information you need. The information was compiled by the federal task force investigating the witness' murders, with input from the CIA and documents provided by the late Deputy Secretary of State, Joe Cunningham. Federal Prosecutor Anita Nicollazzi and Special Prosecutor Joy Phillips will be presented with the same files, after which the FISA judge will issue warrants for the arrest of President Burris, ex-Vice President Borden, ex-Attorney General Ellis Handelman, and several members of the Secret Service."

Ignoring the murmurs and grumblings of his listeners, he continues with his discourse.

"The problem we are challenged with, gentlemen, is how to arrest a sitting President, one who has surrounded himself with ultra-loyal guards who will do anything to protect him and themselves from prosecution.

"I was contacted by FBI Director Decker, because when this hits the fan and Burris is removed from office, I will become the country's acting President. Now, I've thought about our problem, and as former Chairman of the Joint Chiefs of Staff, I know that contingency plans are in place for all types of emergencies. As such, I know that a plan exists for the military to take control of the government in case of extreme emergency. I believe that the only way we can get to Burris while avoiding a confrontation with his personal detail is to create a diversion that is realistic enough to convince them that it is necessary for the military to take control of the White House."

Bradley's comments produce a dead stillness in the room while each member of the group thinks this through. Then the admiral and each of the generals nod at each other in silent agreement.

Vincent Storm, a two-star Marine Corps General, is the first to comment.

"Speaker Bradley, you are accurate in your assessment of the problem, and since the beginning of this President's term in office, the plan you refer to has been tweaked and tweaked again. In fact, I believe that the majority of the personnel behind these hallowed walls are grateful that the plan exists. That plan, codenamed Operation Fallen Eagle, can be altered again and implemented immediately. What do you have in mind?"

"We need to arrange a credible enough set of circumstances that would force the White House to be evacuated. There would need to be a threat to the President or to the building itself. That way, we will be able to act swiftly under Threatcon protocols."

Admiral Reynolds speaks up next. "The USS *Stennis* will be testing drones in the Chesapeake in a couple of days. I think I can arrange a perfect false-flag diversion."

Jack lifts the industrial elevator door that opens onto his loft apartment. As he stares into the dimly-lit room, he becomes aware of the scent of incense and the fragrance of burning candles gently caressing his face. Dropping his luggage at his feet, he peers into the darkness while waiting for his eyes to adjust to his surroundings.

As he gazes through the maze of flickering lights and the smoke of the burning incense, he perceives a figure in red standing at the bedroom door. Walking closer, he centers his attention on Didi, who is leaning against the door in red lace baby-doll lingerie, with all her womanhood showing through. Before he speaks, she holds up a hand to reveal an aerosol can of whipped cream.

"Hurry up, Jack," she murmurs seductively. "I'm hungry. Aren't you?"

William Decker is sitting at his large desk, staring out of a window that overlooks Pennsylvania Avenue, with the White House in the distance. When he looks back into the room, he catches sight of a photograph of President Burris that is hanging on the far wall.

Frowning at the photograph, he is about to make a snide remark when his thoughts are interrupted by a knock at the door. Rising from the chair, he walks toward the door, but before he reaches it, it swings open and reveals a perturbed Anita Nicollazzi.

"Mr. Decker, I was told that you would be contacting me soon, but I did not think it would be this quickly. I'm giving up a hot date for you tonight, so this better be worth my time."

Before he can respond, Joy Phillips walks in and joins them. "I don't have a hot date tonight, but I wish I did. What's this shit all about, Bill?"

Decker smiles. "Let's sit down, ladies. What you're about to hear is going to change your lives. As a matter of fact, it's going to change the entire country. Is that good enough for you, Anita?"

Instantly curious, the two women seat themselves in front of Decker's desk while he slides around them to stand behind it. Reaching down out of sight of his guests, he picks up three large files from the floor and places them on the desktop.

"Shall we begin? I am about to present evidence to you that directly links President Burris, ex-Vice President Borden, and past Attorney General Handelman to murder, treason, and a terror attack upon the citizens of the United States of America, with multiple sub-charges a mile long. The evidence encompasses these files, copies of several DVDs, forensic evidence, and the verbal testimony of others who are involved with them.

"I have proof that President Burris was behind the murders of key witnesses who were scheduled to appear before Congress at his impeachment investigation hearings, namely John Hastings, Joe Cunningham, and Joe Conway. He is also involved in the assassination of Juan Gutierrez."

Decker ignores the gasps of disbelief coming from his guests and continues to recite the litany of charges.

"Burris plotted the bombing at the Lincoln Memorial with an elite group of Secret Service agents, and he named that operation Blue Falcon. The explosion was arranged for the express purpose of redirecting the American people's attention away from the Administration's botched operation in Sudan, and ultimately toward a war with Iran that the President hopes will stop all inquiries into Ambassador Kingston's death.

"He wants to keep a lid on the ambassador's murder because it was the direct result of another clandestine White House operation called Skyhook, which was chaired by Vice President Borden. Skyhook involved the smuggling of military aircraft parts to Iran in the misguided hope that the leadership would stop their nuclear enrichment program in return for these 'gifts' from America. Secretary of State Canton, who as you know, is now incapacitated and near death, is also implicated in Skyhook.

"There is even a third operation called Vaya con Diablo, which implicates Ellis Handelman."

Decker's listeners are shocked and speechless. In open-mouthed astonishment, they gape at each other, and at Decker.

After a moment, Anita shrieks, "Holy shit on a shingle, Bill! This is going to tear the country apart! But what are we going to do about it? There's no precedent for arresting a President while he's still in office!"

Decker sits down at his desk and takes a deep breath before launching into his next surprise.

"The fact that there's no precedent is not our

concern. What is problematic is that Burris has surrounded himself with an extremely loyal group of Secret Service agents who are ex-members of military special ops teams. I have had firsthand knowledge of how far these thugs will go, and I am convinced that they will protect Burris at any cost. Some of them recently attacked my car in Baltimore, and if the CIA hadn't intervened, I wouldn't be here now."

"Bill, what if..." begins Joy Phillips, but Decker holds up his hand to silence her.

"The SUVs they used in that attack were traced back to an exotic car rental dealer near Camden Yards and were found abandoned near that business. The perpetrators used counterfeit IDs to reserve the vehicles, but we were able to pull a print off one of the one-hundred-dollar bills they used to pay for them. The print was matched to Jason Goodie, a Secret Service agent who is on the President's personal detail. We believe there will be a bloodbath if any outright attempt is made to arrest Burris."

"So what are we going to do?" asks Anita.

"Well, several persons have already met to discuss this mess, and during the discussion, both of your names came up. It was suggested that you, Anita, would file the warrants, and that Joy would prosecute the charges in court. The indictment of Burris needs to be handled through the FISA judge so we can maintain complete secrecy before we're ready to go public. I'll get you the names of the Secret Service agents who need to be included in the warrants."

Anita shakes her head in amazement. "But how the hell are we going to get close enough to the President to arrest him?"

"We knew he was dirty," chimes in Joy, "but this? Anita is right. How do we get to this man and still respect the office of the President?"

Decker reaches into a file marked "Praetorium," and takes out one of the DVDs. He walks over to the widescreen TV on the adjacent wall, inserts the DVD into the player, picks up the remote, and presses "Play."

"Ladies, here is an example of the 'respect' that Burris is showing to the presidency."

The women gasp at images that are reminiscent of the extravagances of the Roman Emperor Caligula, and Decker shuts down the show after only a few minutes.

"Speaker of the House Bradley has been brought up to speed on everything, and he is conferring with several officers at the Pentagon whom he trusts. They are all working on a course of action that will grant us unfettered access to the President. The rest will be up to the two of you."

CHAPTER THIRTYFIVE

The next morning, Didi is making French toast in the kitchen while Jack is taking a shower. When he emerges from the bedroom wrapped only in a towel, his chiseled torso, shining and wet, catches Didi's attention. Turning off the burners, she tosses the half-cooked breakfast into the sink, grabs Jack by the hand, and leads him back into the bedroom.

In the nation's capital, David Percal and FBI Director William Decker are sitting in Decker's office, waiting for the arrival of House Speaker Clifton Bradley to update them on the Burris situation. However, when Decker's office door finally opens, it is Admiral Anthony Reynolds who walks in, not the Speaker.

"Good morning, gentlemen," greets Admiral Reynolds. "Speaker Bradley thought it would attract less attention if I met with you instead of him. Shall we commence?"

Decker closes the office door and joins the men who are already seated in plush chairs at the center of the room. The admiral waits until Decker is comfortable, and then proceeds.

"We have come up with a plan to acquire your target. In forty-eight hours, the Navy will begin testing new drones in Chesapeake Bay, just south of Reedville.

As you know, we have already deployed the Joint Land Attack Cruise Missile Defense Elevated Netted Sensor System barrage balloons over Maryland. That JLENS system of converging radar sensor arrays continuously monitors the Washington, Baltimore, and Virginia areas for any unusual ground or air activity.

"During the drone tests, we will secretly run an unplanned simulation of a drone attacking the White House. We will claim that an anarchist group hacked into our control systems and took control of one of the armed drones, but only a handful of trusted men will know that it's not the real thing.

"Under the protocols outlined in Threatcon Delta, if the White House is threatened, Marines stationed in D.C., along with military police from Joint Base Andrews, will be dispatched to evacuate all White House personnel, and they will transport the President to one of the safe bunkers located outside of D.C.

"But the President will not be taken to a safe bunker. Instead, he will be taken to Camp David, where he will be arrested and placed under military guard.

"Now, gentlemen, you realize that because of this apparent attack, much of D.C. will also be shut down. All civilian and governmental personnel, from the Capitol Building to the White House, will be evacuated from surrounding buildings, and all tourists will be forced into underground Metro stations. Military troops with armored vehicles and local and state police from Maryland and Virginia will be ordered to key intersections along Pennsylvania Avenue and the National Mall. F-18s will be dispatched from Andrews, and all air traffic from BWI to Reagan and Dulles will be grounded or diverted to nearby airports.

"The F-18s will provide air cover and backup in case the rogue Secret Service agents present a problem. During the city's lockdown, we will simulate an emergency medical crisis, which we will use as cover to transport a doppelganger for an injured President Burris to Walter Reed National Military Medical Center. There, the 'President' will be declared incapable of carrying out the duties of his office, and Speaker of the House Bradley will be sworn in as the interim President. All subsequent legal proceedings will occur at Camp David, where the involved parties will be protected and guarded by the Marine Corps.

"We are calling this mission Operation Hannibal. The cancer in the White House needs to be uprooted, and we are committed to seeing this through. Any questions?"

William Decker stands, lost in thought. As he paces the room, he muses aloud, "Forty-eight hours? That's all? How the hell will we be able to pull this off in only forty-eight hours?"

"First," answers the Admiral, "you need to get the warrants and proper documents filed. Then, you need to have Willard Stumps, the Senate Sergeant at Arms, accompany you to arrest Burris. He's the only one with the authority to arrest a sitting President, so he must go with you. We will create our own false-flag operation and get this done, got it? We will get the President, but it is up to you to get Borden and Handelman. General Bradley has already put things into motion, so remember—Semper Fi, gentlemen, Semper Fi."

With a curt nod to Decker and Percal, the Admiral places a copy of the detailed plan on Decker's desk, and departs.

Stunned, Percal and Decker stare unblinking at the large file. Neither of them is completely confident that they will be able to pull this off.

Joy Phillips and Anita Nicollazzi stand calmly before FISA Judge Edward McNeil while he signs the warrants to arrest President Burris, former Vice President Borden, and former Attorney General Handelman.

With the help of many brave patriots, the United States will be reformed, and the Constitution will be upheld within the next thirty hours.

Although the morning is almost over, Didi is still dressed in her baby-doll lingerie. She is back at the stove, cooking French toast for the second time, and this time it may actually get eaten. Jack is sitting quietly at the breakfast counter, drinking coffee and perusing the daily newspaper.

Suddenly, Jack remembers his phone, which is still buried in rice. Walking into the bedroom, he removes it from the bag in his luggage, connects it to the charger and plugs the charger into the wall. Holding his breath, he pushes the power button, and with a chime and a jingle, the logo of the cell phone's wireless provider appears.

"Well, I'll be damned! It worked!" he cries.

Calling out from her place at the stove, Didi asks, "What worked, Hon?"

"My cell phone! It took a bath in Baltimore Harbor, but the forensic guys at the FBI rinsed it with fresh water and placed it in a bag of rice to dry out. It worked, and the phone is reborn!"

Sniffing the aroma of breakfast coming from the kitchen, he asks, "We got any maple syrup for your famous French toast?"

"In the fridge, Babe."

Jack loves Didi's French toast. She creates it by dipping cinnamon bread into a mixture of eggs combined with cream.

While Jack scarfs down his breakfast, his cell phone chimes regularly from the bedroom, notifying him of all his missed messages.

Putting his fork down, he walks over to the phone and scrolls through the long queue of messages, nearly choking when he sees that he missed a call from Dave. "Damn! I got a call from Percal!"

Hastily unplugging the phone from the charger, he returns the call while walking back to the kitchen.

"Hey, Dave," he addresses his FBI partner, "I just got my phone working again. What's up?"

"You missed a lot, Jack; the shit is about to hit the fan! Get your ass back to D.C. by tomorrow morning, or even sooner. "

"That soon? We are going after Caligula?"

"Yeah, it's a full-scale military operation."

"Wow! I guess I'll have to take the train from Penn Station, since there's no way I'll be able to get a flight on such short notice. I'll leave ASAP."

Overhearing Jack's end of the conversation, Didi gives him a fair impression of his cold, sniper-like stare.

"You're fucking taking off again? When?" she gripes.

"Later today, Babe. It should all be coming to a head tomorrow. Finish your breakfast, and I'll drive you down to the boutique."

Ignoring Jack's request, Didi saunters over to him and pulls him and his chair away from the counter. Facing her husband, she climbs onto his lap and grins at him seductively.

"You know, you don't have to wait until tomorrow for it to 'come to a head.' "

Smiling widely, Jack grabs his wife's ass.

CHAPTER THIRTYSIX

Jack had wanted to spend a few restful days at home with Didi, but Dave's urgent call to action has placed him back at work sooner than he had expected.

At the moment, he's walking through Union Station, D.C.'s major train station, looking for Percal. Near the Center Cafe Restaurant, he spots his colleague walking into the building from Massachusetts Avenue.

"Did you get any well-deserved sleep last night, Jack?" smirks Percal, knowing full well what his answer will most likely be.

"What I got was well-deserved, but there was very little sleep involved," says Jack, confirming Percal's hunch. Changing the subject, Jack asks, "What's Bradley got in mind?"

"I'll fill you in once we're in the car," replies Dave confidentially.

Jack follows Percal out to a black sedan that is waiting for them at the curb. He expects Dave to fill him in as soon as the doors close, but the FBI agent doesn't speak again until the driver has pulled out into the heavy D.C. traffic. Then he turns to Jack and smiles.

"We enlisted the help of a federal prosecutor to file the charges and get arrest warrants for Burris, his posse, Borden, and Handelman. Tomorrow at 1400 hours, a full-scale military 'operation' will begin in D.C. It's actually a false-flag diversion set up by the Pentagon to get Burris out of the White House, and to enable us to arrest the Secret Service agents involved with him."

"Exactly how will this go down?" asks Jack.

"One of the thugs who attacked us in Baltimore was Jason Goodie, a member of the President's posse. During the confusion caused by our 'emergency security' event, Burris will be intentionally separated from his vigilantes and escorted to Camp David. At the same time, Seal Team Seven will round up Goodie and the other goons and take them into custody.

"I will be at the White House with the military detail while all of this is going on. Jack, you'll be in charge of arresting Handelman at his home in Columbia, Maryland. Several agents from the Bureau will accompany you there. Borden will be arrested by FBI agents at his house in Dover, Delaware."

Dave reaches into an attaché case on the floor of the car and hands Jack a copy of Operation Hannibal.

"Here," he says, "you have homework. Memorize this tonight."

Wide-eyed, Jack stares at the folder. "Who's the federal prosecutor with the balls to do this?"

"Anita Nicollazzi."

"Hmm, I know that name. She was a prosecutor in New York; one tough bitch, if I remember correctly——and she hated Burris."

"Yeah, doesn't everybody?"

"But how are we going to get the President to resign? He won't give up power easily. And arresting a President is going to stir up a whole pot of shit."

"Read the file, Jack; it will all fall into place. Speaker Bradley chose wisely. Just read the file."

When the driver stops the car in front of the

Grand Hyatt Hotel, Dave instructs Jack again.

"Okay, here's where you're staying. Your room key is at the desk. Make sure you read the file, Jack. And this time, get a good night's sleep. We don't want any mistakes tomorrow. I'll pick you up at 9:00 in the morning."

Within fifteen minutes, Jack is sitting in his room in a large chair next to a king-sized bed, reading Operation Hannibal.

All of the usual hotel amenities are available, including a well-stocked mini-fridge and a microwave, but Jack focuses on his reading--until the background aroma of disinfectant gets the better of him.

When he finally looks up at the clock next to the bed, he is surprised to note that it is 9:00 p.m. Putting the plan aside, he grabs a bottle of water from the fridge and downs it within seconds. Then, he picks up the phone and orders room service.

"Damn," he mumbles as he dials, "tomorrow is going to be epic!"

Before his dinner arrives, he takes a quick shower. Then he watches a local TV news station while he eats. When he's finished eating, he puts his dinner tray in the hall and places a call to Didi.

"Hey, Babe, how are you? I'm getting ready to hit the sack now, so I'm calling to say I love you, and I miss you."

"I love you, too, Honey. When do you think you'll be home?"

"I don't know. I can't give you any details, but be sure to watch the news at two o'clock tomorrow."

A few more minutes of small talk ensues, and then Didi gives Jack a kiss through the phone before they both hang up.

Alone in their New York apartment, Didi reflects on her husband's line of work.

"Like a shadow," she muses. "It follows him like a shadow."

The next morning, Ellis Handelman is having breakfast with his wife, Judith, in their 5,000-square-foot mansion in Columbia, Maryland.

They are sitting at opposite ends of a large oak dining room table. Ellis digs into a plate of eggs over easy, while Judith enjoys a bowl of hot oatmeal.

"So, Ell," she asks, "now that you're unemployed, do you have any plans for the day?"

Ellis puts down his cup of coffee and grins.

"Well, I wasn't going to tell you until later, but the law firm of Jonathan and Smith has been looking for a new partner, and they've offered me the position. I have a dinner meeting with them tonight at six. Until then, I'll probably do some lawn work and catch up on my reading. What are you doing today?"

"I'm volunteering at Walter Reed. I'll be there all afternoon."

A similar situation is occurring in Dover, Delaware, where Jeffrey Borden is sharing breakfast with his wife, Joan, in their 6,000-square-foot Tudor home on Stuart Drive.

"Jeff, you have that appointment today with your cardiologist, don't you?"

"Sure do. I have an echocardiogram at four today,

but I'm going to work on my memoirs until then. You still headed for your mother's?"

Joan nods her head. "We're going shopping, and then out to lunch. I should be back before you leave."

The best-laid plans of mice and men oft go awry.

On the Lower East side of New York City, Didi has finished her breakfast and is now driving Jack's Roadrunner out of the parking garage. After giving Jack's signature sound of two quick beeps of the horn, she turns the vehicle toward her boutique, mindful that at two o'clock, she needs to listen to the news.

At the same time, President Burris is on his elliptical machine, trying to complete a workout of at least seven miles. He has a staff meeting at 11:00 and a late lunch with the ambassador of Israel at three, but nothing in D.C. is written in stone.

At the Capitol Building, Speaker of the House Bradley has asked his staff to clear his meetings for the day. At noon, he will go to the Pentagon and wait.

The government of the world's greatest power will soon undergo a coup.

Jack had intended to arrive on time this morning, but traffic in D.C. is never predictable. When he finally enters Dave Percal's office, Dave looks up from his desk and snaps, "You're late. It's almost 9:30."

Jack grunts a reply, but Percal shrugs it off. "I have the warrant for Handelman's arrest. The three agents who will accompany you to Columbia are waiting outside. Go to the Howard County, Maryland Police Department, and ask for Lieutenant George Simpson. He's coordinating the operation to arrest Handelman.

I want this to go down between one and two today. Agents in Delaware will pick up Borden around one, so try to snag Handelman at the same time."

"Who's involved in Burris's arrest?"

"Marines from the D.C. barracks, Air Force military police, and Seal Team Seven will lead the way into the White House to neutralize and then arrest the Secret Service agents."

"How the hell did you get the Seals involved in this?" asks Jack with raised eyebrows.

Dave shakes his head and smiles. "Bradley made a few phone calls after I told him that Secret Service Agent Goodie was involved in the attack on Decker's car, and that we added his buddies O'Neil and Travis to the warrant after we got the testimony from Smithfield. So, because we don't know what kind of shit we'll be stepping into, we decided to take all of the White House Secret Service agents into custody at the same time—with help from the Marines and the Seals. 'Might as well round up everyone now and sort it all out later,' is a direct quote from Bradley."

He offers a folder to Jack.

"Here's the paperwork for Handelman's arrest. Get your ass over to Columbia and stand ready."

In Dover, Delaware, FBI Agent Bruce Longston is preparing for the arrest of Jeffrey Borden. Three agents and a contingent of Delaware State Police Officers will accompany him to Borden's house.

The fall of the Burris Empire is scheduled for one o'clock Eastern Standard Time.

CHAPTER THIRTYSEVEN

"Agent Longston? This is Jack Stenhouse. It's now 1230 hours—time to boogie."

"Ha! We're going to boogie the whole way there! Have fun, Stenhouse."

Jack placed the call to Longston on the way to Ellis Handelman's house, accompanied by Lieutenant Simpson and a contingent of police officers from Howard County and the State of Maryland.

Within minutes, the convoy arrives at Handelman's house. The quiet of the tree-lined neighborhood belies the tension that will soon ensue when the U.S. Constitution and the resolve of our nation are tested.

Jack and Lieutenant Simpson quietly approach the front door of the stately home while three police vehicles, blue lights flashing, block the street from both ends like a blood clot.

Warrant in hand, Jack reaches out to ring the doorbell. When there is no response, he looks questioningly at Simpson. "Didn't you have this guy under surveillance?"

Simpson nods and motions to one of his officers.

"Get me Handelman's current status from the van across the street."

A few minutes later, the officer's voice is heard through Simpson's radio. "His wife left, but Handelman is still here."

"If he's here, why isn't he answering the door?"

queries Jack. "what I'd really like to do is break this door down and go in and get him, but let's play it safe and check around back first."

Agreeing, the Lieutenant orders a few officers to accompany them to the back of the house. However, they don't get far. A high wooden fence with a gate that opens from the inside blocks them from entering the backyard.

Jack peers through the fence at the gate's locking mechanism and takes action. Inserting the blade of a knife between the fence slats, he uses it to lift the locking arm and open the door.

The group rounds the corner of the house, and immediately comes upon a greenhouse attached to the home's back wall. Inside it, they notice the figure of a man moving around.

Using hand signals, Simpson orders his men to hang back while he and Jack approach the structure and open the door. They startle Ellis Handelman, who is watering his orchids.

"How did you get in here?" Ellis sputters. "What's going on?"

Ellis looks at Lieutenant Simpson and Jack, and then, seeing past them, notices the rest of the officers waiting outside. "Well, speak up!" he barks. "What do you want? Why are you here?"

Jack takes a deep breath before speaking. "Ellis Handelman, I'm NYPD Homicide Detective Jack Stenhouse. I'm assigned to a special federal task force with the FBI, and I have a warrant for your arrest."

Ellis Handelman's eyes widen, and his face loses all its color. "W-what do you mean; you have a warrant for my arrest?"

"Sir, you are charged with murder, the conspiracy to commit murder, and attempted murder related to the terrorist attack at the Lincoln Memorial. You are also charged with bribery and gunrunning. Sir, you have the right to remain silent. Anything you say or do can and will be used against you in a court of law. You have the right to an attorney..."

Ellis cuts him off before he completes the Miranda warning. "Yes, I know all that. I know my rights. Who do you think you're talking to?"

Lieutenant Simpson grabs Handelman's arms and cuffs his hands behind him.

"We know who you are," responds Jack. "You're a fucking asshole! And we know all about Blue Falcon and Vaya con Diablo. But even so, you have the right to an attorney. If you cannot afford an attorney, one will be appointed to you. Do you understand these rights as they have been read to you?"

Handelman glares at Stenhouse. "Fuck you!" he spits out with contempt. "And all the rest of you peons, too!"

Jack and Simpson follow the former Attorney General as he is being led out to the waiting police vehicles. At the front of the house, Jack stops and places a call to Percal.

"One down, two to go," he asserts.

The FBI is taking point in Delaware. With a group of police officers lining the street in front of Vice President Borden's home, FBI Agent Bruce Longston, three field agents, and six Delaware state troopers are walking past a white van emblazoned with the logo of the local telephone company, on their way to the front door.

But before they can get too close, a Secret Service agent steps out of the house and stops them. With a cold, piercing stare, he challenges their presence at the Vice President's house.

"What's this all about?" he demands with barely-disguised hostility.

Displaying his ID, FBI Agent Longston states, "We need to speak with the Vice President."

After inspecting the proffered identification, the security agent responds, "He's in the library, but he cannot be disturbed."

"Well, this is a matter of national security, and we're going in whether you like it or not. So lead, or get out of the way."

A tense standoff ensues between Longston and Borden's security agent, until the Vice President appears at the door.

"Can I help you, gentlemen?" he asks.

Stepping around the Secret Service goon, Agent Longston approaches Borden with his three fellow agents as the Delaware state troopers form a defensive line between them and Borden's guy.

"Mr. Vice President, I am FBI Agent Bruce Longston. We need to talk. Please, may we go inside?"

Nodding his head, the Vice President steps aside to allow the FBI agents to enter his large foyer.

As they file in, another member of Borden's security detail walks in from the kitchen, but two of the assembled FBI agents intercept him and block his approach.

Agent Longston turns to the Vice President. "Sir,

we are here to place you under arrest for murder and attempted murder, as well as treasonous acts against the United States of America involving your knowledge of and participation in Operations Skyhook and Blue Falcon."

Borden's face drains of color when he realizes that what he hoped would remain hidden forever has been exposed.

Longston recites the Miranda warning and handcuffs Borden, who is reacting as calmly as can be expected under these circumstances. But before Longston concludes, Borden interrupts him.

"No need to continue, Agent. I will cooperate with you as much as I can. Just tell my wife that I love her. And please, I beg of you, take off the handcuffs. I won't run off." His eyes take on a desperate, pleading look. "I don't want anyone to see me handcuffed. Please!"

Longston pauses, and then makes a quick decision. Uncuffing Borden, he grabs hold of one of his arms and directs another agent to grab the other arm. Together, the two men escort a cuffless Vice President to a waiting vehicle. Inside the house, the Secret Service agents are calling the incident in to their headquarters.

The VP will be taken first to the FBI office in Baltimore, Maryland and then transferred to the agency's headquarters in D.C.

On the drive back to Baltimore, Longston looks at his watch and notes that it is now 1330 hours, or 1:30 PM. Placing a status call to Percal, he proclaims, "Borden is in custody. Good luck!"

"We interrupt our regular broadcast for this special news report.

"This is Sam Storm, ABC News, reporting from the Capitol Building. Dozens of armored military vehicles, along with local and state police, have flooded the streets here, from the Capitol Building to the White House. Intersections and cross streets from the Capitol to the Washington Memorial have been cordoned off, including the National Mall. All pedestrians have been told to seek shelter, and the Metro trains have been stopped at every station. Police and military personnel are directing people to the underground stations. We have received reports from the FAA that all flights scheduled to depart from the three regional airports—Dulles, Reagan, and BWI in Baltimore——have been grounded, and all incoming flights have been diverted to other airports. We are switching now to a joint emergency statement from Secretary Olsen of Homeland Security, and Admiral Anthony Reynolds at the Pentagon."

"My fellow Americans," states Secretary Olsen from a secure room in the Pentagon, "*Washington, D.C. is on full alert at Threatcon level Delta. We have confirmed that a terrorist attack against the White House and the President of the United States is imminent. Military personnel have been deployed from both Joint Base Andrews and the Marine Barracks here in Washington. Admiral Reynolds will provide further details about the threat. Admiral?"*

The men proceed to switch places at the podium, and then the Admiral lays their fictional problem on thick.

"Earlier this morning, the naval destroyer USS Sten-

nis, which is currently deployed in the southern half of Chesapeake Bay, was field-testing two of our new Jupiter-class drones in real-case scenarios. Twenty minutes ago, the ship reported that their control system was hacked and that it lost control of both drones, which were armed for the test.

"Jupiter-class drones are unmanned, low-flying, stealth aircraft that can cruise at a maximum speed of 100 knots per hour for almost ten hours. The Aryan Nation anarchist group has claimed responsibility for the hack, and for taking control of these weapons. The JLENS defense balloons deployed over Baltimore are tracking both weapons, and F-18s have been scrambled from Joint Base Andrews. The F-18 pilots have been ordered to intercept and destroy the drones at will.

"The Aryan Nation has stated that it is targeting the Capitol Building and the White House. Therefore, we are currently evacuating all personnel from both buildings, and armored military units have been dispatched to the White House to relocate the President to a secure location. FBI units and teams from Homeland Security have been deployed to known Aryan Nation locations in Utah and Montana. We will attempt to neutralize the drones over unpopulated areas; however, due to their ground-hugging ability, armed military personnel are at the ready to intercept and destroy them, if necessary. Further information will be provided as it becomes available."

When the feed from the Pentagon ends, the TV station returns to Sam Storm, who is standing in the middle of Pennsylvania Avenue.

"Our nation's capital is under attack! The normally bustling city is virtually devoid of people, except for armed military personnel who are patrolling streets that are littered with thousands of abandoned vehicles.

"Wait... several armed servicemen are telling us that we need to leave. They are escorting us off the street now. We'll return to the airwaves as soon as possible. This is Sam Storm, signing off."

Fifteen minutes earlier, Homeland Security Secretary Olsen contacted the Secret Service Command Post at the White House to inform them of the approaching threat and to order a mandatory evacuation of "The People's House". Now, David Percal and a convoy of Humvees and Mine-Resistant Ambush Protected Vehicles, better known as MRAPs, are converging at 1600 Pennsylvania Avenue.

Surrounded by the anti-aircraft weapon platforms that are deployed on the White House roof and lawn areas to protect the President, Percal and a unit of Marines and Navy Seals in full battle gear surge into the White House. The first Secret Service agent to encounter them is Jason Goodie. He tells them that the President is in the Oval Office and turns to show them the way, but he is immediately neutralized by the Seals. Splitting up, the teams move swiftly through the corridors and expertly take into custody every Secret Service Agent they run into without incident.

While the soldiers are searching the building, Percal and two armed Marines make a beeline toward the Oval Office. When they burst into the office of the most powerful man in the world, they find President Burris sitting at his desk, as if nothing is wrong.

With the howl of a low-flying F-18 filling the room, the Marine sergeant in charge shouts urgently, "Mr. President, you need to leave now!" But when the President doesn't move from his seat, the men are perplexed—until they see Victoria Johnson's head pop up from under the desk.

Calmly adjusting his pants, Burris rises from his chair and leaves Victoria kneeling on the floor.

"Let's go, gentlemen," he says nonchalantly.

Percal's eyes are opened wide in shock, but when he looks over at one of the Marines, the soldier only says with a chuckle, "It's not like *that* never happened here before. At least this time, the dress isn't blue."

Swiftly driving the President forward, the two Marines escort him out to their Humvee while others take Victoria Johnson to one of the MRAPS.

Although Burris obediently allowed himself to be escorted into the back of the Humvee with Percal and a Marine sergeant, as soon as he is seated, he questions their mission.

"Why are we leaving the White House?" he demands with authority. "There's a secure bunker right here. The nearest secure facility is in West Virginia."

When he receives no answer, he looks around him and realizes that the speeding vehicles are not traveling toward West Virginia. Alarmed, he shouts, "Wait… where are we going? What the hell is going on? And where is my security detail?"

With a smirk, Percal replies, "Mr. President, you are under arrest for crimes committed against the people of the United States. Does Blue Falcon ring a bell?"

Wide-eyed, Burris stares at the floor for a moment, and then raises his eyes.

"Oh, brother!" he laughs derisively. "This is all bullshit, isn't it? But you can't arrest me, and I won't resign; there's no one left to run this country!"

Suddenly, his face pales when a thought occurs to

him. With a scowl, he shouts, "BRADLEY!"

At that comment, the person sitting in the front passenger seat turns around to face the President.

"I can arrest you, Mr. President," declares Willard Stumps, Senate Sergeant at Arms, "and I am going to do just that. On the orders of the Senate, you are hereby placed under arrest for crimes against the homeland."

Deflated, Burris slumps in his seat.

With a grin, Percal places a call to Decker. "We're done. All is good."

Following the call, Percal directs his attention and disdain toward Burris.

"Mr. President, or shall I say, Mr. soon-to-be ex-President, we have also arrested Ellis Handelman, Jeffrey Borden, Jason Goodie, and the rest of your Secret Service posse. We will also round up your staff and question Victoria Johnson at length."

Regaining some of his bluster, Burris demands to know the extent of their evidence against him.

"We have proof linking you to Operations Skyhook, Vaya con Diablo, and Blue Falcon, and we also have data that incriminates you in the deaths of Juan Gutierrez and the witnesses who were scheduled to testify against you in the Congressional impeachment proceedings. The Vice President has promised to give us his full cooperation in exchange for a reduced sentence. He will testify against you, your posse, and your 'friends' at the Praetorium."

"Where are you taking me?"

"For as long as necessary, you will be held under house arrest at Camp David." Narrowing his eyes, Percal grins smugly at their prisoner. "Today, forces loyal to the Constitution have successfully rescued this nation from the evil and moral bankruptcy that you have been subjecting us to. And what I'm going to say next is something that I've wanted to say for a very long time."

With obvious pleasure, Senior FBI Special Agent David Percal recites the Miranda verse, and at its conclusion, adds, "You will be held accountable for your actions, Mr. Burris."

But even though Burris has just heard the reading of his rights, he remains as defiant as ever.

"Ha! You can't prosecute me! I have executive privilege! And Bradley can't do shit to me!"

Percal stares at Burris. "Mr. Burris, I have also wanted to say *this* for a very long time: SHUT THE FUCK UP!"

CHAPTER THIRTYEIGHT

After the initial booking at Howard County, Maryland's police facility, Stenhouse and three FBI agents take Ellis Handelman to Joint Base Andrews, where he will be held temporarily. Handelman placed his one phone call to his personal attorney, who tried in vain to have bail issued. But there will be no bail, no mercy.

At the other end of town, Agent Longston and three other FBI agents are transporting ex-Vice President Borden to their office on Pennsylvania Avenue. Later, he will be transferred to Camp David to begin his questioning.

When the news is leaked that President Burris is no longer at the White House, the "main scream" media goes wild.

"This is a CBS News Special Report. Washington is under siege, and the Constitution is being put to the test.

"President Burris has suffered a massive heart attack, and is currently in a coma in the intensive care unit at Walter Reed National Military Medical Facility. The heart attack occurred while he was being escorted to a secure bunker away from the White House in compliance with protocols during the recent national threat.

"Because the office of the Vice President is currently empty, Speaker of the House General Clifton Bradley has been sworn in as Acting President. Bradley was brought to the office of Chief Justice Eleanor Fink, where he took the

oath of office a few minutes ago. We are currently standing by for a statement from Acting President Bradley, and we will bring that to you live.

"In addition to this crisis, former Attorney General Ellis Handelman and former Vice President Jeffrey Borden have been arrested, along with several members of President Burris's Secret Service detail. We are currently awaiting a joint press conference by Federal Prosecutor Anita Nicollazzi and Special Prosecutor Joy Phillips to explain these actions.

"As you know by now, the Capitol Building and the White House were evacuated and the streets of D.C. were cleared earlier today due to the threat of drone attacks on the city. Local and state police, as well as military personnel, ushered citizens, tourists, and government workers into the underground Metro terminals, and all commuter services were stopped—all bus, rail, and taxi services, as well as all air traffic at Dulles, Reagan, and BWI airports.

"Evacuations were ordered after the software guiding two Jupiter-class drones being tested by the USS Stennis in Chesapeake Bay was hacked by the Aryan Nation. The hack re-directed the armed drones' flight paths toward the White House and the Capitol Building. As this video shows, one of the drones was successfully shot down over the Potomac by an F-18 dispatched from Joint Base Andrews, and the second drone was destroyed by anti-aircraft fire from the White House lawn.

"FBI raids at Aryan Nation locations in Provo, Utah, and Billings, Montana, have resulted in the arrest of twenty-five people. This attack on our nation was successfully prevented due to the vigilance and resolve of our military and the Department of Homeland Security.

"As you can see from the live streaming video on

your screen, thousands of people are now exiting the Metro terminals, and Washington, D.C. is slowly returning to normal. But several questions remain, and chief among them is, Will our country return to normal?

"This is James Hunt. We now switch you to a statement by Acting President Clifton Bradley."

The image changes to an unknown location and centers on Clifton Bradley, who is standing at a podium emblazoned with the Presidential seal, with an American flag beside him.

"My fellow Americans, our prayers go out to President Burris and his family during his time of need. The President is receiving the best medical care the nation has to offer, and we are hopeful that he will recover from this medical crisis. Bowing to the family's wishes, we will strive to respect the family's privacy as much as possible while we also provide the nation with regular reports on the President's condition.

"I want to assure you all that our nation remains secure, even though our Constitution has been put to the test in recent days. To ensure that the day-to-day operation of the people's business will continue uninterrupted, members of my congressional staff will join me at the White House to replace the staff that has been taken into custody.

"Following my address, FBI Director William Decker will hold a press conference to address the details of this latest attack on our great Capital. I would like to thank the vigilance of the members of our armed forces, who reacted swiftly and without prejudice to ensure the safety of our President, our members of Congress, and the citizens and tourists in Washington, D.C. this day. They are the men and women who stand at the ready to go into harm's way to protect us all.

"Despite the panic of the morning, this day is ending as a good day for America. With the smooth transition to a new Administration, our system of checks and balances is proving to be worthy of the test of time. I am sure that after President Burris recovers in the coming days, we will all breathe a sigh of relief and be thankful that our forefathers were vigilant and astute enough to give us such a venerable system of government.

"God bless you all, and God bless the United States of America."

The video feed switches back to an image of television reporter James Hunt.

"That was Speaker of the House Clifton Bradley, who was sworn in to fill the office of President while President Burris is incapacitated. It is unusual that he did not mention the arrest of former Vice President Borden and former Attorney General Handelman."

Suddenly, James stops speaking and places his hand over his right ear. After listening for a second, he says, *"I have been told through my earpiece that Anita Nicollazzi and Joy Phillips are about to begin their press conference. We switch now to our feed from the front of the FBI building. Don't change the channel. We'll be right back after the press conference with commentary and reaction to these events."*

The on-screen image changes to reveal Anita Nicollazzi and Joy Phillips approaching a podium covered by microphones. Joy moves to the side as Anita speaks.

"Good afternoon. In association with Special Prosecutor Joy Phillips, who has replaced the late Juan Gutierrez

as chair of the impeachment hearings against President Burris, I have issued warrants for the arrest of Ellis Handelman, Jeffrey Borden, Victoria Johnson, and various members of President Burris's Secret Service detail. A federal task force headed by FBI Agent Maria Assante, who lost her life in the investigation of this Administration, uncovered evidence incriminating these suspects... "

While the nation listens to Anita speaking in Washington, it is almost possible for them to hear the church bells that are ringing in respect for Maria Assante at her burial in a sleepy Central Florida town.

While FBI agents slowly lower her casket into the ground and a lone bagpiper mournfully wails "Amazing Grace," Maria's parents sob and throw roses on their daughter's casket. Circling overhead, but invisible to the attendees, are the angels of deceased law enforcement personnel who are welcoming their newest member.

Back in D.C., the press conference continues.

"... also, Ellis Handelman and Jeffrey Borden have been charged with crimes against the citizens of the United States. Their charges include murder, attempted murder, treason, and sedition. Also implicated in crimes are Presidential Advisor Victoria Johnson and several members of the Secret Service. No formal charges have been made against President Burris at this time; however, Special Prosecutor Joy Phillips is investigating actions by this President that may be impeachment-worthy, and she will now address possible charges against him."

Moving to the side, Anita motions Joy Phillips to the podium.

"Thank you, Anita. I am honored to continue the search for truth that was begun by my late partner, Juan Gutierrez. Together with Juan, a Federal task force led by New York Police Homicide Detective Jack Stenhouse and late FBI Agent Maria Assante, was involved in investigating the mysterious deaths of key witnesses who were called to testify in the impeachment hearings against President Burris. That task force discovered evidence incriminating President Burris in the murders of those witnesses, and it also uncovered information implicating members of President Burris's Administration in criminal acts against the people of the United States.

"As of today, no charges have been filed against President Burris, and due to his current medical condition, any potential charges will be put on hold pending his recovery. In coming days, our offices will reveal the information that has been obtained against everyone involved, and we will release further information as is deemed necessary."

When Joy stops speaking, a multitude of reporters beg answers to their questions, but the two prosecutors ignore them and quickly leave the stage.

All of the main players in the corrupt Burris Administration are out of sight for now.

While most of the world believes President Burris is incapacitated and in the hospital, he is actually under house arrest at Camp David's Hickory Lodge, and Vice President Borden is on his way there as well. Victoria Johnson, Ellis Handelman, and the disgraced Secret Service agents are at Joint Base Andrews.

Jack and David Percal are also at Camp David. For as long as necessary, they have been assigned to individual units at the Hemlock cabins, near the contingent of FBI agents who are guarding the Camp's notorious "guests."

Today, the men are waiting for Vice President Borden and Victoria Johnson. While the VP has been given his own rooms at Camp David, Victoria is being transported there for her interrogation.

Jack's Hemlock cabin is a comfortably-furnished wood-paneled bungalow with a large stone fireplace. The floors throughout the structure are mostly highly-polished wood, but there are several areas of plush carpeting.

Jack and David are together in Jack's cabin, watching the conclusion of the Nicollazzi/Phillips press conference. When they hear a caravan of cars approaching, David walks over to the window and parts the curtain. Calling to Jack, he declares, "It's Acting President Bradley."

Rushing to the door, the men stand ready to greet Bradley and his entourage of Secret Service protectors, but when the Acting President enters, he dismisses them with a curt, "Sit, gentlemen. This is going to be short and sweet."

While Bradley's protective detail takes up positions inside and outside the cabin, Bradley, David, and Jack seat themselves on the sofas and chairs grouped tastefully around the living area.

Not one to waste time, Bradley launches into his discussion as soon as they are all seated.

"I came here to speak with both of you before I meet with Nicollazzi and Phillips," he states without preamble. "Our criminal indictment of Burris's Administration will rock this country and the world, and while the evildoers must be punished, we cannot prosecute the President for murder, or for his involvement in Blue Falcon. We just can't."

Incredulous at this news, Jack speaks out freely, as he always does.

"Mr. President, we cannot let that scumbag get away with this! He's responsible for killing and maiming hundreds of people, and he's also responsible for killing a close friend of mine. What the hell are you saying?"

Studying Jack closely, Bradley asserts, "Burris is scum; we know that. But he was President of the United States, so we need to deal with him carefully. Instead of blaming him directly, we will choose a scapegoat to pin most of this on, to lessen his responsibility for these actions."

Livid at the thought of Burris getting away with what he's done, Jack's blood pressure reaches an explosive level. He jumps up and paces the room, watching for the reactions of Bradley's Secret Service agents out of one eye.

"This is bullshit, sir! Maria and all the others must be avenged! Are we really going to let that man get away with murder—the murder of hundreds of innocent people? What the fuck is going on here?"

Rising to his feet, Percal tries to calm Jack down.

"Jack, sit down and clear your head," he urges. "This is the President of the United States... "

"Bullshit! He's the *Acting* President, and a politician as phony as the rest of them! This is all smoke and mirrors! It's another cover-up!"

Acting President Bradley also rises from his seat and gestures to the two men. "Sit down and hear me out," he pleads. "Please."

After a long pause, Jack reluctantly sits back down and glares at Bradley, who is towering over him.

"Go ahead and state your case," he says through clenched teeth. "But it better be good."

Sighing audibly, Bradley solemnly recites the names of the fallen.

"Assante, Gutierrez, Hastings, Wilkens, Conway, Cunningham, Ambassador Kingston, everyone who was harmed by the Lincoln Memorial bombing and Operation Vaya con Diablo. These and all the other victims will be avenged. You must continue your investigation, and I want you to thoroughly interrogate Borden, Handelman, and Johnson. And I strongly suggest that you single out Victoria Johnson as the one to work on the hardest."

Pausing, he takes a deep breath before continuing.

"This nation may not be able to withstand the indictment of a President on charges of this kind. I assure you that all will be resolved; everything will become clear to you after I meet with the prosecutors. Now, I'm scheduled to speak to Congress and the nation next week. Gentlemen, please believe me—everything will be resolved."

Bradley concludes his discussion by thanking David and Jack for their vigilance and tireless work on the case.

Before leaving, he shakes Jack's hand and whispers, "Jack, the bastards will pay. Trust me on this. Everything will be taken care of."

After Bradley and his detail exit the cabin, Percal turns to Jack. "What did he say?" he asks.

Before answering, Jack stares out of the window for a moment and then looks over at Percal.

"Take cover, my friend. More shit is about to hit the fan."

CHAPTER THIRTYNINE

Standing in front Acting President Bradley's desk in the Oval Office, Anita Nicollazzi and Joy Phillips are wondering why they were summoned.

"Please sit down, ladies," says Bradley. "Would you like something to drink? Coffee? Soda? This meeting shouldn't take long. I know you're both very busy, so I don't want to keep you."

"I'm fine, Mr. President," responds Joy. "Anita and I just had a late lunch, so I'm sure she's as ready as I am to find out what you need from us."

Bradley looks at the federal prosecutor, who nods her head in agreement.

"Good. Very good. I'll get right to it, then. I've read the case files and your warrants, but I must strongly recommend that you do not indict President Burris—for the sake of the country. Burris will be dealt with in another way. We will offer him a new identity and announce that he died from a massive heart attack. We'll throw in plastic surgery and relocate him to another country."

He gazes intently at the two women, who appear very uncomfortable, and look as though they are about to object.

"I will state that in another way. We cannot prosecute a President of the United States. Joy, after the announcement of his 'death,' you will conclude your impeachment proceedings, stating that it is prudent to abandon them for the sake of bringing the country together, even though the overwhelming evidence assures impeachment.

"I also strongly suggest that Vice President Borden be given immunity for agreeing to cooperate with our investigative teams. Now, under executive privilege, I have contacted the NSA and obtained the telephone records of Victoria Johnson. Her conversations implicate her as the architect of the Blue Falcon bombing at the Lincoln Memorial. You will continue with your plans to prosecute her and Handelman, who is involved in the Vaya con Diablo gunrunning fiasco."

The women open their mouths to protest, but Bradley holds up his hand to silence them.

"Let me be perfectly clear. Each of the evildoers will be held accountable for their actions, but if we do it this way, the nation will be able to recover and become stronger. Have I made myself clear?"

In unison, the ladies answer, "Crystal clear, Mr. President."

Minutes after the prosecutors leave the Oval Office, Acting President Bradley greets another visitor——Steven Hobbs, Director of the Central Intelligence Agency.

Bradley guides his guest to a chair some distance away from his desk and takes a seat opposite him. Silent for a moment, the Acting President stares thoughtfully at a painting of George Washington on the far wall, and then looks intently at the CIA director.

"Steve, we got some shit that needs to be cleaned up and sanitized for the good of the nation. I need 'Specter.'"

Leaning toward the Acting President, Steven

Hobbs asks, "How can we help you, sir?"

"Not me, the country. Here's a list of names that need to be looked into. I assume you know what I mean by that, Steve. I will be giving a speech to Congress on Monday, and I want all of this taken care of before then. The country needs us to put this to sleep. This assignment will be the last, and will conclude Operation Hannibal. Just get to it, and put this whole mess to bed."

Hobbs takes the list from Bradley. "I understand, sir, and I will take good care of each name on the list. It shall be done exactly as you say," he declares with fervor. "Good day, Mr. President."

David and Jack are expecting Vice President Borden and Victoria Johnson to arrive at any minute. Each of them will be interrogated before Handelman is brought into the mix.

"Jack, you just got married, right?" asks Percal while they wait.

"Yeah, why do you ask?"

"Oh, just making small talk. Maria spoke very highly of you. Were you married before, or is this your first time?"

"I've been down that road a few times before. Had too many vices for it to work out back then, but I sort of mellowed out after a while. It's Didi's first, though."

"Got any kids?"

"Nope, got fixed when I was in college; too lazy to buy condoms. Besides, I'm not dad material."

"Yeah, but your wife seems like she would be a great mom. We had a long talk at the wake. She's a great lady, Jack. Don't fuck this one up."

"I know. But damn, Dave, if she had to breastfeed any kid, she'd drown 'em!"

"Can't say that I noticed," says Dave with a grin, before he laughs out loud.

The conversation is interrupted by a knock at the door and the entrance of Borden and an FBI agent.

"Detective, this is Vice President Borden. Mr. Percal, we took Victoria Johnson to your cabin next door."

Percal nods meaningfully to Jack and then exits the cabin to interrogate Victoria Johnson. The FBI agent remains with Stenhouse to record the questioning of Vice President Borden.

But before things can get started, the door opens again to reveal a man standing in the doorway. He's wearing a suit that's two sizes too big and he looks like a kid fresh out of high school. Giving the stranger his famous squint, Jack barks, "Who the hell are you?"

The man clears his voice and attempts to speak in an assertive manner, but his voice cracks as he responds. "Ah... uh... I'm with the Federal Prosecutor's office. I'm working on this case with Ms. Nicollazzi, and I'm here to assist with the interrogation of the Vice President."

Lowering his head, Jack shakes it in disbelief. "Name, Slick. What's your name?"

"Oh! Uh... Larry... Larry Thomas."

"Well, Larry Thomas, come in and join the party. Hungry? Would you like some milk and cookies?"

Larry ignores the sarcasm, and with head lowered, enters the cabin. He sits down at the table and takes a file and a digital recorder out of his attaché case. Then he looks at Stenhouse, Borden, and the FBI agent, who are all staring at him.

"Shall we begin?" he asks with uncertainty.

Chuckling, Stenhouse motions for everyone to take a seat.

But before anyone can ask the first question, Borden clears his throat to get everyone's attention.

"I have something to say," he states to the group. "I already told Decker and Ms. Nicollazzi that I'll cooperate with you one hundred percent. I'll answer every question I can, and I'll testify as needed. Ms. Phillips gave me complete immunity, so please let me tell you what I know."

After obtaining nods of agreement from everyone in the room, he launches into a narrative of his recollection of events.

"First, I will detail the plot I have the most knowledge of—Operation Skyhook. The scheme was hatched by President Burris and Victoria Johnson, but it was originally proposed by Johnson, who as you all know, was born in Iran. Both Hilda Canton and Joe Cunningham were closely involved with it.

"It came about because Johnson felt that Burris's agenda and legacy were crumbling around him. The healthcare program was being dismantled by Congress and the rise of the caliphate in Iraq and Syria was making a mockery of his failed foreign policies. The operation they conceived was supposed to provide Iran's Air Force with the vital replacement parts they were banned from obtaining in the hope that they would agree to stop enriching uranium. They also hoped that by giving the Iranians what they wanted, they would help us battle the caliphate.

"Well, the Arab nations and Israel, in an unprecedented show of cooperation, vigorously objected to this plan. On one of my many visits to the Middle East under the guise of negotiating a nuclear treaty, I discovered that they all knew of this operation, and they told me to shut it down. When I informed the President and Victoria Johnson about their demand, Johnson went ballistic and basically told me to give the finger to our allies in the Middle East. When I delivered the message, our allies were furious. They notified the radicals in the area about the operation, and the rest you know.

"The radicals retaliated against us by launching an attack to capture Ambassador Kingston and our embassy. I assume you all know that Kingston was gay. Why we sent a gay ambassador to a Muslim country goes beyond the pale. In my opinion, they captured and tortured him just because he was gay. They hated him because he was gay. Kingston repeatedly asked for more security, but it was denied by Canton and Burris. When the call came in for support during the attack, Burris ignored it and went to bed, and Canton was too drunk to care. They tried to blame a stupid video, but that was all bullshit.

"What I know of Handelman's gunrunning case is that he and Burris were getting a cut-back from the cartels with support from the Mexican President. Somehow, Cunningham, Hastings, and Sansone got ahold of all that info."

"What do you know about Ellen Vanierri?" asks Jack.

"Ha. Ellen Vanierri. She was in love with the President. It started when she was Allen, one of Burris's

Secret Service bodyguards. She took it upon herself to kill Joe Cunningham because he was a threat to Burris's legacy, but from what I've heard, Burris encouraged her to continue with the others when he found out what she did to 'protect' him."

Jack stares at Borden in wonder of all of the corruption and deceit he was privy to.

"Was Ellen, or Allen, part of his elite protective detail? And what do you know about the Praetorium?"

Borden sits back in his chair and sighs. "Burris was a hound. He's bi, and he makes Caligula look like an altar boy. I was never part of the group at the Praetorium, but the list of people who participated in their 'gatherings' includes governors, members of Congress, and well-known lobbyists."

Larry, who has been silent until now, chooses to this moment to speak up. "How about Victoria Johnson? How does she fit in with the Praetorium?"

Borden screws up his face in disgust. "Johnson is a sexual deviant, and so is Burris. Damn... Burris would screw a snake if someone would just hold down its head. She has a nickname among the staff...they call her the 'head' advisor, if you know what I mean. Handelman, the Secret Service, Johnson, Conway, and Vanierri—they were all involved."

"What about Blue Falcon?" ask Jack and Larry at the same time, startling them both.

At the mention of Blue Falcon, Borden becomes visibly upset. He attempts to compose himself by standing up and walking around the cabin's living area. "Those fuckers! Those fuckers!" he snarls several times. Then, with a heavy sigh and a swipe at his eyes, he retakes his seat.

"The Administration was going down in flames," he resumes. "Special Prosecutor Gutierrez was getting close to exposing us all, so Johnson and Burris came up with that doomsday Blue fucking Falcon scenario. It was supposed to divert attention away from the scandals and bring the nation together against terrorism and Iran. They added Iran to the plot after we found out they weren't going to dismantle their nuclear program after all."

"Those two—they killed innocent Americans!" shouts the VP. "Jason Goodie and the rest of Burris's posse set a poor sap up to be the bomber. They erased his past, made him a 'ghost,' and set Johnson's plan into motion. Burris approved it, and here we are."

Jack asks, "If you were so involved with everything, why did you resign?"

"When we learned that you guys found Cunningham's files and deciphered the code, Handelman and I had lunch, and we both decided to resign. We knew we were toast."

Jack gives him a piercing stare. "How did you find out about the Cunningham files?"

"I have eyes and ears in the Bureau. I was tipped off about the find in the canal, so I told Handelman. That's when we bailed."

"Is that it?" asks Larry, who is poised to turn off the recorder.

When Borden responds in the affirmative, Larry stops the machine. He jots down a few more notes and then says, "Jack, Handelman will be questioned at Andrews tomorrow, but Johnson is being interrogated right now, by Percal. Go ahead and join Dave next door. Another prosecutor like me is there with them. I'll conclude the interrogation here, and release Borden under house arrest. He'll be sent back to his home in Dover."

Jack gets up to leave, but before he does, he gets in one last shot at Larry.

"Will the prosecutor at Percal's cabin be old enough to shave?"

At that, the FBI agent bursts out laughing, and since he was drinking coffee at the time, the liquid flies out of his nose, but he continues to laugh. Borden just shakes his head.

"I'm twenty-four years old!" retorts Larry angrily, causing everyone to laugh uproariously.

Roaring, Stenhouse adds, "I drink bourbon older than you!"

CHAPTER FORTY

"Fuck, its Bradley," mutters President Burris as he watches a convoy of black SUVs pull up outside of the building he is being held in at Camp David.

Surrounded by a group of Secret Service Agents, Acting President Bradley exits his vehicle and walks up to Burris's makeshift cell. When he comes face-to-face with the man he replaced, he motions to a chair and states, "Howard, sit down. We need to talk."

"Why are you here, General?" snarls Burris furiously. "What the hell is going on?"

Bradley stares incredulously at the President, and then walks up to him and stands nose to nose.

"Look, you asshole, you have no authority to issue commands anymore. You're in a coma, remember? Just sit down and shut up!"

With the help of a Secret Service agent, Burris is made to sit rather abruptly on a love seat in the living room while Bradley remains standing.

"Howard, you have been charged with murder and treason against the United States and its citizens. Vice President Borden is cooperating with our investigators, and his testimony will hang you as a traitor and a murderer. You will NOT be tried for your crimes, however, because the country may not survive your trial and subsequent conviction."

The beginning of a grin appears on the President's face, but it quickly disappears when Bradley continues speaking.

"Don't be too happy. There was no terror threat in D.C., Howard. That was a ruse arranged by your friends at the Pentagon to arrest you and take you here, but you won't be here for long. The American people have been told that you suffered a heart attack during the evacuation and that you are now in a coma at Walter Reed Hospital. In a few days, they will be told that you did not survive your illness."

Burris's eyes go wide. "Are you going to kill me, Bradley?"

"The government of Kenya has agreed to give you asylum, and we have arranged a new identity for you. But you will not be a free man in Kenya. The government has allowed you entry, but more significantly, they have agreed to our most important request. You will be housed in a large compound and isolated from the rest of the world for the rest of your life."

Burris jumps up from his seat in defiance, with fire in his eyes.

"You fucking asshole! You took over the government and my presidency! You won't get away with this! Someone will eventually leak all this bullshit out!"

"Look, you stupid ass," retorts Bradley. "You are a dead man, do you understand that? I can have you shot right now, and no one would ever know. According to the news, you are at Walter Reed Hospital. Your family has already been informed that you probably won't survive your heart attack. They are outside of the ICU right now, praying for you, along with a large group of people who have set up a vigil outside of the hospital.

But officially, you are now a 'ghost.' Your former identity no longer exists!

"On Monday, four days from today, I will make a speech before Congress where I will detail all of the scandals in your Administration, and you will be declared dead. Victoria Johnson, your Secret Service posse, Ellen Vanierri, Hilda Canton, and Ellis Handelman will all be held responsible for their crimes. But Vice President Borden will be given immunity."

Poking Burris in the chest with his forefinger, Bradly states firmly, "The Constitution will prevail. This country will prevail. And you? Well, you will become a memory. You will be regarded as the most corrupt President this country has ever had. Your legacy will be sexual perversion and crimes against the people of the United States. So... enjoy your stay here, because on Monday, you will leave for your new home... after your 'death' is announced." With a short laugh he adds, "Damn, you're going to miss your own funeral!"

Speechless, Burris drops into his chair and bows his head—a broken man.

"Keep a guard here until Monday," commands Bradley to his guard. "If he causes any problems, shoot him."

It is late, near dusk, and Jack is walking from his cabin to Percal's. Suddenly, he stops and looks around at his surroundings, realizing with clarity that he is at Camp David, where powerful people from the world stage are usually relaxing with a game of golf or tennis. *Instead, we are interrogating murderers and terrorists,* he muses.

When he enters Percal's cabin, the first thing he notices is that Victoria Johnson appears to be taller and nicer-looking in person than she does on TV.

"Who is this fine gentleman?" Victoria purrs when she catches sight of the new arrival.

Pulling up a chair, Stenhouse joins the group of people sitting around the dining room table.

"Name's Detective Stenhouse, NYPD," he responds.

Johnson licks her lips and gazes at him seductively. "Welcome aboard, Detective. What can I do for you?"

"Do for me?" growls Jack. "Not a fucking thing! Just answer our questions, *capeesh*?"

Miles away, Anita Nicollazzi and Joy Phillips are sitting at a metal table in a stark white room, across from Ellis Handelman and his high-powered attorney.

"Mr. Handelman," begins Anita, "you have been charged with crimes against the people of the United States. We have testimony from Vice President Borden, as well as emails and recordings from other sources that confirm your guilt. What do you have to say for yourself?"

Ellis confers with his lawyer, and then retorts defiantly, "I have nothing to say. I am innocent of all charges, and I have pled my innocence to the court. I will fight this imprisonment, and I will be granted bail! Then I will leave you all here to pound sand!"

Bursting into Handelman's tirade, Joy Phillips declares, "Look, Mr. Attorney General, we have copies of bank records that list the deposits that were made into your account from Mexican sources. We also have written and verbal testimony that links you to the drug cartels in Mexico that were working with you in your Vaya Con Diablo gunrunning scheme. In addition, we have testimony that you had knowledge of and participated in implementing Operation Blue Falcon. So Ellis, you are far from innocent. Now, answer our questions: Was it you or President Burris who initiated the operation to send guns over the border, when did you first hear about Operation Blue Falcon, and who belonged to Burris's posse?"

"I'm taking the Fifth. On counsel's advice, I invoke my right under the Fifth Amendment not to answer on the grounds that I may incriminate myself. Take me to trial. Try to convict me of these trumped-up charges that you and your so-called 'President' Bradley have created. I'm through talking to any of you."

Handelman stands and yells to the Marine guard who is standing just outside the interrogation room. "Guard! Get me out of here! I'm through with this nonsense."

Immediately, a Marine sergeant enters and escorts the former Attorney General and his attorney out of the room, leaving the two prosecutors alone.

Anita stares at her file, feeling her blood pressure about to explode. Seething, she mutters, "Handelman thinks we won't go to trial. He thinks we won't let the public know what the hell went on over the past few years. What an ass!"

Joy sighs deeply. "This is going to be brutal. The trial is going to try the resolve of this nation. We don't have an Attorney General right now, and no one is going to be appointed to take his place any time soon. We need to talk to Director Decker, and then meet with President Bradley to get his take on all of this. Thank goodness Jason Goodie and the rest of the Secret Service posse have all pled guilty. It's unfortunate that they're all asking for clemency in exchange for their cooperation."

"I'll meet with Decker in the morning, and I'll schedule a meeting with Bradley," responds Anita. "Today's Friday. Bradley wants to speak to Congress about all of this shit on Monday, so we have to stop it from hitting the fan before then. Victoria Johnson is being questioned at Camp David as we speak, but she doesn't know that she's going to be thrown under the bus. Tomorrow, we'll announce the formal charges against her. I'll go for the death penalty on this bitch. Bradley wants all of this cleaned up and tied in a bow before Monday."

Jack is quietly observing as Percal continues his line of questioning.

"So again, Ms. Johnson, we will begin with the latest accusations and work our way back from there. You were implicated by Vice President Borden in Operation Blue Falcon, and we have recorded phone conversations courtesy of the NSA to corroborate your involvement. Who was behind Blue Falcon?"

Johnson responds, "Blue Falcon? What is that, a lost Humphrey Bogart movie? Look, you've been holding me here and questioning me without my attorney... "

"Hey!" snaps Jack, "We got forty-eight hours before we have to announce charges. You're sitting in a cabin at Camp David and enjoying a cup of coffee. Not exactly a harsh environment, but it's your status with the past Administration that's giving you privileges here, not your oral abilities. Know what I mean? So, answer the question. Your name is associated with crimes against the United States and innocent citizens of this great land."

He ticks off a list on his fingers. "We know all about Blue Falcon, the posse, the Praetorium, Skyhook, Vaya Con Diablo, Ellen Vanierri, and President Burris, your ex-boss, who we know was called Caligula. I don't care who you knew, or who you blew. So, with no pun intended, spit it out. Now."

All of the men who are sitting at the table with Stenhouse--Percal, a federal prosecutor, and another FBI agent--are now laughing. But Victoria is not laughing. As she listens to them, her previously coy evasiveness turns harsh and confrontational.

"Okay!" she screeches. "Now I'm going to tell you all something! You have no idea why we did what we did, do you? We were trying to preserve this Administration's goals and President Burris's legacy! Do you realize that what we accomplished was for the betterment of this nation? No, I need to change that. It was for the betterment of this world! All of us are patriots! Don't you know that we're at war with the bankers and capitalists who are trying to destroy the New World Order?"

Pointing her finger at those assembled around the table, she snarls, "The people of this country are stupid, and you are all pawns of the establishment! What are a few deaths and casualties? They're nothing but trophies and placards that showcase our success. The Iranians gave us their word, and then they fucked us. We were trying to disarm them, but they betrayed us, so we couldn't let the failure of Skyhook be known. The deaths in Sudan? They were casualties of the cause. We needed to punish Iran for their deceit, and we needed to raise President Burris up as a wartime commander. Blue Falcon was a glorious triumph for our cause, and Ellen Vanierri was a tool that we used as needed. The rest of those in the group were just pawns to be used and then set aside. As for the Praetorium, it was fun, a diversion... good times for all!"

Victoria stands and walks around the table behind all of the seated men. As she passes each of them, she runs her hand along the backs of their shoulders. When she reaches Stenhouse, she bends over and whispers into his ear.

"Wish you had been at the Praetorium. It would have been glorious!"

When she blows in his ear, Jack jerks his head away in disgust and watches as she walks around the table. When she reaches her chair, she pulls it out and turns it around so she can sit spread-eagled toward the men, revealing that she has gone commando.

Immediately, Percal stands and fires an order to his agent.

"Get her out of here!" he demands. "She can rot in her cell at Joint Base Andrews until we need her again."

While an agent leads her out to the car, Victoria's haunting laughter echoes throughout the cabin. The men look at each other warily, but Jack just shrugs his shoulders.

Turning off his recorder, the assistant federal prosecutor stands and stretches his arms above his head.

"Well, that was something, wasn't it?" he says to no one in particular. "Anita is going to announce charges against this bitch, so we should talk to Sansone and Smithfield, and... "

Before he can finish, he is interrupted by a phone call.

"Yes... yes...," he says, and then listens quietly while the caller speaks. "Okay, I'll be right there."

"That was Nicollazzi," he announces. "She called an emergency meeting for tonight because she's going to formally charge Johnson in the morning. The Acting President set up a breakfast meeting Sunday morning with her, Joy Phillips, and Director Decker." Looking at David and Jack, he adds, "You two have also been asked to attend. Be at the White House at 9 a.m. on Sunday."

The prosecutor gathers up his belongings and leaves the cabin.

"What the hell does Bradley want from us now?" asks Jack. "This case is just about finished. All I want is to go home, take a hot shower, and clean off all this Washington crap."

"Well, it looks like you won't be able to do that until after we hear more crap on Sunday."

CHAPTER FORTYONE

"Good morning, this is Bill Stone, ABC News Washington, with a special report. We are saddened to inform you that President Howard Burris, who is currently on life support in the ICU at Walter Reed Medical Facility, has been declared brain-dead. Family and close friends are at his side, and they will now need to decide whether to discontinue life support. Acting President Bradley is meeting with cabinet members as we speak.

"We also mourn the death of Secretary of State Hilda Canton. Her ex-husband, former President Bob Canton, was at her bedside as members of her family made the decision to take her off life support early this morning. Details of funeral services will be announced later today.

"In other news, Federal Prosecutor Anita Nicollazzi has announced federal charges of terrorism, murder, and attempted murder against former presidential advisor Victoria Johnson and her co-conspirators, former Attorney General Ellis Handelman, and the Secret Service agents who were on the Presidential detail. Those agents have been identified as Jason Goodie, Sharon O'Neil, and Leon Travis.

"Additional charges of money laundering and gun trafficking have been leveled against Ellis Handelman, relating to his involvement in Operation Vaya con Diablo. As you may remember, that operation was being investigated by Special Prosecutor Juan Gutierrez before he was assassinated while chairing the impeachment hearings against President Burris.

"We have reached out to former Vice President Borden's office for comments on his involvement in these scandals, but we received a statement from his attorney indicating that the VP has received immunity in exchange for his cooperation with investigators, and will not comment on an ongoing investigation.

"Acting President Bradley is scheduled to address Congress and the nation at one p.m. on Monday on these very issues.

"We will bring you the latest information on Hilda Canton and President Burris as it becomes available.

"With the extreme ill health of President Burris, the death of Secretary Canton, and the indictments of past Administration officials, it is a sad day for the United States. This is Bill Stone, ABC News."

After interrogating the VP and the special advisor to the President, David and Jack have left Camp David and are now at separate locations. Percal is at the secret site where agent James Smithfield is being kept under house arrest, and Jack is waiting for Frank Sansone at FBI headquarters on Pennsylvania Avenue.

While Jack waits for the CIA whistleblower, he texts a message to his wife.

Mornin' Babe. As you can tell from the news, this case is just about finished. Should be back soon, maybe Monday or Tuesday. ILY.

After hitting SEND, he looks up to see Sansone standing in front of his desk.

"Why are you still in D.C., Stenhouse? I thought you'd be back in New York by now."

"How's it hangin', 'Benny'? Hey, should I still be

calling you 'Ben-Hur'?"

"Yeah, I'm getting used to it by now," responds Frank with a hint of a smile.

Returning the smile, Jack replies, "I'm just wrapping up some things here, but after that, I got nothing to do until tomorrow morning. Gotta breakfast meeting with the Prez, so I'm thinking about checking out the Smithsonian later today. But hey, I never got the chance to thank you for that rescue in Baltimore. Nice job, 'Ben'!"

"You're welcome, partner. Ya gotta do what ya gotta do, ya know? Did you hear that Homeland Security Secretary Olsen is shaking up the Secret Service? He just announced changes that will clean up their house, including the big white one."

"Huh. That's like closing the barn doors after the horses leave. But better late than never! Hey, Frank, I got a couple of questions for you before I can wrap this whole thing up about Burris and Victoria Johnson. I need your insight."

"Yeah, man, whatever you need."

Before the conversation can continue, Dave Percal storms into the room, and he's furious.

"Smithfield committed suicide! Can you believe it? We found him in the shower. He slashed his wrists and bled out before anyone noticed!"

Unperturbed, Jack takes a sip of his coffee. "That figures," he says calmly, "and it's no great loss." Raising his cup in a toast, he adds, "Here's to you, Maria!"

"Jack," says Percal, "he left a note saying that everything was Burris's idea. He said Victoria Johnson merely did whatever he wanted."

"Fuck 'em all!" reply Jack and Frank in unison.

Grimly, Frank continues. "From what I've been able to learn about Burris, it seems that while he was still in law school, he was groomed by a Marxist professor to enter the world of politics. Then, when the left-wing progressives of his party picked up on his Marxist beliefs, they pushed him into the Presidency." He blows out a sigh. "Burris's radical beliefs and narcissism nearly destroyed the Republic. If it weren't for the conservative talk radio networks and Fox News, the mainstream media would have continued to cover up for their 'hero', and we would never have known what he was doing. Patriots like Cunningham, Hastings, Gutierrez, and unnamed agents of the CIA uncovered all of this garbage, and also some of the other novel ideas he wanted to inflict on us."

"What other ideas?" asks Dave.

"Oh, like abolishing the Electoral College and reducing the influence of the First and Second Amendments. And so, here we are. Everyone on Burris's staff was involved in his schemes, except for the lower-ranking employees. Allen or Ellen Vanierri, Victoria Johnson, Joe Conway, Ellis Handelman, Jeffrey Borden, and Burris's posse—all of them have blood on their hands. It was well-known among all of them that Burris, Vanierri, and Johnson were sexually involved with each other, and that they collaborated on various issues. And as his code name implied, Burris acted like a deviant...like a modern-day Caligula. It really sucks that we can't bring him to trial."

"Yeah, no kidding," says Jack. "I would have loved to see him try to explain his decisions!"

"Ha! That would have made for great TV! But the stain of his actions will remain on our flag forever. The only good thing is that at least he's out of office, and his Administration is finished. The new Administration is going to pin everything on Victoria Johnson. She's going to be the scapegoat."

"Well, maybe we'll get some good TV out of her testimony!" laughs Jack.

"Yeah, I'm looking forward to that!" Frank joins in the laughter.

"Oh, you know what, I've been curious about something," he says, looking at Jack and Dave. "After your swim in the harbor, did you guys rinse your phones with fresh water and bag them in rice?"

"Yeah," answers Percal, "but the salt water got in before that. My phone is working now, but it has issues, so I'm going to upgrade to a new one. Jack, how's your phone?"

"It's fucked. It was fine for a while, but now it will only send text messages. I was going to wait until I got back to New York to get a new one, but I'll probably have time today to go down to my carrier's store. Didi needs a new phone, too, so maybe I'll surprise her."

"If I were you, Jack, I'd get another a pay-as-you-go phone. Just sayin'."

"Good idea, Frank. I think I'll do that."

Rising from his seat, Frank prepares to leave. "Well, guys, it's been fun, but I gotta go now," he says. "With all the shit going on with Burris, the Company is kinda busy these days."

"Thanks, bro. Maybe we can have some drinks at my hotel before I leave. Are you busy Sunday night? My flight leaves Monday morning. Dave, can you join us?"

Frank nods. "Eight o'clock Sunday is fine with me."

"Sunday looks good for me, too. I got meetings with Decker today, but I'm free this weekend. What are you going to do after you go phone shopping today?"

"I'm going to play tourist. I may hit the Smithsonian Museums and the Washington Monument. I've had enough of the White House and Congress!"

Amid guffaws of laughter, the men shake hands, and Jack leaves the FBI building.

On the drive back to his hotel, he thinks about Didi and wonders where he can purchase some new phones.

He doesn't notice the black sedan that is following a few cars behind him.

After taking a few minutes to freshen up in his room, Jack took the elevator downstairs and asked the desk clerk for the location of the nearest cell phone store. When he found out that it's only a few blocks away, he decided to walk there, and then head over to the National Mall.

Purchases in hand, Jack is now strolling casually along the streets of D.C. As he nears the Mall, he begins to encounter the crowds of locals and tourists that regularly fill the area.

Enjoying the role of tourist, he is marveling at all of the iconic buildings, until he is suddenly brought back to reality by the loud sounds of a collision between two taxi cabs on the street just behind him. Turning toward the commotion, he watches the two drivers jump out of their vehicles and shout at each other while pointing furiously at their cabs. As the spectacle continues, his eyes wander randomly over the crowd until he focuses on a man in a brown suit who has also stopped to watch the unfolding drama. With a sense of unease, he remembers that he saw that same man in the cell phone store. Now on high alert, he turns away and continues toward the museum.

Crossing the National Mall, he heads directly toward the popular museum, and once inside, quickly ducks into a hallway near the men's room. He leans nonchalantly against a wall, and scans the crowd as it moves through the building's rotunda and around the large elephant on display at its center.

Within seconds, he sees the brown suit walk in. Unseen by the stranger, Jack studies the man as he looks around and walks over to the information booth.

Jack took his time off this afternoon seriously. He has replaced his usual business attire with typical tourist apparel—an oversized Hawaiian shirt over faded jeans, and his favorite Tony Lama boots. But Jack's casual style doesn't mean that he's let his guard down. His loose shirt is convenient for hiding his Glock and Kevlar vest, and his NYPD badge and the temporary ID issued to him by the FBI are tucked away in the pockets of his jeans.

Still out of sight near the men's room, Jack keeps an eye on the brown suit while he plans an escape route. Before long he sees his chance: a large group of Boy Scouts has just entered the rotunda and is gathering loosely around the large elephant.

Using the group as cover, Jack leaves the hallway and quickly exits the museum. When he's a safe distance away, he takes out his new cell phone and places a call.

"Frank, this is Stenhouse. I'm on the Mall, heading toward the Air and Space Museum, and I'm being followed. Is it one of your guys?"

Frank is concerned, but not overly surprised. "No, he's not ours, Jack. Go to the café in the Air and Space Museum. I'll meet you there in about thirty minutes."

Jack disconnects the call and heads to the Air and Space Museum. But when he enters the building, a black sedan pulls around in front and spits out another brown suit, who walks in right after him.

Spotting the museum café, Jack realizes that he's getting hungry, so he decides to make use of the time until Frank arrives to grab a bite to eat.

After paying the cashier, he looks around for a place to sit and notices an empty table at the rear of the restaurant. He carries his meal tray over and seats himself with his back to the wall, and watches the café entrance while he swallows his tuna melt sandwich and cup of coffee.

A short time after he sits down, he spies a different brown suit than the one at the Natural History Museum enter the café, with Frank Sansone right behind him.

Glancing around the small snack area, Frank quickly spies Jack sitting in the back, and when their eyes meet, Jack nods toward the brown suit. Catching that look, Frank glances over, nods back, and orders a cup of coffee.

When the clerk hands him the cup of hot liquid, Frank turns around and comes face-to-face with the brown-suited man, who is standing in line behind him. Stumbling clumsily, Frank falls against his target and spills his hot coffee all over the front of the man's jacket. With a look of surprise, the man steps backward and exclaims, "What the hell? Look what you did, you idiot!"

Apologizing profusely, Frank grabs several napkins and attempts to clean off the coffee, but when he uncovers the weapon on the man's belt, he shouts as loud as he can, "GUN! HE HAS A GUN!"

In response to the recent events around D.C., heavily-armed guards have been posted at all government buildings, museums, national monuments, and other tourist attractions.

When the guards patrolling the museum hear the word 'gun,' two SWAT-types rush into the snack area. Without warning, they firmly grab Frank Sansone and the coffee-soaked man and then quickly and efficiently walk them both out of the café. A third guard attempts to quiet the agitated crowd.

The only person in the area who doesn't seem bothered by the commotion is Jack. He remained seated throughout the confusion and is now calmly finishing his snack.

When he's done eating, he exits the café and finds Frank Sansone waiting for him in the lobby.

"You've become quite the popular guy around here, Jack."

"That was nice work, Frank. Who the hell was that?"

"He belongs to a special security detail attached to the Acting President. Bradley sent him and a few others to watch over you. Needless to say, I had to calm him down a bit; he's not happy with our little ruse. I assume Percal is also being followed and has his own brown shadows."

"What the fuck? This town is bat-shit crazy!"

"Look, Jack, be thankful they're looking out for you. Burris may still have some friends out there."

Jack shakes his head but agrees with Frank. "Thanks again, bro. I guess I'll continue doing my tourist thing. I don't have to be anywhere this afternoon."

"You know what? My day is basically shot now. Mind if I join ya? We can have some dinner later."

Jack accepts Frank's offer, grateful for the company, and the two men set out to tour the National Air and Space Museum. Some distance behind, a "clean" brown suit follows them both.

Across town, justice was swift. Jason Goodie, Leon Travis, and Sharon O'Neil pled guilty to all the charges leveled against them, and are now on their way to the federal prisons where they will spend the rest of their lives.

Two white prisoner transport vans are currently leaving FBI headquarters with their charges. One van holds Jason and Leon, who are on their way to the United States Penitentiary in Lee County, Virginia, and the other contains Sharon O'Neil, who is being taken to the Secure Female Facility at the United States Penitentiary in Hazelton, West Virginia. Each of these disgraced former Secret Service agents has been sentenced to death for being an accessory to treasonous acts and multiple murders. They will be held in isolation in their respective facilities until their sentences are carried out.

Meanwhile, former Attorney General Ellis Handelman is still fighting for bail. He is being held in isolation at Joint Base Andrews and remains defiant in the face of overwhelming evidence against him. During Bradley's speech on Monday afternoon, he is scheduled to be transferred to the Federal Correctional Institution in Gilmer, West Virginia to await his trial.

Victoria Johnson will also be transferred to prison during Bradley's speech. She is also at Joint Base Andrews, but will be moved to the Federal Correctional Institution in Danbury, Connecticut until the commencement of her trial for crimes against the people of the United States.

Vice President Borden is the only one who is not in prison. Although he was sentenced to house arrest at his luxurious home in Dover, Delaware, he is not entirely comfortable there. After the media reported that he will testify as a material witness against Ellis Handelman and Victoria Johnson, the Vice President had to be provided with 24-hour surveillance, and now U.S. Marshals and armed guards continuously surround him, inside and outside his home.

CHAPTER FORTYTWO

Jack is in his rental vehicle, waiting for the Marine guard at the White House's West Wing entrance to check his ID and confirm his appointment with the Acting President. When his meeting is verified, he is instructed to park the car in the visitor's lot.

At the entrance to the White House, he is stopped by the Secret Service, who conduct a thorough search of his person and possessions. Jack volunteers his service weapon and backup piece to the agent, who thanks him and places them in a secure locker for later pickup. Then a second agent leads him up a narrow staircase to the first floor, where they pass the Roosevelt Room and enter a corridor outside of the Oval Office. But instead of being shown into the imposing chamber, Jack is directed into a nearby dining room, where David Percal, FBI Director Decker, and Special Prosecutors Phillips and Nicollazzi are seated at a large table, waiting for President Bradley to join them.

Unaffected by the high caliber of people in the room, Jack pulls out an empty chair between Dave and the FBI director and greets the assembled guests. While a waiter pours him a cup of coffee, he whispers to Dave, "Sorry I'm late. Got stuck in traffic."

"No problem," responds Percal. "President Bradley is running late, too, but he should be here within a few minutes. His aide told us that they'll serve breakfast as soon as everyone has arrived."

Jack nods and takes a sip of coffee from a gold-rimmed cup. Then, he asks, "Well, what's for breakfast?"

When President Bradley walks in, all heads turn as he replies to Jack's question with a smile. "Just grits, scrambled eggs, and your choice of bacon, sausage, or Virginia ham."

To respect the office of the President, everyone in the room stands to greet Bradley, who says cheerfully, "Good morning, everyone. Please be seated. Thank you for coming."

As the guests take their seats, the waiters start bringing in the food, which they place on the table in large platters and bowls that are meant to be passed around, family-style. The effect of the informal presentation is that the breakfast feast takes on the atmosphere of a friendly gathering, rather than a serious business meeting. Bradley allows the group to build camaraderie while a waiter fixes his breakfast plate. But after taking just a few bites, he begins the meeting.

"Welcome, everyone. I called you here to thank each of you for your perseverance and professionalism in conducting your investigations into the crimes committed by the previous Administration. We will right all their wrongs, and everyone involved will be held accountable for their actions against this country, the Constitution, and the people of the United States.

"Our most pressing problem at this moment is the pending action against Iran. Therefore, in an attempt to pursue every avenue for peace, after this breakfast I will meet with the ambassador of Iran to try to find a way to avoid military conflict. Thankfully, the leaders of Congress have agreed to postpone their vote on military action until after my meeting. I am confident that on Monday evening, I will be able to assure the people of the United States that all is well.

"Now, as some of you may know, Victoria Johnson, Ellis Handelman, and several members of the Secret Service are being transferred to federal penitentiaries to await their trials. Both Johnson and Handelman remain defiant, however. Although they continue to insist that they are innocent, Vice President Borden will testify against them in each of their trials. The VP is under house arrest at his residence and is being guarded there by U.S. Marshals.

"At this time, I would like to give homage to our fallen comrade, FBI Agent Maria Assante. I have invited her parents to dinner at the White House to show my appreciation for her service to the country."

Pausing, Bradley looks around the room. Then he says, "But that's enough business for now," and picks up his spoon, with a smile at those seated around him. "Let's eat."

Instead of eating, Prosecutor Nicollazzi takes the initiative to remind the Acting President of a few details.

"Mr. President, I would like to point out that the guilty Secret Service agents are also on their way to prison. Leon Travis and Jason Goodie will spend time in isolated cells at Lee until their dates of their executions. And Sharon O'Neil is on her way to Hazelton to await the same fate."

President Bradley swallows his grits and takes a sip of coffee as he listens to her. "Thank you, Anita. I forgot to mention them. Yes, I know that they are being transported to prison as we speak. Our system of justice works. Now, will someone please pass me the butter?"

Two U.S. Marshal Prisoner transfer vans are idling at the guard house at the entrance to Joint Base Andrews. They are on the way to the special brig where the two officials from former President Burris's Administration are being held.

"What is your business here, gentlemen?" asks one of the MPs on duty.

"We have orders to transfer three prisoners to federal institutions."

The MPs look over the papers and then hand them back to the drivers. "Sorry, gentlemen, those prisoners were picked up by Homeland Security over an hour ago, by order of Secretary Olsen."

Puzzled, the marshals pull the vans off to the side and huddle together.

"Seriously?" questions the higher-ranking agent. "Why did Homeland Security pick them up when they knew we were on the way? Something's not right." He places a call into the office to verify what the MP told them, and the response he receives is exactly what he didn't want to hear.

"Okay, it's true, Homeland's got 'em," he informs his colleagues. "They're transporting them by separate vans instead of the chopper we had on standby. Those guys are prisoners now, and they're gonna be really uncomfortable sitting on metal benches for their rides to the pen."

Just outside of Manassas, Virginia, the prisoner van carrying Jason Goodie and Leon Travis exits I-66 onto VA-245 N, and stops in the town of The Plains.

Shackled to the floor in the back of the vehicle, the prisoners are unaware of what's going on outside. When they hear the front doors open and close, they expect someone to let them know why they stopped, but there is nothing but silence. After a few minutes, Leon turns to Jason.

"Where the fuck did they go?" he asks.

There are no windows in the back of the van, except for a small opening into the driver's compartment. Jason slides along the metal bench as far as his shackles will let him, and peeks into the front. It is empty.

Suddenly, both men hear warning bells and a train horn. Peering through the small opening again, Jason looks through the front windshield and sees a crossing gate coming down across his line of sight.

"Fuck it! We're on a railroad track!" he shouts.

In a panic, both men start yelling and pounding on the walls of the van, but there is no response to their cries, and the speeding train is rushing closer and closer.

Jason desperately tries to free himself, but only succeeds in causing blood to gush from under his shackles. On the opposite bench, Leon seems resolved to his fate, because he is just sitting back and laughing.

A few minutes later, the freight train impacts the van, crushing it and sending it down the tracks.

At about the same time, the van taking Sharon O'Neil to Hazelton has stopped at a traffic light at the intersection of King Street and Clubhouse Drive just outside of Leesburg, Virginia. Sharon also hears the front doors of the van open and close, and that is the last thing she hears before a cement truck heading east runs across the intersection and hits the van. The collision ends with exploding gasoline and death.

President Bradley is about to begin his meeting with the Iranian Ambassador. But before it starts an aide walks in, approaches the President, and whispers in his ear. Bradley smiles in thanks and turns his attention to the ambassador.

"Mr. Zarcasian, the Congress of the United States is about to authorize the use of military force against your country and the radical caliphate in Syria and Iraq. When that happens, I assure you without any doubt that your country will be annihilated.

"I'm sure you know that Russia and China are backing our cause. You have no allies, sir; the attack on our Capital sealed your fate. Now, it is not my concern whether your country participated in that attack or not. This is the time when your government needs to make a decision.

"The best decision they could make is to banish the caliphate, take your troops out of Iraq, abandon Hezbollah, and dismantle your nuclear program. Period. If you do not do those things, the full power and might of the combined military forces of the United

States, Israel, France, Great Britain, and Germany will wipe Iran and the radical caliphate from the face of the earth.

"You have forty-eight hours to make your decision, sir. Tuesday morning, Congress will most likely vote in support of military action. Advise your leaders to choose wisely, Ambassador, for the fate of Iran rests on what your government decides. Disavow the caliphate, condemn them, and comply with our demands. Only then will you be spared destruction.

"This meeting is now over. You have much work to do, so I suggest you begin as soon as possible."

When Dave Percal and Frank Sansone join Jack at the bar in the lobby of his hotel, he orders Daniels neat all around. The group is uncharacteristically silent while they wait for their drinks.

After everyone has taken at least one sip, Sansone breaches the silence with some news that he believes will lift their spirits.

"So, guys, as you know, earlier today, Goodie, Travis, and O'Neil were transported to federal penitentiaries. But what I don't think you know is that they all died in separate 'accidents,' " he says, using his fingers to make air quotes.

When there is no reaction by Dave, Sansone looks at Jack, who merely shrugs and says, "Nothing changes; everything remains the same—it's government as usual. My guess is that they won't be the only 'accidents' we'll be hearing about. But before we go into the dining room for dinner, let's give Maria and everyone who died one last toast."

Raising their glasses, they drink a toast to their fallen comrades, and then exit the bar toward the dining area.

On the way to their table, Jack texts Didi. He expects to leave D.C. at noon the next day and arrive home by 4:00 p.m.

On the receiving end of the text, Didi smiles. She has some special news for Jack.

CHAPTER FORTYTHREE

On Monday morning, President Howard Burris is driven out of Camp David at the same time as Acting President Clifton Bradley is preparing to leave the White House.

While the Acting President delivers his historic speech to Congress, Howard Burris will board one of two private military jets that are waiting at Joint Base Andrews. One of the jets will fly him to Kenya to begin his exile there, and the other will take Victoria Johnson to the Federal Correctional Institution in Danbury, Connecticut.

Ellis Handelman, the other major player in the country's tragedies, is already in transit to the Federal Correctional Institution in Gilmer County, West Virginia, via a black Secret Service SUV.

Meanwhile, in the D.C. hotel that has been his home for longer than he preferred, Jack is trying to finish a late breakfast before the shuttle arrives to take him to Reagan National Airport. He is not paying attention to anything other than making sure he finishes his meal, so when a news flash is issued by Walter Reed National Military Medical Facility, he is not aware of it.

The extraordinary news that interrupts all radio and television programming is delivered by a somber hospital representative.

President Burris has passed away.

The barrage of questions that follows the announcement obliges the spokesperson to reveal details of the President's demise. Then, at the first opportunity, he yields his time to a government official, who announces that the President's body will be laid in state in the United States Capitol Rotunda on Wednesday morning.

Unbeknownst to all but a select few, however, the body that will be mourned will not be the President's—it will be the body of someone who looks very much like him.

Still unaware of the momentous news, Jack gives his wife a call when the shuttle van arrives at the hotel.

"Hey, Babe, I'm leaving for the airport now, and I'll take a cab home. See ya later. Love ya."

"Okay, Jack, see you soon. Love you, too—always."

Didi hasn't heard the news, either, and she won't be going to work today. She's planning to take the day off to welcome Jack home and prepare his favorite meal.

Ex-President Burris is the only passenger in a private jet bound for Nairobi and permanent exile. As the aircraft taxis down the runway, he stares solemnly out of the window and bids a silent farewell to the United States and everything he has known.

By reason of the extreme secrecy necessary to get the ex-President out of the country, the aircraft is carrying a very limited number of people. Besides Burris, the only other persons on board are the crew and one Secret Service agent. Unbeknownst to Burris, however, the crew and the agent are all CIA operatives who were specially selected to enact 'Specter.'

As the plane takes off, Vice President Borden is letting out his line on a fishing boat five miles off the coast of Delaware, unaware of the destination of his former boss. Although the VP is supposed to be confined to his residence on house arrest, his position affords some leeway, and his security detail has permitted this outing.

At the airport, Jack is fidgeting in his seat at the terminal gate. Never the patient one, he checks his watch for the tenth time while he waits to board his flight to LaGuardia. Noting the time, he muses, "Hmm, Bradley is just about to begin his speech to America. Most of the country will probably be tuning in to hear what he has to say, but they have no idea that what they're about to hear is complete bullshit. I'm glad I'm missing it."

Off the coast of Maryland, the USS *Stennis* is conducting a training exercise with the Navy's new Regis Class Ship-to-Air Defense Missile.

Tracking the target, the ship's senior fire controlman announces, "Captain, target is acquired and locked."

"Fire, son," is the Captain's terse reply.

With a blast of exhaust, the missile bursts from its casing and zones in on its target, twenty-five miles down-range.

Thirty thousand feet above the Atlantic, President Burris has been alone with his thoughts for a while. When he finally puts his reveries aside, he looks around the aircraft's cabin and wonders why he hasn't seen any crew members since take-off. He remembers seeing the pilot, the co-pilot, a Secret Service agent, and a steward at departure, but he hasn't seen any of them since.

He rises from his seat and walks to the front galley to look for the steward, but there is no one there. Turning to the cockpit door, he knocks loudly but receives no response. Alarmed, he tries the cockpit door handle and is shocked to see that it is unlocked. When he peers inside the flight deck, he is further alarmed.

There is no crew. No pilot. No one.

Terrified and puzzled at the same time, he snatches the small sheet of paper that is stuck to the instrument panel. On it is a hand-written message: "THIS IS YOUR BLUE FALCON."

Wide-eyed, Burris realizes that he's going to be killed. Just as he arranged the deaths of so many innocent bystanders at the Lincoln Memorial, someone has arranged his death.

Screaming "BRADLEY!" over and over, he struggles to take control of the aircraft but cannot, since it's being controlled remotely.

When the enormity of his situation comes into focus, his demeanor changes, and he enters into a state of calm acceptance. Turning around, he stops at the bar in the galley to pour himself a Scotch, neat, and then heads back into the cabin. When he arrives at his seat, he looks out of the window just in time to see the approaching missile. Raising his glass, his last words are, "Well played, Bradley."

At that moment, a voice on the USS *Stennis* announces, "Captain, we have a confirmed hit. Target is destroyed."

"Mr. Speaker, the President of the United States," announces the Congressional Sergeant-at-Arms.

A hearty round of cheers and heartfelt applause fills the Senate chamber as Secret Service agents lead President Bradley slowly but surely up to the dais. His progress is delayed considerably by the handshakes and kisses that he bestows freely upon the fawning legislators along the aisle.

"This is William Gent, ABC News. President Bradley has entered the Senate chamber. We believe that his speech tonight will address the scandals that have gripped Washington and reassure the nation that all corruption will be rooted out and destroyed. We also believe that he will announce his choice for Vice President tonight.

"The President is now at the dais. He is waiting for the cheers to end so that he may begin."

"Mr. Speaker," announces the Acting President, *"distinguished members of the Legislature, honored guests, and the faithful and steadfast people of the United States, I am here to tell you all that the nation is secure and the republic will survive..."*

Former Vice President Borden is uninterested in listening to Bradley's speech. With the complexities of political life behind him, he is more than happy to indulge himself in one of his favorite pastimes. At this moment, he is happily struggling to reel in a yellowfin tuna.

With the sun reflecting off the surface of the water like sparkling diamonds, all is calm and serene in his world. That is, until the impostor Secret Service agent onboard his boat walks up behind him, and puts a bullet into the back of his head.

After pushing the VP's body overboard, the phony agent grabs the fishing rod from the rod holder and reels in the yellowfin that's been dangling on the line. When it's aboard ship, he turns to the boat captain and yells, "Oh, yeah! We're gonna eat good tonight!"

A few minutes later, a go-fast boat pulls up alongside the vessel. The captain and the fake agent abandon the fishing boat and head back to land with the go-fast operator. When they are about 200 feet away from the fishing boat, the boat explodes.

A quick call on a satellite phone puts it bluntly. "Done. Heading back."

"... and let it be known that the people of the United States are strong. We will remain vigilant against any and all terrorist threats against the Union. Members of the Senate and the House must now unite to do everything possible to rid the world of the evildoers in our midst. As Commander in Chief, I pledge that I will act without prejudice

and will bring swift justice to any person, or any nation, that seeks to harm America.

"As your President, I have come here to tell you about the progress I have made in keeping our great country safe. Through information we have sent out on social media sites such as Twitter, tens of thousands of people are now gathering in the streets of Tehran to demand free elections and democratic rights. Like the people of Egypt, the people of Iran have awakened, and they have the full support of the United States.

"To appease the demonstrators, Iran will announce later today that they will dismantle their nuclear program. They will also renounce radical factions of Islam and terror networks such as Hezbollah."

When the congressmen and women from both sides of the aisle leap to their feet in loud applause, Bradley is forced to wait until they quiet down. After several minutes, he continues.

"Now I will address the scandals of the past Administration. First, for those who may not have heard, former President Burris passed away this morning. Funeral arrangements for the late President will be announced later today. Let us now have a moment of silence for the repose of his soul."

After a suitable moment of reflection, Bradley resumes speaking.

"Recent investigations into the actions of the past Administration have resulted in the arrest of key personnel. I am here to tell you that the guilty will be prosecuted for their crimes against the people of the United States."

At that announcement, the chamber erupts in more applause.

"I have made arrangements with the National Shrine

of the Immaculate Conception and the Washington National Cathedral to chime their bells in remembrance of and respect for the brave people who lost their lives in this investigation. As I read off their names, the sound of tolling bells will fill the skies over our fair Capital."

As the bells toll, President Bradley recites, *"Maria Assante. Juan Gutierrez..."*

Victoria Johnson is being processed for entrance into the Danbury Correctional Facility. After being handed an orange jumpsuit, she is directed toward the communal showers before she will be escorted to her cell.

A correctional officer waits outside the shower area as Victoria enters an empty stall and disrobes. When she turns the water on, she closes her eyes under the lukewarm spray. She doesn't notice that the officer has left his post.

A minute later, a female inmate enters the shower area and disrobes. Walking up behind Victoria, she boldly places her body against Victoria's and caresses one of her breasts with her left hand. Shocked and aroused at the same time, Victoria is about to turn around to face her new "friend," when suddenly the inmate jerks her left hand up to Victoria's jaw while her right hand slashes a shiv across her jugular vein.

Choking and shuddering, Victoria slumps to the floor. As the clear water turns red, Victoria's life flows quickly down the drain.

"...Joe Conway. John Hastings. Laura Leonard..."

The Acting President continues to read the names of the fallen while the church bells toll their eerie sounds over the nation's capital.

Just outside of Charlottesville, Virginia, the black SUV transporting Ellis Handelman to the correctional facility in Gilmer County, West Virginia pulls into a gas station. The back of the SUV is sealed off from the driver by a bullet-proof shield, but there is a small opening for conversation between the compartments.

Leaning into the opening, the driver tells Handelman, "I have to take a leak. I'll be right back."

Handelman calls out, "Hey! What about me?" but the driver ignores him.

After exiting the vehicle, the driver presses a button on his key fob that locks the van's doors so they can't be opened from the inside. Handelman curses, but resigns himself to waiting for the driver to return. Unknown to Handelman, however, a dump truck that was travelling south has just swerved to avoid a car that had cut him off. Careening out of control, the truck heads into the gas station and plows directly into the black SUV.

The small explosive charge that was placed strategically on the vehicle's gas tank explodes on impact, and the SUV bursts into flames.

"... Joe Cunningham. Sue Wilkens. Ambassador Charles Kingston. I can continue to name all the other agents and private citizens who have lost their lives as a result of the actions of this corrupt Administration, but there are far too many. All of their names will be forever memorialized on a plaque that will be placed inside the rotunda of

the Lincoln Memorial, once it is reopened to the public later this week.

"People of the United States, we are resolute in our desire to return this country onto the right track. I will place before you the name of Senator Mitch Collins from the great state of Montana as my choice for Vice President. Please confirm him quickly so that normality can return, and the process of healing can continue.

"God bless you all, and God bless the United States of America."

A standing ovation accompanies the President as he solemnly leaves the chamber.

Although he is tired from his day of traveling, Jack is happy to be back in New York City.

After exiting a cab in front of his apartment building, he hauls out his luggage and pays the driver. Then he makes his way into his building's industrial elevator for the short trip up to his apartment.

When the elevator stops, he pulls open the door and finds Didi waiting for him with a Jack Daniels and a smile.

"Welcome home, honey!" she gushes. "I made your favorite meal! My special meatloaf and mashed red potatoes."

Jack drops his luggage, gives his wife a kiss, and grabs the drink.

"Wow! Besides sex, what more could a guy ask for? I get a beautiful wife, a good drink, and a great dinner!"

Didi smiles again and follows her husband toward the dining area.

Frank A. Ruffolo

When he places his drink on the dining room table, Jack immediately notices something odd. There are three place settings on the table instead of the normal two.

"We expecting someone for dinner?" he asks.

Grinning widely, Didi looks deep into Jack's eyes. "In a way," she replies. "Remember the night with the candles and the whipped cream?"

Jack closes his eyes and smiles. "Yeah. Boy, do I."

"Well, Jack, I'm pregnant."